It moved closer, searching wildly. The smell of rotten meat filled my nostrils, almost making me gag. It looked right at me but could not see me with its milky-yellow eyes. I held my breath, afraid to even blink. The creature moved frantically, its black-blue tongue licking its fangs. Its closeness made my skin crawl.

It was becoming more difficult to hold my breath. I could push the creature and try to run, but They were so fast it would catch me before I could reach the door.

IN THE AFTER

DEMITRIA LUNETTA

HARPER TEEN
An Imprint of HarperCollinsPublishers

HarperTeen is an imprint of HarperCollins Publishers.

In the After

www.epicreads.com

Library of Congress Cataloging-in-Publication Data

In the After / Demitria Lunetta. – 1st ed.

p. cm.

Summary: In a post-apocalyptic world where nothing is as it seems, seventeen-year-old Amy and Baby, a child she found while scavenging, struggle to survive while vicious, predatory creatures from another planet roam the Earth.

ISBN 978-0-06-210546-2

[1. Survival–Fiction. 2. Monsters–Fiction. 3. Science fiction.]

I. Title.

PZ7.L9791155In 2013 2012038127

[Fic]–dc23 CIP

AC

Typography by Laura DiSiena

22 23 24 25 26 LSB 11 10 9 8 7

First paperback edition, 2014

Acknowledgments

There are so many people involved in making this book come to be. I want to thank my amazing editor, Karen Chaplin, who made me dig deep and helped me build such a wondrously frightening world. I would also like to thank everyone at HarperTeen–my supportive editorial director, Barbara Lalicki, and always-helpful editorial assistant, Alyssa Miele; my fantastic designer, Cara Petrus, who made the book come alive in such an amazing way; the detail-oriented production department, including production editor Jon Howard, who corrects my sometimes-incorrect use of grammar; and the awesome marketing and publicity departments, including Kim VandeWater, Lindsay Blechman, and Olivia deLeon. You have all done such an incredible job. This book would not be what it is today without all of you. I couldn't ask for a better team.

I'd also like to thank Maria Gomez, who responded so positively to my book. I'll always remember our first phone conversation in which she was as excited about *In the After* as I was.

Lastly, I'd like to thank Katherine Boyle of Veritas Literary. You're, quite simply, Awesome with a capital A. You're the best agent anyone could ask for.

PART ONE

AFTER

CHAPTER ONE

I only go out at night.

I walk along the empty street and pause, my muscles tense and ready. The breeze rustles the overgrown grass and I tilt my head slightly. I'm listening for Them.

All the warnings I remember from horror movies are wrong. Monsters do not rule the night, waiting patiently to spring from the shadows. They hunt during the day, when the light is good and their vision is at its best. At night, if you don't make a noise, they can shuffle past you within an inch of your nose and never know you are there.

It's so very quiet, but that doesn't mean that They are not near. I walk again, slowly at first, but then I pick up my pace. My bare feet pad noiselessly on the cracked sidewalk. Home is only a few blocks away. Not far if I remain silent, but it may as well be miles if They spot me.

I've learned to live in a soundless world. I haven't spoken in three years. Not to comment on the weather, not to shout a warning, not even to whisper my own name: Amy. I know it's been three years because I've counted the seasons since it happened. In the summer before the After when I'd just turned fourteen.

A branch snaps in the distance and I stop immediately, my body tense. I shift my bag slowly, carefully adjusting the weight so the cans inside don't clank together. Every little noise screams at me that something is wrong, but it could be nothing.

Clouds shift and moonlight suddenly brightens the street. I glance around, searching, studying an abandoned, rusted car for any signs of the creatures. When I don't spot Them, I almost continue on, but at the last second I decide to play it safe. Stepping into an abandoned yard, I disappear into the shrubbery. I'll wait until a cloud passes in front of the moon and darkness reclaims the night.

I can't take any chances, not with Baby waiting for me. My bag holds the food we need to survive. We only have each other. I found Baby shortly after the world failed, when I still believed things would return to normal. I no longer hold that hope. Nothing this broken can ever be fixed.

CHAPTER TWO

This is how I think of time: the past is Before, and the present is the After. Before was reality; the After, a nightmare.

Before I was happy. I had friends and sleepovers. I wanted to learn how to drive, to get a jump start on my learner's permit. The worst thing in my life was math homework and not being allowed to date. I thought my parents were so clueless; my dad with all his "green" concerns (I told my friends he was an eco-douche), and my mom, who was never home except for Sunday-night family dinner. I was kinder to my mom, though, and only called her a workaholic. Her job was with the government, her work very hush-hush.

I always thought of myself as smart, and I was definitely a smart-ass to my parents. I loved seeing them squirm, letting them know that I didn't buy into their "because I said so" crap. I was good in school. I could always guess the endings of movies and books. Now there is no school, there are no more movies, no new books, no more friends.

The creatures arrived on a Saturday. I know it was a Saturday because if it were a weekday I would have been at school and I would be dead. Sundays I went with my father to visit his parents at Sunny Pine, and if They had come on a Sunday I would also be dead.

I remember that the electricity flickered and I was annoyed because I was watching TV. I had wondered if my father was on the roof screwing around with the solar panels. They didn't require much maintenance, but he liked to hose them off twice a year, which always messed with all our electronics. I checked the garage. His electric car was gone. He was at the farmers' market, probably overpaying for organic carrots.

I microwaved some pizza bagels (the ones my mom hid from my dad at the back of the freezer) and sat back in front of the TV, flipping through the channels mindlessly.

I'd wished my parents would listen to me and upgrade to the premium cable package. I thought life was so unfair. My mother had bought my father a brand-new electric car for more money than I would probably need for college, but she wouldn't spend fifty bucks extra a month to get some decent television.

I checked my cell phone but there were no calls from Sabrina or Tim. I was supposed to go to a movie with them later. Tim had been madly in love with Sabrina forever but her parents would only let her go out with him if I tagged along. I joked with Sabrina about being the old spinster in a nineteenth-century novel. "No secret love child for you two," I'd tell her with a wink. "Not while Matron Amy is on duty."

I didn't really mind being their chaperone; they never made me feel awkward or like a third wheel. Sabrina hadn't even decided if she was all that into Tim. I'd been friends with her since fifth grade, when I was the weirdo who skipped a grade and she was the nice girl who didn't treat me like I had the plague. Pretty soon we were friends and stayed besties through middle school and into high school.

I tossed my phone on the coffee table and kicked up my feet, giving my full attention to the TV screen for the first time. But I noticed that even when I changed the channel, the picture stayed the same. I paused, curious. The president was making a speech. Boring. I ate my snack, only half listening.

"It has come to our attention," the president droned, "that we are not isolated in this attack."

I sat up, my bite half chewed. Attack? I was too young to remember the string of terrorist attacks at the beginning of the century, but my mother worked for the government and was constantly talking about our "lack of counterterrorist mechanisms."

I turned up the volume. The president looked exhausted, bags under his eyes, makeup caked on for the cameras. "The structure landed in Central Park early this morning," he said into twenty microphones. "As of now, the fate of anyone residing in New York City and the surrounding suburbs is unknown. We are working to find the cause of this interruption in communication as soon as–" He was cut short. The breaking news logo flashed across the screen.

I took a swig of soda. It was strange that the network had interrupted the president. I didn't understand what they were talking about, didn't know what it all meant yet. I glanced at the screen and what I saw nearly made me choke on my soda. They had footage of the "structure" in the park. Something emerged, turned toward the camera, stared. Still coughing, I pressed PAUSE on the DVR remote and stood.

That was the first time I saw an alien.

CHAPTER THREE

After They came, I did not leave my house for three weeks. The broadcasts stopped after the first few days, but they were not helpful anyway. They kept repeating the same things. Aliens had landed, they were not friendly, half of the planet was dead.

They were horrifyingly fast, traveling across the globe at an alarming pace. They didn't destroy buildings or attack our resources, like in so many crappy Hollywood movies. They wanted us. They hungered for us.

That first day, I was slow to understand what was happening.

My hands shook as I desperately tried to call my friends and family. My father didn't carry a cell phone. He didn't believe in them, said they gave people brain cancer. My mom had one of those fancy touch-screen phones that her job paid for, but she never answered, and her office line went straight to voice mail. Sabrina's phone just rang and rang. So did Tim's. I tried my cousin in Virginia and my mom's parents in Miami. No one answered. I went through the phone book on my cell, furiously calling one number after another. Eventually I could no longer dial out. I kept getting a recorded message. "All circuits are busy. Please hang up and try your call again at a later time." Soon I couldn't even get service. I stared at the screen for a minute, then, frustrated, threw the phone against the wall.

I curled into a ball on the couch and tried not to cry, but I couldn't hold back the tears for long. When my father didn't come back after a few hours, I had to admit to myself that he was dead. He had camping skills, but I could not imagine him holding his own against an alien attack. My mother might be okay, her government offices were high security, surrounded by soldiers. But I had no idea how to reach her, and could soldiers really protect her from those repulsive creatures? I had to face the reality that my parents could both be gone.

I stayed on the sofa and cried until I had no tears left and not enough energy to sob. I eventually crawled to the fridge and grabbed my dad's Ben and Jerry's from the freezer. It was the one junk food he allowed himself. He said life wasn't worth living without Cherry Garcia. I gorged myself on ice cream and ended up vomiting purple-pink onto the floor. I fell asleep there, exhausted and miserable.

When I woke several hours later, I couldn't figure out why I was on the kitchen floor. I opened my eyes and saw the mess I had made, instantly remembering everything. I wanted to stay there, but the smell finally got to me. I sat up and rubbed my deadened arms. Sobbing hysterically wouldn't help my dad or my friends. It wouldn't help me. Something inside me shifted or maybe just broke. I had to take care of myself.

I stood carefully, my legs still shaky, and went to retrieve the cleaning supplies from under the sink. When I was done cleaning the mess, I numbly grabbed a book from the shelf and hid in my room, unable to face my own thoughts. I needed to escape, if just for a short while, into a story from long ago.

My first night alone, I still assumed things would settle down. I stayed glued to the TV, watching the news report the same thing over and over. People were dying, and I was sick with grief, but I knew that we would overcome the invaders or whatever they were. We were the strongest nation on earth.

The second day passed and the TV was out, but there were still people on the radio. I was comforted by their voices, even though they spoke of mass chaos. People tried to run away, but They were everywhere. People tried to hide, but They found them.

Then on the third day, the radio went silent. I stayed in my room and obsessively read one book after another, to keep my mind on anything other than what was happening. I'd always escaped into books, but now reading had become something more. It allowed me to be somewhere else, to feel something else, not just the numbness that overtook my body and made me wonder if I was still alive.

My father loved Shakespeare; he would read passages with me and discuss all the intricacies. I reread *Romeo and Juliet* and cried my eyes out over their loss. Before I'd always argued with my father that the star-crossed lovers were idiots who should have coordinated their plans better, but this time they got to me. I completely broke down and crawled into my parents' bed. Draping their covers over my body, I sobbed myself to sleep. I was like that back then; my mood would swing between an almost hysterical sense of loss and having no feelings at all.

On the fourth day, I made myself eat and then tidied the house, trying to do the normal things that people do. I put out all the pictures I had of my friends and parents, gluing a collage to my bedroom door. I ransacked every photo album, placing each picture with great care, keeping my mind occupied. It was so much easier than facing reality. Sometimes I found it hard to concentrate, what with the world ending and all. I wanted so badly to leave the house, to see if anyone else was around, but I was scared of Them.

I finally decided to go out on our rooftop deck, and watch Them chase people down the street. They were faster than I'd thought possible, a blur of green, the color of pea soup. Glowing yellow eyes sometimes caught the light and flashed gold. The creatures pounced, not bothering to kill their prey before feeding. They ripped skin and flesh from their victims, who screeched in agony. The cries always brought more of Them, eager for their next meal. Those first few days were full of screams. It was terrible, but the real terror came when there were no more shrieks, when the world went quiet. I thought I was the only one left on the planet. There was only me and Them.

The fourth night, I turned on all the lights in the house. My block was dark, except for our home, my home. No one else had electricity, but I still did. I silently thanked my father who wanted to live footprint-free by installing solar panels and insisting we always put more into the grid than what we took out. We were as close to self-sustaining as current technology allowed.

I didn't know then that They were drawn to the lights, like moths to a flame. I didn't know that they couldn't see very well. They were attracted to anything bright, especially once they realized that where there was light in the darkness, there were humans, which for Them meant food.

The electric fence saved me, and that was my mother's doing. Even though we lived in an excellent, safe neighborhood in Chicago, she needed to protect the work she brought home. She had the fence installed behind our beautiful iron gate, the one They ripped up and destroyed in just a few minutes. She needed to make our house a "secure area." My mother and father were so different I wondered sometimes how they managed to stand each other at all. Still, they were so in love. Their public displays of affection were always embarrassing and I used to make gagging noises to try and get them to stop. Now I regret the way I acted toward them. I regret a lot of things that happened Before.

CHAPTER FOUR

After those first few days, I quickly learned to keep the noise to a minimum and the lights off when it was dark outside. They hid at night, but were still attracted by light and sound. Even small noises would bring Them to the fence, their green skin sparking as They tried to tear through the electrified chain links.

I spied on Them through my dad's nature binoculars, carefully watching, mesmerized by their grotesqueness, their snarls and sharp teeth. They had two arms and two legs, but that is where their similarities to humans ended.

They were hairless; all the same shade of yellow-green, like sunburned grass. Most were naked, though some wore torn shirts or pants they must have scavenged from the dead. One sported a dirty Cubs hat, at which I couldn't help but laugh. My sense of humor was very different in the After.

I spotted them at the fence sometimes. They heard me if I was too loud, or occasionally They wandered over aimlessly. They didn't seem to be very curious in general, not concerned with anything but the pursuit of food. I tried to ignore Them when They rattled the fence, braving the electric shocks in search of meals. I'd go and hide in my room, but eventually I developed a sick fascination with Them. I decided to study one up close, determined to know what they really looked like. One day I gathered my courage, took a deep breath, and walked into the backyard. Humming softly, I waited.

Within a few seconds, one made it to the fence. It grabbed the metal with both hands and was jolted back by a painful shock. Shaking its bald, dull-green head, it quickly got up and tried again to attack, never taking its eyes off me. Again and again it came after me; either it couldn't learn from the earlier shocks or it just didn't care. It gnashed its teeth, pulling back its thin lips to reveal yellow fangs. It had practically no nose, only two holes where a nose should be. Puke-green flesh hung loosely from its body like baggy clothes. I could smell its burning flesh as its hands became blackened from the electric current. As long as I was within sight, it would pursue me single-mindedly.

I was frozen in place, terrified yet fascinated. I called out, "How have *you* destroyed *us*?" The sound of my voice only made the alien struggle harder against the wire of the fence trying desperately to attack me.

Finally I left it, snarling and slobbering, relieved and confident that the fence would hold. I went back inside and watched from the window, my shaking hands wiping the nervous sweat from my forehead with a kitchen towel. It would forget in a moment why it was there, what it was that drew it to that place. It would wander off in search of food again, live meat. I went to the basement, huddled in the corner, and read, pretending it was still Before, when little green men were just a joke and couldn't eat you.

CHAPTER FIVE

After twenty days I ran out of food. My father had a small rooftop garden, but none of the vegetables were ready, and I couldn't live on carrots and tomatoes for the rest of my life anyhow. I went a whole day without eating before admitting to myself what I needed to do.

I walked to my parents' room, into their closet. I took down the box that my mother thought I didn't know about. I'd put it off, hoping I wouldn't need to leave the safety of the house, that all the carnage would stop and that I would be saved. My hunger made me realize that I would have to face the world as it was; life-threateningly full of Them. For that, I needed protection.

"Most households that keep a firearm end up hurting a family member or someone they know." I heard the echo of my father's concerned voice as I took the gun from its case.

"I would like to see those statistics," my mother had replied. "What studies are you citing, exactly?" she'd asked with a wink. He tried not to smile, but his eyes betrayed him. He'd always pretended to be stern but would give in so easily. He put his hand on the back of her neck and pulled her forward for a kiss. I remember being amazed. Even when they were arguing, they still made out. They didn't notice me in the doorway. Even then I was good at being quiet.

They kept the gun, thanks to my mother's stubbornness. My father surrendered, as long as I learned how to use it properly and knew it wasn't a plaything. I was ten. My father came up with some lame excuse about wanting me to gain a better understanding of the world, but I knew it was because he feared I would find the gun hidden in the closet and think it was a toy.

I never thought about the gun, not after my lessons at the shooting range were finished. That day, however, when I needed to leave the house for the first time since They arrived, all I could think about was how grateful I was that my mother was super paranoid, that her work demanded it.

I loaded the clip into the gun and smiled, putting the holster on, slipping my arms through the straps. I packed my backpack with a flashlight, a knife, and my wallet, unsure of what I would find outside. Looking back, it just goes to show how clueless I was.

I waited until sunset, when there would be less of Them. It took me twenty minutes to work up the nerve to open the front door. The lock clicked open, painfully loud. I checked to make sure They weren't waiting for me at the fence. We lived in a nice neighborhood: big expensive houses with well-manicured lawns. Ours was the only one with a fenced-in front yard. I unlocked the electric gate, checking for the hundredth time that the key was safely tucked into my pocket for when I returned. To lock myself out now would most certainly mean death. I felt sad remembering when I'd done it a couple of times Before, when the penalty was only heading over to Sabrina's house to mooch junk food until one of my parents got home.

I took a deep breath and steadied my shaking hands, willing myself into calmness, pushing my terror away as I stepped past the rubble of what used to be our outer gate.

I had decided I would start out simple; venture to the corner store a block away, have a quick look around, grab some canned ravioli, and haul my butt back to my house. I was careful to walk quietly.

"Slow and steady wins the race," my father had always said. *He is such a dork,* I thought automatically. It made me want to cry. My father wasn't anything anymore. No one was anything.

I walked slowly, carefully placing each foot on the sidewalk to avoid making noise. The night was windy, which made me jumpy. Any movement of a bush or tree and I froze. After constant stalling, I had to force myself to calm down again. I didn't want the sound of me hyperventilating to bring Them. *The shadows are just shadows,* I told myself. *They are all sleeping now,* I reasoned. But I wasn't very convincing.

As I walked, I noticed a few of the houses had broken windows or open doors. Cars had been abandoned in the street, some with blood on the windshield. I tried not to look at these things too closely, not to let them psych me out. I had survived an alien invasion, I wasn't going to starve to death because I couldn't overcome my fear.

I made it to the store without spotting any of Them.

Cautiously I pressed at the door, expecting it to be locked, but it gave way with little trouble. The smell hit me first, musty and rotten. I stood for a moment with the door open, breathing shallowly until I became used to the stink. When I stepped inside, my shoes squeaked on the linoleum floor, making me cringe. I slipped them off and left them by the door.

This is the market that Sabrina and I would sneak off to, to buy junk food when she stayed at my house. There used to always be customers here, buying munchies or lottery tickets, sipping on sodas in supersize cups. The outside world was empty now, but being in that vacant store was somehow worse.

I made myself focus into the darkness and went straight to the canned food aisle, frantically filling my backpack with corn, soup, tuna fish, anything I could get my hands on. The cans clanged loudly when I hoisted the bag to my shoulders and I froze. There was no way I could make such a racket and get home alive. Quickly I repacked the bag, placing candy bars and bags of marshmallows between the cans.

But now not all the cans fit. I don't know why I didn't leave them on the floor, but it didn't seem right. Your mind does funny things when you spend so much time alone. I stocked them back on the shelf, one by one. Anxiety was flooding my body, and my hands were shaking with fear and hunger. I dropped a can on the shelf and it fell into the other ones and onto the floor. My eyes followed it as it rolled toward the front of the store. I stepped forward and instantly froze. There was one of Them at the store entrance.

I took a step back as quietly as I could. The creature's head pushed through the door, its body jammed in the opening, unsure of where to go. Finally it made its way inside; its head rocked clumsily from side to side, trying to see in the dark. They shuffled around when there were no people in sight, wandered aimlessly. They weren't fast until They had reason to be, when They detected their prey.

The creature's foot touched my shoes where I'd left them by the door. In a flash it dropped to the floor and sniffed at my sneakers. I continued to back away, my socks soundless on the cold tile. It moved forward, crawling on its hands and knees. Something settled in my bag with a thud. Its head snapped up in my direction and in a flash, it ran toward me. Without thinking I grabbed a jar of tomato sauce and hurled it at the creature.

I aimed for its head, but the jar sailed over it and smashed against the floor. That made it stop. It looked back and forth, unable to decide if it should investigate the new, louder noise.

I stood as still as I could. *Please don't see me. Please don't see me. Please don't see me.*

The gun was at my side in its holster. I could reach it and shoot before the thing reached me, but that would draw every one of Them within earshot.

It moved closer, searching wildly. The smell of rotten meat filled my nostrils, almost making me gag. It looked right at me but could not see me with its milky-yellow eyes. I held my breath, afraid to even blink. The creature moved frantically, its black-blue tongue licking its fangs. Its closeness made my skin crawl.

It was becoming more difficult to hold my breath. I could push the creature and try to run, but They were so fast it would catch me before I could reach the door. Its teeth were unbelievably pointy, too big for its mouth. Hot, putrid breath blew onto my face.

It edged closer and I took a small step back, sickened. I clenched my teeth, willing myself not to give in to my terror and run. My foot hit a can, hard. It rolled down the aisle, away from me. The creature rushed toward the noise, almost brushing against me as it went by. I made myself as small as possible, knowing if we touched, if the creature discovered me, it would be the end.

Luckily it knocked over more cans on its way, creating a clatter, confusing itself. I used the diversion to run toward the exit. My socks made no noise on the hard floor.

I silently jerked open the door and power-walked home, looking over my shoulder every few seconds. My heart in my throat, I was convinced the thudding in my chest would be loud enough to bring Them all running.

I finally reached my house and fumbled with my key. I panicked when I couldn't get the gate open immediately, but taking a deep breath I managed to find the keyhole. I unlocked the gate and slammed it behind me, no longer caring how much noise I made. I was barely able to turn the interior bolt before the creatures smashed into it.

I ran for the door and once inside, a sick curiosity made me look out the window. There were three of Them at the gate, milling around, unsure in the darkness. They hadn't known I was there until they'd heard the slamming iron. They were so fast. I would have easily been caught if it were day.

I rummaged through my pack, gorging myself on candy bars and canned ravioli. My father would have had a fit. I'd always been annoyed when we shopped at the natural food store, just wanting to eat "normal food." It wouldn't be long until I pined for an endless selection of fresh vegetables.

Much later, I realized that I should have dropped my pack the minute one of Them appeared. But I desperately needed the food in my bag. My shoes were gone, left at the store, but I decided soon after that shoes were dangerous. They made too much noise. I started wearing just socks, but my feet would grow calloused and rough before long, making footwear unnecessary altogether.

Looking back on that first trip, knowing what I do now, it was a miracle I survived at all.

CHAPTER SIX

I was incredibly lonely that first month, before I found Baby. I stopped keeping track of the days. Whether it was Monday or Wednesday seemed meaningless in the After.

There were whole days when all I did was read. Sometimes at night I'd listen to my TuneZ player turned down low, headphones in my ears. I listened to my dad's playlist, full of bluegrass and oldies. I told myself that it was a good way to honor his memory, even though I could barely think of him without breaking down.

I went about my routine, venturing farther and farther

away from home. There was a large supermarket only five blocks away. As far as I knew, there weren't any other survivors, so I had my pick of overprocessed food, filled with the toxic preservatives that my father always ranted against. Now they were keeping me alive.

It was so creepy, to walk through the empty aisles, to "shop." I avoided the produce section, quickly turning to compost. Even so, the supermarket smelled awful, but I began to get used to the stink. I'd never realized how sanitized my life had been, how clean and contained. I thought about how dirty the After would be, how the world would change without constant maintenance.

I visited the supermarket often, wanting my cabinets to be full of nonperishable food. It became routine. One night, though, I had the greatest shock since the After began. I discovered Baby in the produce section, her chubby fingers shoveling rotten, month-old grapes into her mouth, hands and face stained with purple juice. She could not have been more than three or four. Her dirty, blond hair was matted into pigtails, pink hair ties still in place. She had been injured; her skirt was stained the rusty brown of old blood.

I took a step toward her and immediately her large, brown eyes were on me. She didn't cry out or even flinch.

As quiet as I was, she'd heard me approach. After studying me for a few seconds, she padded silently in my direction, her arms outstretched. How was this tiny being still alive?

I almost left her there. I was already hardened from what I'd witnessed. Instead I picked the girl up and carried her home. I decided that if she cried on the way, I would leave her. If she squirmed, I would just drop her. If she so much as whimpered, I would have tossed her aside for Them to find. How much I had changed in just a few short weeks of living in the After.

But the girl had not made a noise. I've witnessed Baby cry many times since that day. Her lips tremble like any other child, her nose wrinkles, and tears run down her cheeks, all in silence. I watch her sometimes while she sleeps, guilty at what I almost did all those years ago. I don't want to think about what my life would be if I had given in to my heartless thoughts. I don't know what I would do without Baby, left alone with only my memories of Before.

When Baby came, it was like starting over in the After. I was no longer alone. I still wonder how she survived for so long, since she was so young. It helped that she was quiet and had good instincts. She knew not to make a sound. She didn't whine when I cleaned her wound, pouring hydrogen peroxide to kill the germs. A chunk of flesh was missing from the fatty part of her thigh, but it seemed to have healed over enough to prevent infection. After I'd cleaned and wrapped her leg, I checked her for other wounds, but the only other abnormality was a strange diamond-shaped scar at the nape of her neck, just near her hairline.

Even though she looked in good shape, I still walked to the pharmacy and scavenged antibiotics to give her as a precaution. I figured she could take the same pills I was given for my skin infection the year before. I also scavenged some new clothes for her, and when I returned, she was waiting silently at the door.

I gave her the antibiotics, guessing at the dosage. I also gave her a bath and washed and combed her hair. After that, Baby became my shadow, following me silently around the house. Sometimes she'd stop and stare at a window or wall and I assumed she was damaged from the After, unable to focus. Once she stopped mid-step, suddenly turning and running to hide behind the couch, and a few seconds later I heard the fence spark. I realized that she knew They were outside and was frightened. She could hear them, often when I couldn't.

I tried to comfort her, but I knew I needed some way to

communicate with her. Vocalization was out of the question, voices always drew Them, and I did not want Them constantly testing the fence. It seemed easier just not to talk, and Baby was smart enough to understand this. Or maybe what she had witnessed had shocked her into silence permanently.

I dug out my dad's book on sign language and began to teach her and myself. Through the years we've modified our language to fit our purpose. We sign into each other's hands when we're near. Now, we can have an entire silent conversation moving only our fingers, but when we started I used only a few simple words. *Food. Quiet. Bad. Good. Baby.*

Calling her Baby seemed to fit; for all I knew she was the last toddler on earth. She took to the signs remarkably well, mimicking my every action. She became my constant companion. She wanted to be everywhere I was and do everything I did. If it had been Before, I would have been annoyed, but I was starved for human interaction. Baby didn't just become my family, she became my entire world.

CHAPTER SEVEN

Amy. Baby wakes me by signing onto my face. Three years have passed, so she's a child now, not a baby, but my label has become her name.

What? I ask crankily. *I'm sleeping.*

I saw it again, she tells me, her fingers move with a desperate swiftness. *The ship.*

I sit up and look into her eyes, large and shining. She should be afraid, but instead she is excited. Her lips curve slightly, almost forming a smile.

Show me, I demand.

She grabs my hand and we hurry to the roof. I don't bother to get dressed. Years ago, Before, I would never have gone out on the roof deck in my underwear. Years ago, I would have been careful of the neighbors. But now, in the After, there are no neighbors.

See? There! Baby hands me the binoculars. I look out over the houses. Sure enough, there is another black object, hovering in the distance. When we first spotted them, I told Baby they were ships, for lack of a better word. The sign in the book is actually "boat," but Baby doesn't know that. The signs are what I make them, a visual representation. I didn't know how to explain "spaceship."

The ship looks more like a helicopter, anyway, except without the tail end. No windows either. I can't hear the engine from where we are and I wonder at the single blade, keeping it airborne. What differences in technology do They possess? The ship's material looks odd: it's not metal; it can't be. It doesn't throw the light back. Even in the early morning predawn glow, it should still reflect something. I'm impressed Baby noticed it at all. She must have been on the lookout. We've only started seeing the ships recently and any break from the norm is a cause for excitement. I scan the ground to see if any creatures are on the prowl yet, but there are none.

I look back to the ship, which hovers in the distance, unmoving. If it is a spacecraft, why would They wait three years to reveal their mode of transportation? If it isn't a spaceship . . .. But I don't even entertain the idea. I've never seen anything like them before. The ships had to have been brought by Them.

The craft lowers itself slowly in the distance. A few blocks away, maybe more. I map it in my head: Oz Park. It landed in the park.

I'm going to go have a look, I tell Baby. *You stay here.*

She shakes her head no and points at the sky.

It's not quite daybreak, but if I leave now I will be pushing it. I can get out to the park before sunup, but I doubt I'll be able to make it back home again. I will have to be very careful.

I run downstairs and put on my camouflage pants and hooded sweatshirt. They are from years ago and the pants no longer fit me properly, my ankles stick out the bottom. *Floods,* my dad would have joked. I bought them when army greens were in style and haven't been able to scavenge any that fit better. Designers probably didn't take into account an imminent postapocalyptic scenario; they had no idea how useful these would be. With the creatures' poor eyesight, the camouflage pattern helps me blend into grass or shrubbery. But I've never tried it in daylight before.

I grab my pack, with the gun tucked inside. In three years I've never shot it, but I like having it close. I sometimes think about taking a few of Them out, lessening their population, but there are so many, it wouldn't do much good.

Before I run out the front door, I kiss Baby on the forehead. *Stay here,* I say with a look. The last thing I need is to worry about her following me.

I jog barefoot to the park. I've been practicing running at home on the treadmill in the basement and have developed a way to breathe silently. My mouth gapes open strangely, but who is around to judge? I run through the streets, staying close to bushes and trees. Everything is overgrown now, which provides plenty of places to hide from Them. The sidewalks are already beginning to crack, with tree roots pushing upward toward the light of day, and the roads are filled with leaves and debris. I can feel the unevenness under my feet. It doesn't make much difference to me since my feet are so calloused at this point I can walk through the rubble of the After unfazed.

Oz Park used to be beautifully maintained. My parents, more often just my father, would take me here when I was little. I loved the swing set, which is now overturned and rusting away. Most of the grass has died, leaving pitiful weeds and sandy soil. I make my way through the park, careful to stick to covered areas, pausing under trees and along fences to survey the area.

When I reach the southwest corner, I sprint up the hill and flop down on my stomach. I crawl the last few feet through the uneven sand and try to get a better look.

The ship has already landed. It sits in the middle of an old baseball field, its blade continuing to swing around and around. There are no windows, no door. I scan the area, keeping my head low. None of Them in sight. But why? I listen carefully, my ears strain for even the smallest noise, but I hear nothing. The ship is soundless.

An opening suddenly appears in the side of the craft, more like a hole than a door. Three of Them stumble out, snarling. The gap closes and the ship takes flight, straight up into the air, silently, before vanishing.

I start to crawl back, but quickly realize that They are headed toward me. I pull my hood over my head and lie perfectly still, my hands tucked under my body. It's still dark out, but first light is coming fast.

Crap, I think as I hear them approach. They crest the hill and shuffle by me. I wait silently until They are out of sight and consider my options. Unfortunately I don't have many. I scramble to some nearby trees and climb one easily. Settling in, I guess I will be there for a while.

The sun is rising, but it looks like clouds are rolling in from the lake. I pray for a storm. They hate storms, especially loud ones with thunder and lightning. I can make it home easily in the rain. I remember being in the park on a similar day long ago. My mother had a rare moment for us and had asked me what I wanted to do. I insisted on a picnic, even though the weather was dreary. We wore our rain gear, yellow boots and plastic coats, and ate egg salad sandwiches in the rain. It's one of my favorite memories of my mother. I couldn't have been older than four or five.

I wait for the downpour and consider the ship. Clearly it's theirs, but I can't imagine one of Them flying it. Maybe there are different kinds of Them? It's possible that the ones I've seen are the mindless drones, sent to rid the planet of us pesky humans. Maybe there are smarter ones, ones that can build things like that ship. Ones who have plans. Perhaps the ones

I've seen are only the first wave, sent ahead to destroy us.

The rain starts, but only a drizzle. The newly lit morning sky is starting to darken and I let my mind wander to my other experiences with Them, one in particular that made me truly understand that there was no going back to Before.

CHAPTER EIGHT

It was before Baby, but not long before. Now, three years ago seems like a lifetime. Only a month into the After, I'd started searching houses, looking for signs of life. Most were simply empty, although some had a few bloody pieces of clothing in a bedroom or broken belongings scattered in a hallway. *This is where They had gotten the occupants,* I often thought.

It was well after dark, so though I was cautious, I was also confident. I used the sidewalk, instead of keeping to the shadows. I chose houses at random, tried the doors. Most were unlocked. A few were missing altogether, torn apart by Them. People left all kinds of useful things behind, food being the most important. I also liked looking through their books. As much as people loved e-books, there were always paper books around. You can tell a lot about people by the kind of books they owned.

I'd taken to pilfering to alleviate my boredom and keep sadness at bay. You could see just how far a family had gotten, how prepared they were. There were a lot of half-eaten lunches, a few packed suitcases. There were never any bodies, which I was glad for, but there were plenty of questionable stains, and a few odors that I'd rather not have walked nose-first into. At first I was afraid I'd run into Them, but you would never find Them in an empty house. They preferred to be in the open during the day, hunting, and at night . . . well, I didn't know where they went at night. There just weren't very many around when it was dark . . . unless you made a lot of noise.

I never pilfered houses directly around where I lived: somehow that would have been wrong. I'd known those people. They weren't the faceless masses. They were neighbors, my parent's friends, and with associations would have come memories, which I didn't want. In those early days, before I'd hardened, my only chance for survival relied on maintaining tight control over my emotional life. Breakdown would have meant death, but sometimes a memory would open the gate a crack.

I found a promising house a few blocks from home, with no broken windows but an open door. I had hope that maybe the family that lived there made it out of the city before They showed up. Whoever stayed there had clearly tried to hurry, probably left at the first sign of trouble. I stepped inside, quickly helping myself to their canned goods. I searched the bedrooms for winter clothes, unsure if I would be able to use the heat in the winter. I'd been stockpiling blankets and coats.

One bedroom was painted all lavender and I assumed it belonged to a teenage girl. I went to the closet, hoping the clothes would be my size. On the floor next to the closet was a yearbook from my high school. I sat on the floor and thumbed through it. It was from the previous year, so my picture was in the freshman section. I paused over Sabrina's photo, feeling my throat catch at the sight of her smile. I remembered being so jealous that her picture came out better than mine. One of my tears hit the page and I quickly flipped to the front section, which had scrawled notes to *have a great summer* and *good luck in college.*

Trembling, I quietly closed the yearbook and set it back on the floor. Whoever owned it would not be in college now, and they certainly did not have a great summer. I wiped the tears from my face and composed myself, my stomach aching from the unexpected glimpse of what was.

I left there with my bag of cans and walked toward my house, exhausted and ready to call it quits for the night. That's when I saw a house with a light on in the basement. *A light? Someone's home.* I stopped, stunned. Someone else had a generator or solar panels. Someone else was alive.

I crept toward the window cautiously, painfully aware that light attracted Them. I looked all around me; something was very odd. For some reason, I glanced up. Over the basement window, about eight feet up, hung a refrigerator suspended from a cable. It was a trap. I smiled. A trap for Them.

I backed away slowly, not wanting to trip over whatever mechanism would spring the trap. I searched my pack for a pen and ripped out a blank page from one of the books I'd taken.

My hands shook as I scribbled, *I'm alive too. I'll be back here at midnight tomorrow.* I looked at the paper and added, *Please.*

Elated, I placed the note under a rock just in reach of the light from the window. Whoever rigged the trap would see it when they came to check if they were successful. I figured I could return for a couple of nights.

When I came back the next night the trap was sprung, but the note was still there. Whoever set the trap had not yet returned. I placed my note closer to the fallen refrigerator, glad that the creature underneath was almost entirely covered. Its feet stuck out awkwardly and I thought of the Wicked Witch's sister from *The Wizard of Oz*. We're sure as hell not in Kansas anymore, Toto.

I had to suppress a laugh, but then the creature's leg twitched and I realized that its slaughter was recent. I backed away, cautious that others could be close by. I walked home, slightly disappointed but also hopeful, knowing I could return the next night.

For two days I waited, with no one in sight. I wondered if they kept track of time or owned a watch. I still wore my dad's old-school digital. More for the memory of him than anything else. I wanted to wear my mom's Cartier, but the ticking was too loud in the absolute quiet. Each night I began to doubt my plan. I wondered briefly what the person or people were like; what if they were avoiding me on purpose?

What if they were unfriendly? The thought of being able to interact with another human being made me desperate.

On the third night, there was someone waiting, crouching in the bushes. I was used to watching for Them, so I spotted him at once.

"I can see you," I told him in the loudest whisper I dared. "Hello? Please come out."

He stood and looked me over. I couldn't see him well in the dark, but he was tall and his shaggy hair framed a face I couldn't quite make out. Backing away, he waved for me to follow. I almost couldn't believe that there was another human alive. I wanted to yell or hoot, but I swallowed my enthusiasm and tried to calm myself. Even so, I was shaking slightly as I trailed behind him to an apartment building a few blocks away. He unlocked the entrance door and motioned me inside.

We went up several flights. Some of the stairs creaked, making me uncomfortable. It wasn't long ago that I would never have dreamed of following a man to his apartment.

At the top floor, the man unlocked the door and went inside. I looked up and down the hall, hesitating for just a moment before going in after him. He shut and locked the door with a *click.* Then he flipped on a switch and I was startled by the sudden brightness. I looked to the windows but they were blacked out, keeping Them from spotting the glow. A gentle hum sounded from another room.

"You can talk. They won't hear us," he told me.

I looked at him clearly in the light. He wasn't young, but he wasn't old either, probably about my father's age. Fortyish. I wrinkled my nose. In his enclosed condo, I could smell him for the first time. It was likely he hadn't showered since Before. His shaggy, blond hair almost covered his eyes and an unkempt beard framed his face. I guessed he hadn't shaved since Before either.

"Who are you?" I asked. "I mean, what's your name?"

"Jake." He held out his hand and I shook it. His hand was firm, his skin rough. It was strange to touch another person.

"I'm Amy," I said, my voice unsure. He still hadn't released my hand, so I pulled it away awkwardly.

"Sorry." He grinned. "I'm just surprised to see another live human around. It's a shock."

"How . . . You set that trap by yourself?" I asked.

"Construction worker by day." He grinned again. "Drummer by night. Well, I *was* a drummer. There's no band anymore."

"There's not anything anymore," I said quietly.

"Whoa, negative Nancy." He ran his fingers through his greasy hair. "We're still here."

I bit my lip, ashamed. I didn't want to alienate my first human contact. "So, you were in a band? That's fan."

"Fan?" he asked.

"Fantastic . . . It's what my friends and I used to say," I explained. Sabrina and I started it as a joke, to make fun of the people at our school who insisted on talking in text-speak. Sabrina and I had whole conversations where we pretended to be bubbleheads and only used the first syllables of words. The rest of our friends got annoyed with us real fast, but subbing *fan* for *fantastic* stuck.

"Fan." Jake tilted his head and stared at me. "I like that."

"What kind of music did you play?" I asked, mostly because I didn't know what else to say to him. I read in *Cosmo* once that you can put people at ease by asking them questions on topics that interest them. The problem was Jake seemed completely comfortable, I was the one who needed to chill. I had wanted to see someone for so long, but now it all felt so strange and unreal.

"Death metal," he told me with a grin. "We used to make a ton of noise in here." He motioned toward the walls. "That's why we can talk; I had the place soundproofed. The neighbors were always bitching about the noise."

I looked around, uncertain of what to say. Jake's condo was nice. He had fancy furniture and paintings on the walls. One in particular caught my eye.

I gawked. "Is that . . . ?"

"A Picasso," Jake shrugged. "I know what you're thinking, but it would have just sat abandoned in the Art Institute. Besides, we have to enjoy the finer things in life, otherwise what's the point of surviving?"

"I suppose." I was uneasy about it but wasn't sure why it bothered me. Why not take priceless art? . . . It was hardly stealing. There was no one else around to enjoy it.

"What about you, Amy?" he asked. "How did you survive? You look like you're about twelve."

"I'm fourteen," I corrected him. I wanted to add that I read at a college level and was very mature for my age, but I didn't. It would have sounded stupid, and what did that matter now?

"How have they not gotten you? They've gotten everyone else."

"My parents," I explained. "One was a hippie and one was paranoid."

Jake frowned, not understanding.

"My mother put in an electric fence; my father made sure we had solar panels, a vegetable garden, a rainwater basin. . . ."

"You have running water?" he interrupted me.

"Mostly . . . when it rains anyway. The filters work because of the solar panels."

He stared at me. "Where do you live?" I felt my body tense. There was something in his tone that I didn't like.

I looked at him, unsure of what to say. "Lakeview," I answered vaguely. "But you have electricity too," I quickly pointed out.

"A generator. It runs on gas . . . plenty of cars lying around to siphon fuel from. I also hooked a couple up in empty houses to attract those things."

"Why?" I asked, truly curious. There were so many of Them, what would killing a few stray ones do?

"It makes me happy." He scowled, looking anything but happy. "I feel like I'm actually doing something. Every night I go on my rounds, up to the lake and downtown and back. I check on the traps every third night."

He stepped toward me and I backed away. I smiled awkwardly. Something about him had me on alert.

"I'm just heading to the fridge," he told me, his hands

up in the air. He opened the door and grabbed a couple of bottles. "Do you want a beer?"

"Uh . . ." Out of habit, I hesitated. "I don't know. . . ."

"In case you haven't noticed, society is in shambles. Our government has collapsed and we've been overrun by creatures from another planet. I don't think the drinking age applies anymore," he told me with a smirk.

He was right. There's no reason why I shouldn't drink. "Sure, I'll have one," I said, feeling a little embarrassed.

Jake returned from the kitchen and held out the bottle to me. I reached for the beer uneasily. As I stretched out my fingers the bottle slipped. The glass crashed to the floor and shattered, the noise startling me. I stared at the broken bottle, the beer fizzing in a puddle. It was unsettling not to be silent. Everything felt all wrong.

"I'm sorry," I told him lamely. "Do you have a towel or something?"

"Don't worry about it." He took a swig of his beer and went to get me another one. Suddenly I was struck by an overwhelming urge to leave. "Actually, I should get back," I said. "I wanted to do some more scavenging before dawn."

"Oh. Okay." His face fell. He looked at the floor, clearly disappointed. "But maybe I can see you again tomorrow," he said, perking up slightly. "I mean, we have to stick together. There aren't many of us left."

"Have you seen others?" I asked excitedly. Somehow I just didn't like the prospect of being stuck with Jake as my only human companion for the next fifty or so years.

"A few. There are even rumors that a whole town survived, though no one seems to know where it is." He sipped his beer, unwilling to say more. Then he gave me a look that made my skin crawl. "You can stay here if you want. Or I can come to your place. I'd love to take a hot shower." He beamed. "A shower would be fan."

"Yeah, fan," I agreed. Jake's use of my friends' slang sounded like when my dad tried to buddy up to me and said things like *cool* and *hip*.

"So, we can hang out at your place for a bit?" He was suddenly standing very close to me.

"Maybe." I was careful not to commit to anything. "We can talk about it tomorrow." I backed away toward the door.

"All right," he said, though clearly it was anything but. "Should we meet up tomorrow at our spot? Midnight?" he asked. A shiver ran down my spine. His use of "our spot" freaked me out.

"Sure, sounds good," I agreed, just wanting to leave. I

reached for the door and struggled with the handle. Jake stood over me, making the muscles in my neck and jaw tense. He reached past me and undid the lock.

"Thanks," I mumbled, and hurried down the stairs, out the door, and into the night.

My hands shook slightly and I felt queasy. I had such high hopes for our meeting. I thought he'd be younger, less creepy. I wanted us to click and become friends. But up there, in his apartment, all I wanted was to escape. I guess it takes a certain kind of person to survive an alien invasion; I was just lucky my parents were a little wacky. I had no guarantees with strangers.

A noise behind me snapped me out of my thoughts and I stood still. I quickly stepped into the bushes and hid. I expected one of Them to shuffle by, as they often did at night, unaware of things that were not directly in front of Them. Instead there was nothing.

It took me a few moments to realize it wasn't one of Them. It was Jake. He'd followed me. He wanted to know where I lived. He wanted to see my setup and decide if it was better than his. My heart thudded in my chest. And what if he did think mine was better? My house was secure. It had running water and electricity. What would he do when he saw all that? My mind was racing. He would try to take it.

I waited in the bushes for him to make a move. His progression was not loud, but I'd learned to listen for even the slightest sound. As he made his way closer, I froze, uncertain of what I should do: run or stay hidden. I didn't have long to decide.

Too late, I chose to bolt. I was still in the bushes when a hand grabbed my arm tightly. Jake pulled me roughly from my hiding spot. He took my backpack and slung it over his shoulder, holding my arm in a death grip. He hugged me to his chest.

"If you scream," he whispered, his hot breath in my ear, "the creatures will come and kill you." He shoved his arm under my shirt and squeezed. The pain made me exhale loudly.

"If you like that, just wait." He pulled my hair, yanking my head back with a jerk. Forcing his face to mine, he kissed me roughly. His teeth rammed into my lips, cutting painfully at the soft tissue. He pulled away slightly and I tasted blood, sharp and metallic against my tongue.

I reached my arm around and pulled the gun from its holster. I was grateful my clothes were baggy and Jake hadn't noticed I was carrying it earlier. I shoved the barrel in his stomach and unhooked the safety with a click.

"Back off," I said, careful to keep my voice low. I could hear the panic in my tone, and my hands were shaking. Jake took several steps back and stared.

"If you shoot that gun, every one of those things within four miles will be on you." He started to come toward me again. I quickly reached in my pocket and screwed the attachment onto the end. I'd practiced at home for speed.

"Silencer," I hissed, forcing a smug grin. I really just wanted to puke.

"You know, silencers aren't all that quiet. . . ." he whispered, though he didn't sound very convinced. He backed away, looking me up and down. He still held my backpack. "I'll see you around, honey." He winked at me before he turned and began to jog away.

Then I remembered the object in my pocket. Since that day with the creature in the store, I'd come up with a getaway plan. A way to distract Them if They had me cornered, something more complex than a can of corn. I pulled out the remote and stepped back into the bushes. I paused for only a second before hitting the button.

About half a block away, the siren sounded. I heard a few run by, not the mindless shuffle but the full gallop They developed when They thought humans were near. And then I heard Jake scream. There must have been a few closer. He would have been shocked at the noise. It would have taken him too long to realize it was coming from the bag. Even if he had tossed it in time, he could not have outrun Them. He wouldn't have had enough time to hide.

The screams continued and I put my hands over my ears. He'd be dead in less than a minute. I just wanted the noise to stop. The alarm was still going, but I figured They would tear that apart soon enough as well. I didn't want to do it, but I already had to worry about Them. I couldn't live wondering if a psycho survivor was out to get me as well. I cried silently, hoping Jake was not the only other person alive on the planet. Did he lie about seeing other people? About the town of survivors?

The creatures shuffled around for a while, satisfied with their meal. Exhausted, I waited for what seemed like hours, cold and miserable until the area cleared and I could walk back to my house. The first thing I did when I got home was rig another bag from the car alarms I'd scavenged.

I didn't know then that the awful exchange with Jake would be the last real conversation I would have for a very, very long time.

A clap of thunder brings me back to reality, away from the past. I scan again for any new ships, but the sky is empty except for dark gray clouds. The heavier rain will come soon. I'll be able to climb down the tree and return home before long.

I try not to think about Jake and what happened that night. But I had learned a few very important things about survival. I also learned where They go at night.

While I hid in the bushes all those years ago, I watched Them shuffle back from their kill. One by one, They lay on the ground and slinked down a rain gutter. I would not have thought it possible, but they are small and bend in incredible ways. Even their bones seem flexible. That's where They will be now, while the sky is darkening and the heavy downpour threatening to burst through the clouds. They will head underground to the sewers.

As soon as the drizzle turns into a torrent, I slide down the tree and jog home. Baby is happy to see me. She greets me with a towel and a change of clothes.

Did you see it? she signs, her quivering hands betraying her concern. *The ship?*

I nod.

Is it Them? she asks.

Yes.

Where did it come from?

I don't know, I say, no longer sure that I want to find out.

CHAPTER NINE

We spot the ships weekly now, their presence becoming more common. So are our run-ins with other survivors. It used to be once a year, when the weather turned warm. Now I spot other people about once a month, usually when the moon is only a sliver in the sky, providing the most cover of darkness. They are coming to the cities from the country. They figure if anyone else is alive, this is where they'll be. They don't seem to understand that it is also where the creatures prefer to live and feed.

I develop a system for dealing with strangers. I never

show myself to groups of people. A group is more likely to turn on me, try to steal my resources for themselves. I read a book once about mass hysteria, how people can do anything if others are doing it too. In the After, even three people can be considered a mob, and I'm not taking any chances.

I avoid lone men for obvious reasons. I sometimes make my presence known to women, depending on how scrawny they look, how much they seem to need assistance. I don't speak to them, but I let them see me. I nod and motion toward a sewer drain, make a cutting sign across my throat. They get the picture. I also point in the direction of the lake and pretend to drink a glass of water. I always make Baby hide when there are people around. You never know who you can trust.

Poor Baby. I look at her sometimes and think about my own childhood. I used to go to the zoo and shop on weekends with my friends. Baby tags along with me to silently scavenge dead people's homes. I had pizza and home-cooked meals. She has canned food and badly charred squirrel that we catch in rattraps. I had two loving, if a little wacky, parents. She only has me.

Most important, I had sunlight. Now we both live in a dark world. We go to the roof sometimes, during the day, but

I find it eerie. The silent city, Them shuffling underneath us. At night we can at least make some noise. We discovered that They ignored the hum of the air conditioner or the heat pumping through winter, but they came running when the microwave beeped. I was confident the fence would hold, but I didn't know for how long, so it was better not to test it. We learned to do everything as quietly as possible. We live like monks. Silent, pasty, scared monks.

What's this one about? Baby asks, handing me a book. I glance at it: *Pride and Prejudice.*

It's about two people who love each other but are too stupid to figure it out until the end of the story.

Baby looks disappointed. *But,* I add, *the woman is very smart and the man is very handsome.*

What's that? She points at the cover: Mr. Darcy on a horse. I grab the sign language dictionary and look up the word *horse* to show her.

They're from Before, I tell her. That's what I usually say when I don't know how to explain something, like airplanes and Christmas.

She nods and looks at the horse longingly. I smile. I guess every little girl wants a horse, even ones who don't know what a horse is. I wonder if there are any horses left. It's been a long time since I've seen a dog. There are cats around, ones feral enough to make it on their own. Cats have the right combination of animal characteristics to survive Them. They are silent and like to hang out in trees. Birds do well, too. Dogs and larger animals, not so much.

And this one? Baby asks.

Too old, I tell her. I'm not up to explaining the entire plot of *The Merchant of Venice.* Greed, revenge, and racism are topics for another day.

Baby tugs on my sleeve, points to a new book. I scan the cover. *This one is about a monster,* I say without thinking, pausing at Baby's horrified expression. *Monster* was the word I'd assigned to Them.

Not a monster, I correct myself. *I meant a thing.* . . . How could I explain *Frankenstein* to someone who has seen real monsters?

It's a story from Before. I take the book from her and place it high up on the shelf. *Now, this is a good one.* I hand her a picture book that I loved when I was growing up, one I asked to be read to me every night for a year. *The Little Mermaid.* I let her look at the pictures and tell me how the story goes. Her version is a lot happier than the Hans Christian

Andersen one and much less gory. My father was pleased how much I appreciated the tale; he said it taught children consequences and that not all endings are happy.

Baby, though, ends with *They all lived happily ever after,* just like I taught her.

I hope, she tells me, *that we can live happily ever after.*

I hug her, trying not to cry. *You and me both,* I think, kissing the top of her head.

I like this one, Baby signs into my hand. She holds up a candy bar, its wrapper dusty and crinkled.

Is it sealed? I ask. At this point everything in the grocery store is expired, but things last a lot longer than companies let on. It's all those preservatives. I taught Baby to check for rancid chips and candy and to only gather cans that have no dents and aren't all bulgy. We have stomach medicine at home, but I don't want to trust treating botulism with three-year-old pink bismuth.

Yes, it's sealed. Baby smiles up at me. *Also, I found this.* She holds up a box of macaroni and cheese. She manages to move the box without all the noodles crashing together like a maraca.

Fan, I tell her. *Good job.* I taught Baby "fan" as very good.

I made up the sign: hand just below your face, gesture like you're fanning yourself on a hot summer day. I like keeping the word my friends and I always used. It's like having a bit of Sabrina with me at times. It hurts, but in a strange way it makes me stronger.

Baby beams. She loves being helpful. As she grew older, I let her come with me more often. We'd soon pilfered everything in the corner store near my house and had to walk farther and farther for supplies. She can carry a surprising amount for a child, and I never have to worry about her making noise. She is excellent at staying quiet. She also has exceptional hearing, sometimes alerting me to Them before I'm even aware They are near.

What's this? she asks me, holding up a plastic cell phone filled with candy.

Candy, I tell her.

No, the outside. Baby wants to know about everything. It's annoying sometimes, but I'm secretly glad she isn't traumatized by our lifestyle. I would have thought a little kid like that would shut down completely when faced with Them.

It's something from Before, I explain. *People used it to talk.*

Like books?

I shake my head. *No, with their mouths.*

Baby smirks slightly and raises her eyebrows. She thinks I'm joking. It's been so long since she's heard anyone speak, she doesn't remember what it's like.

I try to explain. *Before They came, everyone didn't use their hands to talk. They used their mouths.* Well, except for deaf people, but I don't want to confuse her.

Baby's face scrunches in disbelief and confusion. Then it turns suddenly to stone. *Noise,* she signs.

Baby and I immediately grab our bags and back quietly away into the aisle. We hear footsteps. We look at each other. Footsteps mean shoes. The creatures don't wear shoes.

I'll look, Baby signs into my hand. I nod once. She soundlessly drops her bag and doubles around to the side of the store. I don't like sending her off, but she is excellent at spying.

I listen to the footsteps. They're coming from the front of the store near the registers. They are not slow and they are not cautious. Anyone who went around making a racket like that shouldn't have survived this long.

Baby touches my elbow. She's returned silently. *A woman. Alone.*

I think for a moment. *Grab your bag.*

Are we going to meet her? Baby asks, wide eyed.

No. It could be a trap.

Baby nods. *She's very loud. Does she want Them to come?*

Maybe, but even if she doesn't, they'll be here soon. Let's go.

We take the long way around, avoiding the footsteps and their owner. We are almost to the door when I feel a tickle in my throat. I swallow twice trying to fight the urge. The tickle climbs up my throat to my sinuses. I try to hold it in but I can't help the small noise that escapes me as I sneeze.

Baby freezes.

"Wait," I hear from somewhere in the store.

Go, I tell Baby. *Fast.*

"Please, wait." The woman runs toward us, yelling. "Don't leave me here."

I grab Baby's hand and hurry to the door. Whoever the woman is, she has zero self-preservation skills.

We make it through the door just as a car alarm sounds. Baby stops, startled by the unnaturally loud noise. I think for a moment that it's me, that I accidentally triggered the alarm I carry in case I need a diversion. The noise isn't coming from my bag, but blaring from across the street. When the realization takes hold, I notice that Baby is still frozen in place. I pull Baby's arm and push her into some overgrown bushes. I crouch down, searching for the source of the noise.

A red pickup truck across the street is loaded with men.

My jaw drops. There are ten of them at least, each with a rifle. It's the largest group of people I have seen since Before. One of the men stands on top of the truck. He holds up a bullhorn and clicks it on with a *beep*.

"COME ON, YOU SLIMY GREEN BASTARDS!"

It has only been a few seconds since the siren sounded, but already They are running toward the truck. The men form a circle, facing outward, their weapons raised and aimed at the creatures' heads. If They are merely wounded they continue to crawl forward, even when they are missing arms and legs.

Baby shakes next to me, her head buried in my arm, her eyes closed tight. I'm glad she isn't watching. She doesn't need to witness a massacre.

As more and more of Them arrive, the men are forced back against the truck. *Please don't die,* I think. I don't want it to end this way. They shouldn't throw their lives away just to take a few of Them out. It isn't worth it.

It's not long before the situation begins to look hopeless for the men. The creatures are about to overwhelm the truck. There are too many to continue fighting, but the men keep shooting. They take out several more of Them, but others take their place.

Finally the men retreat. As quickly as they arrived, they jump into the flatbed of the red truck, still shooting. The man with the bullhorn hurries to the driver's seat and steps on the gas. The truck is surrounded, but they plow through the mass of creatures taking at least ten of Them out. I smile. They are not on a suicide mission. They are guerrilla warriors.

The truck drives away, tires screeching. The creatures follow, running after it as fast as they can, which is sickeningly fast. The silence that follows is frightening after so much noise.

Is it over? Baby signs.

Yes, but we have to wait here until it's clear.

Baby raises her head to look out. *Talking with your mouth is scary,* she says, referring to the man with the bullhorn.

It is. But it wasn't Before. Our brief encounter with chaos makes me homesick for that other time. I try not to think about Before.

Amy. Baby touches my elbow urgently.

A pair of legs appears before our hiding space. I look up. It's the woman from the grocery store, who I'd forgotten about during the commotion.

"Don't leave me," she shrieks. I'm furious and

panicked–she is going to bring Them right to us.

I pull her down into the bushes and put my hand over her mouth. I hope she doesn't struggle, but as soon as she is within the cover of our hiding place, her body goes limp. I leave my hand where it is as a reminder to be quiet.

We're lucky. After the commotion, They don't react very quickly to the woman's outburst. They are too busy gnawing on the remains of the creatures that were killed. It is dark, so as long as we stay quiet, they won't find us.

They feed for a long time, eating every bit of their dead, their sharp teeth chewing through skin, muscle, and bone. Their feeding noises sicken me, slurps with the occasional crunch. Two fight over an arm, wrestle on the ground. I hope they hurt each other but one eventually relents.

I glance at the woman. She's more of a girl really, maybe a few years older than I am. Her face is slack, her eyes dull. I take my hand off her mouth and rest it on Baby's trembling shoulder. I need to distract her, to distract myself.

What was that story, from the other day? I ask. *The one about the mermaid.*

Baby puts her hand in mine. *The fish princess lived in the lake, where no monsters could reach her.* Baby's eyes are closed, her lips parted slightly.

For the moment she is at the bottom of the sea with the mermaid, not hiding in a bush watching aliens pig out on other aliens. She expands on her earlier story, explaining in detail the lives of the little mermaid's sisters. "Sister" was the sign I'd taught Baby for what we are to each other.

I feel her fingers move against my hand, relaying her story in a language only we understand. The movement is comforting, but I remain tense and anxious as we wait for Them to leave. I have no idea what to do with the girl lying beside us.

It is almost dawn before the creatures clear out. Baby has fallen asleep, so I shake her awake. I stand and stretch, my muscles sore from sitting in the same position for too long.

What about her? Baby points to the girl, awake but unmoving. I shrug.

Leave her. My main concern is getting Baby back to the house before first light.

We can't. Baby's eyes plead. *She's* . . . I can see Baby search for the right word . . . *She's sick.*

I want to tell Baby no, that the girl can't come with us, but I look into her eyes and I can't. I think of the time I found her in that grocery store, when I almost left her. The guilt is too much.

I reach back into the bushes and grab the girl by the wrist.

"What . . ." she starts to speak. I put my finger over my lips and breathe out slightly. If this girl isn't going to be quiet, I am going to leave her, no matter what Baby wants.

Luckily the girl gets the idea and follows us, her shoes thumping on the pavement. I stop her and point at her feet. She looks at me blankly. I hold out my own foot, bare and calloused.

She quickly slips off her shoes. She holds them in her arms, waiting. I motion for her to follow and we make our way back home.

"Swanky," the girl says once we are inside. I look at her, unwilling to speak. Her dark eyes and hair contrast sharply with the whiteness of her skin. She is painfully pale, but then, so am I.

We should give her food. Baby suggests. I nod and Baby runs to make us breakfast.

I show the girl to the basement. It used to be my dad's work space, but Baby and I made it our reading room. I scavenged a ton of pillows to give it an *Arabian Nights* feel.

The girl sits on my beanbag chair, unsmiling but not

appearing overly distressed. I cross my arms and stare her down.

She scratches her nose and looks back at me, expecting me to speak. Her dark hair is flat against her head, dirty and oily. She is thin, but not painfully skinny, like most of the survivors I encounter.

"Look, I didn't know those guys. . . . Well, actually, I knew one of them. He's my brother, I . . . do you even understand me?"

I nod.

She starts again. "My name is Amber." She pauses, waiting for me to respond. When I don't, she narrows her eyes. "I don't know what all this silent treatment is about, but I don't like it."

I sigh. My silence has kept me alive. I'm not about to break years of habit for a stranger. I lick my lips, my mouth painfully dry . . . besides, I'm not even sure if I can talk anymore, it's been so long. I go to my dad's desk and scrounge around for a notepad and pen. I write, *We have to be quiet, the creatures are attracted to noise. They know that voices mean people. There is safety in silence.* It would be foolish to drop our guard now, to begin speaking aloud. It could be deadly.

I hand it to Amber and as she reads, understanding dawns on her face.

"It all makes sense now," she whispers. Her voice carries through the room, making me nervous.

Where have you been? I write. *Whisper as quietly as you can.*

"My brother, Paul, and I were shut up in a bomb shelter until a few days ago. My parents . . ." She falters. "My parents died right away, my little sister too. Paul and I had lots of food down there without them. My parents were end-of-the-world nuts, you know."

I nod. I had a great aunt who was like that. She always thought everyone ought to be prepared in case something crazy happened. Like an alien invasion, I suppose. Too bad Aunt Ellie died before she was vindicated.

"We ran out of food," Amber was saying, "a few days ago. There was only supposed to be enough for a year, but with the rest of my family not making it . . ." She trails off and stares over my shoulder before snapping back. "We probably should have left way before then. We had water but the sewage system stopped working a long time ago. We couldn't shower and had to . . . use a bucket for a toilet.

Paul went first, to see what was going on. He came back last night with those psychos. They said something about creatures, but I didn't understand. They sent me into the store to look for food. I didn't know. . . ." She pauses, a look of realization emerges on her face. "Oh, I think I was the bait."

Bingo.

"Oh God, I can't believe Paul left me there." Amber begins to cry softly.

I feel for her. I can't imagine emerging from a safe, secure place completely unprepared for what the world has become. Amber is so helpless, so loud. There is no way she can survive on her own.

Baby joins us with a tray and three plates piled high with breakfast. She places it on the table in front of Amber. Baby has gone all out. Baked beans, eggs from the pigeons that roost below our solar panels, and Twinkies: the breakfast of champions.

Eat, she signs. Amber nods. Even an idiot can decipher that one. She begins to shovel beans into her mouth, the brown juice running down her chin. She wipes her face on her sleeve.

Can she stay here? Baby asks as if Amber is a puppy. Baby's eyes are wide and hopeful.

I think for a moment while Amber eats. She unwraps the Twinkie and shoves the whole thing in her mouth.

"These *do* last forever," she says. Her mouth is so filled with yellow cake that she spits some out onto the floor. "Sorry," she apologizes loudly. I hear the electric fence spark. It is day now, and They will be out in full force.

I make the "shush" sign again, pointer finger pressed to my mouth.

Amber nods, exaggerating the motion. She's finished her meal and licks the plate clean. I give her my share. I'm not very hungry, still unsettled by the bizarre massacre and the arrival of Amber. Baby, on the other hand seems to have forgotten about the commotion. She eats her food slowly, more occupied with staring at Amber curiously.

When they are done eating, Baby stands to clear the plates. Amber grabs her wrist. I move forward to stop her.

"Thank you," she whispers. I realize she doesn't mean Baby any harm and I relax.

Baby looks at her blankly. She hasn't heard English since she was a toddler. By now she's probably forgotten all she ever knew.

Amber turns to me. "How do you say 'thank you'?"

I show her. I put my hand to my chin and gesture out and down in a small arc.

Amber turns back to Baby and makes the same motion. Baby's eyes shine and she smiles.

You're welcome, she signs, her face glowing as she retreats upstairs.

I give Amber a pillow and a blanket. *Sleep,* I tell her, using another easy sign. She lies down on the couch and closes her eyes. She must have been exhausted because she falls asleep almost immediately, her breathing slow and deep.

I walk upstairs to talk with Baby. I know she likes the idea of Amber, and I do as well. She is another person to scavenge with us, someone else to watch our backs. We can teach her our language and how to survive in the After. She needs us.

Unfortunately I know that liking the idea of something and dealing with the reality of it are two very different things. What if Amber is more of a burden than a help? What if she never gets the hang of being quiet? What if she can't deal, turns schizoid, and kills us in our sleep? I stop and take a breath. Amber doesn't really seem like the murdering type.

Baby is in the kitchen, loading the dishwasher. It is one of those energy-efficient ones my dad insisted on, which works out great because it runs super quiet. I think of Amber and realize how easy I have it. It is the end of the world and we have a dishwasher, not to mention all the other appliances I take for granted. Sometimes if it hasn't rained in a while we have to go without washing clothes or taking showers, but never for very long.

Even though I don't make a noise, Baby senses me behind her and turns.

What do you think? I ask her.

She's so . . . Baby thinks for a moment. She shakes her head. *She's so loud!* She throws her arms up to illustrate her point.

I know. We have to show her how to be silent.

Baby grins and I notice one of her baby teeth is missing, the front one that was loose. She must have lost it during the commotion. No tooth fairy for her, though. She wouldn't understand.

Can she stay? Baby asks.

We don't have a choice. But we do have a choice. We can send Amber packing. Good-bye and good luck. Don't let the electric gate hit you on the way out. *She can stay,* I decide.

Fan. Baby holds her hand up to her face and waves, overjoyed.

I smile at her enthusiasm, but I can't help but think, *Fan-fricken-tastic. Please, don't make me wrong about Amber.*

CHAPTER TEN

I'm unsure about Amber at first, mainly because everything about her annoys me. She is the kind of girl I would have never been friends with Before. My friends and I competed in class. We went to poetry readings and volunteered for political candidates we were too young to vote for. We ran track and thought it was the only acceptable sport. So much of who I used to be was about being good in school and having friends who were also good in school. We were, to put it simply, arrogant little know-it-alls. But I miss that.

Amber, on the other hand, is the girl who hung out with

the football players. She is the one who squeaked by with a D average and was thrilled to get the occasional C. She didn't think about college, and probably never faced the eventuality that high school would one day end. I would have made fun of her behind her back, while I secretly envied her popular, carefree life.

But we aren't in high school, and having to deal with a self-centered dimwit can have deadly consequences. I have to make her understand.

The first thing I show Amber is the electric fence and warn her not to touch it. I am a bit dramatic with that, pointing at the fence and then clutching my hands to my neck, my tongue hanging out. I am pretty sure she gets the idea. Then I show her the small area around the lock where it is safe to touch.

In actuality, the fence won't kill her, or anyone. The shock isn't pleasant, and if you hang on for long enough it will take you out of commission and leave you unconscious. I tested it out once when I was twelve and my arm was numb for a couple of hours. My dad totally freaked out on my mom then, told her he didn't want us living in a "gold-plated prison." I thought for a little while they were going to get divorced over it, but they made up eventually, like they always did.

The fence's real purpose was to stop people from trying to break in. It was hooked up to an alarm system that alerted the police if someone touched it. There is no one to come running now when They try to get through, but the shock seems to stop Them, move Them on their way. Unless, of course, we are standing right in front of the creatures' beady yellow eyes; then nothing can break their focus. I don't want to test just how much damage the fence can take, so I still need Amber to be quiet.

We set her up in the basement with the couch as her bed. I let her wear my clothes at first, but I eventually allow her to raid my mother's closet. Amber is beside herself. My mom had good taste and bought expensive things, but I'd always thought of it as "middle-aged fashion." Amber loves it all, especially the Dolce & Gabbana skirts and the DKNY jeans. That is another thing that shows we would not have been friends Before. I would not have been caught dead wearing designer anything. My dad always assumed it was because I shared his eco-sensibilities, that I would rather spend the money to plant a tree or save a whale. Truthfully not all my friends were as wealthy as we were and I didn't want them to know how much money we had. I didn't want them to think I was a snob, especially Sabrina.

It's weird to see Amber wear my mother's shirts or scarves, but I find it strangely comforting too. I've avoided going through my parents' closet for years; mostly I stay away from their room altogether. It's all too painful, but giving Amber free range of my mother's things breaks that spell.

After Amber picks out her new wardrobe, I show her the rooftop garden and she gets to work at once, which I am grateful for. The garden is a chore I never enjoyed, even though I recognize the need for fresh vegetables. Amber seems to know what she is doing and I leave her to it. She likes to be up on the roof, especially during the day. She comes downstairs, sunburned and glowing. Three years without any sunlight is a long time.

At first, I am afraid to leave her alone with Baby. I imagine every horrible thing that can happen. Amber accidentally letting Them inside. Amber convincing Baby to eat some questionable canned food. Amber letting it all get to her and going crazy, maybe trying to end her own life and not caring who she hurts in the process.

All these thoughts rumble around in my head while I watch Amber playing with Baby, eating our food, doing her chores. I pay close attention to how she interacts with Baby and even check on her when she's sleeping. She curls on the basement couch, mouth open, breathing loudly. I'm glad we set her up downstairs because if she were in one of the upstairs bedrooms, her snores would bring Them.

After about a week, I start to relax. Amber doesn't seem like she is on the verge of a nervous breakdown, in fact she is making an incredible effort, especially with Baby. Sometimes she looks out the window, staring at nothing. She was abandoned by her brother. I'd be a little depressed too.

I don't know when it is exactly that I start to like Amber, but one day, I just do. It's nice to have someone around who is about my age. She takes such pleasure in our life, in our home. She sits and watches the dishwasher run. She helps Baby make a pillow fort. She plucks a pigeon without complaint. I am especially glad that she gets the hint after that first night and stops talking. Well, mostly stops talking. We speak to her in a broken language: *Amber sleep now,* or *Amber go up, eat now.*

She understands more each day. Baby and I sign in front of her, trying to let her see as much as she can so she can learn to communicate with us. I show her which appliances are "safe" and which can only be used if all the doors and windows are shut, to lessen the noise. She falls in love with the shower and I have to limit her to only ten minutes a day, unless it is raining. Otherwise our water supply will run out and we'll have to trek to the lake for drinking water.

It doesn't take very long for Amber's presence to feel normal. Baby loves her at once. She wants to be near Amber all the time. I am a little jealous at first, but I get over it. Baby is Amber's shadow and signs to her constantly; explaining this or that, or sometimes just telling her stories she's made up. Amber likes to watch Baby sign, though sometimes I notice she zones out. Baby doesn't seem to mind, though, and continues signing, glancing at me every once in a while with a smile.

What this? she asks one day of the mark on Baby's neck. Amber enjoys brushing out Baby's hair, styling it into different looks. She studies the strange, barely perceivable diamond, traces it with her finger.

I shrug. *Baby, show her your scar.*

Baby grins and hikes up her skirt to show Amber the scar on the fleshy part of her thigh. Amber lifts up her face and shows us a fine white scar under her chin.

Was fallen . . . She struggles and goes to grab a pen and paper. Amber often writes me notes when she doesn't have the vocabulary to sign what she wants to say, or when Baby's hands are going a mile a minute and Amber is lost.

Cheerleading, she scrawls. *I was dropped and needed five stitches,* she adds proudly.

I try to explain to Baby, but give up when I realize I'd have to describe sports and crowds and girls in short skirts screaming at the top of their lungs to lead other people in screaming at the top of their lungs too. She wouldn't understand . . . to be honest, I never really understood. I turn to walk away, but Amber stops me.

What's that thing she just called me? Amber writes, showing me the motion.

I take the pen and paper from her and write what Baby has said. Amber glances at the paper and starts to cry.

Baby has called her sister.

I'm in my room reading when Baby appears at the door. *I just heard the trap snap,* Baby informs me happily.

I smile. *Squirrel or pigeon?*

She cocks her head to the side, hearing what is beyond my ability to sense. *Can't tell, but I hope it's not a squirrel.* So do I. Squirrels are a lot of work for very little meat.

Where's Amber? I ask.

Baby listens intently. *In the basement. I can hear her moving around.*

I head downstairs and find Amber dancing around with her headphones on. I roll my eyes. When she turns to me, she yelps with a start.

She puts her hand to her chest. *Amy scared Amber.*

Sorry, I sign. *Come.*

She follows me upstairs and out into the yard. I show her the no-kill rattrap. Just another thing she has to learn.

Dinner, I tell her.

She scrunches up her nose. I show her how to open the trap, pleased that it caught a rabbit this time. They sometimes burrow under the fence without getting shocked. I reach in quickly and pull it out by its neck, while it squirms. I put one hand on its head and twist as Amber watches, horrified, and I remember the first time I had to kill an animal. I placed the trap, baited it with peanut butter, and waited. It was a pigeon that time. My hands shook when I tried to kill it; I nearly gave up. I almost let it go. I cried afterward and didn't set another trap for a week. All I could think about was bird-watching with my father and his constant concern with preserving nature and the environment. Now all I am concerned with is self-preservation.

Amber looks like she is about to be sick. *It has to be done,* I tell her. The little meat we get, no matter how scarce, is welcome. I show her how to skin and clean the rabbit, but I let her go after that. She is a bit pale and looks like she can use the break. I salt the rabbit and place it in the oven to cook.

When I go to the basement, I find Amber and Baby deep in conversation, as deep as two people who don't understand each other very well can be.

"You would like my brother," Amber whispers. "He's real good with little kids." She signs what words she knows, which are only *real, good,* and *like.*

Baby thinks she is talking about her and grins. *I really like you too, Amber.*

I wonder how often Amber whispers to Baby. If she keeps it up, Baby will begin to understand English. I wonder if she'll start to talk then, or if the silence has become a part of her.

I step to back away, but Baby hears me and looks up. She narrows her eyes at me, and I'm shocked to realize that she's unhappy that I'm there. She wants to be alone with Amber. I feel as if I've been spying.

It was a rabbit, I sign.

I know, Amber told me. Her guarded look fades, but I'm still left with an uneasy feeling.

No whispering, I sign to them both. Baby nods quickly, ashamed, while Amber just shrugs.

Not bad now. She means there is no harm in whispering in the basement.

Whispering is always bad. Always bad. I repeat it so she gets the picture. I go upstairs and sit at the kitchen table. For the first time ever with Baby, I am the outsider.

It is a couple of weeks after Amber's arrival before we need more supplies; I've put it off for as long as I can. I wanted Amber to settle in before we left her alone, but we need more food. Amber has used most of the shampoo and soap, and Baby is starting to complain that her clothes don't fit. She grew like crazy as soon as the weather warmed up, getting taller and thinner. Also, we have to start collecting and hoarding supplies for the winter, although it is months away. Once it snows, it's impossible to walk outside without making noise.

I write Amber a note, explaining that Baby and I need to get supplies. I watch her read it, her smile disappearing as her face changes from excited to disappointed.

You leave Amber? she asks unhappily.

Yes, we have to. We need food. I point back at the note. I've explained it all.

Amber come. She starts to walk toward the door where Baby stands, ready to go.

I put my hand on Amber's shoulder. *No.*

Why?

I look at her. She's learned a lot about how we live day to day, but she is still clueless about the world outside our house. Our home is paradise compared to the real After. Amber is like a child, and even Baby has better survival skills.

It's dangerous. Dangerous is a word she knows. I've used it often.

Please, she signs. "I can't stay here alone," she whispers desperately. Her forehead wrinkles with concern, and her eyes are already welling up.

My jaw tightens. This behavior just proves that she isn't ready to face the outside again.

Amber's nose scrunches and her lip trembles. I look away from her, ashamed of myself. It's not fair to leave her on her own when she is just getting used to being part of our family.

Okay, fine, I sign and she immediately brightens. I take the note from her and find a pen. *But you have to watch us and do exactly as I tell you,* I scrawl across the back.

Yes, she quickly agrees, relieved.

I hand her a backpack and give her some socks. She walks around the house barefoot, but she isn't used to walking on pavement scattered with twigs and stones that could damage her feet. The socks will offer a little cushion without added noise.

Is it safe? Baby asks as we open the door and head toward the gate.

We'll take a short trip, something easy for Amber.

We only go a block. There is a big house on the corner that I've avoided exploring, since I knew the people who lived there. They had children, a little boy and a girl about Baby's age. I hope their daughter's clothes will fit Baby, otherwise we'll have to take a much longer walk to the stores downtown. We have to plan ahead for that one, and Amber definitely can't come. She isn't ready for a silent, eight-mile hike.

The door to the house is locked, so we walk around to the side yard. Their back door, sliding glass, is smashed to pieces. A shredded blue curtain moves with the breeze. I turn to Amber and Baby and point out the glass shards. Baby follows with Amber close behind.

The living room smells of mildew. The open doorway

has allowed the rain to damage the walls and floor, leaving black mold on the carpet that has crept halfway up the nearest wall. The paint has peeled in long strips. Even so, you can still tell that the former occupants were well-off. The living room is furnished nicely, intricate wood chairs and a plush cream couch, now on its side and spotted with dirt.

Baby, you check the kitchen, I tell her. *I'll take Amber with me to look upstairs.*

Baby nods once, all business. I smile sadly. At that age I complained about cleaning my room and thought my parents were mean when they made me clear the table after dinner. I sometimes wonder what kind of child Baby would be if none of this had happened. Would she be that weird kid in the corner of the playground who never spoke to anyone, or would she be the daredevil on the jungle gym?

Where Amber go? Amber asks. She is looking around uncertainly. Her eyes rest on a dark spot on the carpet. Even though the blotch is several years old, there is no mistaking the black-red stain. Someone has died there. Amber stares at the unpleasant splotch, her forehead wrinkled. I realize I should have warned her about what to expect.

I wave my hand to get Amber's attention. Her gaze lingers on the spot of blood for another moment, then she focuses on me, eyes glassy.

It's okay, I tell her. I grab her hand and lead her across the living room. We need to find the daughter's room and grab some clothes for Baby while she searches for canned food. I don't want to take longer than necessary.

We find the staircase past the dining room. I test the stairs first, making sure the water damage doesn't extend to the wood. I don't want to fall through and hurt myself since there isn't anything I can do if I break a bone.

The stairs are solid, though a couple sag. Two squeak loudly. I make a mental note of which ones, so I can avoid them on the way back down. I motion for Amber to follow. Her face is pale, her lips pressed firmly together. She's still shaken from the gore on the carpet and imagining what took place there.

I take her hand again and lead her slowly up the staircase. The wall is lined with family photos. One is pushed sideways, a picture of the little girl taken at the lake. She wears a bright pink bathing suit, grins at the camera. I had a blue-and-white-striped suit when I was her age. "Cheese-it," my dad used to tell me before he snapped a photo.

I reach out to straighten the picture but suddenly change my mind. At the corner of the glass is a smudged red fingerprint. After being attacked downstairs, someone tried to escape up here, to hide. I try not to think about it. I've had to survive my own horrors; I don't need to live the terrors of others. I squeeze Amber's hand. There will be more bloodstains upstairs.

At the top of the stairs, I scan the hall for signs of what happened there, but there is no broken furniture, no gory scene. I know better than to feel relieved. The hallway is full of doors, any of which could lead to the room in which They caught their prey.

The door closest to the stairs is the only one open. The wood is littered with deep scratches and the door handle is missing. I glance through the doorway but can't make out anything in the dark.

Stay, I tell Amber.

I walk the few feet, holding my breath, and step inside a large bathroom. A shower curtain lies across the floor, ripped to shreds. I sniff the air. It leaves a metallic taste in my mouth. The plush bathroom rug feels strange between my toes. It is too soft and fluffy for the After.

I force myself to look into the tub to confirm what I already know. Someone tried to hide from Them in here, but wasn't quiet enough. The white ceramic is splattered with blood. The spots are brown with age, and hair is sticking to the porcelain sides. I swallow hard.

When I back out of the room, closing the door firmly behind me, Amber stares, her eyes asking, *Well?*

I shake my head no and try the next door down the hall. The room is big, with a king-sized bed and fancy carpet–definitely not a kid's room. I almost move on, but I notice a bookshelf against the far wall and my curiosity takes over. Amber keeps to my side as I browse the titles, deciding which to take. After a while, she grows bored and wanders to the walk-in closet.

Suddenly Amber shrieks.

I turn to the closet, my heart pounding. Is one of Them in there with her? I've never come across one in an empty house, but that doesn't mean it isn't possible. I back toward the bedroom door, ready to sprint and hide. If it found Amber, it will be distracted for a while and I can grab Baby and get out before it's done feeding.

Something moves in the closet and I brace myself for a disgusting green head and glowing yellow eyes. Instead, Amber appears in the doorway, her face jubilant. She holds up a bag.

"Prada," she says with a grin, not bothering to whisper.

We have to leave, now. I grab her arm and drag her toward the door. If They heard her, we don't have much time. Amber cries out slightly as I pull her down the stairs, my fingers digging into her skin. I don't care that I am hurting her. Baby is downstairs, alone. We need to find her and get the hell out.

I step over the two squeaky stairs, but Amber steps heavily on both. Either she doesn't remember or she doesn't care. I can feel my face grow hot with anger. I shouldn't have brought her; she isn't ready. If we all die, it will be my fault.

I pause at the bottom of the stairs, quickly scanning the room. I don't see any of Them. I lead Amber cautiously through the dining room. I stop again. In the next room there is a sound. The noise is faint but distinctive: shuffle, shuffle, sniff. Amber's outburst brought one inside. It is in the kitchen, where I told Baby to stay.

Wait, I sign to Amber. *Danger.*

Her eyes close tight with fear. She pushes herself flat against the wall, trying to become invisible. I let go of her arm and hope she has enough sense not to make a sound.

I remove a box of snappers from my bag. I take one, rolling the small, papered bundle in my fingers. I used to love throwing them on the Fourth of July. They were just the right amount of safe and loud that my parents could reach a compromise on. No real fireworks for me. It was a good day when I found an unopened box of snappers in the attic. I had my mother to thank for that once again, since she didn't like to throw things away.

I duck into the kitchen and throw the snapper as hard as I can against the far wall. The creature is sniffing around the kitchen table, but runs toward the popping noise at full speed. Terrified, I nevertheless fight the urge to laugh hysterically as it smacks into the wall where the snapper hit. I take a deep breath, try to calm myself. It will not help if I panic. If I die, Amber won't last long and Baby will be on her own.

The creature is now studying the wall, touching it with its fleshy green hands, wondering what the noise had been. It doesn't immediately turn and focus back in on the room. It knows something was there, something loud, but does not understand where it went. I hear Amber move in the other room and the floor creaks. The creature's head snaps in the direction of the doorway, exactly where I'm standing.

I'm exposed. It is a cloudless night. Moonlight filters in the window, bathing the kitchen in a soft, silver glow. I can't risk moving back into the shadows. I try to stay absolutely still.

Most people probably lose their nerve when they are this close to Them. They run or scream, not in control enough to realize it will get them killed.

But I am calm. I am collected. I am nothing more than a statue, a decoration. The noise was just the house settling, a breeze through the window.

I hear a low *thump* in the backyard past the shattered glass door. The creature's face twitches.

Go check it out, I think at the monster. *Maybe it's a tasty rabbit.*

Before I even finish my thought, I am blinded by a brilliant white light. I have to squint against the sudden brightness, which is so intense it makes my skin tingle.

"What the . . ." Amber says from her hiding spot.

The creature focuses on me, no longer wondering if I am there or not. It might as well be broad daylight. It can see me perfectly. It growls, muscles flexed to run.

It rushes at me and there's no place to go. Too late I think of the gun at my side. I'm panicked, and there is no way to reach it in time. *I'm sorry, Baby.* I fall to my knees. My hands instinctively fly in front of my face.

But nothing happens. A long second ticks by. I peek past my fingers.

The creature is barely a foot away, completely covered in some kind of net. It is being dragged back slowly while it tries desperately to escape. It pushes against its bonds and snaps its teeth at me. It is not happy it has missed its meal.

I scramble to the doorway and hide behind the wall, where Amber still stands, shocked. I lie on the floor and poke my head out to watch. The creature is being reeled into a ship, the same dark, soundless ship that I witnessed landing in the park and have seen many times since then. It beams the light everywhere.

The creature does not stop fighting, but it cannot break free. I can see just inside the doorway of the craft. There is a tall figure, clothed in black from head to toe. The figure holds a rope attached to the net that encases the creature. It pulls the still-struggling alien into the ship. The door shuts behind Them and the bright light goes out.

The sudden darkness is a shock. By the time my eyes adjust, the ship has disappeared without making a sound.

I get to my feet. We still have to go, and quickly. The light, no matter how brief, will attract more of Them like a beacon in the darkness. I run into the kitchen but Baby is not there.

Panicked, I search around the chairs and under the table.

Where would she have hidden? I freeze in the middle of the room and crouch, my head in my hands. What if she didn't have time to hide? My eyes scan the room frantically. There is no blood, no sign of a struggle. She must have escaped somehow.

A dish towel on the floor catches my attention. It is pushed out away from the sink. I rush to the cabinet and pull open the door. Baby looks up at me, relieved.

I grab her and haul her out of the cabinet, hugging her tight. My whole world would collapse if I lost her. I can't lose her. I pick her up, even though she is much too big now to be carried.

Are you okay? I sign onto her arm.

Yes. I was scared, though. Baby smiles weakly, putting on a brave face. She can deal with a lot, but this was a close call. *I hid as soon as Amber made that terrible noise.*

I put Baby down, squeezing her one last time. *We have to go,* I tell her.

She nods knowingly.

I find Amber and we all walk slowly, careful to be silent. Even so, Amber walks way too loudly, her sock-covered feet padding on the sidewalk.

When we get to the gate, I unlock it as fast as I can,

making sure Baby gets inside first. I shove Amber after her, pulling the gate shut.

Inside the house I scold Amber. I sign at her furiously, call her names she doesn't understand. We don't have words for "stupid" or "idiotic," I'd never needed language like that with Baby. Instead I say she's useless. *Bad Amber,* I claw the words at her.

I'm sorry. I'm sorry, I'm sorry, she tells me over and over. She clutches the designer purse to her chest.

It's not her fault, Baby pleads. *She doesn't understand.*

I look at Amber. How can she not comprehend the danger we face every day? How can she jeopardize our safety for a stupid bag? I glare at her and she begins to sob.

She's from Before, Baby says.

I sigh. I place my hand on Amber's shoulder. *It's okay.* I force a smile. *Go to sleep. We'll try again tomorrow.*

Amber sniffles and nods. She gives me a weak, half smile and creeps downstairs to her bed. I feel a stab of regret.

Baby is right. Amber is stuck with her head in the Before. She doesn't understand that expensive clothes and shoes are not as important as staying alive. She spent all those years in a bomb shelter, dreaming of a life that is no longer possible. If she doesn't let go of her fantasies, she'll kill us all.

Are you angry? Baby asks.

No. I was just scared that you were hurt, I explain.

What happened?

I shake my head. Baby won't understand. To her, things are only as good as far as they are functional, so one bag is the same as another, as long as it isn't ripped or doesn't have holes. She wouldn't get that Amber wanted something because it was a famous brand.

Amber found something that people used to think was very fan.

Something we can use? she asks, probably wondering if it is as good as a dishwasher or candy bar.

No, something that reminds her of Before. She was very excited and forgot to be quiet.

Baby nods her head, pretending like she understood. She wants to believe the best of Amber, and I don't want to shatter that illusion. I can't just tell her, *We almost died today because Amber is a shallow idiot.*

What about the light? she asks. *I saw it through the crack in the cabinet.*

I tell her about the ship and how they captured the creature with a net. I describe the figure inside, how it wore some kind of black suit.

Why would They capture Themselves?

I don't know. Now that I've had some time to think about it, it really doesn't make sense to me either. *Maybe the creatures were sent to get rid of us so the other ones could come and take over.*

You don't think that, do you?

I honestly don't know what to think. If They are supposed to get rid of the human race They did a pretty bang-up job in the first few weeks. Why would the cavalry wait years to show up? Maybe it just took them that long to get here. Send in the troops, wait for total destruction, then call in the clean-up crew.

If the other kind comes and takes away all of Them, that will be fan. Baby smiles, imagining a world without monsters.

I nod. But even if They are eliminated, what will replace Them? I don't want to worry Baby, though, so I suggest we eat some of the new food she gathered. She didn't drop her bag during the commotion, and I am proud of her. At least *her* priorities are straight.

After we eat, I tell her the story of Rapunzel, who I decide will run away and go to college instead of being rescued by a prince. Baby falls asleep with her head full of fantasy and I hope she dreams of a better place.

I stay up long after Baby has gone to bed, reading to keep my mind occupied, not ready to close my eyes. Every time I do, I see the ship and the figure in black, reeling in the creature for capture. I don't understand any of it and I don't like the not knowing. The last few years have been awful, but I now know how the After works and how to survive. With the arrival of the ships, I am lost again, just like in those weeks when They first came.

I wake at dawn, sobbing. I'd been dreaming about the night's events, only this time we were not so lucky. In my nightmare, Amber's screams brought Them straight to Baby. I saw it all in slow motion, Baby bitten and clawed as she called out for help, but I couldn't help her. I was paralyzed with fear.

I get out of bed and check on Baby, awake in her room. *I was asleep,* she explains. *Something woke me.* A noise outside. She is always waking at the slightest sound, when a tree branch falls or a bird sings.

Want a story? I ask, but she shakes her head no. I sit with her until she falls back asleep, then go to make myself some tea. I've had time to calm down, and I want to blame Amber for all this, but I know I can't. I shouldn't be so angry at her; it wasn't really her fault. It was mine. I should not have let her come with us. My dream is still fresh in my mind. Baby could have died. I don't think I can stay in the After without her.

I decide to see if Amber has fallen asleep yet. I want to apologize for being so harsh to her. I grab a package of long-expired, but still-good Oreos to use as a peace offering and tiptoe down the basement stairs.

Amber has made the room hers, decorating it with construction paper chains and Baby's crayoned pictures. The room is still and I am amazed at how quietly Amber is sleeping, when she can't even walk around in socks without stomping like a baby elephant. She also snores more often than not.

She isn't snoring now, though. I walk across the basement floor with a strange feeling in my stomach. Something isn't right. I pull back the blankets.

Amber is gone.

CHAPTER ELEVEN

I broke the news to Baby as soon as she woke up, after I checked to make sure the gate was locked and Amber hadn't taken anything important. Baby is crushed. We don't say it, but we both think Amber is dead. She couldn't make it a block on her own, much less live out in the city with no comfy, secure house. With no one to feed her and take care of her, she would be alien lunch in no time.

You're glad she's gone, Baby accuses, her face dark with anger.

I shake my head. *I'm sorry I yelled at Amber, but she put*

us in danger. I needed her to understand. I try to put my hand on her shoulder, but she pulls away, her arms crossed. She's never been difficult like this before and I'm worried.

Baby's lip quivers. She turns away, not wanting me to see her cry. I reach out to hug her, but change my mind. Maybe she just needs some time alone. She doesn't remember ever losing anyone.

I go downstairs to the basement. Amber taped up a bunch of Baby's drawings and pictures cut out from old magazines. I start to take these down, grimacing at long-dead models and TV heartthrobs.

I fold up the blankets and place them to the side. The papers I gather and put in a plastic bag. I'll throw them away on our next outing. Baby doesn't need to be reminded of Amber every time she comes downstairs.

I sit on the couch and put my head in my hands. I'm not that horrible. It was all just a coincidence. I should have exercised more caution, but I can't blame myself, even if Baby resents me. Whether or not I meant for all this to happen, I still have to make it up to Baby somehow. There are other survivors. I can watch a few, see who is trustworthy. I can invite people to live here. We don't have to be alone.

I feel a tap on my shoulder. I turn to find Baby glowering

at me, angry. She is so damned quiet. I didn't hear her come down the stairs.

What are you doing? Her little fingers move furiously. Sometimes I forget how young she is.

I'm just trying to clean up, I explain.

Baby grabs the bag of drawings and cutouts. *Amber and I made these.* She crumples them against her chest.

I know. I thought it would be better . . . I stop signing. I've never seen Baby so mad. Once again I've made the wrong choice. I should have left Amber's room the way it was, for Baby to sort out when she was ready.

I'm sorry. I don't know what else to say. I'm not perfect. I don't have all the answers. I'm just trying to keep us safe. I start to cry softly. *Please.* I hold out my hand. *Please don't hate me.*

Baby's face softens. She places the bag of papers on the floor and sits next to me on the couch. I hug her close.

I don't hate you, she tells me. *I just feel* . . . She searches for the right word. *I feel empty.*

I rest my head on top of hers. *I am so sorry.*

Baby nods and scoots onto the floor. She opens the bag of papers and begins to sort them into piles. *Can I put these in my room?* she signs, without looking up. *For when Amber comes back.*

I place my hand on her shoulder. *Yes.* I don't tell her that Amber is almost certainly dead.

Baby no longer sleeps in my room. She is more withdrawn. She likes to sit alone and look at her picture books. She isn't even very excited when I bring her new, better-fitting clothes. She glances at me, shrugs, and puts them in her closet.

Don't you want to try them on? I ask.

Maybe later.

I go to my room to read. Baby doesn't want me around and I don't want to force her. I wonder if my parents felt the same way; I never wanted to hang out with them either. Not once I turned ten and decided they were lame. I wish I'd done more things with them, not given them such a hard time. I try not to think about it too often because it's too much. How was I supposed to know I'd never see them again?

I start to read my *American History* book from sophomore year. I always liked history; it was like ancient gossip. I sometimes go back over old homework, try to remember what I was learning. Everything except math, that is. I could never get the hang of precalculus. The only good thing about the After is that I never have to worry about math homework.

I doze off. I dream I'm at the zoo with my parents. I'm about Baby's age, six or seven, except I'm not myself. I *am* Baby. I have a balloon and a little plastic cup with a lion on it. I love the zoo.

Suddenly my parents are gone. Everyone is gone. I run around looking for people, but I can't find anyone. I begin to cry.

"Be quiet," someone tells me, but I can't see them so I keep on sobbing. "Shut the hell up!" comes the same voice, except this time I recognize it. It is my voice. I haven't heard it in a very long time.

I see why I'm supposed to be quiet. The lion is no longer on my little plastic cup. It is standing in front of me. It roars, showing off its sharp teeth. I am frozen with fear. Suddenly the ground begins to shake. I try to regain my footing, but I fall to my hands and knees. The quake continues. The earth splits apart. I open my mouth to scream but nothing comes out.

I open my eyes. I'm in my bed and I'm me again. Only the vibration continues.

I turn over. Baby is shaking me. I push her hands away, but then I see the look on her face. Her eyes are wide, her jaw clenched. Something has frightened her and it takes a lot to scare Baby.

I sit up. *What is it? What's happened?*

I hear someone at the gate. Baby jumps on me. *Maybe it's Amber.*

I push her to the side, onto the bed.

I go down the stairs and peek out the window. There is a man in army fatigues studying the gate. He picks up a stick and throws it at the fence. It sparks where it hits and then falls to the ground. He looks at the window and I duck down, hoping he hasn't seen me. When I look again, he is gone. I have an empty feeling in the pit of my stomach.

I run back up to my room. *It's not Amber; it's a man,* I tell her. *I need you to get a bag together. You'll need some food, a change of clothes, and your pocketknife.* I know she will listen to me. Even if she's been surly lately, she knows that this is serious.

Baby nods, still frightened. *Can I bring my books?* She already understands that we might have to go.

No, I tell her. She looks at the floor, frowning, but doesn't bother to beg. The sight is enough to make me feel guilty. *One book,* I relent. She needs to have something familiar.

Where are we going? Are we leaving now?

No. I just want us to be ready. Just in case. I try to smile reassuringly, but Baby isn't buying it. *Go, now. Put your bag by the back door when you're done.* Baby runs off to her room.

I start to pack my backpack. Some clothes, a water bottle. I take a can opener from the kitchen too. I grab the gun and holster from my nightstand and put it on. We have to be prepared for every possibility.

We keep the bags ready, but after four days the man doesn't return. Baby talks about it constantly and I've run out of ways to distract her.

Is he going to hurt us? she asks, signing one-handedly. In her other hand she clutches a fork. She's eating peaches from a can. The juice dribbles down her chin and stains her shirt.

I won't let that happen. I hand her a napkin. *Stop making a mess.* "You don't have a maid," is what my mom always used to tell me, even though we did have a housekeeper. When I pointed out the obvious to her, she would say, "Do *you* pay her wages?"

Amy, if that man comes back, are you going to hurt him? Baby asks, eyeing the gun that I have not taken off since we spotted the outsider, except to shower.

If I have to, I tell her. She stops eating, her fork paused midway between the can and her mouth. I don't want to frighten her, but she needs to understand that we could be in danger. All of Them are monsters, but not all monsters are Them.

Maybe he was just lost, she ventures.

Maybe.

Maybe he's nice.

I frown at her. *I doubt it.*

Amber was nice.

Eat your peaches. You have to get going soon.

Baby shovels the rest of the fruit in her mouth, chewing carefully. I told her that tonight she can go scavenging on her own. We need food again and one of us has to stay home, in case our visitor comes back. I debated leaving Baby with the gun, but I don't think she can shoot someone if push comes to shove. I'm not all that confident that I can either, but I'm willing to try.

Baby keeps smiling and pushing her head up tall. She is excited; I can tell by the way she won't sit still. I hope she can channel that energy later, but I'm not overly concerned. She is a smart girl, fast and quiet. She can take care of herself out there, for a few hours anyway.

Baby clears her place and grabs her two bags. One almost

empty to hold food and supplies, one filled with garbage to drop down the block. She stands by the door and hops up and down silently.

Do you have everything you need? I ask, unwilling to let her go just yet.

Yes. She rolls her eyes.

You have the key for the gate? I've already checked twice to make sure it was in her pocket. I can't stand the thought of her stuck out there, even though I'll be watching from the window.

Yes, yes. You know I do.

Okay, I sign. *Then what are you waiting for?*

She grins and opens the front door, quickly stepping out into the night. A few feet away she comes to a halt. She turns back to me, no longer smiling.

What? Is one of Them at the gate?

Baby's mouth opens. For a second I think that she is going to scream, but she doesn't. She's just surprised.

There's someone at the gate again, she signs.

I look past her to the fence. The man has returned and he is fiddling with the gate. Large black gloves cover his hands, protecting him from the electricity.

Get inside now, I order.

Baby hurries past me and I slam the door as loud as I can. I want to bring Them to the gate. I need that man to be gone.

I head over to the window and watch. The man not only has protective gloves, he has other tools as well. In one hand, he holds large shears. He is going to cut the fence so he can get inside. We'll be completely exposed to Them.

I try to think. What can I do? I reach immediately for the gun and hold it in my hand. I don't want to kill him. Maybe if I just show him I have it he will go away.

Stay here. Don't look out the window, I tell Baby.

I jerk open the door and an idea strikes me. I reach over and flick on the porch light. Even if the door slam doesn't bring Them running, the light will. They love the light.

The man looks up briefly, but continues to work. I hear a low snarl, and smile. They will be coming soon.

"Circle in," a voice in the distance yells. I squint against the light. Other figures gather around the first man. He is not alone.

I run back inside and up the stairs at full speed. I need to get to my bedroom window, where I'll have a better view. Baby looks at me questioningly as I run past, but stays where I told her to.

From the window upstairs, I can see that there are several men, at least five. I spot a few of Them down the street, running toward the light. They will be at the house in a matter of seconds. One of the men sees Them and holds up a gun.

I breathe a sigh of relief. The guns will only bring more of Them. The men will be finished in a few minutes. The damage to the fence looks minimal. We're safe.

The first creature reaches the semicircle of men and falls without a sound. I blink. Another creature goes down and another. I pound my head against the glass of the window. I want to cry, but know I don't have time for a nervous breakdown.

The men have guns, but they have something else too. From where I sit, I can see one pull something long and white from his bag. He holds it up to a black metallic object and shoots. Crossbows. They have crossbows. Where did they get crossbows? They must have raided a hunting supply store. They are handling themselves like seasoned hunters, either that, or they've had a lot of practice in the After.

Without the additional noise, all that's calling to the creatures is the porch light. It won't draw them like gunshots. The men just have to hold Them off until they can break through the gate, then they can turn off the light.

I look again at the man with the gloves. He is being extremely careful, terrifyingly precise. They don't want to damage the fence because they want to live here. Once they get inside, what will they do with me and Baby? Best-case scenario, we have to share our space with men we don't know–rough, hardened men who would expect us to be at their beck and call. Worst-case scenario, well, I don't want to think about that.

I aim the gun through the glass of the window, seeing what kind of shot I can take. It will be hard to get them all. I'll have to open the window without them noticing. By the way they are killing the creatures, I can see they are experienced marksmen. I'd only ever practiced shooting at paper targets a long time ago. I'd never actually shot a living thing.

I weigh my options. If I manage to kill some of them, but not all, Baby and I can still escape, but they will look for us. If we leave quietly, they might just be content to stay and enjoy their newfound home. They won't bother looking for us when all they want is here. I put the gun back in its holster. My mind is made up. It is too risky to fight.

I'm heading downstairs when something out the window catches my eye. Just out of reach of the light is a red pickup truck. It looks like the same red truck we saw that night we found Amber. My face burns and I can feel my jaw clench. *What has Amber done?* Did her brother abandon her or was she just a spy all along?

I run back down to Baby, taking two stairs at a time. Seizing her arm, I yank her to her feet.

We have to leave, now, I sign furiously. I take her hand and drag her to the back door.

For how long? she signs into my hand.

Forever, I tell her. I feel her stop, her weight dead against my pull.

I turn and look into her eyes. She stares at me. She understands why we have to leave, but this is the only home she's ever known. I grasp her shoulder.

It's not safe here. I am telling her what she already knows, but she doesn't want to believe. *Those men, they are going to get inside. If we stay, they'll hurt us.*

You don't know that. She tries to convince me, convince herself. *They could be good. Like Amber.*

I close my eyes as my fingers dig into Baby's shoulder. I tried to protect her, but led these horrible people right to our doorstep. I've failed her. I open my eyes to see Baby's face twisted in pain. I let go of her shoulder.

If we're still here when those men break through the gate, they're going to do very bad things to us.

Baby nods, finally admitting that she understands. I hug her for a second, kissing her forehead roughly. When I let her go, she moves to the back door without direction and picks up her bag of supplies.

I take my own bag and sling it over my shoulder, double-checking to make sure the gun is still at my side. On the way out the back door, I remember that I haven't packed a picture of my mom and dad. I run back into the living room and snatch the one of them on their honeymoon in Hawaii. My mom is wearing a long, flowing dress with bright purple flowers in her hair. My dad stares at her and grins like an idiot. I shove the picture in my pack.

We creep out the back door and edge along the wall, inching toward the back gate. *There might be a man back here,* I sign to Baby. If they planned the whole thing out, then Amber will have told them about the back gate.

Amy, careful. I see someone. Baby motions with her hand.

I look to where her finger points. Where the moonlight shines against the gate, a shadow moves back and forth, pacing.

I have an idea, I tell her. *Give me the key and be ready to follow.* Baby digs in her pocket and hands me the key. She steps behind me and I pull out the gun and hold it tightly in my right hand. I stalk toward the back gate, my feet barely making a sound on the soft ground. In one motion, I put the key in the lock, turn it, and pull with all my might.

I jump through the opening into the alley, aiming the gun at the figure. I'm lucky. He's only a few feet from the entrance. I move as fast as I can and place the barrel to the man's temple.

He sucks in a breath. "Please. Don't," he whimpers.

He isn't a man. He's a boy, fourteen or fifteen at the most. I almost feel bad for him, but then my anger flares up. These men are taking away our home.

The boy holds a handgun limply in his hand. I grab it from him and shove it toward Baby. Baby cradles it to her chest and watches us. Pushing the boy down to his knees, I press the barrel of my gun right up against the back of his head.

I could kill him. I have the silencer. The creatures might sniff out his body before his friends break through the fence. They might never know we've killed him, assuming instead he is a victim of Them.

Baby's hand on my back brings me back to my senses.

The boy is blubbering and he smells like urine. He's pissed himself. I can't kill him, but I can't leave him to run back to his friends and tell on us. We need a head start.

I raise my arm and hit the boy as hard as I can with the butt of the gun. He falls over and slumps against the gate.

Baby backs away from me, horrified. *Did you kill him?*

No. He's just asleep, I assure her.

She looks at me doubtfully. She steps forward to inspect him. She moves his arm with her foot. The boy moans and his head jerks slightly.

She steps back, satisfied.

He won't be asleep for long, I warn her. *Where's the gun I gave you?*

Put it in my pack.

Good. We have to go.

Baby runs toward me, her hand outstretched. I grab it and lead her away from our house, through a neighbor's yard, out onto the street.

Where are we going? she asks.

I don't answer. I have a few houses in mind, none very secure. Night is only just beginning. We have plenty of time to find somewhere to hide before daylight. Baby is safe for now; that is what's important.

Together we jog in the direction of the lake. There is a house I pilfered a few months ago that has a largish attic. It is musty and crowded with boxes, but it will be a good place to spend the day. It's not far, maybe half a mile.

We make it there long before dawn. I find some old blankets in a closet and spread them out on the floor. It isn't super comfy but it will still pass as a bed for Baby.

Eat something now, I tell her. *We can't make any noise during the day. At all.*

Baby unwraps a candy bar. Even as quiet as she is, the wrapper crinkles. We are not protected here. We have no fence to keep Them out now.

After Baby eats, she looks at the book she packed, turning each page with care. She falls asleep clutching it close to her body and I carefully take it from her hands and place it back in her bag.

At dawn, I watch from the attic window as the streets fill with Them. I can't stand the sight and sit next to Baby. I try to sleep, but can't.

I pull the picture of my parents out of my bag, taking the photo out of the heavy frame. I feel the smoothness in my hand. I touch the happy image, leaving white fingerprints all over their faces.

Everything I had is now gone. I am feeling so sick and numb inside. I look at the picture until it blurs, tears falling down my face.

Once again, my world has ended.

CHAPTER TWELVE

We stay in the attic a couple of nights, but I soon realize that we need to keep moving if Baby and I are going to remain sane. We can't stay in one place and pretend it's our home. It's too much like being trapped. We have to get used to a completely different life.

There is no fence to protect us if Baby accidentally drops her book or if one of us coughs. I long for summer to end, for the days to be shorter. But then I remember that we won't have any heat. Maybe we can find a room to burn a fire, keep the light inside somehow. I have some time to figure it all out. As of now, we have to wait until nightfall to even use the bathroom.

Not that there are working bathrooms to use. When I explain to Baby that she will have to go to the bathroom and not flush the toilet, she looks at me like I am insane.

There's no water, I explain. *And even if there was, the flush would be too loud.* At our house we only used the bathroom in the basement. You couldn't hear it from outside. I realize I have to stop thinking of our house; we can't go back there.

We also have to get used to not bathing regularly.

You smell, Baby tells me after a week. We are holed up in a basement near the park, waiting for day to end.

You're not exactly lemon fresh yourself, I inform her.

We need to wash our clothes too. She tugs at her shirt, stained with sweat and dust.

I agree. I feel so gross. It's taking me a while to work things out. *We can go to the lake tonight and take a swim,* I suggest at last. It is creepy to be out in the open like that, but I am pretty sure They don't like large bodies of water. We've gone to the lake to retrieve drinking water, but I don't want to run into any other survivors. Not yet anyway.

I don't know how to swim, Baby signs.

You don't have to swim. We'll go to the beach. You can just stand in the water. It will be like a big tub.

Can we bring soap? Baby asks.

Sure. Why not?

But we drink that water. She shakes her head. I smile. If she knew the sign for *duh*, she would have made it.

We'll bathe far from where we get water for drinking. It's a big lake, Baby.

Maybe–she looks at me slyly–*you can teach me to swim.*

No. It would be too much noise, I explain. Baby frowns and twirls her hair. She's started pulling out strands lately. I tell her to stop, but she still tugs at it when she thinks I'm not looking.

Leave your hair alone. Do you want to be bald?

She pouts. She looks at her book for a while, then signs, *I'm hungry.*

It's not dark yet. You can't eat. Usually before daybreak I unwrap some food for us to eat, but I didn't have a chance to last night. We barely found the basement in time. It is the closest we've ever cut it to being out at first light.

Baby pulls at her hair again. I don't know if it is from the stress or the boredom, but she needs something more than surviving the day. I need something more too. We are stuck.

The lake is beautiful at night, even a dark, cloudy night like tonight. It's strange to see the city skyline illuminated only by faint moonlight. Gone are the days of light pollution, and I wish I could remember the last time I saw the city at night from the lake, and who I was with. Fourth of July with my father? Out during the summer with Sabrina?

We avoid the harbor area, where boats, half sunk, jut dangerously from the water. They could not survive the first winter in the ice-covered lake. Later I may look for a lifeboat or a dingy, something to take Baby out farther into the water.

It's cold. The way Baby moves her hands is the sign language equivalent of shouting.

It's good. I've already dunked myself in the water and am trying to convince Baby to wade in deeper than her ankles. *If you just come in a little more, you'll get used to it.*

She folds her arms across her chest and moves a little farther into the water. She's shivering. I hold out my hand to her. She was happy to strip down for relief from the sweltering, humid heat, but when faced with the cold expanse of water, she shied away.

Come on, don't be afraid.

I'm not afraid. She inches forward, taking small, dramatic steps.

If you come out here I'll wash your hair. I hold the bottle of shampoo up and shake it temptingly.

Oh, all right. She plunges into the water, splashing slightly. I eye the shore. We aren't being very loud, but I'm still concerned. I don't know if They can swim.

Baby's eyes are distractingly white, reflecting the moon. I can't help but think how eerie it is, as she makes her way toward me. She blinks and her eyes look normal again, a trick of the light.

I stand where I know her head will be above the water. Her teeth chatter slightly with the shock of the cold and she opens her mouth wide to stop the noise.

You'll be warm once you get used to it, I tell her. I squirt the shampoo into my hand and massage it onto her head. We can do this every night in the summer, but maybe we will get used to a bath once a week during the cool months, and not at all in the winter.

I scrub Baby's scalp with my fingers while she holds the shampoo bottle. She squeezes it to make bubbles in the water.

Okay, now hold your nose and dunk your head.

She takes a deep breath, puffs out her cheeks, and holds her nose. She slowly lowers her head into the lake, her eyes open wide. She wants to see what is under the water.

Close your eyes, I quickly sign. *You'll get soap in them.*

She snaps her eyes shut just as her head disappears. I see her outline under the water, her hands in her hair trying to rinse out the shampoo. When her head breaks the surface, she grins.

Feel better? I ask.

I like taking baths in the lake. Her blond hair shines in the moonlight.

Baby, would you like to learn how to float?

She nods eagerly. I put my hand on her back. *Lie flat.*

On what?

On the water, like it's a bed. Take a deep breath first.

Baby gulps in some air and moves back into my hand. I push up slightly and Baby's feet rise. She instinctively holds her arms out on the water's surface. When I feel she is stable, I let go, holding my hand above her face so she can see my gestures.

See . . . you're floating by yourself.

Baby smiles, afraid to move.

Keep breathing and you won't sink, I promise.

I wash my hair while Baby drifts. It's nice to feel clean. The cold water is refreshing, especially after the heat of day.

We are stuck inside without air-conditioning and it's so hard to sleep when it's hot.

Baby jerks upright suddenly.

What?

I felt something, against my leg. She looks down into the water, searching.

It was probably a fish.

What if They live under the water? She starts to head back to shore.

They don't. They don't like the lake.

What if there is a new kind, like the ones in the ship. What if They like being in the water? She looks around wildly, unsure of where to head to safety.

They couldn't live down there. I try to calm her.

Mermaids do. She is already to our pile of belongings, putting her dirty clothes on over her wet body. I follow her over.

Mermaids are just a story, I tell her.

She looks up at me, tearful. *No they're not. Mermaids are from Before. Like horses. You said horses could live in the sea.*

Seahorses aren't horses that live in the sea . . . I start to explain but stop myself. It doesn't really matter if she has the Before straight in her head. She can believe in mermaids and horses that live in the sea if she wants.

You're right, I tell her. *But mermaids and seahorses have a special way of breathing under the water. The monsters don't.*

Baby looks out over the lake, searching for creatures or maybe for mermaids.

I rummage in my bag and hand her a bundle. *You can leave those smelly old clothes.* I pilfered the house while she was asleep.

Baby takes the clothes and examines them. We have to wear dark, neutral colors so we won't stick out at night, but I found a practical brown dress, something that will keep her cool in the summer heat and still be good to run in if we need to escape. Baby holds it out in front of her, smoothing down the fabric. She pulls it on over her head.

It's a little too big, but Baby doesn't seem to care. She twirls around, making the bottom of the dress billow out into a bell shape.

Thank you, Amy.

You're welcome. I also took clothes for myself, some dark jeans and a black T-shirt. I got the shirt from a stuffy, messy room plastered with rock posters, a dusty guitar in the corner.

Before I get dressed, I motion Baby over and hand her a pair of scissors. *I want you to cut my hair short,* I tell her.

How short? Baby wants to know. We usually trim each other's hair every few months.

Short short, I tell her.

Why? Her own blond hair is sort of thin; it never gets tangled.

Because it's too hot. I just don't want to be bothered with it. I haven't combed it in a week and it is starting to turn into dreadlocks.

You'll look funny, she warns.

Not if you do a good job. I kneel next to her and hope she can make it sort of straight.

She starts to snip away, tentatively at first, but then she gets into it. I feel the hair drop down my back and all around me. Already I feel lighter. Baby steps back to examine her work.

How does it look? I ask.

Not bad. She bites her lower lip. *Not good either.*

I slip back into the lake to rinse myself off. My fingers slip through my short hair. I can't see it but it seems like Baby made it even on both sides, close to my scalp until just above my ear, then a bit longer on top.

I look like a rock star from Before, I try to convince myself. In truth, I already miss having long hair, but it just isn't practical. Who is there to impress anyway?

I dress in my new clothes, strapping my gun back over my shirt. Baby gathers her things, carefully placing the gun we took off the boy at the house at the top of her bag. I want her to carry it, to use it if necessary. I showed her how. It makes me feel a little safer to know she has it, in case something happens to me.

I heft my bag to my shoulder. *Let's look for a place on the lakefront tonight. We can find a mansion.*

O . . . Baby pauses mid word. *Did you hear that?*

Hear what? I ask, puzzled. I look around and then I see it. A ship, landing.

I turn back to Baby. *Run. Now.* I sign as the blinding light appears.

Before I have time to turn, I hear a *swoosh*, and Baby is knocked into me and we fall. Her body weight presses against my chest. I gulp for air. We are a tangle of arms and legs, held tightly inside a strong web of netting. Luckily Baby is mostly on top of me, so I don't have to worry about crushing her small body.

We begin to move. I twist my head so I can see through the netting. We are being dragged toward the ship, just like the creature, that night with Amber. I can't reach my gun, but I feel Baby's hand within my grasp.

Desperately I sign to her. *Baby, where is your bag?*

Here. She shifts her weight slightly, maneuvering the bag into my hand. I undo the zipper and reach inside. I feel the cool metal of the gun against my fingers. I don't know what happens inside the ship but I'm going to be ready.

We are almost to the ship doorway, the gaping hole in the side of the craft. We are lifted from the ground and sway within the net for a moment before being deposited roughly onto the floor. I can barely see anything in the dark, but I feel a presence come closer.

Suddenly the net falls away and my hands are free. I roll over Baby into a crouch. The creature looms over us, covered in a shadowy black material from head to toe. I raise my arm, gun in hand, and fire into the creature's body.

It's not the recoil of the gun that surprises me. I'm ready for the gun's push against my arm, the memory of childhood shooting lessons still etched in my mind. What shocks me is the noise. I've forgotten how loud things were Before. In the enclosed space, the noise is amplified and my eardrums feel as if they will shatter.

The creature jerks back and clutches its chest where the bullet struck. I pull Baby to standing but cannot see a way out of the ship. It's small and cramped with no windows, and the door has already closed tight. I can't even tell where the opening is. We are trapped.

Baby grabs my hand. *It's not dead.*

I look back to the creature. It didn't fall over; it doesn't even look very hurt. It seems to study us, debating what to do.

I shove Baby behind me and fire again. Now I'm prepared for the deafening boom. The bullet hits the creature's shoulder, and I watch closely. There is no tear in the creature's suit; the bullet just falls to the floor with a *clink.* I can't believe it. *They aren't smart; They are mindless killers.* How can They design a bulletproof suit? How did They even make it to our planet?

The creature lunges at us and I throw myself in front of Baby to take the brunt of the hit. I'm knocked off my feet into the wall of the ship. My shoulder crunches sickeningly and the pain brings spots of light in front of my eyes.

I attempt to stand, but the creature is already on top of me, wrestling the gun from my hand. Out of the corner of my eye, I see Baby ready to jump on its back.

I ram my fist upward, into the creature's jaw. I know I can't hurt it, but I need to fight back, even if it only distracts the creature for a few seconds to give Baby a chance. I punch again, a little lower this time, hoping to find a tender spot under its chin.

I hear the creature choke inside its suit. I've gotten its neck. I shove it, trying to get away, but it forces me back down, pressing on my shoulders. It reaches for its head and pulls at the black material. It's going to eat me here and now, no matter what its original purpose was for capturing us. I made it angry and it isn't going to wait.

As it removes the material from its face, I close my eyes. I can't bear to see its green skin and pointy yellow teeth. I wait for the pain. I want to die quickly.

"What the hell did you do that for?" a woman yells.

I open my eyes and stare into two very pretty, dark brown eyes.

She is beautiful. She is human.

CHAPTER THIRTEEN

I lie on the floor, dumbfounded, not knowing how to react.

I still can't believe that underneath the strange black material is a woman. A regular, human woman. Her features are Asian; her accent is American.

"You're the first person to ever shoot me," she tells me, "and I think you broke one of my ribs." She pushes herself off my body roughly and stands. I sit up, looking for Baby. She hurries to my side and sits down on my lap. I hug her close.

"What are your names?" the woman asks. I shake my head, unable to speak. It's too much. Why have they captured us?

"Do you understand English? *Español? Français?*" She places her hands on her hips. "I'm pretty sure you're not Japanese . . . *Nihongo*?" she asks. I'm shaking and I can't stop.

We stare at each other. "Well, that's all I've got," she says eventually. "I think you can understand me just fine, but have it your way."

She puts her hand to her ear and pushes a slim black earpiece. "We've got a couple of hostile post-aps here," she says. "I've secured their weapon but they're unresponsive to questioning. We're going to have to skip the meet and greet and put them straight through to psyche-eval." She listens for a minute, looking us over.

"Two female children, a Class Three and a Class Five." She pushes against the wall of the ship and a drawer pops out. She places the gun inside and moves a few feet back. She presses the far wall this time and an opening appears. I can make out the head of another person through the doorway. The pilot. The woman disappears into the cockpit and the door slides shut behind her.

What is happening? Baby asks.

I don't know. I hug her to my chest, ignoring the pain in my shoulder. I'm so very tired. The adrenaline has left my system, draining my energy reserves. *I think we've been rescued.*

Like the princess in my book?

Sort of . . . Are you scared? I stroke Baby's hair and hope we are being rescued and not just captured.

No. I was at first, but that woman isn't one of Them. She won't hurt us. She is so sure, even though the woman *has* hurt me. I rub my throbbing shoulder, the pain getting worse with each passing second.

Are you scared, Amy? Baby asks, needing reassurance.

No, I lie, pulling her closer.

Why didn't you let that woman know you understood her? Baby asks. *You know loud speak. You understood Amber.*

I think we should wait and see before we tell them anything. I try to explain. *Maybe it will be better if they think we don't understand them.*

Okay, but I think that everything is going to be happily ever after.

I hope for her sake she's right. If not, we have a backup plan. I touch the small bulge at my side. They took away Baby's gun, but I still have mine.

I adjust Baby's weight so she isn't pressing against my aching shoulder. I rest my head on hers and wait.

"Wake up."

I open my eyes with a start. The woman in the black suit is shaking my extremely sore shoulder. I pull away and glare at her.

"We're here, sunshine," she tells me with a smirk.

I narrow my eyes at her and scowl. She tilts her head, studying me for a moment. Even annoyed as I am, I am struck by her beauty. She is about my height, but with more delicate features. Dark hair, dark eyes. All business, she reaches down and pulls me to my feet. She is stronger than I would have thought and I mentally scratch the idea of this woman as delicate.

Baby stands without help, and I hold her hand firmly.

The door to the ship opens, revealing a warmly lit room. The woman steps out into the light. Baby and I look at each other. She smiles nervously, excited. I sigh. I can see no other option but to follow.

I walk forward, squinting against the brightness. My bare feet make contact with the soft ground. I feel the grass between my toes and think it is pleasant before my heart jumps into my throat.

We are outside in the daylight.

Baby panics. She tears her hand away from mine and tries to climb back into the ship, but the door has already closed behind us. She runs to me and buries her head in my waist. I search frantically for someplace to hide.

The woman crosses her arms and watches us with an amused grin. "This is a secure area. There's no threat."

In the light of day, I can see her features more clearly. She is gorgeous, but there is something else just under the surface that mars her beauty. There is a cruelness in her voice and I can see it again and again, in the way her lips curl, in her deep brown eyes.

"The Floraes, the creatures, they can't get to you here," she tells me. When I don't react, she continues, "I think you can understand me just fine," she says, staring into my eyes. I look at the ground, unable to meet her gaze. "You need to follow me, now." She turns.

We have to get out of the open. Baby clings to me, desperate to find a safe place to hide.

The woman said that They can't get us here and I believe her. What choice do I have?

Baby nods, her eyes still searching. I have to admit that I am unnerved too. There is grass and a few white buildings, but no creatures as far as I can tell.

Where are we? Baby asks into my hand.

I think we're about to find out. Let's keep our signs a secret for now, okay? I want to learn as much about our captors as possible before revealing anything. Signing using only one hand limits what we can say, but we've always had leeway in our language. If you live closely with someone long enough, a deep intuition develops; Baby and I are always on the same page.

We follow the woman away from the ship toward a large, squat building. We are led through a black door into a small room. The woman pushes a button on the wall and speaks, "Kay here with those two post-aps."

A scratchy voice replies almost immediately. "Kay, you know you're supposed to bring them to orientation. Dr. Reynolds is at lunch."

"Look, Rice, I radioed in that they were hostile and gave you our ETA." She looks over at me and winks. "These two aren't fit to be among the general populace. What's the holdup?"

The voice on the intercom pauses. "Bring them in," he responds in a defeated tone. A buzzer sounds and the woman pushes a panel on the far wall. A section moves, sliding open to reveal a doorway.

The woman, Kay, motions us through. "Come on, girls, time is money."

I smile. There is no money anymore. Time is nothing anymore. Kay catches my smile and I immediately regret it. Now she knows for sure that I understand her.

We walk through the door and everything is white, sterile. We wind our way down several passageways, occasionally going through a door or up a flight of stairs. Nothing is distinguishable. Finally Kay opens a door and directs us inside a large room, painted a pale blue. After the white blandness of the hallways, I welcome the color change, but I realize that is what whoever is in charge wants. Kay has pegged us as hostile and blue is a calming color. I scan the rest of the room, empty except for a metal table and four matching chairs. It looks like a police interrogation room from a movie, Before.

Kay doesn't follow us inside. "You guys hold tight, all right?" she says with a smile bordering on sincere. "You'll be okay, kiddo." Maybe she isn't cruel, just a little malicious. She shuts the door and Baby and I are alone.

What's that noise? Baby asks. *There's a strange humming.*

I go to the door and try the handle, but it won't budge. *I don't know, maybe the lights?* I didn't think it would be unlocked but it was worth a try. I trudge back to the table and sit in a chair.

Baby shakes her head. *It's loud and . . .* She's struggling with her chair. *I can't move it in,* she says. *It's stuck.*

I look at where the chair meets the floor. It is bolted down. So is the table. I sit back and shrug. *It's so we can't take them,* I tell her.

Really?

No, it's so we don't throw things around when the people come to question us.

Oh. Baby looks disappointed. *When are they coming?* she asks, suddenly excited. She realizes that we are going to meet more people.

I don't know. It's cold in the room and I can hear the air conditioner running. I look at the ceiling and notice a medium-sized vent big enough to push Baby through if I have to. I hear the door lock release before it swings open. *No open signing,* I remind Baby. She nods.

"Hello there," a teenage boy stumbles into the room, holding a stack of papers. He reminds me of the boys I went to school with Before. Not the jocks or the popular kids. The geeky ones, who looked a little socially uncomfortable, but you always knew they were going to go to Harvard and change the world. He looks up and I wonder who decided it was a good idea to throw him in a room with potentially hostile people. He looks only seventeen or eighteen. From what I gather, we are here for our psychological evaluation, but this boy looks nothing like a trained psychiatrist. He's tall, bigger than I'd first thought, and kind of cute. He's wearing a white lab coat and jeans. He makes me feel a little better about this place; the jeans make it all seem harmless.

The boy dumps his papers on the table and starts sorting through them. "Now where is . . . oh, here." He looks up at me, flushed, and I see that his eyes are a piercing bright blue. He takes a pair of glasses from his coat pocket, cleans them with his shirt, and perches them on his nose.

"Oh yes, Kay's report. You two are the hostiles?" He looks doubtfully from me to Baby. "You don't seem very threatening . . ." He catches me staring at him and I look away. ". . . and if you are hostile, then Kay should have handcuffed you to the table."

He takes out a pen and scribbles on a piece of paper. "Now, what are your names?"

I stare at him blankly. Baby takes my hand under the table. *What does he want?*

Our names.

Are you going to write them down for him?

No, not yet.

Is he a great-man? She means is he important.

No. A white coat doesn't make you an expert. But it definitely suits him, showing off his broad shoulders.

"Ummmm, do you understand?" he asks, not looking directly at me. His face is very red and his shaggy, blond hair resembles a mop. It looks like he hadn't bothered to comb his hair today, or any day this week for that matter. There is no way he is in charge of anything, so I decide to wait and see who else they will send. My mother always did say I was arrogant.

"Look, I can get you situated, but you have to help me. . . . I . . ." He shakes his head. "You don't understand anything I'm saying, do you?" he mutters.

He touches his hand to his ear, and I see he has a black earpiece similar to the one Kay wore. "Hey, Rice here. We're going to have to save these two for Dr. Reynolds. I've been unable to get a verbal response. They seem harmless." He listens. "Yes, that is my initial evaluation despite the Guardian's concerns. Let's keep the Class Five for further study, and let the Class Three mix in with the current observation group." He pauses. "Yes, come get the child."

I stand and pull Baby off her chair. I shove her behind me with one hand and reach under my sweatshirt with the other. I feel for the gun, pulling it from its harness. I don't want to harm him but I point it at the boy. There's no way he's taking Baby anywhere. His mouth drops open. With his hand still to his ear he makes a squeaking noise.

He closes his mouth and swallows. "Yeah," he says, eyeing us. "You need to get Dr. Reynolds up here, now." I realize he is still speaking to the person on the other end of his earpiece. "I don't care," he tells them between clenched teeth. "Then get the director. They have a *gun*."

He moves his hand from his ear and puts both arms above his shoulders. "Look, there's no need for that. I'm just trying to help you." His voice trembles. "I promise."

I lick my lips. It is a safe place here, from Them anyway. I don't have to be quiet. I can ask him questions, get answers. But still, I can't bring myself to speak. I have lost my voice and am so very exhausted.

I hear the door unlock once again and see it begin to swing open. I point the gun at the opening.

"It's just the director," the boy assures me. "She won't hurt you."

A woman steps through the door. She is tall with long,

brown hair, and I instantly picture her with bright purple flowers in her hair. The kind you wear in Hawaii when you are on your honeymoon. I lower the gun and freeze.

Then, for the first time in three years, I find my real voice.

"Mom?"

PART TWO

NEW HOPE

FOUR MONTHS LATER

CHAPTER FOURTEEN

"Are you feeling better?" A woman's voice wakes me and I sit upright in bed. She is standing by the door, a meal tray in hand. I don't recognize her, but she looks commanding, her gray-blond hair tied back into a tight bun.

"Who are you?" I ask groggily. "What day is it?"

"I'm Dr. Thorpe. Do you know where you are, Amy?" She sets the food down, retrieving a small paper cup from the tray.

"I'm . . . I'm in the Ward, aren't I?" I ask tentatively, my brain in a fog.

"Yes, very good. You were brought here after your breakdown. Do you remember?"

I shake my head no. I know who I am. I can recall blurred faces, me being taken from someone. Who are they all? While I struggle to think, Dr. Thorpe hands me the cup, which contains three pills. "What are these?" I ask.

"They'll help you." She takes a larger plastic cup from the tray, walks to the sink, and fills it with water. She sits next to me on the bed and offers me the cup of water. I hesitate, then take it.

"I'm not sure I should take anything without talking to my mother first," I tell her, uncertain.

"Your mother is well aware of your course of treatment."

"Where is she? When can I see her?" I ask, unsettled. I take a deep breath, trying to calm myself.

"I will have to consult with Dr. Reynolds." She sounds kind, but something in her voice just isn't right.

"Is he the one who prescribed me these?" I shake the cup of pills. She nods, smiling reassuringly. "What are they?" I ask again, confusion clouding my head.

"Medication to help you get better."

Get better? What exactly is wrong with me? "And if I refuse?"

"I'm sorry, but that's not an option, Amy. I'd prefer you take the pills now. Otherwise I'll have to call an orderly in here. I know you don't want that." The doctor's kind manner has turned cool.

I hold the cup to my mouth and shake the pills in, trying to conceal them under my tongue as I swallow all the water. I give the empty cup back to the doctor, but she just walks to the sink and refills it.

"Let's try again, shall we?" she asks, handing the cup back to me. I frown, considering an alternative. There is none. Eventually I give in and swallow the pills. After the doctor checks my mouth to be certain I'm not hiding them, she brings me the tray of food.

"Now, you must eat all of this," she tells me firmly. "And if you refuse, you'll be force-fed, and I know you don't want that either." She gives me a pointed look before she leaves, the door clicking shut loudly behind her.

I pause for a moment, looking around. My room is sterile—white walls, a small sink and toilet in the corner, and the bed I'm sitting on. I'm still trying to figure out what is going on—to remember what brought me here. I look down at my food and, unwillingly, I make myself eat it, my stomach already queasy. Either the drugs aren't settling well or it's the stress. After

I finish, I push the tray onto the floor and lie in bed, clutching my stomach. Despite the pain, I fall into an uneasy, pill-induced sleep.

When I wake, I don't know if it's been hours or days. I can't help but wonder: Where did it all go wrong? I struggle to think back to when I saw my mother for the first time in years.

• • •

"Amy?" My mother looked at me, unbelieving, her hand covering her mouth. She walked forward slowly. "Is that you?"

I nodded. I'd already begun to cry. Not the silent tears that I'd developed in the After, but loud, blubbering sobs. Baby held tightly on to my waist. I could tell she was agitated.

My mother crossed the room and instantly I was in her arms. It was strange yet comforting. She smelled the same as I remembered: fresh and flowery. I bawled onto her shoulder. She rubbed my back, and I got lost in the feeling.

Eventually I could breathe again. I raised my head and wiped my nose. My mother gazed at me, beaming. Tears had stained her face.

She touched my head and studied my newly cut hair. "You always did want a Mohawk," she said. I managed a laugh.

"Baby cut it." It was strange to finally talk, to say Baby's name out loud. I'd only ever signed it. As soon as I said it, though, I noticed she was no longer clutching my waist. I turned to find her crouching on the floor against the wall, her hands covering her ears. I went to her quickly, bent down, and touched her arm.

"Are you okay?" I asked. Then I realized she wouldn't understand what I was saying and signed it instead.

She looked at me like I was a stranger. *Yes. You talked loud,* she accused.

I did Before. You know that.

It just scared me.

I'm sorry. I smoothed down her hair. *We're safe here. I promise.* I was sure.

Did the princess tell you that?

Princess? I turned and looked at my mother with a smile. *She's not exactly a princess. She's my mom.*

Baby stared at me, astounded. She was as amazed as I was to see my mother in front of us, alive. I took Baby's hand and helped her stand up.

My mother placed her arm around my shoulder. "I have so much to tell you. Let's go, you and . . ."

"Baby," I offered.

"You and Baby can come with me. I'll show you where you're going to live."

"Mom, where are we?" I felt like at any moment I would wake up and discover it had all been a dream.

"You're in New Hope, the largest postapocalyptic community of survivors in the Northern Hemisphere."

I smiled at the words: *hope*, *survivors*, *community*. Baby and I followed my mother back down the corridor and into the light of day. We were home.

We saw very little of New Hope that day. We were poked and prodded by doctors, since my mother insisted on a complete medical evaluation. She stayed by my side the entire time, fawning over me. It felt so good, almost unreal, having my mother back. I'd always hoped she was alive, but after so many years, the hope had seemed more like fantasy. My mother rubbed my back and played with my hair. She whispered how much she'd missed me as tears welled up in her eyes.

I was in a hospital room for several hours while they took my blood and conducted a full physical. My shoulder turned out to be sprained, and I was warned to be careful with it for a while. Then came all the medicine. I explained shots to Baby and how they were a good thing, despite the pain.

"Richard," my mother told the boy from earlier. "Do a complete workup on the child."

"Yes, of course." He took Baby's hand to lead her to another room.

"Wait," I said tentatively, the word not as forceful as I had hoped with my newly found voice. "I want to stay with her," I insisted.

The boy smiled. "Sure. I can examine her in here, if it makes you more comfortable," he offered. Grateful, I gave him a faint smile back. Baby looked around uncertainly.

"It's okay," he told her kindly.

"She doesn't understand you. We never spoke out loud at home. She'll have to learn. . . ." I paused, thinking of Amber whispering to Baby secretly. "I'm not sure if she remembers any English. . . . It's been a long time and she was only a toddler when I found her."

My mother took charge of Baby and helped her onto a hospital bed. "A lot of the children we find don't talk at first," my mother told me. "They've learned to be quiet to survive and have a hard time adjusting. We'll put Baby in a language class and I'm sure she'll regain her ability. You'd be surprised at how strong the language instinct is in children." She returned to my side and hugged me close. I nodded but still wondered. Baby had never even attempted to speak.

The boy examined every inch of Baby, pausing only for a moment at the nape of her neck, peering closely at her scar. He glanced around quickly, placing her long hair back over the mark. He caught my eye and for a moment I saw he was afraid, but the look passed quickly and I wondered if it was really there at all.

"Is everything okay?" I asked.

"Of course," he smiled, adjusting his glasses. "Do you know how she got this wound?" He motioned to her leg.

"No. She had it when I found her." I licked my lips. I was sweating, although the room was chilly.

"Probably a dog bite," the boy told my mother, but he called several other people over to Baby's bed, where they all made a commotion over the scar on her leg. My mother examined it herself, taking photographs and measurements. I held Baby's hand and signed to her that everything was going to be okay, although the attention being paid to her was making me nervous.

After they took her blood and gave her a few more shots, my mother informed us that we were in good health, if a little malnourished. "Time to go home," she said, stroking my hair.

"Excuse me," the boy addressed my mother, his tone surprisingly authoritative, "but I believe Dr. Reynolds wanted to complete a psyche-eval."

"It can wait," my mother said firmly. "I'll speak with Dr. Reynolds tomorrow about rescheduling. Right now I am taking my daughter home."

My mother took my hand and I took Baby's. As we walked out of the room, I glanced back. The boy was staring at me. He smiled, but he had a worried look in his eyes. He raised his hand to wave. I nodded and smiled back, then turned as my mother led us down a corridor and outside, into the sunlight. I shrank back, but she put her arms around my shoulders and whispered, "Be strong, Amy. I'm here."

I mostly stared at my mother's face as we traveled in a golf cart on a short ride to her apartment. Her building was large and white and looked like every other structure in the town, which seemed more like a college campus with bland buildings and shabby, weed-infested lawns.

My mother's apartment was a few floors up. She paused as we walked in the door, hugging me. Inside there was little furniture, but it looked cozy.

I was home.

•••

When Dr. Thorpe comes again, I've been awake for what seems like several hours. My head pounds and I know that something is very wrong. I'd tried the door, but it was locked. Why did they need to lock me in? I don't belong here. I've decided to refuse my medication.

"This is all for your own good. You aren't going to get better if you continue to refuse treatment," she tells me.

I stare at her, upset. "You're drugging me. I don't even remember how I got here. How is this helping?" I ask. "And why is the door locked?"

"You've had a very traumatic experience. It's better this way. . . . You can't handle everything you've been through. This treatment should stabilize you."

I ignore her, focusing on a spot on the wall over her left shoulder. I hate not being able to remember, but if I concentrate, I get flashes of memories; a small man with silver hair, a toddler playing with a toy truck, a blue-eyed teenage boy with glasses and shaggy, blond hair. Baby's smile.

I stay stubbornly motionless and eventually Dr. Thorpe sighs and puts the tray with the pills down next to the sink.

"I didn't want it to come to this," she says sadly. She

leaves the room and I steel myself for what is about to happen. I hope I am strong enough to resist.

•••

I sat on a couch in the living room while Baby rested her head on my lap. She'd long since fallen asleep, after I'd talked for hours about my life in the After. How I found Baby, how we survived. Now it was my mother's turn.

"I was at the lab when it happened," my mother explained. "We were on lockdown immediately. That's what saved us. We had a secure perimeter, electric fences, top-notch security team. We weren't allowed to go outside for a month. Luckily there were plenty of researchers who lived on the compound premises. We had supplies and sleeping quarters. I tried to call the house, but none of the outside lines were working." She stared through me, haunted by her memories.

"It was clear by then that the Floraes had taken over." The people in New Hope called the creatures "Floraes," short for Florae-sapiens, what the remaining scientific community had named them. "There weren't many people left out there, in the cities and rural areas. Maybe one in a million survived. We'd been in contact with the military research division at this university and decided this was the best place to relocate. That was nearly six weeks after the first Florae sighting. I . . . I ordered a search team to look for you before we left."

She paused and gazed at me. "When they said the electric fence was intact, but you weren't there, I was sure that you went with your father to the farmer's market that first day. If you were outside, you wouldn't have had a chance." She began to tear up at the memory and I couldn't help but cry too. *How did they miss me?* What was I doing while they searched the house, gathering cans . . . pilfering books? If I'd only been home that night I could have avoided years of fear. I could have been here, with my mother. But then, where would Baby be?

My mother continued through her tears. "Researchers in the private sector with facilities on the college campus were working on a stealth helicopter for the army. You would have been picked up in one." I nodded, instantly understanding that this had to be the ship. "It was incredible. They were developing a silent technology just when we needed it. Hover-copters. We could go out to other secure facilities and bring survivors here. We could remake society.

"After a while we sent out patrols, to check on the Floraes, to see how many were left, what they were doing, how they were surviving. But the patrols weren't just finding Floraes; they were finding people, living out there in silence, just like you. We started a program to integrate them into our systems and it's worked amazingly well . . . although, you were the first to ever pull a gun on my assistant." My mother shook her head at me, incredulous.

"He was going to take Baby away! I didn't know what was going on yet," I explained.

"Usually we send post-aps to an orientation to clarify things and ease people in, but you were classified as hostile, so you were going straight to your psychological evaluation. You should have been handcuffed and you definitely should not have had a gun." She was no longer amused.

"That woman, Kay, took one of our guns away as soon as she captured–I mean rescued–us. I was fighting with her. I think she assumed we only had one."

"It doesn't matter what she assumed, she knows that she should search everyone, even children," my mother said firmly. Her tone again pulled me back to my memories of her, how she was always the stern one. She sent me to my room when I was bad as a child and it was always my dad who let me out after she went to work.

"You know, it scared the hell out of us, that hover-copter

thing and the secret agents in their black suits. We thought they were the aliens, a new kind sent after the first.

My mother blinked at me. "You thought the Guardians were aliens?"

"They don't exactly look human. What are those black suits they wear?"

"It's a protective fabric. . . . They scared you?" she asked, concerned.

"Yeah, I mean, if you're looking for survivors you might want to write something on the side of the copter like 'we're here to rescue you, don't try to shoot us' or even just a symbol that everyone knows, like a peace sign or smiley face or something," I said.

My mother put her hand on my head and stroked my short hair. "We'll certainly take that under consideration," she said. "You know, I thought about you every day, Amy. I had the security team bring me a photo album from the house. Would you like to look through it?"

"I would, but I'm exhausted." And the memories were still too much.

"You and Baby can sleep in Adam's room," my mother told me.

"Who's Adam?"

My mother took a deep breath and sighed uneasily. "He's my child, Amy . . . your brother."

"Oh." It was too weird. "How old is he?"

"Two." She held my hand. "He's two years old."

I stared at the floor, suddenly furious. "You didn't waste any time," I mumbled.

My mother sighed. She took my head in her hands and made me look into her eyes. "It's not how it seems. I know you're exhausted now. If you want to get some sleep, I can explain everything tomorrow."

"Do, um, I have a stepfather?" I asked, feeling shaken to my core. My face burned.

"No . . ." My mother shook her head. "There's only me and Adam." She put her hand on my cheek. "And now you." She looked as if she was about to cry again.

I didn't want to see her sad. "Can I meet him?" I asked, the bitterness gone from my voice.

At that my mother's face softened. Her smile, still so beautiful. "Of course," she told me. "He'll be back from school at five."

I was quiet for a while, thinking about all I'd learned. "Mom, do you miss him?" I blurted out before I could stop myself. Her head snapped up. She knew who I meant.

"I miss your father every day," she said quietly.

My eyes stung. I desperately wanted my father to be remembered.

"But no matter how much it hurt me to lose your father, it was only a tiny fraction of the pain I felt when I thought you were gone."

The tears rolled down my cheeks then. I leaned into my mother, hugged her tightly. She kissed the top of my head and wiped my face with her hand before wrapping her arms around me again.

"If you want to get some sleep," she said, "I'll stay here while you and Baby rest."

"I think sleep would be good. We've had to take in a lot today," I said, which was the understatement of the century. I put my face in my hands and massaged my temples. In one day everything I knew about the After had changed. I didn't think I could handle much more.

•••

When Dr. Thorpe returns again a few minutes later, she is trailed by a couple of large men wearing all white. I stay still, my eyes open but unfocused.

The orderlies approach my bedside, where I continue to lie motionless. As soon as they are close enough, I jump up, hitting the nearest one in the nose with the palm of my hand. Blood squirts all over my clothes and splatters the bed.

Stunned, the second orderly doesn't have time to react. I crouch low and sweep his legs out from under him. My muscles seem to know what to do before I can think it. And suddenly I flash back to a gym—I'm training with Kay, a Guardian. She flickers into my mind, her expression sour, but her eyes full of kindness. In a flash as quick as lightning, her face is gone, leaving a blank void where the memory had been.

All this takes place in seconds, and the orderly I've tripped is still falling sideways. His head makes a loud knocking sound as it bounces against the floor. I spring forward and sprint to the door. I'm going to escape. I'll find Baby and someone to help us, maybe the woman I recalled through my haze. What was her name again? Once I'm out of here, I'll be able to think. My fingers are on the door handle when I feel a sharp pain in my neck. I look up to find Dr. Thorpe standing over me, flushed, a needle in her hand.

I try to open the door and run anyway, but my arms and legs have turned to jelly. I fall back, into Dr. Thorpe's arms. She lowers me to the floor and before I black out, I hear her say, "It's okay, Amy. You will get better. I will make sure of it."

•••

I woke at midnight to find Baby already up and watching me. I rubbed my face; my hand came away wet.

You were crying in your sleep, Baby told me.

Why didn't you wake me?

I thought maybe you were happy. You cried when we found Mom today.

I shivered slightly and shook my nightmare from my head. *Why aren't you asleep?* I asked her.

I can't sleep. It's too loud here.

I listened to the noises of the building, the buzz of the lights, the settling of wood and metal. That was all normal. We had those gentle noises at home. I listened harder and noticed that there was more. Voices from far away, sounds like a television program. There were footsteps in the hall, laughing outside. The ticking of the clock on the wall. I tried to tell Baby what all the noises were, but she shook her head.

There's a humming underneath it all. She explained. *It makes my head hurt.*

I wondered what it was she was hearing that I couldn't. *We have to get used to it here. It's our new home,* I told her. I was wide awake. *Are you thirsty?* I asked, rubbing my neck. She shook her head no, but I went to fetch myself a glass of water. My throat was raw from talking so much.

I walked through the apartment. Out of habit I was completely silent. In the living room, I noticed kids' clothes on the couch, a toy truck on the floor. My mother must have taken Adam to bed with her, not wanting to disturb us.

I quietly opened the cabinet doors until I found a glass and filled it with water from the pitcher in the fridge. The cool water soothed my throat and I drank it greedily. I drained the glass and filled it again to the brim. Then I brought it back to Baby in the bedroom in case she wanted some later. After I put the glass on the nightstand, I snuggled with her under the covers.

When I woke again, it was eight o'clock, and light was streaming in the window. Uneasy, I got up and surveyed the view. My mother's apartment looked down on a smallish park area that people were walking through on their way to other buildings. The area had the same look as the structures, minimally maintained.

I closed the blinds and shivered with the strangeness of it all. There were dozens of people down there. A pregnant woman read while several children ran around her, playing. I wondered, *How many people live in New Hope?*

I made my way to my mother's room, hoping to spend time with her before she left for work. I looked for my old clothes but they were gone. In their place were two jumpsuits. One was Baby's size and was a bright yellow, and the other, larger one was red and must have been meant for me. Underneath them were two pairs of shoes, the same colors as the jumpsuits. Both pairs were way too small for me and too big for Baby. I placed them on the floor. We didn't need shoes anyway.

I woke Baby and showed her the new clothes. She loved the yellow color, but all I could think was how impractical it was. You couldn't blend in; you couldn't hide. It was like wearing a big flashing sign that said, "Come eat me."

I buttoned up my own jumpsuit and looked in the mirror. It was big and the extra material billowed out, making me look several sizes larger than I was. I rolled up the sleeves and pant legs and resigned myself to looking stupid for a while.

My mother wasn't in the kitchen or the living room, but I found a note on her bedroom door.

I'll be back at eleven to show you around. You can watch TV until then. Snacks in the fridge. Love you, Mom.

My mother the workaholic, just like Before. Unnerved, I put the note on the counter and turned on the TV. Ours at home could still play videos, and sometimes Baby watched with the sound off. I flipped through the channels, finding only five stations. One had old sitcoms, another one showed cartoons, and there was even one with movies, all from Before.

The last channel was a news station, minus the slick studio feel. The "anchor," an older man, sat at a plain metal desk with nothing but a white wall behind him. I turned up the volume, and Baby covered her ears. The man spoke directly into the camera: "Grave news today, another Guardian has lost his life while defending New Hope. We will honor his memory Friday night at Memorial Hall."

I was startled by a death, after all my mother's assurances that we were safe here. How often did it happen? I listened to the news for a while, understanding very little of the context.

"And finally we have a breakthrough in our post-ap research, thanks to Director Harris." I stared at the screen as the camera panned left. My mother looked back at me.

"This is indeed a bright day, for I believe that we are close to realizing the dream that so many of us share." This is the mother I knew, professional and commanding. "We would like to put out a call for volunteers, once again. Any interested citizens should report immediately to the clinic for suitability testing." Suitability? For what?

After fifteen minutes the news repeated itself, so I turned the volume way down and flipped to cartoons for Baby. I searched the fridge, which was pretty bare except for some questionable-looking plastic bowls, their contents even more questionable. *Great snacks, Mom.* I did find a block of cheese wrapped in a cloth. On the counter was a loaf of coarse, homemade bread. Cheese sandwiches it was.

I toasted the bread and cheese in the oven and it smelled delicious. I hadn't had real cheese in a very long time. My mouth started to water. The oven dinged and I transferred the sandwiches to a plate. The smell of melted cheese filled the room and suddenly I was brought back to another time. I was watching TV in our old house, eating pizza bagels. I saw an alien for the first time.

I was no longer hungry.

I handed the plate to Baby, who automatically took a large bite, her eyes glued to cartoons. The food was hot; she blew on it and took a sip of water to cool down her mouth. As she chewed she turned and stared at me.

What is this? she asked.

She'd never had unprocessed cheese. The only bread we had was the kind I made at home which always came out hard and dry. I never got the knack for baking.

It's food from Before.

This is the most fan food ever. She turned back to the TV and wolfed down the rest.

My stomach growled, but I ignored it. I was way too on edge to eat. My mother would be back soon to show us around New Hope. I thought about her on the news. She was the director, but who, or what, did she direct? Before, she worked in a research lab for the government.

Maybe she could tell me more about the creatures, about where they came from and why they were here. It couldn't just be coincidence or a mistake. Why were they so vicious? And why us? Why now?

I glanced at the clock. My mother couldn't answer my questions if she wasn't around for me to ask them. I tried to watch cartoons with Baby, but I was unsettled. I sighed and willed time to go faster, which only made it worse.

CHAPTER FIFTEEN

"Hello again, Amy." An older, doughy man sits in a plastic chair across from me, smiling. I rest on my bed, my feet thrust under the covers. I'm uncertain about most things, my thoughts are murky, but I know I like my room. Even groggy, I feel comfy here.

"Hello . . . Dr. . . ."

"Dr. Reynolds," he tells me helpfully.

"Yes, of course." I know this man, I'm sure of it, but I can't quite place him. I'm finding it hard to concentrate.

He looks in his notebook and scratches his bald head.

"How are you feeling today?" he asks pleasantly. He seems nice enough. Maybe he's a friend? But that doesn't seem quite right. I feel bad for not remembering him.

"Good," I tell him. "I like it here."

"That's great." He scribbles something in his notebook and looks up brightly, which makes me smile. "You're not planning any more escape attempts, are you?" he asks in a joking tone.

"No . . . . ," I assure him, not certain what he's talking about. I want his approval, so I add, "New Hope is fan!"

Dr. Reynolds laughs lightly. "Well, I think so too, Amy. New Hope is everything I've always wanted."

"It's safe," I offer. I hear my mother's voice saying it again and again. "You're safe now, Amy." I scowl because I know, somehow, that she was wrong. I also remember another voice, a male this time. "I'll keep her safe," he promised. "I'll protect her."

Dr. Reynolds studies me and I lose my train of thought, my face softening into a smile. "New Hope is safe," I tell him again.

"Oh, it's so much more than that, Amy." He closes his notebook and sits back. "New Hope holds all my ambitions for the human race. It's our destiny."

I nod sleepily. A glint of a memory forming in my mind. A boy who made me promises. I let the spark flare. I need to remember him.

• • •

Someone's at the door, Baby told me moments before I heard a knock.

I hurried to the door and looked through the peephole. A teenage boy was standing on the other side.

"Yes?" I asked through the door.

"I . . . your mother sent me," he said loudly. "I'm supposed to show you around. The director said . . ."

I jerked open the door.

"She said . . ." He lowered his voice. "She'd meet you for lunch." He smiled crookedly, which softened his striking features and wild blond hair, making him look kind. When I noticed a pair of glasses shoved in the pocket of his white coat, I realized he was the "psychiatrist" from our arrival.

"Oh." I put my hand to my mouth, suddenly remembering. I'd pulled a gun on him, frightened him half to death. "Look, about yesterday, I'm sorry."

He shrugged. "It's okay. The director explained your situation." He said *director* like it was the president or something.

"Did she?" I wondered what my mother told him, what she was telling everyone about her long-lost daughter.

"We have a lot to cover, though, so we really should get going."

"Right. Okay," I motioned to Baby, who turned off the television and hurried to my side. She bounced slightly on her toes, eager to explore.

"Um . . ." He stood in the doorway awkwardly.

"Oh, sorry. I'm Amy and this is Baby." I introduced us, though we already unofficially met yesterday and I was sure he knew our names.

"I'm Rice." He held out his hand and I shook it.

"Rice?" I asked. I signed to Baby *He says his name is Rice.*

Rice? Why would he be named after food? she asked, scrunching her nose.

I started laughing. The tension in me was breaking–or finally overflowing–I wasn't sure which.

"What did she say?" Rice asked.

"She wants to know why you're named after a food," I explained, still giggling.

Rice smiled politely. "My name is Richard. Richard Kiernan Junior. My dad used to call me Rice and I absolutely hated it, but . . . well, he died, so I decided . . . you know."

I nodded, understanding completely. We stood for a moment, waiting. "So, should we go?" I asked eventually.

"Yeah, sure, um, it's just . . ." He glanced down at my feet.

"Shoes," I said, smiling. "Right. Wait here." I felt a little embarrassed as I ran to my mother's closet and scanned her few pairs of shoes. Like Rice was picking me up for a first date and I picked out the wrong outfit. Not that I knew what that felt like, since my parents never let me date in the Before. In the back of the closet I found some black rain boots, not too chunky.

I pulled them on; they were a bit big but not unbearable. It was so strange to wear shoes and I tripped as I left the room.

"Are you okay?" Rice asked, putting out a hand to steady me.

"Yeah," I said sheepishly. I wiggled my toes in the boots. Even though they had plenty of room, I felt trapped. "I'm not really used to wearing shoes." I took a deep breath and tried to calm down.

"What about for 'Baby'?" he asked. He said it like it wasn't really a name. I guess it really wasn't. To be fair, neither was Rice.

I shook my head. "I don't have any for her. The ones

my mother left looked way too big." Just like my ugly, red jumpsuit.

"The director had to guess your sizes. . . . We can stop by clothing appropriation and get her a pair."

"Fan," I said, making the fanning motion with my right hand so Baby could understand.

Baby smiled. *This whole place is fan,* she signed. I wished I felt the same.

"Fan?" Rice asked, confused.

"You know, like fantastic," I explained. "It's a thing that Baby and I say."

"Oh." Rice laughed and led us downstairs and outside into a courtyard. People meandered around, enjoying the sunshine. Baby clung to my arm. I gave her hand a reassuring squeeze, trying not to show her how overwhelmed I felt. I wasn't comfortable being out in the open during the day. The day belonged to Them.

"This is the Quad," Rice told us. "We're going to head to the north building, where the nonperishable goods are stored. You can get clothes and shoes and any other stuff you need." He led us to a large, white building that looked like the others.

Inside, it seemed like a campus bookstore, minus the

books. The shelves were full of random items, from soap and toothbrushes to backpacks and clothes. A few dozen people wandered the aisles, shopping. An older teenage girl looked from one skirt to another, deciding, while a young, pregnant woman grabbed some cloth diapers and put them in her cart.

"Usually people are assigned a time to come and pick up the essentials," Rice explained, "but since you're new to New Hope, you two are allowed an unscheduled visit."

"You have to make an appointment to shop?"

"Yeah, if people didn't keep to their appointments, a hundred people might show up at once and clearly"–he motioned around the store–"it would be too crowded. Besides, it gives the store time to restock between appointments. We have a big warehouse of nonperishable items that we've gathered from the surrounding . . ." He paused, looked at me. "Are you okay?"

"How many people live here?" I asked shakily.

"Three thousand five hundred and thirty-three," he answered matter-of-factly. My jaw dropped and I made a strangled coughing noise.

"They give a daily population update on the news," Rice explained. "Population growth and human expansion are our primary concern, for obvious reasons."

I found a bench nearby and collapsed on it. Baby still held my hand and pressed her cheek to mine.

What's wrong? she asked.

Nothing. I never imagined so many people survived.

"Rice, where are we? I mean, where is New Hope located?"

"Geographically?" he asked, sitting down next to me.

I nodded and noticed he smelled clean, like soap.

"This was a university in Kansas, but I don't think state boundaries apply anymore."

"It looks less like a college campus and more like a military compound," I said.

"It would. You've mostly seen the buildings devoted to research and development. They were working on some pretty important high-security projects here."

I looked at him, a frightening thought nagging at me. "Rice, what keeps Them out . . . the creatures? I didn't see any fences."

He looked back at me, smiling. "There aren't any," Rice said proudly. "It's perfectly safe. We've developed a sonic wave that keeps the Floraes away. They have sensitive hearing and can't tolerate it."

"That must be what Baby heard last night. She complained about a humming."

He frowned, turning toward Baby. "That's impossible. It's beyond the range of human hearing." He gazed at her intently, an odd look on his face. I didn't like the way he was gaping at her, as if something was wrong with her.

"Noise keeps Them out? So, if you know how to get rid of them, why don't you broadcast that sonic wave thing across the country, around the world?"

Rice snapped his attention back to me. "It doesn't kill them, Amy. It just makes them unhappy, hurts their auditory nerves, their 'ears' so to speak. It makes them want to get away. What would that accomplish? If they had nowhere to go for relief, they'd wander everywhere just like they do now. Then we wouldn't be safe here."

"Is that why you capture Them?" I asked. "To find a way to hurt them, instead of just annoy them?"

Rice flinched slightly. "We don't capture the Floraes," he said slowly.

"Yes you do. Baby and I saw someone, in a hover-copter. They caught one the same way they got us."

Rice looked around, then back at me. "I wouldn't go around telling that story to anyone," he said quietly. "Please."

He pressed his lips together and searched my face, his blue eyes penetrating. "Sometimes, the post-aps are unfocused. . . . They have to have extensive psychiatric treatment. It's for their own good," he assured me hurriedly. "But I don't want you getting sent to the Ward."

A chill ran down my spine, and Rice looked worried that he'd upset me. "I'm sorry," he said, reaching out to touch my arm. "I don't want to scare you. It's just, you're one of the first girls my age brought here in a while. I wouldn't want anything to happen to you."

I looked down, feeling myself blush.

"If this is too much for you, we can go back. Maybe when the director has the time, she can take you around, if that would make you feel more comfortable."

I shook my head. "When does my mother ever have spare time?" I asked.

He smiled at that. "She's very busy. But hey, it gives us time to get to know each other."

His leg jostled against mine and I got goose bumps. I wasn't used to anyone but Baby touching me.

I turned to Baby and tried to explain to her about the population. She could only count so high, but I knew she could conceptualize larger numbers.

Think of the largest number that you know, I told her. *And double it again and again and again.*

Baby looked at me like I was crazy. *There's that many people?*

Yes. More. I felt Rice's eyes on me. I turned and caught him staring. He blushed bright red and looked away.

"I was just . . . ," he stammered. "That's not standard American Sign Language."

"No, we've modified it a lot."

"Baby, she's so quiet." He smiled at her and she watched him with her big, brown eyes. Even if she didn't understand him, she knew he was talking about her.

"It's why she isn't dead."

He nodded. "And you really don't know how she got that scar on her leg?" he asked.

"No, she was already hurt. I didn't see how it happened." I told him the entire story of how I found her, wounded and alone in the supermarket. "She also has a strange mark on the back of her neck," I mentioned.

"Yes, but that was nothing of significance," he told me quickly, even though I knew he looked closely at it yesterday.

I studied him while he watched Baby taking in the people around us.

"How old are you?" I asked.

He paused. "Seventeen."

"Seventeen? And you're my mother's assistant? But you're so young."

"You have a lot to learn about New Hope," he told me, fiddling with his name tag.

"I don't doubt it," I agreed, standing. "I think I'm over my initial shock, though. Let's go get Baby some shoes."

• • •

Dr. Reynolds is still talking. I've zoned in and out of hazy memories, but continue to nod my head dutifully. I tune back in to the sound of his voice, trying to concentrate on what his words mean.

"It's a fresh start. We have an opportunity to isolate all the best that humanity has to offer and weed out the worst. New Hope is a society that will be spoken about as the birthplace of a new civilization. When humans reclaim the earth, they will look back here and know this was the foundation for a new world."

He is talking with such passion the skin on his face jiggles slightly. I laugh despite myself.

"Is that funny?" His smile fades to a scowl.

"No . . . I'm just . . . excited." I don't want him to know I

wasn't really paying attention to his prepared speech. I don't want him to be angry. Worry begins to creep into my thoughts.

"It's all right, Amy. You can go back to your nap now."

"Thank you, Dr. . . ."

"Reynolds," he reminds me.

"Yes, thank you." I lie down and pull the covers up over my head, welcoming the ease of unconsciousness.

• • •

"Let's try these." Rice pulled a couple of pairs of shoes down off a shelf for Baby.

"Why are they yellow?" I asked as Rice bent down, placing the shoes next to Baby's feet to size them up.

"Class Three is yellow," he declared, holding up a pair triumphantly. "I think these should fit her."

"What's all this 'class' business?" I asked.

"That's how we keep track of children. After the Floraes showed up, there was a core group of survivors. Mostly researchers and military, people who were in secure, easy-to-defend areas."

"My mother mentioned that last night."

"Well, the post-aps . . . the ones left"–he motioned vaguely–"out there. The ones who really survived the Floraes, they're mostly children."

"Children? I never saw any children, except for Baby."

"You were in a city," Rice explained. "High concentration of Floraes, hardly any post-aps. In other areas, where there was less population density, children were the ones more likely to survive. Adults probably kept them concealed, took extra measures to protect them. And of course children are good at hiding. Once their instinctual survival skills kick in, they know how to be quiet."

"They believed in the monsters before the monsters showed up," I whispered.

"Exactly. That's why when we bring in the post-aps, we usually don't have a problem with them. We place them in a structured environment. They fit right in."

"What does that have to do with Class Three or Four or whatever?"

"It's just how we organize the kids. Newborn to toddler is Class One. They don't get a color. Three to five years is Class Two and they have to wear pink or blue based on their gender." He cleared his throat. "Kids aged six to nine are Class Three; they all wear yellow. Age ten to twelve is Class Four–they wear orange–and thirteen to sixteen is Class Five . . ."

"Let me guess. Class Five is red." I tugged on my

oversized jumpsuit. "Only the kids are assigned a color?" I asked.

"Yes."

"But I'm seventeen years old." It was strange for me to say it. Seventeen. I'd never had a sweet sixteen. I'd never gotten my learner's permit. I didn't get to do all that normal stuff that teenagers used to do.

"Oh. Maybe your mother was just confused," Rice offered unconvincingly.

My mother was not easily confused. My heart sank as I wondered if she'd forgotten how old I was.

"Well, let's let Baby try these on." Rice held the shoes out to her, but she just looked at him blankly. She didn't seem to get that they were hers now, even though she stared at them longingly.

Go on. Put them on your feet, I instructed her.

Baby took the shoes and carefully held them, fingering the laces. *Do you want me to help you?*

She nodded. I knelt and showed her how to put on the shoes and tie the laces. *First you make a bunny rabbit.* I held the knots with one hand and signed with the other. *See the ears? Then the rabbit goes through the rabbit hole.* I finished tying the bow.

What are you talking about? she asked, puzzled.

That's how I learned to tie laces. My dad taught me.

But Baby wasn't paying attention. She was engrossed in the feel of her shoes. She held out her foot and shook it.

Feels heavy, she said, taking a few awkward steps. The shoes thumped dully against the linoleum floor. She looked at me and wrinkled her nose. *Why is everything here so loud?*

I laughed, surprised it was the way I used to laugh in the Before, not careful to be silent.

"What did she say?" Rice asked.

"She wants to know the point of shoes when they make so much noise."

You don't have wear them now if you don't want to, I told her, wanting Baby to be as comfortable as possible in her new surroundings. She slipped the shoes off her feet and clutched them to her chest.

"I told her she doesn't have to wear them today. That's okay, right?"

Rice gave me an uncertain look. I got the feeling he had a hard time breaking rules.

"What's the next stop?" I asked to distract him.

"School. You don't have to go yet," he assured me, "but I'll show you where it is."

"Fan!" I smiled, trying to sound enthusiastic, but inside I was worried. Baby had never played with kids her own age and I didn't know how she'd react.

We reached another large, nondescript building that looked more like a prison than a school. Inside, each door was painted a color to correspond with the jumpsuit colors. The doors even had windows, so I peeked in a yellow one as we walked by. A cluster of children, all wearing yellow, were sitting quietly, while their teacher lectured from a chalkboard.

"This is where all the kids go during the day. The bottom floor is classrooms for children under twelve, the second floor is for Class Five, and the top two floors are the dorms."

"Dorms?"

"For children without a parental claimant."

A parental claimant? Those must be the kids who were found wandering around without their parents. Kids who had watched their families die.

"How awful," I whispered, looking at Baby.

"They're very well taken care of," Rice assured me. "You shouldn't be worried."

I signed to Baby everything Rice told me as we walked up the stairs.

What if I don't like it? Can I leave? she asked.

No. You're supposed to learn things, even if you don't want to. She nodded, trying to understand, but clearly confused.

"This is where the Class Five students study," Rice said as we reached a set of red doors.

"I guess I won't be attending classes, since I'm not the right age."

"Oh no, you still can. Your mother said you were a wiz in school. We can test you in. You may even qualify for investigative study."

"Investigative study? Is that like college?" I asked, excited despite myself.

"Sort of. You can do your investigative study in biological chemical engineering, civil and environmental engineering, advanced physics, nuclear science and engineering, genetics, aeronautics, medicine. . . ." He paused when he saw my blank expression. "The sciences are extremely important if we're going to rebuild society. We need better equipment, better vaccines, people who can design buildings. . . ."

"Not the people who like to study plays, poetry, and novels." The truth of what I was saying had sunk in. The arts were probably pointless now that everyone was focused on survival. I thought back to all my time alone, reading, as the world crumbled around me. It was the only thing that gave me solace and hope.

Rice seemed to read my mind. "That's not true," he insisted. "We need people with all kinds of talents. Under the director I'm learning how to engineer a society in which all the members are valued for their unique abilities."

"You sound like a propaganda poster," I told him, secretly relieved.

He looked embarrassed. "Sorry. I just want you to understand what we're trying to do here."

"No, I get it. It's just a little much," I said, trying to hide my frustration. "Maybe we can skip the tour and just meet up with my mother?"

Rice looked at his watch. "We still have some time to kill; it's an hour before we meet the director for lunch." But he cut short the lecture and took us around the side of the building to a playground. Small children sporting either blue or pink jumpsuits wobbled around, attended by several older women who all wore purple T-shirts. We sat on a bench and watched them. I never liked little kids much, except for Baby, but I now felt drawn to them. It was relaxing, seeing them play and struggle.

Baby grabbed my hand. *Amy? Why does that little boy look*

like you? She pointed and my eyes followed her finger to one of the blue-clothed children close to us.

He was playing with a bright yellow truck, filling it with sand and emptying it out in a heap. When he stood, I could see him better: he had my dark hair and eyes, my round chin. He did look like me and my breath caught. Staring, I watched as he joined a line for the slide, impatiently hopping from foot to foot. When he reached the stairs, he rushed up, took a misstep, and fell forward.

"Adam!" someone yelled. One of the teachers rushed to his side and scooped him up. She checked him and comforted him, wiping the tears from his face.

I could feel Baby's eyes on me. Rice's too. I must have looked terrible or at least in terrible shock.

"I think that's my brother," I whispered, also signing my words to Baby.

The color drained from Rice's face. "Oh my gosh, how could I have been so stupid? I'm so sorry, Amy." He put his hand on my arm and I didn't pull away. "I should have thought. I knew the director's son would be here. I should have prepared you."

Baby buried her head in my side and wouldn't look up. I pushed aside my own distress. *What's wrong?* I asked when I finally managed to place my hand in hers.

If you have him, you don't need me, she said, her worst fear coming to light. With all the events of the past day, I hadn't thought about how Baby would react to my "new" family.

You're my sister, I told her. *It doesn't matter how many other people we love, we'll always be sisters.*

Baby nodded, still with her head on my side. She didn't want to let go of me, and I didn't mind. She anchored me to who I was.

I looked up at Rice and smiled. "We're okay," I assured him.

"Great," he exhaled loudly, genuinely relieved. He clearly wanted to move on. "Let's get some chocolate milk." He grinned at Baby. "Would you like that?"

Baby raised her eyebrows and half smiled. She didn't understand him, but she knew he was excited about something and wanted her to be excited too. She waved her hand in front of her face.

"Fan!" Rice shouted, pleased. I smiled. The tension melted away, though I was still unsettled.

I like him, Baby told me.

Me too. He's . . . nice. I wasn't sure how I felt. His knowledge of this place was comforting, and he did make me feel at ease–which was something I hadn't felt in a long time. He was also cute, and something dipped in my stomach every time we were close. But after being on my own for so long, I wondered if I would recognize a crush if I tripped over one.

"Can you teach me more of the words in your language?" Rice asked, snapping me out of my thoughts. "It's fascinating, all the modifications you've made, especially how sometimes you sign into each other's hands when you don't want people to know you're communicating."

"Oh, you noticed that?"

"It's not obvious," he assured me, "but sometimes you hold hands and tell me what she's saying. Either she's letting you know somehow or you're a mind reader."

I bit my lip. "You wouldn't believe the latter, would you? You shouldn't underestimate my psychic ability."

"I'll believe it if you guess what I'm thinking right now." He turned and looked intensely into my eyes. I noticed again how good-looking he was. He and I stared at each other, not saying anything, for what felt like minutes. I smiled, a real smile this time, not the forced, tense imitation of a smile I'd been wearing all morning.

It was strange. On some level I genuinely felt comfortable with Rice, almost like he was a friend from Before. I raised my thumb and pointer finger to each temple. "You are thinking . . ." I feigned concentration. ". . . that you wish you didn't have to babysit two post-aps when you could be off somewhere engineering chemicals."

"Clearly you are not a mind reader." He grinned, turning to Baby. "I'm actually enjoying this. You and Baby are . . . different."

"Thanks," I said sarcastically.

"No, I mean in a good way." He looked at me again. "I'm really glad you're here. And I won't tell anyone about you two being able to communicate through touch."

"Thanks," I said again, and this time I meant it.

We walked to another large white building that turned out to be a standard cafeteria. A smell that made my knees weak hit me immediately.

Burgers. Not pigeon burgers. Not squirrel burgers. Not rat burgers. Honest to goodness hamburgers. I sniffed the air. There was another scent, just as heavenly: French fries.

My stomach growled loudly. I looked at Rice and grinned. "I skipped breakfast."

"We're supposed to wait for your mother . . . but go ahead, if you want."

We made a beeline for the servers and I grabbed a tray.

But before I got in line, I stopped.

"I don't have any money," I told Rice.

"It's okay, we don't use money here. We have enough resources for everyone, at least for now. If you live here, you get whatever you want."

"Fan." I smiled and piled plates onto my tray, thinking of what Baby would like to eat as well. Hamburgers, fries, a baked potato, three slices of pizza, some kind of burrito thing, and two pieces of crude-looking apple pie. I made my way past a table of kids my age, all dressed in red, and another table of pregnant women, talking excitedly. I brought the food to an empty table and signed to Baby that she shouldn't place her shoes on the tabletop. She dropped them under her chair and looked at me expectantly.

Well, dig in, I told her with a smile. I ate until I was in danger of bursting. Baby was on her second slice of pizza. Rice just watched us, trying to make conversation.

"You know, you're not really eating beef."

"You could have fooled me," I mumbled, my mouth full.

"It's a synthetic protein that we manufacture from soy and a chemical compound."

"Sure tastes real. My dad used to make us eat soy burgers all the time and they weren't half as good as these are."

"We've perfected the formula this past year," Rice told me, obviously pleased. He went on to explain how there was a nearby dairy farm that they were able to save when the Floraes arrived and how they kept the cows fed a steady diet of a synthesized organic compound that maximized milk output with minimal caloric intake. I tried to listen, but I was lost in the euphoria of the banquet in front of me.

CHAPTER SIXTEEN

Days seem to go by here, but there are no windows in my room and I am unsure about the passage of time. More often than not, I am unable to focus. I can't think very well. When I ask questions, no one answers. I've learned that probing just confuses me and I keep forgetting why it is important in the first place. I've stopped asking for my mother, for Baby. If either of them came to see me I do not remember their visit.

I am brought meals and medication by Dr. Thorpe or one of the nurses. I dutifully swallow the pills and whatever food they put in front of me and fall asleep soon after. I like being asleep. When I'm awake my head is foggy.

Eventually Dr. Thorpe encourages me to leave my room and visit the common areas and the small cafeteria. There I eat with the other inhabitants of the Ward. They don't talk and neither do I. I leave them alone. I don't want to cause any trouble.

There is a large window in the common room and I sit and look out it sometimes. There is nothing to see really, the glass is thick and covered in bars, but past that I can make out some trees. I like the color green. It goes on endlessly. When the wind shakes the leaves, it seems as if the world is rattling.

Sometimes, when I'm lost in the trees, I feel someone there, sitting next to me, holding my hand. The hands are rough and much larger than mine, but gentle and masculine at the same time. I feel like they belong to someone I should remember. Sometimes he doesn't hold my hand, but I still feel him there, watching over me. When I turn to look, though, he's gone and I wonder if he was really there at all.

•••

He stares at you when he thinks you're not looking.

Maybe it's the fan haircut you gave me. Crossing my eyes, I stuck my tongue out at Baby. *I can't help that I'm beautiful.*

He's looking at your face, not your hair, Baby told me with a slight smirk. I realized she was giving me a hard time. I made another face at her, but I inwardly smiled and tried to hide my blush. I looked up and saw Rice watching us, trying to figure out what we were saying. He raised his eyebrows questioningly.

"Baby was just talking about my awesome haircut," I lied. "She did it herself."

Rice smiled widely. "She did an excellent job . . . very . . . even." He gave Baby an enthusiastic thumbs-up.

See, he likes it. I told her. *Maybe you should get your hair cut just like me.*

Baby's eyes widened, and she nodded her head vigorously. *Then everyone will know we're sisters!*

"And that?" Rice asked, echoing Baby's excitement.

"She wants her hair cut just like mine so people will say we look alike."

Rice's amusement faded. "I don't think that's the best idea."

"Why not?" I touched my Mohawk self-consciously.

"It's just . . . not the style for children here. You wouldn't want to make her too different. . . . I mean . . ." He struggled for the words to explain, but I understood.

"More different than she already is?" I muttered.

Baby was still looking at me expectantly. *Well? When will you cut my hair too?*

Maybe later.

Baby pouted, not understanding. She'd never had to deal with social norms. I wanted to cheer her up, so I turned to Rice.

"There was mention of chocolate milk, for Baby," I reminded him. I wanted some too. I hadn't had fresh milk in a long time.

Rice nodded and practically jogged over to the counter, returning with two glasses.

Drink it, I told her.

What is it? She wrinkled her nose. *It's very brown.*

It's good. I took a sip to show her. As the sweet creaminess hit my tongue I was transported back to my childhood. Before the After. I gulped down the milk, not even pausing to breathe. The liquid added uncomfortably to my already full stomach, but I tilted the glass until the last drop trickled into my mouth. Rice and Baby stared at me as I put the glass down and wiped my lips on my sleeve.

Baby took a tentative sip. Her eyes widened. She drank slowly, holding the glass with both hands, staring at the milk, unbelieving. Suddenly someone jostled her from behind and she dropped her glass. It hit the table before it rolled onto the floor and shattered. The noise startled her and she jumped up into the mess.

Adrenaline filled my body and I was at her side in seconds. *Are you okay?* I checked her feet for cuts.

"Why isn't that child wearing shoes?" someone asked.

"Is she all right?"

"Where's her Minder?"

Baby crouched and put her hands over her ears.

I was flooded with a sick panic. "Can you all just be quiet?" I pleaded. "Do you have any idea how loud you all are?" I looked around the cafeteria, overwhelmed. There were too many people, too much noise. I suddenly couldn't deal with it.

I grabbed Baby's hand and we ran, desperate to escape the racket. Outside was the Quad, which I knew was very close to our building. I stumbled across the pavement, focused on getting Baby away from the noise. I found our building and yanked her up the stairs to our apartment.

Inside, I put her on the floor and sat next to her, hyperventilating. Her face was wet with silent tears and she reached for my hand.

I'm sorry, Amy.

It's not your fault. It was too much, too soon. I held Baby tight. *Feel any better?*

Yes. It's just, there's this noise in my head. Ever since we got here, I hear it all the time. When everyone talks with their mouths too, I feel like my head is going to burst. She started to cry again, soundlessly. Fat tears rolled down her cheeks.

Whenever you feel that way, you can come find me and we'll come here, where it's nice and quiet.

She nodded her agreement and I let her cry herself to sleep, stroking her head with my palm. It wasn't long before Rice appeared, looking worried.

"Is she okay?" he asked loudly, opening our apartment door. Baby opened her eyes and glanced at Rice before closing them again and drifting back off to sleep. I put my finger to my lips. "Did she get cut?" he whispered.

I shook my head. Baby's feet were strong and calloused. He sat down next to me, with a loud *thump.* I was very aware of his closeness. I tried to relax, to lose my unease.

"It's kind of strange, but I think of things as Before and After," I said at last.

"Before and after the Floraes?"

"Yeah, but now . . . this is something completely different. New Hope, I mean. It's like the After is out there, in the unprotected world. New Hope isn't Before or After. . . . I don't know what it is."

"Maybe New Hope is the now," he offered.

I smiled. "That sounds like another crappy slogan."

"Hey, I'm just trying to help. . . . Do you spend a lot of time thinking about Before?" His voice was full of concern.

"Not really, I think it's better not to. When I lost everything, everybody, it was so surreal. It was a long time until the After felt like reality. By then I'd already accepted that my parents were gone and my friends were dead."

We sat in silence. I tilted my head and rested it on his shoulder. He tensed for a moment, then relaxed. We stayed like this for a while. I needed, at that moment, to feel support–a physical touch that could make me feel this was real.

"You can always speak with someone about it," he said, breaking the silence. "We have trained psychiatrists available for anyone who needs them. Therapy is encouraged here. It could help, you know, instead of keeping it all bottled up inside."

"Sorrow concealed . . . ," I whispered.

"Like an oven stopp'd, Doth burn the heart to cinders where it is." Rice finished the quote. I picked my head up off his shoulder and looked at him, astounded.

"What? I can't know my Shakespeare?" he asked with a little smile. "I'm not just a bio-geek. . . . I'm an everything geek," he admitted.

I sat with my back against the couch, content to be there with Rice. I wished I could stay forever, in the quiet.

"I think I need to rest," I told him. "Would you mind letting us get some sleep?"

"Sure. I know it's been a long morning."

That was an understatement. It was only yesterday that Baby and I were taken from the lakefront, only yesterday I was reunited with my mother, only yesterday I discovered there were nearly four thousand more people in this world than I dared hope.

It wasn't yesterday; it was a lifetime ago.

• • •

"Are you doing okay in here, Amy?" a voice asks.

I smile, my eyes half closed. Why wouldn't I be okay? Everything here is so peaceful.

"Do you recognize me?" The boy inserts himself in front of me, blocking my view of the trees. I try to focus on him. He has shaggy, blond hair and glasses. He looks smart. Is he one of the doctors who take care of me? He seems too young to be a doctor or a nurse.

"You're . . . a friend?" I ask, unsure.

"Yes, I'm a . . . friend."

He is frowning, so I reach out and place my hand on his shoulder. "It's okay. They'll make you better here. That's what they do." I try to reassure him.

He pulls away from me, still frowning. "Oh, Amy, I am so sorry."

I shake my head. I don't understand what he would be sorry for.

Then he leans in and whispers softly, "I'm going to get you out of here. I promise."

My mother's face flashes in my mind. I want to see her and Baby. Why am I here and not with them? *"Maybe you should talk to my mother," I say loudly. "She's the director, you know. She can help you get me home," I tell him excitedly. The boy looks horrified and backs away.*

"What's going on here?" A nurse comes over to check on us.

The boy's expression turns cool. "It's okay. Ms. Harris was just a bit agitated," he tells the nurse calmly. He takes off his glasses and cleans the lenses with his lab coat. "She was asking for her mother."

"Should I inform Dr. Thorpe?" the nurse asks, uncertain.

"No, I'll let Dr. Reynolds know," the boy tells her with finality. After she leaves, the boy leans in again. I think he is going to kiss me on the cheek but instead when his lips brush my skin, he whispers so low I almost do not hear him.

"Watch for Kay." He pulls back and looks in my eyes. There is kindness in his.

Kay. *The name is so familiar. There is a glimmer of recollection before it slips away. He squeezes my hand as I stare out the window and watch the trees tremble in the breeze. As the boy starts to leave, I yell after him, "You should definitely talk to my mother. She would want to help me."*

But something is nagging at the back of my mind and I'm not so sure. A wave of fear washes over me. Why hasn't my mother come for me? Where is she?

• • •

"I came as soon as I heard," my mother said the minute she walked in. "Are you okay?" She sat next to me on the couch, hugging me, then Baby.

"I'm fine. Baby dropped a glass and freaked out because of the noisy cafeteria." I patted Baby's shoulder. "Then I super freaked out," I admitted.

"You're still getting used to things here. It's only been a day." She twirled her fingers through my short hair. "I shouldn't have left you alone so soon."

"It's okay." I didn't mention that we'd gotten along fine

the past few years without her. "Rice is really nice. He was a good tour guide."

"Tonight it will be just us girls." She smiled at us. There was a knock at the door and she corrected herself. "I mean, just us girls and Adam."

My mother went to the door and collected a toddler from a woman wearing purple. "Thank you, Stephanie," she said, shutting the door and carrying the little boy into the living room. "Come meet your brother, Amy." She carefully placed Adam on the floor and watched me expectantly, waiting.

"Oh, okay." I sat on the floor and smiled faintly at my mother. I took a deep breath.

"Adam, say hello," my mother prompted.

"Hello, Amy," he said loudly, his voice surprisingly husky for a child.

"Hello, Adam." I watched as his chubby hands grabbed a teddy bear and then ran it over with the toy truck. "I'm your sister."

"I know. Mommy shows me your picture." He looked up at me. "You're pretty."

I relaxed a little and smiled, amused. "Thank you."

He stood jerkily and fell toward me. He landed against

my chest and I could feel his breath on my cheek. He put his arms around my neck and rested his head on my shoulder.

I couldn't help it. In one clumsy motion, the little boy had inserted himself into my heart.

That evening we talked and watched old movies and ate homemade snacks. It almost felt like Before, except my mother never did any of those things with me Before. She was always working. I half expected her to head back to the lab. She did whip out her computer during one of the movies and occasionally took calls on her earpiece, but mostly she was all mine. Baby loved "girls' night," and played trucks with Adam happily.

Rice stopped by at one point to drop off the shoes that Baby left in the cafeteria. She took them and beamed at him happily. *Thank you.*

"What about for Amy?" my mother asked him. "She told me the shoes I picked out for her were too small."

"I've been meaning to ask you for some normal clothes." I tugged at my red jumpsuit. "Rice explained the color-coded thing was only for kids younger than seventeen."

"Honey, what are you talking about? Your birthday isn't until August."

I paused. Could I be wrong? I never really kept careful track of time in the After; I was only vaguely aware of the passage of seasons.

"What month is it?" I was afraid to ask.

"It's May," Rice informed me, his voice kind.

"So, that means . . ."

"You're sixteen." My mother said gently. "You have four more months before you class out. Then you'll be assigned a job."

"Oh." I paused. Everything in New Hope was wrong. "Can I study whatever I want?" I blurted, sounding desperate. I wanted to go back to the subjects I loved. I wanted to feel normal again.

"Not exactly. I know you were always good at English and you love literature. You can study those subjects, but you'll still have to take basic medicine and everyday science, unless you qualify for advanced study." She smiled. "I know it's confusing, but we have a whole system worked out. If you're put in advanced study you're exempt, which means you don't have to take a part-time job."

"And if I don't qualify?" I asked.

"Then you're nonexempt and you'll have to go on work rotation," my mother explained. "An assignment will be made for you, but you can request something you'd prefer, like working at the library or maybe helping with the small children."

I could live with that. I liked to learn and I wasn't afraid of work. "Maybe I can help with the new post-aps that you all bring in."

"What do you mean?"

"Well, you know I didn't have a very good experience. I mean, you stick some crazy survivors in a room and throw someone young like Rice into the mix. Did you think that was a good idea?" I was still traumatized from yesterday, from everything. I turned to Rice. "No offense."

"That isn't common practice, Amy." My mother smiled tightly. I knew that smile. It was her "things are not going according to plan" smile. I often got that smile Before. "It would be good to get your input about your experience, though. It's not a bad idea to change procedures that aren't working."

She looked at Rice and continued, "Maybe Amy can have a special orientation sometime. That way she can understand the social system we've worked out for New Hope."

Rice nodded.

She turned back to me. "Richard can take you one day. I wish I had the time."

I felt my heart surge a little, the old resentment setting in: my mother the workaholic. "I know you're busy, Mom. I get how it is. Dad always . . ." I stopped myself. My mother's pose shifted, suddenly stiff. I knew it was hard for her to hear me talk about my father. She retreated to the kitchen quietly.

Rice turned back to the front door and I thanked him before he went. "Baby really enjoyed our tour earlier." I paused. "So did I."

He looked at me, his blue eyes shining behind his glasses. "I'm glad I could help," he said. "It was nice to meet you, again. You know, without the weapon."

Suddenly I didn't want him to leave. He was a friend–a comfort–in an unfamiliar place. Instead of shaking his hand, I threw my arms around his neck and hugged him.

"Thank you," I whispered in his ear. When I released him, he was beet red. He mumbled something incoherent and stumbled out the door.

CHAPTER SEVENTEEN

When I'm not sleeping, or staring out the window in the common room, I spend a lot of my time watching old Disney movies. Everyone enjoys the cartoons, so there are always other people here, around me, but I don't pay attention to them. They sit quietly, watching contentedly, and I do the same.

One day I am deep into Snow White *when I hear someone repeating my name. I turn from the television. My mother is sitting in the chair next to me. I hadn't even noticed she'd arrived.*

"Hi, Mom."

She smoothes my hair, petting my head. There are tears in her eyes. I don't understand why she is so upset.

"Oh, honey, I'm so sorry. I came as soon as they said you were stable. You had a dissociative mental break." She glances around the room and lowers her voice. "I didn't tell him what you learned about the Floraes."

"What about them?" I ask. Something pulls at my mind and I feel like I should understand her, but I don't know what she's talking about.

My mother stares at me. "It's . . . it's nothing. I just wanted to let you know that I love you." She hugs me.

"I love you too, Mom." I turn back to the cartoon.

"It might not seem like it, but you're getting well here. You're getting the help you need." She takes my hand.

"I know," I tell her.

"Dr. Reynolds sounds very positive about your recovery." Her voice quavers and she sniffles loudly.

At the mention of Dr. Reynolds, I get a sinking feeling in the pit of my stomach. I try to ignore it. "That's nice," I say uncomfortably.

She lets go of my hand and kisses my forehead. I don't know how long she stays by my side, but when I think to look again, she's gone.

• • •

It's Baby who elbowed me awake in the morning. My nightmare was still fresh in my mind: the Florae had Baby and she was terrified, screaming. I shook the fear from my mind as I felt for Baby's hand and signed, *What?* still half asleep.

Mom is talking really loudly.

I listened, but couldn't hear anything. *So?*

She's saying your name. I know it in loud speak. Maybe she needs you.

I sat up quickly and silently walked to the bedroom door. Putting my ear to the crack I could just barely make out my mother's muffled voice.

"But Amy has already gone through intake. . . ." She paused, listening. "Yes, I know, but I don't think she requires a full psyche-eval. . . . It just seems unnecessary." She sounded exasperated. "Yes, of course I understand there are no exceptions, even if it is a waste of time." There was another long pause. "I'll have them there at eight."

My mother was quiet, shuffling papers, when I pushed open the door.

"Oh hi, honey." She hastily shoved her papers into her computer bag. "You doing okay?"

"I'm good. Better," I told her. "Still in shock," I added honestly.

She patted the empty spot next to her on the couch and wrapped her arms around me when I sat down.

"It's okay for you to feel disoriented," she assured me. "But it's important for you to know that everything will soon seem routine." She pulled back, then, and gave me a hard look. "You do know that, don't you, Amy? You'll fit in here just fine. You'll be back to normal in no time."

"I don't think I understand what normal is anymore."

My mother frowned, considering. "You should remain optimistic, especially when you speak to others about New Hope. . . ."

"Is this about the psyche-eval?" I asked. "I overheard you talking about it just now."

"Honey, you'll do fine on your psyche-eval," she said brightly, but I sensed something else in her voice . . . anxiety? My mother was never anxious. "It's just that you've had to deal with so much hardship over the years . . . you may have forgotten that things can be pleasant. Not everything left in this world is horrific."

"I know that, Mom." Even the After wasn't all bad. I had Baby, a home, a life of sorts.

"Good. So during your psyche-eval, when you speak with Dr. Reynolds, just make sure you let him know that you feel hopeful, that you're ready to move forward."

"I will," I promised, although I didn't exactly feel hopeful or optimistic. I felt heavy, like New Hope was weighing me down. My mother was looking at me expectantly, so I smiled reassuringly, which seemed to satisfy her.

I wished it were that easy to shake my dark dread.

• • •

I hear Dr. Thorpe talk sometimes, about me and others. I kneel quietly next to my door while she's in the hallway. I don't think she realizes I'm there, or maybe she thinks that I can't hear her.

The medicine hasn't been making me as muddled lately and memories are starting to come back to me. I know I shouldn't be in this place. I wonder how Baby is doing without me. I want to see her. I wish I could talk to her or to my mother.

I back away from the door as I hear Dr. Thorpe come closer. I sit on the bed and wait for her to enter with my food and medication. She pushes open the door and carries in my tray, placing it on the counter. As soon as her hand is free, she puts it to her earpiece.

"Ms. Harris is reacting well to her treatment," Dr. Thorpe says, not bothering to look at me. She talks as if she is making

a recording. "Her mood has stabilized, as has her erratic, violent behavior."

What is she talking about? *She can't mean me. I've never been violent.*

"The paranoid delusions that Ms. Harris was experiencing have completely disappeared, thanks to the antipsychotics prescribed by Dr. Reynolds and the antidepressants I prescribed. Ms. Harris has also been given a high dosage of the sedative ketamine and seems to be at a comfortable level of . . ."

"Excuse me, Dr. Thorpe . . ."

Dr. Thorpe pauses, looks at me as though I've suddenly appeared.

"Yes, Amy. What is it?"

"Who are you speaking to?"

She considers me. "I'm taking oral notes for the other doctors to consult."

"You said I was reacting well to my treatment. If I'm showing improvement, can I go home?"

Her face becomes pinched and her body tenses. She doesn't expect me to ask questions. "You haven't fully recovered yet," she tells me, her voice strained. "You can't leave until Dr. Reynolds approves your release."

I smile uncertainly. "Will that be soon . . . since I'm getting better?" I remember when the boy came to visit he said he would help me, or was that just a dream? He said to watch for someone. Kay. I keep thinking of her, but can't remember who she is.

"We'll have to wait and see what Dr. Reynolds thinks." Dr. Thorpe turns and continues to talk into her earpiece while I watch.

I'll get out of the Ward, no matter what Dr. Reynolds decides.

• • •

"I'm Dr. Reynolds." The pale man offered a hand from his overstuffed chair. His smile seemed genuine, but his dark eyes were sharp, searching.

"I know," I said, shaking his hand. His grip was too tight and I shivered. "My mother speaks very highly of you." I sat across a coffee table from him in an identical chair. I looked around the sparse room, taking in the bookshelves, a desk. I couldn't help but glance at the door. Baby was sitting in the waiting room while I had my psyche-eval. I wondered if she'd be okay, if she needed anything.

"Are you nervous?" he asked, his voice tinged with concern.

"It's just . . . Baby isn't used to being without me." I looked at him fully for the first time. He was average height, normal weight, though his flesh seemed to hang loosely on his frame, giving him a strange, sickly look, like he had only just recently lost a lot of weight. His head was shaved clean. At least he didn't go the comb-over route. The thought made me smirk.

"What's so funny?" he asked, the hint of a smile on his lips, as if he already understood the joke.

"Nothing, really . . . I'm just . . ." I struggled. "I'm just happy to be here in New Hope. I'm feeling really optimistic."

He studied me and scribbled in his notebook, a fake smile still plastered on his doughy face. "It's good to be positive, especially after everything you've been through. New Hope must seem like it's too good to be true."

I nodded, but offered no response. I'd decided that the less I say the better.

"And what do you find the hardest about being in New Hope?" he prompted.

"Excuse me?"

"I hear you had an incident yesterday; Baby cut herself. . . ."

"She didn't cut herself," I clarified, sounding sharper

than I'd intended. I cleared my throat nervously. "I just . . . it's very loud here. It takes some time to get used to."

He tapped his pen against the notebook paper absently, the odd smile never leaving his face. "So you would say the noise disturbs you the most?" He fixed me in his intense gaze. His dark eyes seemed to bore into my thoughts. I crossed and uncrossed my legs, unable to find a comfortable position.

"I didn't say I was disturbed by the noise," I answered carefully. "It's just different here. There are a lot of sounds that we aren't used to anymore." I tried to sit still but I kept rubbing my hands together. Dr. Reynolds seemed to be observing this, so I moved my hands to the arms of the chair, trying not to hold on too tightly.

"You said *we*."

"Sorry?"

"Just now, you said 'sounds that *we* aren't used to.' Why did you say *we* instead of *I*?"

"Oh. I mean Baby. I'm used to thinking of us together. We're hardly ever apart."

"I see." The loose flesh around his chin jiggled when he spoke and I had the urge to laugh again, which I hid by coughing loudly. He glanced down at his notebook, making a few notes. “Let’s talk more about Baby. You see yourself as her . . . friend? Parental figure? Protector?”

I did see myself as those things to Baby, and so much more, but I didn’t want to seem like I was overbearing. “I guess . . . I see myself as more of a sister to her.”

“And what does Baby mean to you in terms of sisterhood?”

I looked down at my hands. I was starting to wonder why he wanted to talk about Baby so much. I swallowed, trying to appear composed.

“I think about her before I think about myself . . . like whenever the creatures were close by. I want her to be safe.” I was rubbing my hands together again and had to clench my fists in order to stop.

“Can she not protect herself?” His tone was steady, like every word carried a double meaning.

I hated how frail my voice sounded in comparison. “Oh no, she can. Baby is amazing. She knows how to be quiet and when to hide. She’s been my rock, really. I think she kept me sane out there. Not that I was insane, I mean who wouldn’t be a little crazy, stuck with only Floraes for company.” I was rambling and my forehead was sweaty. I wiped my face on my sleeve, which I regretted when Dr. Reynolds immediately made a note on his paper.

"Was it distressing, to learn your mother was alive all these years?" He looked at me thoughtfully. "While you were 'stuck,' I believe is how you put it."

"It's . . . surprising. I wish I'd known sooner." I bit my lip, uncertain if I should have said more. After a moment, I added, "Even if I wasn't with her, wasn't in New Hope, it would have been a relief to know she was alive."

He waited for me to continue and when I didn't, he asked, "What word, if you could choose only one, would you use to describe your reunion with your mother?" His pen poised at the ready, eager to judge my response.

"Only one? But there are so many." *Confusing. Frightening. Surreal.* I stare at the ground, trying to think. "I guess, I would choose . . . fortunate." I cringed inwardly. I should have chosen *grateful* or *overjoyed*. "We're just so lucky to be here," I kept on. "I mean I am. I'm lucky to be in New Hope."

Dr. Reynolds studied me. His unwavering smile would be reassuring on some people. On him it just gave me the creeps. "I think we've chatted long enough, Amy."

"Did I pass?"

He froze, and for the first time since we began talking, his phony smile had faded. "This isn't a test. What gave you the idea that it was?"

"I . . . um . . . I just assumed."

He stood to shake my hand, his palm clammy. "Maybe we should have another chat one day soon."

"I'd like that," I lied.

He opened the door leading to the waiting room, and my mother looked up from where she sat with Baby, searching my face.

"How did it go?" she asked, and I shrugged.

"Just fine," Dr. Reynolds said from the doorway. I realized my mother was asking him, not me. "I'd like to see the child now."

"I'll have to translate," I told them. I didn't like the way he was staring at Baby, like she was a lab specimen.

"That won't be necessary." Dr. Reynolds motioned for Baby to step inside his office.

"But she doesn't speak," I explained, concerned. "And she barely understands spoken language." My voice was loud, bordering on frantic. Dr. Reynolds and my mother exchanged a look.

There was a silent understanding in that glance, and my mother said, "Don't worry, Amy, everyone has to have their psyche-eval."

Baby looked to me. I tried to be strong. *Go with this man. He'll make loud speak at you. Be good.*

Baby smiled and disappeared with Dr. Reynolds into his office, the door closing with a loud *thump.*

We sat and waited for Baby in silence. I didn't feel like talking. After a while, my mother got a call on her earpiece. After a quick conversation regarding a corrupted computer file, she grabbed her computer bag. "I'm going to run this down to Richard in the lab. . . . You'll be all right for five minutes on your own, won't you?"

I looked around the waiting area, taking in nothing more threatening than empty chairs and a bored secretary behind the front desk. "Yeah, Mom, I'm great."

She hugged me before she left, a reassuring squeeze that actually did make me feel better. Flipping through an old nature magazine, I wondered if Dr. Reynolds was really as phony as I thought he was, or if I was just projecting.

The secretary stood suddenly, which startled me.

"I'm just going to run to the restroom, hon," she said, looking at me like I was an absolute freak. "Do you need to use the facilities?"

"Um, no. I'm good. Thanks." I sat back down and pretended to read the tattered magazine.

As soon as she left the room, though, I felt like I might need a bathroom, if just to splash some water on my face. I hurried out the door, but barely managed to see the secretary disappear around a corner. I attempted to follow her but every hallway looked the same; I followed one corridor that led to another identical one. When I tried to backtrack, I got turned around.

"Crap," I whispered. I was completely lost.

After a few long minutes, I heard voices down the hall and tried to follow the noise. Again, I turned the corner too late and saw a black door with a RESTRICTED sign closing slowly. I rushed forward and slipped inside just before it clicked shut. The hallway was empty. Where did those people go? I walked forward, my shoes echoing loudly on the hard floor. Out of habit I slipped them off and tied the laces together, draping them over my shoulder.

I slowly continued down the bright hallway. I didn't know what I was doing; I just wanted to find my mother and go home.

I noticed the hallway wasn't like the other ones. One side was lined with black doors, one of which those people must have disappeared through. The other wall had several windows. Curious, I stepped closer to the nearest window and peered through the glass. I looked into a small room, completely white except for a green form against the far wall. The green splotch wasn't part of the decor, though, and it began to move slowly across the room.

It took me a second to realize that I was looking at one of Them. I quickly threw myself against the opposite wall, my heart beating out of my chest. *Why was the creature there?* Breaking into a cold sweat, I realized that this must be where the Floraes were studied. This is where They were kept.

I slowed my breathing back to normal and gathered enough courage to approach the glass again. The creature shuffled unhurriedly, circling its confined space. It had no reason to do otherwise; it clearly could not sense that I was there, that food was near.

I walked slowly down the hall to look into the next room, where a Florae was feeding on a pig. Frenzied, it focused entirely on the task at hand: gore, slash, consume. The walls dripped with blood as the Florae ripped the pig to shreds, gnawing on its flesh.

I quickly moved to the next room. There, the window was oddly bright. The Florae inside didn't shuffle mindlessly, but instead remained still in one place. It looked shrunken, as if its skin were too tight for its body. It was hugging itself, its mouth open in a scream of agony I couldn't hear. Its skin was dry and flaking. I looked to the ceiling and saw that extra-bright lights bombarded the creature. *UV?*

Floraes loved the sun but something very bad was happening to this one. I wondered if there were ways to use this in a weapon, or if there were areas of the planet where they couldn't survive. Fascinated, and heartened by the possibility, I moved on.

In the next room the creature shuffled, as it did in the first, but after a few seconds the floor lit up. The Florae trembled uncontrollably and fell, unable to remain upright. Writhing, its skin sparked where it was in contact with the floor. I'd seen enough Floraes wander into our electric fence to know what was happening. The creature was in agony, convulsing as electricity flowed through its body.

After a moment, the room was back to normal and the creature stood. Jerking slightly, it resumed its shuffle around the room. I waited until the floor lit up again, watching the Florae as it suffered, then resumed its behavior as if nothing had happened, unaware that it would soon again be in horrific pain. I had no idea how long I watched the cycle. It was mesmerizing.

"Amy?!"

I couldn't stop staring at the creature sprawled on the floor again, twisting as it was electrocuted. How much could it take? Why didn't it die?

"Amy. Amy! Look at me." I broke my trance and turned to find my mother inches away. She grabbed ahold of my head, forcing my gaze on her, into her eyes. "Amy?"

I blinked hard. "Yes?"

She didn't ask how I got in or what I was thinking. She simply steered me toward the door, quickly through the maze of hallways, and back into Dr. Reynolds's waiting room.

"Oh, I was wondering where you got to," the secretary said.

"I just took my daughter to get some air," my mother told her. She sat me down. "Amy, put your shoes back on," she instructed quietly.

I was still carrying them over my shoulder. I dropped them to the floor and slipped them on one at a time. My mother was the one who bent down, untying the laces from each other and retying them properly. After she sat back in her chair, I stared at the floor for a while, uncertain of what I should do.

"Mom . . ."

"We'll talk about it later, Amy." My mother smiled brightly at me as the door to Dr. Reynolds's office opened. "And how was Baby?" she asked cheerfully.

"Are you okay?" Dr. Reynolds asked, looking at me.

"My . . . my stomach hurts," I offered.

"Let's get you home," my mother said, helping me up from my chair. "It can take a while to get used to a normal diet."

I reached over and took Baby's hand, not wanting to let her go for even a second. As we walked, I debated telling Baby about the lab Floraes, but decided against it. I didn't want to upset her. Still, I couldn't get the image of the creature being electrocuted again and again out of my head. Tortured.

My mind focused back on Baby, her psyche-eval. *What was it like?* I asked as my mother led us from the building and back to the apartment.

I played with some toys. . . . He didn't even loud speak at me.

Weird.

We had lunch at the apartment while my mother tried to explain the purpose of their experiments. "We need to test their pain threshold, their reaction time, their ability to withstand fire or electricity or . . ."

"I get it, Mom." She didn't need to justify the why of it. I was clearheaded again and more curious about what they'd found out from all their testing, what they'd learned about the Floraes. When I asked my mother, though, she was withholding.

"That is a conversation for another time," she told me. She eyed me intensely. She was the one thing I could trust in this strange place but I knew she was also an integral part of it. She was my mother and the director, both. "And I know I probably don't have to ask, but you know not to mention what happened earlier, right?"

"I won't." I didn't want to get in trouble. Or get my mother into trouble, for that matter.

"Good. All right." She exhaled. "Who wants a cookie?"

Baby raised her hand, excited. In two short days she'd learned to recognize her name, my name, and the all-important word *cookie.* As I watched her eat, I tried to push the visions of the Floraes from my mind. I'd thought, for a brief time, that I was free from Them. I knew then that even in New Hope, They would plague me.

CHAPTER EIGHTEEN

Baby appears at the foot of my bed. At first I think it's a dream. They've increased my medication, and things are getting fuzzy again. The line between my daydreams and reality is blurred. It's hard to keep everything straight. But then I see Dr. Reynolds has followed Baby. He pulls up a chair and watches as she jumps in bed to snuggle next to me.

She grabs my hand. Amy, I've missed you! *Her face is bright and shining.*

I've missed you too. *I begin to cry.*

"Amy, what's wrong?" Dr. Reynolds asks.

I shake my head. "I don't know." Dr. Reynolds now has a strange look on his face, almost a smirk.

I close my eyes. Are you happy crying? *Baby asks. She must be signing into my hand but I swear I hear a child's voice echoing her words. "Are you happy?"*

I open my eyes and study her, hoping that I'm not just hallucinating. That she is real. Baby grins at me, and I glance at Dr. Reynolds. "That must be it," I tell them slowly. "I'm crying because I'm so glad." I don't really know how I feel, other than disoriented.

I focus on Baby and sign, What about you? Are *you* happy?

She looks at me. Things are fan. I go to school and Rice comes to visit me all the time. We talk about you.

Rice? *I suddenly get a flash of a boy's face—cute, blue eyes, shaggy hair, glasses. He'd made me a promise to help me.* You talk about me? About helping me? *I sign, puzzled.*

Baby shakes her head, then looks to Dr. Reynolds. "But he said he would help me," I say, confused.

"Who said they would help you?" Dr. Reynolds asks sharply.

"I . . ." I don't know what to tell him. I don't even know if my memories are real. If only I weren't so dull. I do know that Dr. Reynolds scares me. Real or imagined, I know I can't tell

him what Rice said. I look at him and mumble, "I think it's my father. He sometimes talks to me in my dreams."

"Your father is dead," Dr. Reynolds tells me matter-of-factly. His tone cuts through me and I begin to cry again.

"Do you think I don't know that?" I sob.

Dr. Reynolds looks at me with disdain as he turns to Baby. "Perhaps we should leave Amy to recuperate." He stands and approaches us.

"No!" I shout, taking rough hold of her arm. Dr. Reynolds glowers at me. "Can she just stay a little longer?" I beg.

"I think it's best that we leave now," Dr. Reynolds tells me calmly. "Let go of her."

I look at Baby. She is frightened and I regret grabbing her like that. Reluctantly I release her arm.

Sorry, Baby. I love you. *I start to sob again and can barely see her through my tears. Before she leaves, I swear I hear a child's voice this time saying, "I love you too." But I know it's just my imagination.*

• • •

In that first week we were in New Hope, I barely left the apartment. I'd put off going to school for as long as I could but my mother decided we had to start. I thought we would have longer to adjust. I didn't know if Baby was ready.

"All children in Class Two through Five attend school. It's important that you follow procedure," my mother told me. There was no arguing.

After she left for work, I stood in front of the mirror, noticing again how unflattering my jumpsuit was. I touched my hair, fiddling with the short Mohawk for a few minutes before giving up. Resigned, I made sure Baby was dressed and combed her hair. I made her put her shoes on, even though she'd rather just lug them around all day.

Rice had let himself in and was sitting patiently on the couch, waiting for us to emerge so he could walk us to school. "We're ready," I proclaimed, stepping into the room.

I must have looked uneasy because Rice walked over to me and gave me a half hug. "You'll do fine."

I took a deep breath and nodded as we headed out the door and down the stairs. I was still worried, but I appreciated his effort to comfort us. Soon we were outside the school building.

Rice smiled reassuringly. "Go find an adult; they'll know where you both should be. I'll meet you right back here after school at four. Your mother wanted you both to go to the normal orientation that most post-aps attend. . . . She thought it would help you get a handle on New Hope and she wants to see what you think about the material."

I beamed. My mother valued my opinion. It gave me the boost of confidence I needed. "Okay. See you later, Rice." I grabbed Baby's hand and led her through the door.

There weren't other children in the hall and I hoped we weren't late. I found a yellow door and knocked. A woman greeted us, smiling brightly.

"Hi. I'm Amy Harris and this is Baby."

"Yes, we're expecting her." She opened the door wide. I gave Baby a gentle push into the classroom.

There was no artwork on the walls, no toys on the floor. It seemed more like an office than a classroom. Students were reading quietly. A few looked up at our arrival, but most continued to concentrate on their books.

"Baby can't read," I told the woman. "And she doesn't talk. But she's a quick learner. If you take the time to explain something, she'll get it. She's already starting to understand spoken words. She knows my name and her name and as of this morning she knows the word *breakfast*." I was rambling, desperate for her to understand Baby was special, even if she didn't speak.

"We have plenty of children who come to us unable to read and with limited vocal skills," the teacher assured me.

She was older, her white hair cut in a bob. "We have tests to measure a child's potential, nonverbal tests." She held out her hand to Baby, who looked at me for reassurance.

I didn't want to let Baby go, but I knew I had to. *This nice lady is going to take you now. I'll be right upstairs if you need me.*

What if she mouth talks and I don't understand? What if I have to go to the bathroom but they don't let me?

I turned to the woman. "Baby is concerned that you won't understand what she's saying."

"The director asked us to prepare for her," she told me, making the sign for Baby, followed by the "okay" sign. "I know she uses a modified version, but I think we can make do."

"That's . . . wonderful." I felt a warm wave of reassurance.

Baby, this lady knows how to sign. Not like us, but you should be able to understand her.

Is it safe?

Yes, but you have to do as you're told. I knelt down next to her. *Will you be okay?*

Baby put on a brave face, determined. *Yes.*

"And Amy, you're supposed to wait upstairs." The woman told me. "First door next to the stairs, on the left side. Someone will be with you shortly."

"Okay. Thanks." I hugged Baby before heading upstairs.

The red doors were more intimidating than the yellow and orange ones on the first floor.

I walked to the nearest red door and pushed it. It opened into a small room with a couple of metal desks and a wooden table. I sat at a desk and waited, eyeing a bookshelf filled with classic literature. Eventually an older man entered carrying a stack of papers.

"Hello, Amy. I'm Dr. Samuels." He placed the papers before me, adjusting his bowtie and eyeing me. "Ever take the SATs?" he asked, all business.

"I took an SAT pretest."

"Excellent." He sat across from me. "This is the same idea. We'll just test your basic abilities. Verbal, written, math and science, and potentiality."

"Potentiality?" I asked.

"We used to call it an IQ test. This version is tailored to our current environment. First up is the written portion," Dr. Samuels informed me. He punched a button on a stopwatch. "You may begin."

It was oddly comforting, taking a test. For a moment I felt like I was back Before, sitting in class with Sabrina and Tim.

When I finished all my tests, Dr. Samuels collected my

papers. "I'll just grade these and then we'll place you."

"What happens if a post-ap can't read?" I asked, curious. "What if they can't complete the tests?"

Dr. Samuels considered for a second. "It really hasn't come up yet. . . . This is a Class Five test. . . . I guess in the future . . . maybe in five or ten years it will be a problem."

"Do you think anyone can survive that long out there?" After all, I barely survived. How well would I have done in a couple years when all the canned food was gone and the buildings were crumbling?

"I would have never thought that people could survive this long," he admitted, "but at least once a week the Guardians bring back a few post-aps." He explained to me that although New Hope had been a university, it was affiliated with Hutsen-Prime, a government-funded research facility. Researchers lived on the complex with their families, and along with the university campus, it was its own little town.

"Are there other Class Five post-aps?" I asked.

"Yes, but most don't integrate very well," he admitted, gathering up my papers and organizing them. "We've learned that the recovered post-aps who were teenagers in pre-ap times have a hard time fitting in. The small children don't remember how it was and most of the adults are just happy to be alive. People your age . . . they want things to be the way they were."

"I can relate," I told him. "What happens if a kid doesn't play well with others?" There had to be a couple of trouble-makers.

"Well, it depends. Children aren't really punished, except with extra chores. The kids like to call it Dusty Duty." He chuckled at the silly term. "But honestly, if you need extra help coping, you're admitted to the Ward."

I thought of Rice's strange warning. "What is the Ward, exactly?"

"It's where citizens can go to get the help they need," he explained automatically. "Some people just can't learn to live in a Florae-filled world, even though they're perfectly safe here. They need intensive psychological treatment. The Ward is where they live until they can get better. In extreme cases, troublemakers are expelled, but that doesn't happen very often."

"What does someone do after they're expelled?" I asked.

Dr. Samuels looked confused. "They do whatever they want, I suppose." He stood. "Let me grade this and get back to you. . . . Can you hold tight here?"

"Sure . . ." I grabbed a copy of *Alice in Wonderland* from

the bookshelf, but was too nervous to focus. I kept reading the same paragraph over and over. Finally I shut the book and tapped my fingers on the desk, waiting.

• • •

An older man with a silly, yellow bowtie sits across from me. I've been given papers, a pencil, and a clipboard on which to write. I've never been able to write in my room before and I'm pleased. I begin to doodle on the paper, drawing cubes and circles.

"Now, we're going to test your basic abilities. Verbal, written, math and science, and potentiality."

"Potentiality?" I ask. This term seems familiar. "Have I done this before? Do I know you?"

The older man nods his head. "Yes, Amy, we've met previously. I'm Dr. Samuels. Now, try to concentrate."

I stare at the papers. "I've done this. . . . I remember you." I look up at him. "Why am I taking these tests again?"

"We need to see how your scores have changed since your treatment has begun," he explains slowly. "Do you understand?"

"Yes. You're seeing if I'm getting better?"

He smiles kindly. "We're making sure you're living up to your abilities."

I lick my lips. "Who decides . . . if I've met my potential?"

Dr. Samuels looks at me curiously. "I'll evaluate your tests and share the results with my colleagues."

"Does that include my mother?" I ask hopefully.

"No, Amy, but I can make sure she knows how you're doing," he offers. "If you like."

I nod. "Yes. Please." I take the pencil and hold it over the papers. "I'm ready now, Dr. Samuels."

He punches a button on a stopwatch. "You may begin."

•••

It wasn't long before Dr. Samuels returned and beckoned for me to follow him. "We've found an advanced placement class for you. Come along." I trailed him down the hall, where he stopped at a different red door. "This is where you'll come tomorrow," he explained. "Advanced Theory is an unstructured program and you'll remain here until you class out."

"Advanced Theory of *what* exactly?"

"Anything and everything." He opened the door. The room was big, with a few scattered desks and tables, and only a handful of students. One was scribbling in a notebook. He looked up briefly, squinted at me, and returned to his work. The others were talking, chairs arranged in a circle. They didn't even glance over.

"Yes, but what if cold fusion were possible?" a petite girl with long, dark brown hair was saying. "If we figure out the results of an impossibility, maybe we can find a possible replication of those results." I was fixated on the white scar that ran across her left cheek and down her neck.

"That's bullshit," a blond girl told her. "You cannot theorize based on nothing; we would just be creating a fiction. This isn't creative writing." A few of the students laughed, as did the girl with the scar.

She noticed me standing by the door. "Hello there."

"Hi." I turned back to Dr. Samuels, but he was already gone. I didn't even hear him leave. He would have done well in the After.

"You must be Amy." The scarred girl stood and came forward to shake my hand. "We're just in the middle of what we like to call a 'think tank.' I'm Vivian; that's Tracey." She pointed to the blond girl, then went around the room. "Jacob, Haley, and Andrew, and Hector is the one with his face in his notebook."

Hector looked up once again and gave me a half wave. I smiled at each person in turn. I might like being in such a small class.

"I know you're probably baffled. I was when I first came

here," Vivian told me.

"You were out there, with Them?" I asked, examining her face. The scar was not fresh; its raised, white surface had healed as much as it ever would. I'd never seen anyone escape from a Florae once it got its claws in.

"For a little while." Vivian looked away, clearly not wanting to talk about it.

"I'm sorry." I tried to change the subject. Thinking of the conversation I'd just had with Dr. Samuels, I asked tentatively, "Um . . . what exactly do you do here?"

"We formulate the ideas that the scientists put into effect." She motioned me to a table. The rest of the group had already reconvened and were continuing their conversation.

"So . . . we try to invent useful objects?"

"Objects, ideas, concepts. It doesn't even have to necessarily be based on science. We develop the ideas that New Hope scientists implement for the good of the community."

"Just the ideas, not the concrete things? That doesn't seem very hard."

"You'd be surprised. First you have to come up with a truly indispensable idea. That in itself gets most people. Then you have to take it further. How will it work, theoretically, of course. But yeah, we don't have to make a working model. That's someone else's job."

I was flooded with relief. It wasn't literature but it was the next best thing: something based solely on creativity and imagination.

"Where do I start?"

"Anywhere you want. You can read about technological advances, or you can speak with the others about what they're working on. Generally we like to share our preliminary ideas. It helps us figure out how to develop a concept to its fullest potential."

"That sounds awesome. What have you come up with?" I asked.

"Tons of things, most of which are filtered out by the higher-ups. Others are in production and one of my ideas has been realized."

"She's being modest," Tracey said. I noticed their conversation had stopped and they were all listening to me and Vivian now.

"What was it?" I asked.

"I conceptualized a fabric that was strong, flexible, and extremely thin. Something breathable that wouldn't tear and could stop a bullet."

"The suit that the Guardians wear?" I asked, stunned.

"Yes. I came up with the initial idea for the synth-suit. I can give you a copy of my proposal to use as a model so you'll know how to submit your ideas."

"That would be great." The class seemed like something I might have enjoyed Before.

Vivian showed me where to get supplies: notebooks, pens, calculators. "Feel free to take a walk too, if you want. We're encouraged to let our minds wander, try to achieve that 'eureka' moment, you know."

"Won't I get in trouble for being out of class?" I asked.

"No, everything we do is for the good of the whole. There isn't a need to rebel." Vivian smiled. "This isn't like high school."

I took my notebook to a desk and stared at it while Vivian rejoined her discussion. I needed to think of something that would benefit New Hope, something for "the good of the whole," whatever that meant. It sounded like a slogan. I had nothing. Soon it was lunchtime and I hadn't accomplished anything.

"Don't worry," Vivian reassured me. "They don't expect you to come up with something every day. They just want us to look at situations from a different angle. The more minds contributing to our community, the stronger we all are." Another slogan.

"But what if I don't ever think of anything?" I mumbled.

"If you can't generate useful concepts then you class out and only have to worry about your nonexempt job and doing a few extra chores every now and again. Amy, relax." She laughed lightly. "Kids may call you a Dusty, but it's not the end of the world."

"I suppose not." I didn't really want to scrub toilets for the rest of my life, but I could think of some worse things.

"Come on, let's go get some food," Vivian suggested.

"All right . . . Do you think it's okay if I look in on my sister, Baby? We've never really been separated," I explained quickly.

"Sure, what class?"

"Three . . . I don't know where she would be now, though." I hadn't thought about how to find her if I needed to. I was already losing my edge.

"I'll help you find her," Vivian offered. She knew some of the Class Three teachers and we learned that Baby's class had taken a short field trip to the farm. We continued on to the cafeteria, but I was still distracted. I hoped Baby was getting along okay without me.

Inside the noisy cafeteria, Vivian and I grabbed our lunch trays and made our way through the line. I tried to restrain myself this time, but I couldn't resist taking both a soy burger and a few helpings of vegetable stew. Most of the dishes today looked like vegetarian hippie fare, stuff my dad would have loved.

Vivian steered me to a table with more teenagers decked out in red and introduced me to the group, rattling off names. I smiled, trying to listen politely while I shoved food in my mouth and hoped no one expected me to talk. But I was not so lucky.

"Amy, what was it like seeing your mother after so long?"

"What do the Floraes look like, up close?"

"What did you eat? I've heard a couple post-aps exchange marinade recipes for flame-broiled rat!"

I felt light-headed and swallowed loudly. "Well . . ."

Something touched my back.

I stood in a flash and grabbed the knife from my tray in one motion. Swinging around, I knocked over my chair and crouched to a defensive position, ready to thrust the blade into my attacker.

"Whoa." Rice held his hands in the air. "Amy, it's only me."

I paused, then lowered the knife, my hands shaking from the sudden surge of adrenaline. I stood, mortified. The cafeteria had gone still; everyone was staring at me. But all I could think was how I hadn't heard him sneak up behind me. I was exposed and vulnerable in the center of the large room. It was so loud in the cafeteria, it was hard to concentrate. There could have been a Florae behind me and I wouldn't have known.

I turned and quietly placed my knife back on my tray. The cafeteria noise picked up again as I reached down to right the overturned chair.

"Are you okay?" Rice asked, lowering his hands and looking concerned. I could see that he was trying to minimize the awkwardness of the moment for me.

"Yeah, I'm fine. Sorry about that." I said nervously. "Do you want to sit with us?"

"Rice has already classed out," Vivian joked, helping to break the tension. "He can't eat with lowly Class Five kids." Everyone at the table laughed uneasily.

I faked a smile though I really wanted to cry. "Actually, can you walk me back to class?" I asked Rice softly. I no longer had much of an appetite.

"Of course." He put his hand on the small of my back

and we left. I expected him to walk me back to the school entrance, but we took a slight detour and headed for the Quad. Rice sat on the grass and motioned for me to sit beside him. We rested there for a while, in silence.

"Rice . . . I don't know if I can do this," I confided as I lay back on the soft grass. "I thought things were going okay, but I keep freaking out, like last week when Baby dropped her glass and just now when I almost stabbed you. . . ." I began to tear up.

"You just have to give it time," he said softly, laying his head down next to mine and squeezing my hand. "You'll get used to it."

"What if I don't?" I asked in a whisper.

"Amy, I know what it's like to feel out of place." He turned his head toward me. "I told you that I was named after my father, right? Well, my parents died when I was very young and I was raised in foster care . . . until Hutsen-Prime found me."

"Found you?"

"I won my fourth grade science fair and the next day Hutsen-Prime offered to fund my studies, to put me on a fast-track course. I finished high school when I was twelve and my undergraduate studies in a year and a half. That's why I was here," he explained. "I was in my second year of grad school when the Floraes arrived. In the few days it took them to reach this far into the country, a student working on a sonar project for the Navy discovered the creatures couldn't stand the noise."

"And that student was you?" I asked, enthralled. Rice really was a genius.

"No." His voice was heavy. "I knew her, though. She gave her life to save the campus. . . ." He trailed off.

"What happened?"

"We were setting up the emitters," Rice explained, his face pained. "We knew we had to expand in a circle, keep the Floraes on the run, away from the compound. We thought they were still far away, but suddenly one was right in front of us, at the center of the sonar radius. It didn't know where to run, but as soon as it spotted us, it . . . rushed us."

His eyes lost focus and I could tell he was back there, in that awful place nearly three years ago.

"It reached her first. And I ran. I thought I was dead for sure, the Floraes are so fast, but it stayed with her. I was *lucky*." He sat up as he spit out the word bitterly, as if he were anything but.

"A lot of people here don't understand. I mean, they

know the Floraes are real, that they've killed nearly everyone on the planet, but they've never seen one up close. They were here when it happened. They can't understand what it's like."

I sat up next to him. "I survived outside of New Hope with the Floraes. You couldn't have saved her. You did the right thing by running away." I placed my hand on his arm, my touch bringing him back from his memories.

"Yeah. Well. That was a long time ago." He shrugged. I gave his arm a squeeze before letting go. "We've positioned the emitters to optimize sonic output and we expand the area of New Hope a little each year. We're even working on something for the Floraes. . . . You know, your mother would probably be the one to talk to about all this. I'm not sure what she wants you to know."

"Did my mother tell you I snuck into the lab?" I asked.

Rice sighed. "Yes, she told me. I don't know why you did that. You could have been sent to the Ward or expelled."

"I don't know why I did it either. I saw the black door open and slipped through without even thinking." I paused and looked around to make sure no one was in earshot. I lowered my voice. "I saw all the experiments you're doing. You must have discovered something about the Floraes by now. Where they come from, why they're here."

Rice fidgeted, adjusting his glasses. "Amy, I can't talk about this. I can't share our research with you. Even though you're the director's daughter, you're still just a citizen. You haven't even classed out yet."

"I don't understand why this is all so secretive."

"It's not, just . . . I mean, every citizen of New Hope doesn't need to know every single thing that is going on. It would be too much for some people to handle."

I sighed and rubbed my face.

"How is Baby?" Rice asked, changing the subject. "The director said you two were resting this past week. She's not sick is she?"

"No. She's fine," I assured him. "We're just getting used to sleeping at night instead of during the day."

"I was worried about you two, hiding in your apartment all week."

"We weren't hiding," I told him, though that's exactly what we were doing. I lay back in the grass and let the sunshine pour over me. After a few minutes of peace I sat up and gave Rice a weak smile.

"Feel better?" he asked.

"Yes, thanks. This was . . . necessary."

He stood, wiping the grass from his jeans, then held out a hand and helped me up. He looked down at me, his eyes shining intensely. "I have to get back to work, but I'll see you after class. Okay?"

I smiled and nodded. I walked back to my classroom with a strange mix of emotions. I liked Rice, trusted him. But when I slipped into my desk, I wondered about our conversation. Floraes outpopulated us thousands to one. We had to stop them. Someone in New Hope had to find the answer. I looked around the classroom, at the gifted and talented kids back from lunch, all working quietly on their proposals.

I made my way over to Vivian's desk. She looked up cheerfully. "You doing okay?"

"Yeah . . . about lunch . . ."

"Don't worry about it. People expect post-aps to be a little jumpy," she told me.

"Well, I was just wondering about what you were doing earlier, when I first got to class . . . when you were all talking to figure something out."

"The think tank?"

"That's it. Can I call a think tank?"

"Sure." She stood and started arranging chairs in a circle.

"Come on, guys. Andrew, Hector, Haley . . . Amy needs our help with something."

Everyone gathered in a circle and stared at me expectantly.

"Well," I started hesitantly. "I just have a lot of questions. I guess I want to know . . ." I took a deep breath. "How are there still so many Floraes when their main food source–us–is mostly depleted? How have they not died of starvation, or left, or whatever?"

They considered for a moment.

"They could eat other things," Haley offered.

I shook my head. "I don't think so. I've never seen them eat vegetation. They are definitely carnivores." I told them what I observed from the safety of my electric-fenced home. How they can't see well, but have amazing hearing. What they looked like up close. What they smelled like–damp earth and rotting flesh. How they shuffled along until there was meat, then sprinted with single-minded determination.

"What about their blood?" Hector asked. "Is it red, green, thick, thin?"

"Blackish green. I don't know how thick it is." I remembered the night we met Amber, how that gang of men killed a bunch of Floraes, how their blood splattered against the sidewalk and pooled into the street. "Actually, it's fairly thick, like syrup."

Hector scribbled in his notebook before he looked up at me. "They don't eat anything but meat. I think they get the rest of their nourishment from the sun."

"What?" I asked, doubtful. "You figured that out in five seconds from greenish-black sludge-blood?"

"No, it's been right in our faces the whole time," he explained. "What are they called?"

"Floraes?" I felt dense.

"Florae is short for Florae-sapien. They're plant people. It was so obvious, but they don't educate us about the Floraes."

"It makes sense," Vivian said. "They're green. They need the sun. They like to be underground at night."

"They know," Andrew spoke for the first time. "The people who run New Hope, they don't want us talking about it."

"What? Why not?" I asked. "Any knowledge that the people of New Hope have about the Floraes would only serve to help them. Wouldn't it?"

Hector gave me a pointed look. "I don't know. None of us have ever been asked to study them. Maybe the people in charge decided it wasn't important?"

Meaning my mother decided: she and her creepy colleague Dr. Reynolds.

Suddenly Jacob looked grim. "Guys, maybe we should lay off the Florae talk. We don't want to end up like Frank."

"What happened to Frank?" I asked. A heavy silence followed and everyone looked uncomfortable.

"He was working on an undesirable project and was told to stop," Jacob explained quietly. "He wouldn't, so he was sent to the Ward."

I looked at him. "I thought the Ward was supposed to be for people who were mentally unstable. What was his project?"

"Not sure," Jacob told us, "but I know he wanted to study a Florae up close. It's all he talked about. It became an obsession and I think it pushed him over the edge."

"But they study them," I said. "The Guardians do, in the wild," I quickly added, not wanting to scare anyone, especially after Rice's warning.

"So they must know a lot," Haley chimed in.

"Like where they came from?" I asked. I turned to Hector. "Any clues about that?"

He shook his head.

"The news said they were aliens," Tracey offered.

"But I've seen them, up close. They don't have the intellect to turn a door handle; I don't think they could have manned spaceships."

"Why don't you just ask the director?" Vivian asked me.

"My mother doesn't talk to me about these things," I admitted. "She's a master at changing the subject."

"Amy, she would have the answers," Hector said. "If anyone does."

"If they don't like us to talk about the Floraes and don't want anyone to know that they're studying them, they know something they don't think we can handle," Andrew told us.

"What are they keeping from us?" Hector asked, dismayed.

"I don't know," I quietly replied.

CHAPTER NINETEEN

"I'm concerned about her test scores," the older man tells Dr. Thorpe in the hallway. I heard them out there, muttering, so I got off my bed and knelt down next to the door. "It's not unusual for scores to worsen when a citizen is in the Ward, but Amy didn't even try. She's given up."

"What do you think the problem is, Dr. Samuels?" Dr. Thorpe asks, concerned.

"If your goal is rehabilitation, you should ease up on the sedatives," Dr. Samuels tells her firmly.

"Ms. Harris has been exhibiting some highly erratic

behavior," Dr. Thorpe explains. "Her medication is the only thing keeping her from a complete relapse."

"Then try something else." He sighs loudly. "Dr. Reynolds mentioned to me that he is investigating some alternative procedures. He's had encouraging results with electroshock therapy in several patients."

"Yes," Dr. Thorpe tells him. "Dr. Reynolds also mentioned electroshock to me. . . . At the time I didn't think it was appropriate for Ms. Harris. What's your opinion?"

"Perhaps . . . ," Dr. Samuels suggests hesitantly, "Amy would benefit from such a treatment."

"I'll take your recommendation under consideration and consult again with Dr. Reynolds," Dr. Thorpe promises. "Thank you, Dr. Samuels."

I hear footsteps echoing down the hall and I rest my head on the floor. Dr. Samuels had promised to tell my mother how I was doing. She wouldn't let them do any of this to me, would she? But what if he'd only said that to placate me? I barely know him. He'd only given me a few tests before I was assigned my class.

Suddenly a memory comes to me. Advanced Theory. Vivian, Tracey, Hector, and Andrew, all sitting around talking about the Floraes, and how someone was sent to the

Ward for probing too deeply. Frank. He would be here. Maybe I could find him. He could answer some questions for me.

Or maybe I could get a message to Vivian. If Rice couldn't help me, she would find a way. Vivian's so smart and I know she's someone I can trust. She'll be here for me, just like she was when I first got to New Hope. She'll help me if she can.

• • •

When school was over for the day, Vivian caught up with me outside class and handed me a lumpy brown muffin. "I saved this for you. You didn't eat much lunch."

"Thanks." I nibbled at the bran muffin, not really all that hungry.

"Um, Amy." She looked anxious. "I wanted to talk to you. You might want to cool it on all the questions. Some things are best left alone. You don't want to be sent to the Ward." She was twirling her long brown hair around her fingers. I'd noticed that about her: she was always fiddling with something. If it wasn't her hair, then it was a pencil, or her gold cross necklace.

"What is all this about the Ward all the time? It's starting to sound like a bad joke. What exactly *is* the Ward?"

"It's a place where citizens can go to get better," she said automatically.

"Yes, I've heard that before. But if that's true, then why wouldn't I want to go there?"

She shook her head, her eyes almost pleading. "People don't usually come back from the Ward. If you go there, you go there to stay."

My chest was oppressively tight. I took in a deep breath, releasing it slowly. "But how do they determine if you need to go there?"

"They base some of it on your psyche-eval. . . . You had one, didn't you?"

"Yes."

"Good," Vivian sighed, relieved. "Then you won't have another one for six months." She squeezed my arm. "You'll be fine, Amy. I didn't mean to freak you out or anything. Just remember what I told you–no more questions."

I returned her smile but I didn't feel reassured. Now that I really understood what the Ward was, I felt panicked.

What would happen to Baby if I were sent away?

• • •

Later, the door opens, hitting me on my shoulder.

"Amy!" Dr. Thorpe yells in surprise. "What are you doing on the floor?"

"I . . ." I get up slowly. "I don't know." I should be more careful.

"Let's get you back in bed." Dr. Thorpe helps me over to the bed. "Amy, I have to admit, I'm a little concerned about your behavior."

I sit down and stare at her. The word electroshock *still rings in my ears. I have a flashback to my old house, the electric fence. The Floraes sparking as they touch it, trying to reach me. Trying to kill me. Tears begin to flow down my face. "I'm not going home, am I?"*

"No. Not yet, Amy." Dr. Thorpe frowns. "We haven't decided just yet how best to help you. But we will," she assures me. "We will help you."

I nod unhappily. What if this is it? What if I have to suffer under Dr. Thorpe's idea of help? Being drugged and tortured. Rice promised to get me out of here. Where is he? Where are my friends? Where is my mother?

I rub my arms, trying to suppress the panic rising inside of me. If anyone is coming, they need to be quick about it. I may not live through my treatments. I may not survive the Ward.

"Rice," I whisper after Dr. Thorpe is gone. "Please hurry."

• • •

"Amy!" Rice called. He jogged over to me, pushing up his glasses. His shaggy, blond hair disheveled. I wanted to tell him what I discovered about the Floraes, what I'm sure he already knew, but I decided against it. I trusted Rice just as I trusted Vivian, but her warning had left me spooked and cautious.

Out of the corner of my eye, I saw a yellow jumper. "Baby!" I yelled. She rushed into my arms. I picked her up and swung her around, relieved to see she was grinning.

How was it? I asked, smiling.

Amy, it was sooooo fun! We went to the farm. I saw all the animals from my farm book and I got to ride a horse, a real one. It was big and a little scary, but I want to go back. They said I could, but not for a while.

What else did you do? I asked.

I learned this. She shoved a piece of paper in my face and I looked at it. I wanted to cry. Scrawled across in chicken-scratch letters was B-A-B-Y. *This means my name,* she told me.

I am so proud of you, I said. We didn't have a word for *proud*, but *happy happy at your work* got the point across. Her face glowed with pleasure.

Here, this is for you. She handed me a sealed envelope. My mother's name was neatly typed on the outside, but I ripped it open.

"Amy, should you be reading that?" Rice asked.

"Sure, why not?" I scanned the page. It was Baby's evaluation. She scored a zero for verbal, no surprise there, but was good at reasoning and information retention. At the bottom was a handwritten note. *"Baby" shows a willingness to learn and gets along very well with the other children. We hope to progress quickly with her writing and we will continue to encourage verbalization, which we have yet to witness. She shows an aptitude for handling animals, which we will investigate further. She will, perhaps, in the future, be most comfortable as a farmworker or a veterinarian.*

After one day they were already discussing what Baby would do as an adult?

"Rice, where's my evaluation?" I asked.

"Dr. Samuels gave it to me. I gave it to your mother *unopened*," he stressed.

And Amy, Baby waved to get my attention, *I played a game where you jump over a piece of rope and I fell on my butt. I think I'm okay except I might have a bruise.*

"She's excited," Rice said.

"It was her first first day of school and she's never been around other kids before." I was sick with relief. I let Baby prattle on until she ran out of steam and just grinned happily. Her hair was disheveled so I fixed it, fastening it into a high ponytail. Rice watched me with a scowl and reached over to undo her hair, redoing the ponytail lower so it covered Baby's neck.

"Rice, what are you doing?" I asked.

"It looked a little too tight," he explained crisply.

"Um, okay." It was strange for him to snap like that.

"Sorry, it's just that we should head over to orientation," Rice told me gently. "If we start soon, you can review all the recordings before dinner."

"Sure, sounds good," I said, realizing I must have just annoyed him. Or maybe he was irritated I'd opened the evaluation addressed to my mother.

I shook off my unease as we walked and explained to Baby that she was going to watch a program, then tell me what she understood about it. Baby took my hand, but her fingers were still as she processed her day.

We walked past several white buildings until the road narrowed and we reached a cement path. The buildings started to look less alike, more quirky, and some were brick, but all were badly in need of a paint job. There weren't many people around, and after a while I asked Rice where, exactly, we were going.

"Orientation is on the outskirts. We try to contain the

post-aps until we know what we are dealing with."

"Have there been any problems?" I remembered how Rice and I first met, and smiled sheepishly. "Uh, like mine?" I still felt guilty about pulling a gun on him.

"People sometimes freak. Mostly they're just appreciative. The psyche-eval usually weeds out the troublemakers, though not always."

"What do you mean?"

Rice looked at me, considering carefully what to say. "Last year we found a boy with limited mental faculties. He was about ten, which would make him six or seven when it happened. It was amazing he'd survived so long, but he didn't integrate well into New Hope. He had to be expelled."

"Like, as in, he could no longer attend school?" It didn't seem fair to punish someone who had a disability.

"No, he was expelled from New Hope."

I stopped walking and turned to Rice. "He was banished?" I whispered, horrified. "*That's* what it means to be expelled?"

"He couldn't function here, he couldn't even hold down a Dusty job. He was a complete drain on our resources."

I was stunned at his words. Baby looked up at me nervously, sensing something was wrong. "How could you send him back out there? He was ten years old! What about old people, do you expel them too?!"

"It's not like that. We have a building for elderly care and we have the Ward for people who are mentally incompetent. This boy, he was different. He used to make it out to the farm and kill the animals."

"Maybe he didn't understand that he didn't need to kill anymore, that his food was provided. You don't understand what it's like out there."

"He used to watch the toddlers, Amy. He watched them the same way he looked at the animals on the farm."

"Oh." We walked in silence. When your entire world was filled with Floraes, with terror and silence, and thinking of your own survival, how is anyone normal after that? I squeezed Baby's hand and tried not to think about it.

"Here we are," Rice told us after a few minutes. We entered the short, squat building, and Rice led us to a room with a black door.

"You all love to color code things," I commented. "Don't people ever get confused?"

"No. They don't."

I wondered what would happen if they did, what my punishment would be if certain people found out I'd been in a restricted area. The Ward? Expulsion?

Rice led us into a room painted a pale blue. Instead of tables and chairs, desks were placed in rows, all facing a large screen. He opened a laptop and placed it on one of the tables.

"Have a seat," he said. "I thought you'd like to see this first." He typed away on his computer and on the screen appeared a map of New Hope. We were centralized in the "urban" district where most everyone lives. The residential buildings were numbered, with the lowest numbers near the Quad, the higher farther away. To the east was the dairy farm that Rice had mentioned, with more farmland to the south and west, and a lake to the north. East of the dairy farm was a forest that the map labeled FOR EXPANSION TBD.

"You keep the Floraes out of this entire area?" I asked, eyeing the map.

"We've been aggressively expanding certain areas, like the farm. It was originally just a few acres, with a small number of animals." He pointed to the map. "Now it covers this whole area, and we've maximized livestock breeding through advances in animal husbandry." He glanced at me. "It's really pretty fascinating how much we've accomplished in such a short amount of time."

I looked at the map again. "But there isn't a fence?" I still found it hard to believe.

"No, we don't need a physical barrier. You won't find the Floraes within a two-mile radius of the emitters."

"What about other people? People who might want to come and take all this away?" New Hope was well protected from the Floraes, but what would they do if a guerilla force came to take it over?

"That seems very unlikely."

"It happened to us," I said quietly. I thought of Amber, of what she did to us.

"What would someone gain by destroying us? We welcome all post-aps, offer a functioning society, a way to live without constant fear of death."

Doesn't he know there will always be someone out there who wants to destroy good?

Rice was fiddling with his computer again and the map disappeared. "I'll show you all the recordings, so you can see the version for the little kids, the older children, and the adults."

"Fan." I tapped the notebook I'd brought with me. Rice said my mother wanted my opinion, so I came prepared to take notes.

Rice dimmed the lights and the screen flickered on. The video was for the younger kids and featured small children and an adult. "The adult is called a Minder," Rice's voice came loudly from across the room. Baby, who'd been enjoying the movie, glared at him.

"I don't think you're supposed to narrate," I told him. "I need to see if it's self-explanatory."

"Oh, right," he said sheepishly. "Sorry."

"No worries," I said. It slipped out–something I used to say Before. I looked at him, suddenly wishing I'd known him back then.

The video continued to show the Minder helping the children with their daily routine. At the end, the Minder tucked each child in, then turned on a night-light. The Minder smiled into the camera, and the movie went dark.

Baby turned to me. *I like the lady.*

Good. I think they want you to.

I scribbled in my notebook. *Effective images of comfort to integrate small children, show them who they can trust, who will take care of them.*

"At this point, a Minder will come fetch any child who doesn't have an adult with them," Rice said. "I'm not explaining," he added. "It's something you should know. At first," he continued, "we had a lot of small children, but now it's not that common. Here's the one for older children, Class Threes and Fours."

Baby, this one is for you. Pay attention.

Baby nodded dutifully.

The movie started much the same way as the other film, only this time a little girl was wearing yellow. They again take you through the child's day, demonstrating tasks narrated with simple words, such as *school*, *eat*, *play*, *work*, *sleep*. The children were put to bed in a dorm, only this time they were separated by gender. Once again, a Minder tucked them in and smiled at the camera.

"I thought Minders were only for the small children," I told Rice.

"There are a lot of kids without parents here. Some of the Minders are for the toddlers and some are for the dorms."

What do you think? I asked Baby. *Did you understand?*

Baby looked down at her jumpsuit. *I'm yellow, so I do things with other yellows and go to school through the yellow door.*

Yeah, that's about it.

"Ready for the last one?" Rice asked.

I nodded, eager to see the grown-up version. *This is for adults,* I tell Baby. *Try to follow along, but you may not understand everything.*

This time the film began with a shot of the town while WELCOME TO NEW HOPE scrawled across the screen. A woman began to narrate and I realized that it was my mother.

"You have survived much to get here and we are so very happy to have you," she said. "Over the next hour, we will explain all the workings of New Hope."

The film went over everything, from the Class system, with emphasis on Class Five and red doors, to details about the entry test that placed the adults in their jobs. I discovered that although you may be exempt from having to perform a menial task, that didn't spare you from attending fitness training twice a week or from doing "acts of community improvement."

"Everyone works because everyone is important." To me this sounded like a great way to spin forced labor.

"And in order to ensure the continuation of our society," my mother's voice persisted, "we must maintain genetic diversity and encourage accelerated birthrates." This was followed by a shot of a lab and a woman working with a test tube.

"All babies born in New Hope are the result of careful selection by the Committee for Genetic Diversity. All adult males are required to submit their genetic material for consideration."

Next it showed a happy pregnant woman lying in a hospital bed, her belly swollen. "All adult females are expected to carry a child to term once every three years unless they are medically unfit to do so or have reached the age of forty. No one is allowed to bear a child without genetic consideration and to do so will result in immediate expulsion."

It took me a minute to process what I was hearing but then my chest went cold. They were forcing people to breed. Not only that, people weren't even allowed to decide who they had children with. *That was why my mother had Adam.*

"All adults have the right to petition the Committee for Genetic Diversity if they wish to be parentally responsible for their offspring. Otherwise children produced in New Hope are the wards of New Hope until they themselves become adults. Any adult may choose expulsion at any time."

The film ended the way that the others began: happy children playing.

"Rice." I tried to swallow but my mouth was too dry. "That last bit, about the babies . . . they can't expect women to give birth every three years."

"They do," he confirmed. "Unless there is a medical risk."

"So women don't have control over their own bodies? When do you have to have your first pregnancy?" I asked, my voice trembling.

"Not until you become an adult."

"At seventeen?"

He shrugged. "I submitted my genetic material last year. It's not a big deal. Our population's up; the children are healthy."

"Wait. You have children?" I asked.

"I don't know. I never made an inquiry with the committee. I don't want to petition for parental rights, not until I'm . . . um, settled with someone." He adjusted his glasses awkwardly.

I stood, shaking. "This is too much. I need some fresh air," I told him, motioning for Baby to come with me. When I tried to open the door, it didn't budge.

"It's restricted," Rice reminded me apologetically. He fished out his key card and opened the door, leading us back outside. I sat on the ground, taking time to think. Baby crouched next to me and held my hand. Rice waited patiently a few feet away.

There were so many secrets, so many rules. I understood the need for structure, but how could they decide what a child is going to be when they're in kindergarten? How could they make some people work two or three jobs, while others only have to work one? How could they tell people who they can have children with?

And forcing women to give birth, like we were nothing more than incubators. It made sense, all the pregnant women in the cafeteria, in the Quad. I thought about my mother, who turned forty this year. Adam was two. For some reason, this understanding made me even more upset. She not only helped design our new society, she was also an outstanding member who followed her own rules.

I stood up and walked over to Rice. "Who makes New Hope's rules?" I asked. "My mother is a scientist. . . . I don't understand why she's the director."

"The director certainly has a say on regulations but she isn't solely responsible for the policies for New Hope," Rice explained patiently. "She's in charge of the lab, the scientific sector. Dr. Reynolds is really the one–"

"Dr. Reynolds?" I interrupted him. "The creepy psychiatrist?"

He shook his head. "Dr. Reynolds isn't creepy. And

who better than a psychiatrist to determine how a society should be structured?" he asked defensively. "We're lucky to have him. He was in New Hope when the Floraes came. He headed psy-ops for the military. He's a brilliant man. It's like he can see into the core of people, determine what we're made of. He did it to me. He saw a lost, young orphan in me and decided I had the potential to be more," Rice told me passionately. "He's the one who recommended that Hutsen-Prime take me under their wing. He's the one who has checked on me over the years, made sure I had the best education, the best chance to succeed. And now he's molding New Hope. We have the ability to rebuild the world and make it better."

I looked at Rice, horrified. After the propaganda speech, I didn't think I could stand to hear any more of the party line, even from someone I trusted.

The more I learned about New Hope, the less I saw my place there.

CHAPTER TWENTY

"Did Baby come to visit me today?" I ask Dr. Thorpe.

"No, that was last week, Amy." She hands me my pills and a cup of water, which I dutifully swallow. I hate taking all this medicine. Nothing changes. I'm always confused; sometimes I lose myself in a memory, only to forget a few seconds later what I was thinking about. My time in New Hope is coming back to me slowly, but there's so much I can't remember.

I look at Dr. Thorpe and I know I can't fight her on the drugs. They monitor me all the time. "When will Baby be back?" I ask. "I think it will help with my treatment if I can see her more often."

"I'm not sure. Dr. Reynolds supervised the visit. He said it was too upsetting for you. Maybe she'll come again when you're more stable." She takes the empty cup, absently looking at her clipboard.

"And my mother?"

"Your mother is a very busy woman. She doesn't have time to visit every day."

I try to concentrate. My mother has always been busy, but she'd make time to see me, wouldn't she? Someone came today, but I can't remember who exactly. They held my hand.

"Who was here earlier?" I ask.

She looks up at me, sharply. "That was Richard . . . you know, Rice. You had a very nice visit with him. He likes you very much."

"Yes, yes." I burrow back under my covers. I like having visitors, even if I don't always remember who they are.

"And what about Vivian? When did she come last?" I stop myself, thinking. "She hasn't been to see me at all, has she?"

Dr. Thorpe stops and sucks in a breath. "You don't remember?"

I shake my head while she studies me for a moment, then

turns slightly and touches her earpiece.

"Ms. Harris is not responding as well to her medication as we had first hoped." She talks about me as if I'm not here. Maybe I'm not. "We should start her shock treatments as soon as possible."

I take a deep breath, trying to keep my anxiety in check. "When?" I ask quietly. Either Dr. Thorpe doesn't hear me, or she ignores me. I stand, agitated, knocking into her and making her drop her clipboard on the floor. She backs away from me with a frightened look on her face. "Sorry." I sit back down. "I didn't mean . . ."

"It's all right, Amy. You're not well." She retrieves her clipboard from the floor. "We'll talk more about your treatment another time," she tells me before she leaves the room.

The door shuts with a loud thud, *followed by a single* click. *I stand slowly and go to the door, trying the handle. It's been locked from the outside. Retreating to my bed, I place my head under the pillow and sob myself to sleep.*

• • •

"SURPRISE!"

We walked into the cafeteria and a roomful of people shouted at us. I let go of Baby's hand so she could cover her ears. I was still in shock when my mother came over to hug me.

"I knew you could do it," she whispered in my ear. "Advanced Theory! I'm very proud."

She introduced me to her colleagues and other Class Five students she must have deemed worthy. I lost track of Baby and panicked until I spotted her across the room, in Rice's arms.

There was a flat, slightly lumpy cake and a dark, carbonated liquid that tasted like cola and root beer mixed together. This was really bad timing. I wanted nothing more than to talk with my mother, alone, away from the eyes, and regulations, and colored jumpsuits of New Hope.

"You know, when I made Advanced Theory, I didn't get a party," Vivian said behind me. I turned to catch her with her eyebrows raised mockingly, her brown eyes shining.

"Yeah, this is fan," I say sarcastically.

"What's wrong?" she asked, lowering her voice. "You haven't been asking about the Floraes again, have you?"

"No, I just saw the orientation video. . . . I . . . it really got to me. New Hope. Everything we have to do in order to stay here."

"Yeah," Vivian said carefully. "But it's worth it."

"Is it?"

Vivian grimaced and tugged at her necklace. "I'll take

New Hope any day over being out there with the Floraes."

"You don't mind giving up your freedom?"

Vivian tilted her head. "You always have to give up some freedoms to live in any society."

"But here, it's all or nothing. It's get in line or be sent to the Ward, or worse." I thought of being expelled, forced to leave the safety of New Hope. "They're preying on people's fears to make them conform." I knew I shouldn't be talking about any of this here and now, but it was just flowing out of me.

"Amy, it *is* all worth it," Vivian whispered desperately, wanting me to understand. "I would trade almost anything to be safe. Think about it. What are you really giving up? So, they make you work, make you exercise, make you live up to your potential–is that really so bad?"

"But you can't even decide who you have children with." I glanced around the room, at least a quarter of the women were pregnant. Several looked like they weren't much older than me.

Vivian sighed. "We have to rebuild the human race. Everyone is tested for genetic compatibility. It gives our species the best hope of survival."

I watched my mother from across the room, holding

Adam. She spotted me and beckoned me over.

"Duty calls." I smiled at Vivian.

My mother had me speak with more of her colleagues, eat more cake, fake more smiles. I finally found a quiet corner to hide in when Rice saw me and brought over Baby. She beamed at me, just happy to be at her first party.

"You knew," I playfully accused Rice.

He grinned. "Of course I knew. Your mother had me show you those orientation films to keep you busy while they set up the party."

"But you told me my mother wanted me to watch those videos before I even took that test today, before I was placed in Advanced Theory."

Rice shrugged. "She had high hopes for you."

"She didn't . . ." I paused. "Rice, did I actually place into Advanced Theory, or did my mother pull some strings?"

"No, the director wouldn't do that," Rice assured me. "Your scores placed you. The director wouldn't break the rules."

I thought of Adam, what his existence meant. Of course she wouldn't break the rules. But I wondered. "Not even for her daughter?"

"Especially not for her daughter," Rice said.

Baby tugged on my sleeve and signed urgently, *Amy, I think that's the woman from the ship.*

I looked up and saw Kay. She wasn't wearing her skin-tight black outfit, but it was definitely her.

"Who's that woman?" I asked Rice.

"That's Kay Oh. You don't recognize her?" he asked, surprised.

"No, I do. She brought us in. She's tough." I admired her.

"No, I mean don't you recognize her from pre-ap times. . . . She was a pop star."

I took a closer look at Kay. She did look familiar, but not entirely. The hair was wrong. For some reason I pictured it blue and spiky. Suddenly I had it.

"That's Kay Oh from Kay Oh and the Okays!" I was startled to remember them. They were a pop girl band and Kay Oh was the lead singer. They were everywhere Before.

"Yeah, she's in charge of the Guardians now, believe it or not. It suits her. She likes to cause trouble and kick ass. She scares me," he whispered with a smile.

"Me too," I admitted. "She's the one who captured us." I moved my shoulder up and down. "I still have the bruises."

Rice laughed. "Kay gives your mother a headache, but she's good at her job."

"A headache how?"

"You know, she's just . . . difficult," he said, clearly not wanting to say more.

"Like?" I smiled. "Come on, Rice, you've got to give me something here. *Everything* can't be a secret." I tried to sound like I was joking, but it was really how I felt.

Rice considered, adjusting his hold on Baby. "Kay likes to shake things up. In committee meetings she always plays devil's advocate, doesn't just fall into line. I really shouldn't be telling you this." He looked genuinely nervous.

"Their jobs are pretty demanding physically, aren't they?" I asked, an idea starting to form.

"Yes, Guardians are the only ones who have to work out every day, and they're exempt from almost everything except their psyche-eval. The women don't even have to donate their genetic material unless they want to."

"And how, exactly, do you become a Guardian?" I asked, prying.

"You have to pass certain tests, stealth, speed, weaponry . . ." He stopped and studied my face. "Amy, you don't want to be a Guardian."

"Why not?"

"Your mom would freak, first of all."

He was right. If my mother didn't want me to be a Guardian, I'd have a powerful opponent. On the other hand, her fanaticism for her own rules could work in my favor. She couldn't keep me from doing something I was qualified for because she wanted to keep me out of harm's way. Not when she asked other citizens of New Hope to risk their lives as Guardians.

"Besides," Rice continued, "do you know the mortality rate for Guardians? The odds aren't good. I wouldn't want you in danger like that."

I thought for a moment about the death that was announced on the news. "No, but I do know about Floraes and surviving outside of New Hope."

He sighed. "Look, the Guardians started up as soon as your mother became director. There were some military people here, checking up on their commissioned research, but most of the Guardians are Hutsen-Prime security staff and new recruits. At first everyone wanted to be a Guardian. You get special treatment, you're exempt, and everyone in New Hope treats you like you're royalty. Personally I think they're just glorified couriers."

"What do you mean?"

"The Guardians' main mandate is to get supplies from

the outside world. There's a lot of stuff left out there, canned goods are just now starting to expire and clothing and supplies stored in plastics are as good as new. If New Hope needs new computers, or more solar panels, the Guardians go out and fetch them. It's dangerous and necessary, but they act like they're war heroes every time they come back."

"I thought they were like the police," I said. "I thought the Guardians protected New Hope."

Rice laughed. "The sonic emitters protect New Hope. The Guardians act as our police force. . . . We have some rooms we've converted to holding cells, but we hardly ever use them. Mostly everyone here follows the rules. Almost all the adults were Hutsen-Prime staff. They screened their employees thoroughly, and the children . . ."

"Are indoctrinated."

He looked at me sharply. "Not exactly the word I would use."

"So, what happened? Why don't people want to join the Guardians anymore?"

"There were too many deaths, too many training accidents. That's why they don't even train Guardians until they're adults. We can't have our children getting injured in the hopes they'll make good Guardians."

"So how would I actually become a Guardian?" I was tired of him avoiding the question.

"You have to class out and take the tests. If you do well, they train you until you're ready for the final test. If you pass that, you're in." Rice smiled kindly. "Look, if you're serious about becoming a Guardian, why don't you go talk to Kay? She's the one who knows everything."

I nodded and searched the room for Kay again and saw her slipping out a side door. I didn't want to miss my chance. I turned to go but felt Rice's hand on my shoulder. "I was serious about not wanting anything to happen to you. Be careful what you're asking for."

I nodded again and smiled grimly. Then I hurried to where Kay had disappeared and pushed open the door, stepping into the hot, late spring air.

Kay had vanished, but I didn't want to go back inside just yet. I closed my eyes and breathed, tuning out the noise of the party, the noise of New Hope. To my left I heard a sharp inhalation, then a long, satisfied exhale. I peeked around the corner.

"Hello, Kay."

She looked at me, slightly startled. "Amy." She took another drag on her cigarette.

"Where did you get those? I didn't think cigarettes would be allowed," I said.

She shrugged. "They're frowned upon, but what isn't here?"

"Procreation, apparently," I said.

She smirked. "Enjoying your party?" she asked.

"No, not really."

"You'll be happy to know that attendance was mandatory, for those special few invited, that is."

"Few? It seems like half of New Hope is packed in there."

We stood in silence for a moment. "Did you want a cigarette or something?" Kay asked.

I took a deep breath, building up my courage. "Actually, I want to be a Guardian," I blurted.

She studied me. "And . . . ?"

"I have to learn how to pass the tests. I want you to teach me."

Kay scowled. "And what does Director Mommy think about this idea?" she asked. She finished her cigarette and squashed it underfoot. She then picked up the butt and put it in her pocket.

"She doesn't know, exactly."

"Why should I help you?" Kay asked. "You got me in

trouble when you pulled your little stunt on Rice." There wasn't even a hint of amusement in her voice. "I wouldn't have guessed you girls were packing two guns, although you did seem like trouble."

"That was unintentional," I apologized. I still couldn't read Kay. I didn't know if she was considering helping me or just toying with me.

"What about shooting me? I'm pretty sure that was intentional."

"You were wearing a synth-suit, and you seem fine now." I'd hoped she'd forgiven me for that, under the circumstances.

"It still hurts." She rubbed her side. "I'll have bruises for weeks. You could have broken one of my ribs."

"Well, I thought you were a Florae at the time, if that makes any difference."

To my surprise, Kay nodded. "The people here, they don't really get it. They're safe and secure. They don't have to think about what it's like out in the world now. How empty it is."

"Except for the Floraes."

"Yeah, except for the Floraes." She began to walk away.

"What are They?" I called after her. "I know the Guardians

must know more about Them; they capture Them to study."

She paused, turning slightly. "If you want to be a Guardian, maybe you should focus on that for now," she told me, walking away again.

"So . . . you'll train me?" I jogged to her side and walked with her.

"Yes, but you have to do things my way."

"All right."

"And you can't miss any school, so your mother doesn't catch on."

"Okay."

"And you're not allowed to complain," Kay continued.

"Not at all?" I grinned. Kay was a hard-ass, but I could tell she had a sense of humor.

"Never." She smiled slyly. "Well, I suppose if you break a bone you can complain a little bit."

"Does that happen often?" We were nearly back to the party.

"Yes," she told me bluntly. "Synth-suits can save you from teeth and claws, but not brute force. We train Guardians to deal with everything, all types of attacks. Some don't make it."

"Don't make it, as in are injured, or don't make it as

in . . ." I trailed off when Kay gave me a meaningful look.

"What time does the director leave in the morning?" Kay asked before we rejoined the party.

"Usually by five."

"Perfect, you can get in a morning run and be at the Rumble Room by six. It's the big building across from the Orientation Office."

"Black door?" I asked. "Restricted area?"

She nodded. "I'll wait for you outside."

"I'll be there," I said. She opened the door, and I added, "Thank you."

She paused and turned to me. "Don't thank me, kiddo. We need more Guardians. Each year we get fewer and fewer applicants. We've lost four this year and we have one new recruit: you." She shook her head.

"I won't give up," I said.

She looked me up and down one last time. "We'll see about that, sunshine," she added mockingly before heading inside.

I stood alone outside, wondering if I would ever feel at home in New Hope. Kay's sarcastic voice echoed through my head: "We'll see . . ." I went back to the party, determined to prove myself to Kay, to my mother, and to New Hope.

•••

"Take this, sunshine," a female voice whispers.

"What is it?" I ask the nurse. I look at her closely. She's not my usual nurse, and I always get medication in my room, not in the hall.

"Just take it." She pushes it into my hand. She's strong for someone so petite. "Rice said he'd tell you I was coming."

My mind races. I take a step back, startled. My mouth hangs open in amazement. Kay.

"You've come for me?" My heart is pounding. She's going to help me escape. Relief floods over me. I won't have to suffer anymore. I won't have to live in constant fear of my impending electroshock therapy.

Kay stares at me. "I'm sorry, kiddo, no. I just came to give you the pill."

"But you're supposed to help me." I open my mouth to say more, but she shakes her head, silencing me.

"I set it up so there's a blind spot in the cameras but we only have a few minutes." She glances down at her watch.

"When are you getting me out of here?" I ask, pleading.

"For now, take the pill." Her voice is stern.

I nod and put the pill in my mouth, swallowing it with a dry cough.

"Good girl." Kay leans in. "I'll get you more later. This was all I could manage for now. We need you clear if we're going to . . ." A nurse walks down the hall, past us, and Kay pretends to consult a chart.

"When?" I ask again, frustration in my voice.

"Just be ready," she tells me, looking over her shoulder.

I don't want her to go, not without me. All the exhilaration I felt moments earlier has turned to panic. "Please, take me with you now," I beg.

"It's too risky," she tells me sadly. "We'll come back for you."

I nod unhappily.

"Keep safe," she says before walking down the hall, her head bent low, and disappearing around the corner.

I stare after her with mixed emotions. "We'll come back for you," *she'd said. I can't leave just yet, but it's finally begun.*

PART THREE

GUARDIANS

CHAPTER TWENTY-ONE

My mother comes to visit me today and she brings Adam. I'm happy to see them both. Adam shows me his new toy, a hand-me-down plastic dinosaur he scored from a Class Three boy who'd outgrown it. I play with Adam on the floor of my room while my mother sits on the bed, watching us.

I know the pill that Kay gave me has worked. I'm still a little groggy, but I'm much clearer than I've been in a long time. I turn to my mother and ask, "How long have I been here?"

"It's been almost half a year since you've come to New Hope." She smiles at me encouragingly. "And I'm grateful for every moment."

"No." I shake my head. "I mean here, in the Ward."

She reaches out and fixes a stray hair that has settled on my forehead. "Your hair is getting a lot longer, maybe I can find out about getting you a haircut?" When I don't reply, she sighs loudly. "You've only been in the Ward a little over a month, honey."

So I've lost an entire month. What has been going on in New Hope without me? "Why am I in here?" I blurt.

"You're here to get the help you need." She doesn't even think before she speaks.

"I know . . . but why specifically? Help for what?" I push.

She studies me. "I . . ." She pauses, then says, "Dr. Reynolds believes you need to be monitored. You were acting erratically."

"Erratically? What did I do?" I wish all my memories would come back. I wish Kay could have given me more pills. If I could only have a few days without any medication, without the constant confusion. What did I do that was so bad they

put me in here and drugged me into a zombie?

"Amy . . . let me talk to Dr. Reynolds about this." My mother kneels down on the floor next to us.

"No. I'd really prefer it if you didn't," I tell her, trying to meet her gaze, but she looks away.

"I just want you to get well."

I'm not reassured at all. "But what if I'm not getting better?" I ask.

"Don't say that."

I play with Adam for a few more minutes, then my mother has to leave. She promises to come back soon and kisses me on the head. Adam waves good-bye with his chubby hands and gives me a wide smile.

After a few seconds, I hear my mother speaking to Dr. Thorpe in the hall, about the questions I've asked and about my course of treatment. Dr. Thorpe's voice is strained as she explains I am relapsing. I hear my mother begin to sniffle. She must be crying.

When Dr. Thorpe comes in, she takes my vitals and writes in my chart.

"How are you feeling?" she asks.

"I feel . . ." I don't know what she's looking for. "I feel fine." I say at last.

"And the memory loss?"

"Things are coming back to me slowly."

"Do you remember coming to the Ward?"

"Not yet," I admit, uncertain.

"I'm very concerned," she tells me. "The meds that Dr. Reynolds has prescribed seem to be having an adverse effect. Your condition is deteriorating. I've decided, under Dr. Samuel's recommendation and with the urging of Dr. Reynolds, to begin your electroshock treatments tomorrow."

She sees the horror on my face and continues hastily, "It's not as bad as you might think. You'll have an initial worsening of your memory. . . ."

I shake my head. "No." I can't return to how I was, not knowing the difference between dreams and reality.

"But that will only last for a few days. The therapy could be very beneficial to your psychosis."

"Can I refuse treatment?" I ask, already knowing the answer. I begin to shake, fear and frustration taking over my body. I have no control. I have nothing.

Dr. Thorpe sighs. "Amy, I'm only trying to help you. I didn't mean to upset you. I'll send a nurse in to give you a sedative."

"No, I'm fine." I try to relax, but my body still trembles. I

can't even control my own muscles. Dr. Thorpe leaves and a nurse comes in to give me a shot. I try to stay awake, struggling against the darkness. There is so much I don't remember but what little I do, I don't want to forget.

•••

I got up before the alarm and listened for my mother, who always left the house around five a.m. Two weeks had flown by, between class and training and babysitting. I was finally getting used to waking up at first light, instead of going to sleep at daybreak.

Going running? Baby asked when I got out of bed. Even though I tried not to wake her, she still heard me every morning.

I need to practice, I signed into her hand. She hadn't even bothered to open her eyes.

See you before school. She turned and fell back asleep. I stared at her for a moment, her blond hair barely covering the scar on her neck. I reached out and combed her hair with my fingers, arranging it over the mark, though I wasn't entirely sure why.

I changed into the T-shirt and shorts that I'd scavenged from my mother's closet. I stretched outside the apartment, then jogged in the opposite direction from the Quad. I preferred to be alone, since I didn't wear shoes and my "silent" running technique drew stares. Running around with my mouth wide open made me look like a total weirdo, but it would be a useful skill if I made Guardian.

As I breathed in the humid air, I noticed how, even in the heat, it felt good to be outside. I loved the soft prickly sensation of the grass under my feet and the quiet in the outskirts of the town. I decided to run to the lake, knowing I would have to push it to get back in an hour. The last time I was late for training, Kay refused to even look at me and I spent the session on my own, trying to copy what the other Guardians were doing. Even so, I was relieved to have a focus, to have my days filled with purpose. I was even sleeping better, exhausted from all the physical exertion.

The ground felt cooler under my feet and I could tell I was nearing the lake. A twig broke, making me cringe at the sound in the relative quiet. Every day I had to remind myself that I was safe here. Vivian was right: being safe was worth living in a strange system. I kept telling myself this too.

When I reached the lake, I paused to take in the view, the serenity. A loud noise off to the right made me freeze, my heart jumping into my throat. Something was there; I heard it loping in my direction.

One of Them.

I almost panicked. It was daylight and I was completely exposed.

"Amy?"

I wheeled around and almost collapsed with relief.

"Rice." Instantly I was back in New Hope and out of the world of the After. Rice wore his familiar white coat and jeans and carried a duffel bag.

"What are you doing?" he asked curiously.

My heart was still pounding from the adrenaline. I took a deep breath to calm myself. "I . . . um . . . was out for a run," I explained. "I heard you coming this way and . . ."

He looked at me. "Am I really that loud?" he asked.

"Yeah, you are." I laughed shakily. "I figured you were either a freight truck or a Florae."

"At least I don't snarl." He grinned.

"Or, more important, eat human flesh," I added, suddenly self-conscious of the way I looked. I was drenched in sweat from my run. I wiped my face with my sleeve.

He looked me up and down. "It's nice to see you out here. . . . Why aren't you wearing shoes?"

I shrugged. "It's easier for me to run without them. Where are you headed anyway?" I asked, pointing to his duffel bag.

"I'm going to check on a couple of sonic emitters. I usually do four or five a morning; that way I can make the rounds in a week. . . ."

"Have they ever broken?"

"Once or twice the solar panels shorted. They're strategically placed," he assured me. "If one isn't working, then the others will compensate."

"But what if two stop working?" I asked, unnerved at this new information. No one else in New Hope seemed to think there was any chance the Floraes could break through the sonic shield. They didn't even question it.

"There's no Floraes around for miles anyway. It's more of a precaution." Rice adjusted the duffel bag, slinging it over his shoulder. "Do you want to come check them out with me?" I glanced at my watch. I had thirty minutes before I was supposed to meet Kay, which meant that I had to head back now.

My curiosity got the better of me, though. That and the fact that I really liked being with Rice, liked how he made me feel understood. Alive. "Sure," I said.

He took off walking slowly and I followed him. He kept watching me as we walked, making me even more self-conscious.

"What? Why do you keep looking at me?" I asked finally.

"Nothing. It's just . . ." He smiled. "You're . . . um . . . so damned quiet. It's amazing."

I smiled. "You should see Baby sneak around."

"What do you mean?" he asked, suddenly serious.

"She's just very stealthy," I tried to explain as we walked. "She knows how to move without making any noise at all. . . . You have to if you want to avoid the Floraes."

"Did you teach her how to be quiet?"

"No, I didn't have to teach her anything. Even as a toddler, she already understood. Plus we've had years of practice. I can try to make more noise," I offered, "if that helps."

"No, don't worry about it. We're here now anyway." He led me into a clearing. "We keep all the emitters out in the open so the sun can get to their solar panels," he explained. "They all have backup batteries that are good for forty-eight hours, and a distress beacon in case they are somehow damaged by a storm or an animal."

I expected it to be more imposing, but the emitter was just a two-foot-high box with a satellite dish attached.

"The panels move to face the light," Rice told me as he tinkered with the box panel. "This little guy can cover a four-mile radius."

"Impressive," I said. "I wish I'd had one of these at my house."

"You seem to have done okay without one." He stood, wiping his hands.

"It would have been nice to have neighbors." I was overcome with a great sense of loss for all the years wasted, when I could have been in New Hope. I turned away and put my hands over my eyes but a sob still escaped.

Then there were firm arms around me and I was sinking into Rice's chest. "I'm sorry." I sniffled. "I guess I've been due for a breakdown since coming here."

"It's okay," he told me kindly.

"How do you deal with it? You lost someone right in front of you."

He shifted away a little but kept an arm around me. "I work . . . a lot." He paused. "Does running help you cope?"

"It does . . ." I lifted my head and looked into his warm eyes. "Except when I hear you and think a Florae is after me."

He smiled down at me. We stared at each other, and suddenly he bent his head and kissed me softly. I was startled at first, then felt myself returning the kiss. It only lasted a few seconds. And as he pulled away, he looked in my eyes and said, "It's all going to be okay, you know." I stared at him and nodded, my legs feeling weak with nervous excitement.

"Do you want to help me finish the rounds?" he asked, giving me a last squeeze before breaking away and adjusting his glasses.

I looked at my watch. "Oh, I should really get back." I was already going to be late, but Kay would kill me if I didn't show up at all. "But I'll see you later?"

He nodded and I waved good-bye and hurried to the Rumble Room, where Kay was waiting. I expected to get yelled at, but instead she just smiled coldly. I would have preferred the yelling.

"Here." She threw something at me and I caught it between my fingers: a black cloth, smooth and light. "Go change, quickly. We have a lot to do today."

I was still thinking of Rice, of his lips on mine. I looked down and held out the material Kay had thrown at me. My heart surged. My very own synth-suit.

•••

I lie awake as an orderly rolls a gurney into my room.

"Ms. Harris, you need to lay down here, please."

I stare at him, weak and slow-minded from my last shot. I raise my head slowly, trying to prop myself up. My arms are unresponsive. The man is impatient or thinks I am being difficult to defy him. He picks me up roughly, hefting me onto the gurney. I let him fasten me in without complaint.

As he pushes me out of my room, I wonder why I'm being carted around. "I can walk," I tell the orderly. But he doesn't even glance down at me. I move my hands, testing the straps at my wrists. I pull harder and Dr. Thorpe appears over my face, walking next to my gurney.

"Amy, don't struggle. You'll only hurt yourself." She smiles reassuringly. Her gray-blond bun has come undone into a ponytail that spills across her shoulder.

"Why am I tied up?" I ask her, still puzzled. "I've done nothing wrong."

"Remember, yesterday we talked about trying out a new procedure?" She glances down the hall, then back at me. "That's what we're doing now."

I tug at the straps again, this time more forcefully. "I'll try harder," I tell her.

Dr. Thorpe ignores me. "Make sure she's secure," she tells the orderly. "I'll get Dr. Reynolds and meet you downstairs."

"Wait . . ." I yell. Dr. Thorpe disappears from view as I am wheeled down the hall to an elevator, feeling helpless. I close my eyes tight, terrified.

• • •

"Owwww," I couldn't help but yowl, even though I knew it would make Kay come at me twice as hard.

"Toughen up," she said. She took another swipe at me with her practice knife. This time she got me in the ribs and I gasped as a sharp pain shot through my abdomen.

"Jeez, give the kid a break," Gareth shouted. He was small and wiry, and we often sparred together. I glanced up and noticed they were all watching us now. Even Rob, who wouldn't give me the time of day, since I wasn't technically one of them yet.

"Like the Floraes will?" Kay called. She was right. If she had been a Florae–if one got a claw in me–I'd be dead.

I wasn't used to the synth-suit, the way it clung to my body and muffled my movements. It was lightweight and skintight, which almost made me feel naked. You had to pull it over your body like panty hose. There were pockets too, little compartments to hold things, like a knife or a super-thin compass.

Kay lunged at me. In each hand she clutched a knife, trying to simulate hand-to-hand combat with a Florae. I heard her foot loudly make contact with the mat and I could tell she was off balance. I parried her blow and pulled her arm forward. She fell on her side and I placed my practice knife at her throat, tracing the line of her neck with its rubber tip.

"You're dead," I told her.

"Good job, Harris," Marcus yelled. I looked up and grinned. Marcus was one of the military badasses; to get a compliment from him was just short of amazing. Suddenly the world shifted and I was flat on my back, the wind knocked out of me.

"Don't gloat," Kay told me from where she sat on my chest. "Now, *you're* dead."

She stood up smoothly and offered me her hand, winking as she pulled me up. I was improving and she had just given me the Kay equivalent of a compliment.

"Pair up," she yelled. "Half-hour rumble before we hit the shooting range."

I headed over to Gareth. He's wasn't like the Guardians who were former military; he was more of a smart-ass than a hard-ass.

"You're looking good out there," he said as we began to spar. Gareth wasn't nearly as aggressive as Kay, though he did get a knife to my shoulder. "That synth-suit accentuates your . . . talents."

"You old perv!" I was trying not to blush. He was always

acting flirty with me, even though he'd told me that I wasn't his type, being a girl and all.

"Old!" he yelled, dropping his guard and allowing me to stab him in the arm. I knew that would get him. Although Gareth was only twenty-five, his hair was almost entirely gray. He was living proof that the life of a Guardian is stressful.

"You're getting really good, Amy." He smiled, rubbing his arm. "Even Marcus and the Elite Eight have noticed."

I looked over to where the intense training was going on. The Elite Eight were the military personnel who were on the Hutsen-Prime compound when the Floraes showed up. Kay led the Guardians, but Marcus was her second in command.

"If you care what the Elite Eight think so much, maybe you should put on about twenty pounds of muscle and try to join them," I teased.

"Then they'd have to change their name to the Nimble Nine," he joked. He came up next to me and surveyed the training area. "That Jenny is as fast as a Florae," he observed.

She *was* quick, dancing circles around her partner, Rob. She used her knives as an extension of her arms, lunging, stinging, moving away.

"Floraes are faster," I said, shaking my head. There was no way to fend off a Florae without a gun or a bow. All I really knew was that the farther away they were, the better your chance for survival. "Seriously, Gareth, do you think this will help, if you're actually alone with a Florae?" I asked.

"It definitely helps." I was surprised to hear no doubt in his voice. "It's mostly the synth-suit that will protect you, but not panicking, being able to kill without hesitation, that's what will keep you alive."

"Less talking, more fighting," Kay yelled at us from across the room. I didn't know how she saw me roll my eyes, but she called out, "Amy, come here. I want to demonstrate something."

I looked at Gareth. "Oh, crap."

"You're on your own, honey," he said, holding up his hands and backing away from me.

I made my way over to Kay, debating whether or not to pull on my synth-suit hood to protect my face. I decided against it, hoping she would go easy on me. Bad strategy.

In three moves she had me on the floor. I tried to get up but she hit me twice in the face. I groaned, the metallic taste of blood in my mouth.

"Next time, sunshine," she told me, "wear your hood."

"What happened to you?" Vivian asked, her voice heavy with concern when I arrived twenty minutes late to class.

"Kay Oh punched me in the face," I told her. It was more of a chop than a punch but, either way, my face ached; the area around my eye had already begun to turn dark purple.

"What? Why did she do that?"

"It's a long story. She was trying to help me, if you can believe it."

"Remind me to never ask Kay Oh for help," she said, studying my bruise. "But seriously, why did Kay hit you?" she asked. Then understanding dawned on her face. "You're training to be a Guardian, aren't you?" she whispered.

"No one can know," I said, but I was relieved that she'd figured it out. I'd wanted to tell her, if just to vent, but Kay was adamant that it had to be kept secret.

"I won't tell anyone, I promise. Just be careful." She reached for my hand, squeezed it. I looked at her face–her scar–my eyes tracing the white line.

"Vivian, you never told me. What happened to you?" I asked.

She surveyed the class and then motioned to the door. "Let's go for a walk."

Outside in the fresh air, it was a while before Vivian began to speak. We watched the Class Twos on the playground. I looked for Adam but didn't spot him.

"We were trapped in our apartment building," she finally said, sounding distant. "My parents were out. They probably died right away. We were stuck. We couldn't leave, not with the Floraes on the loose. We barricaded the front doors and the stairs and holed up in the top apartment. It was me, my brother, and a couple of people we knew from our building. We weren't thinking long term, we just wanted to survive each day." Her face was strangely calm though her voice was heavy with misery.

"We had electricity for a couple of days. But you know, the news was so grim, it was almost a relief after the power went out and we couldn't listen to the radio anymore. We had no contact with the outside world. For all we knew, we were the only people left on the planet." Vivian tugged at her necklace.

"We ran out of food after a month. We were careful, basically starved ourselves to conserve what we had. My brother and the old man from 7B went to search the other apartments." Her voice quavered at the mention of her brother. "They never came back. A Florae must have gotten in somehow.

"We heard it eventually, clawing at the door. It wanted

us. One woman wouldn't stop screaming. We . . . there was a man, one of our neighbors; he was going to kill her to shut her up. I tried to stop him, but he was too strong. He knocked me out. When I woke up, the woman was dead, lying in a pool of blood with a slit throat. My face hurt when I touched my cheek." She caressed her face. "It was wet. I thought it was from my tears, but then I looked down and my hand was covered in blood."

"What happened to the man, the one that killed the woman?"

She shook her head. "I don't know. He was gone when I woke up. I thought maybe he felt guilty and jumped off the roof. I couldn't deal with being alone, so I went up there to do the same. Going up those stairs in the dark, I was convinced a Florae would attack at any second." Wiping her eyes, she looked over at me.

"Oh, Amy, I just wanted to die. My parents were gone, my brother; the entire world was dead–but I didn't want a Florae to kill me. I'd rather have done it myself."

I nodded knowingly.

"It's a miracle," she told me. "I was going to jump when I heard a thud behind me. The Guardians saw me on the roof. They came to rescue me."

She fingered the gold cross suspended above her breastbone. "This was my mother's. I always thought all that religious stuff she tried to get us to believe was crap, but standing there on that rooftop, no hope in my heart, and being saved by the Guardians . . . I thought they were angels. I know I was half starved and delusional with grief, but at that moment I believed my mother had sent them to me. I still do. I light a candle every Sunday and thank God I'm alive."

I wrapped my arms around Vivian and gave her a gentle squeeze. I wasn't able to take away her horrible memories, but I could share her pain. Vivian hugged back and when we pulled away she gave me a small smile.

"You'd be surprised how many of these people of science go to chapel every Sunday. People who aren't even religious, they just want a quiet place to pray."

"I'm not surprised, it being the end of the world and all."

"I don't think it's really the end, you know. Just something new," Vivian said.

"I hope you're right," I told her.

• • •

"I feel very positive about this." I hear Dr. Thorpe say, somewhere in the room. My body and head are secured; I can only see the ceiling.

"How many treatments before we can hope to see signs of recovery?" comes another, older voice. Dr. Samuels.

"It truly depends on the patient," Dr. Reynolds says. My stomach drops at the sound of his voice. "With some, there is noticeable progress after one session. Some take more than twenty, and some never improve at all."

"And the memory loss?" Dr. Thorpe asks. "What are the chances that Ms. Harris will be affected? She was very concerned about that when I spoke with her."

"Retrograde amnesia can be a side effect. So can cognitive impairment and death. No treatment is without risk."

I hear footsteps and the hum of a machine. I open my mouth to protest and something is placed in it. It's rubbery and smells like old leather. Dr. Reynolds's head appears above my face for a moment. He licks his lips, a look of pure joy in his eyes. "Let's begin," he says loudly.

The pain hits me like a lightning bolt and my entire body seizes. Every nerve, every synapse is on fire. I am burning from the inside out. I bite down on the piece of leather in my mouth, wishing that I were dead, that the excruciating agony would stop. Anything to make it stop. When I lose consciousness, I welcome it. The darkness will end the torture. The blackness is a relief.

• • •

"Keep your focus," Marcus yelled at me.

"Watch your back!" Gareth shouted.

"Where is your head today?" Kay spit.

They were watching me fight three of the Elite Eight, who had been instructed to behave like Floraes. That meant they would run at me at top speed and try to slice me with their knives. Not the rubber-tipped knives I trained with at first, but real ones with sharp, shiny metal blades.

I felt someone stab at my back, and it could only be Jenny, because I had the two boys in my sights.

I thought wearing the synth-suit's hood would hurt my hearing and obstruct my vision. The hood is attached to the back of the suit, but you can pull it down over your face where it fastens seamlessly to the neck material with a strong, Velcro-like fastener. It's as strong as the rest of the suit, but so thin, it didn't hinder my senses at all. It amazed me that the concept for this started in our class. Vivian was a genius.

I heard Jenny approach again at a run from behind and I crouched down low at the last second. Kay taught me that trick. Jenny tripped over me and fell on her side. I pushed her on her back and traced my knife across her neck. According to the rules, she was dead. We learned that if you were going to fight a Florae with a knife, your best bet was to slit its throat, sever its spinal cord. Stabbing it anywhere else would just piss it off.

I backed away from Jenny, who played dead on the ground. Nick and Rob didn't waste any time rushing me, taking me down. They stabbed at my face and torso. Now *I* was dead. They backed away and Jenny got to her feet. She pulled up her hood.

"Not bad." She smiled.

I pulled up my hood, feeling a little disappointed in myself but also frustrated with the setup. "You know, this is completely unrealistic," I told them.

"Don't be a sore loser," Nick said. He hadn't taken off his hood, so I couldn't see his expression.

"No. If you all were Floraes," I explained, "I'd have been dead in five seconds. But if I had managed to kill the Jenny Florae, you two would have been on her instantly, and I could have made my escape . . . or killed you both while you were feeding. I mean, you capture the Floraes, right? Don't you study them? Learn how they behave?"

There was silence as Kay and Marcus exchanged an uncomfortable look.

"Amy, can I speak with you?" Kay said quietly.

I walked over to them with my head held high, though I really wanted to hunch over and stare at the floor.

"How do you know that we capture the Floraes?" Marcus asked.

"I saw you, before I came here." I lowered my voice. "One was about to kill me, actually, before it was captured." I didn't tell them about being in a restricted area and seeing the Floraes being tortured.

Both of them were quiet. Finally Marcus gave me an intense stare. "Listen, Amy, we keep the Floraes in a secure facility on the base. Most citizens of New Hope would not be comfortable to know they're here."

"But you do study them?" I asked, wondering how much they would tell me.

"Yes. We study them for a number of reasons. They're crucial for perfecting our training techniques. We watch the way they move, how they react to prey. . . ."

"You mean people."

"I mean any mammal." He glowered at me. "What, do you think we feed bad children to the Floraes?"

"No, of course not. I just wonder why you don't know how they act in groups. . . ." I stopped, remembering that the

Floraes I saw were kept alone, one to a room. "They're too dangerous in groups," I whispered.

"We can only study one at a time," Kay confirmed. "Otherwise we couldn't contain them."

"But you go out, into the . . ." I was about to say "the After," but I realized they wouldn't know what I meant.

"We go and collect supplies and the odd survivor. We have our hover-copters, our guns. We avoid places that are teeming with Floraes, unless our purpose is to capture one. Then we're in and out."

"Then why all this training?" I asked.

"In the Marines," Marcus told me, "they push you to your limits and expose you to every imaginable horror. They gas you. They half drown you. You're afraid, but it's only training. The next time you're not so afraid. You know what to expect."

"We can't have Guardians freezing up the first time they encounter a Florae face-to-face," Kay clarified. "We depend on each other, so everyone has to function. There's no alternative."

"I get it," I told them.

"Shall we continue practice?" Kay yelled, loud enough for the others to hear.

"Can I be a Florae this time?" I asked hopefully.

"Not until you're a real Guardian, sunshine." Kay smiled wickedly. I pulled my hood back on and made a face she couldn't see before walking back to the practice mat. Then I took extra pleasure in pretend-killing Nick and for-real elbowing Rob in the face. It didn't even matter that in the end I was, once again, the loser. You just couldn't win against the Floraes.

After several hours, I stepped out of the Rumble Room, exhausted from my training session. That's why I didn't see him until he called my name.

"Amy?"

I turned to find Dr. Reynolds watching me, a strange smile on his lips. "I wasn't aware you had clearance to be inside a restricted area."

"I . . ." I froze, lost for words. Thankfully Gareth was next out the door. He took in Dr. Reynolds and me with my mouth hanging open like an idiot.

"Thanks again, Amy," he said quickly. He was wearing civilian clothes, jeans and a T-shirt. He looked so different from when he was in his synth-suit–much less intimidating, and even with his almost completely gray hair, much younger.

"Yeah . . . no problem," I responded slowly, still frozen in place.

"Dr. Reynolds." Gareth nodded at him pleasantly. "What brings you out our way?"

"I just wanted to observe the Guardians in training, but I suppose I'm too late," he said, the same eerie smile surfacing again. "Your psyche-evals are coming up soon."

"Again? It's been six months already?" Gareth asked. "Seems like my head was just shrunk last week."

Dr. Reynolds chuckled. "Well, let's just hope you've solved some of your relationship issues."

Gareth grimaced. He'd mentioned to me he'd recently broken up with his boyfriend, but didn't go into details. It must have ended badly. I could tell Dr. Reynolds's comment cut him deeply.

Dr. Reynolds turned his gaze back to me. "Amy . . ."

"Amy was invited here by Kay," Gareth said irritably, no longer pretending to be friendly. "She was telling us more about her experiences with the Floraes in the field. She's an invaluable resource."

"I'm sure she is." He studied my face. "In fact, I hear you've been talking quite a lot about the Floraes." My blood turned to ice.

"Yes." My voice cracked and I swallowed before trying to speak again. "I was trying to prepare for my presentation to the Guardians," I bluffed, trying to follow Gareth's lead. "I didn't want to leave anything out."

"Of course not."

"Well, I have to get to class." I turned to go.

"Amy, I . . . ," Dr. Reynolds began.

"I'll walk with you, Amy," Gareth said, cutting him off. He nudged me so my legs would start working. I tried not to look back, but when I did, Dr. Reynolds had already disappeared into the Rumble Room. I exhaled with relief.

"That man is creepy," I whispered to Gareth.

"You don't know the half of it," Gareth told me. "He must know you're training with us."

"How?"

"My guess is Marcus. . . . Kay has thought he's a spy for Dr. Reynolds for a while."

"Why would he need to spy on the Guardians?" I couldn't help but look behind me again, making sure we weren't being followed.

"When the Guardians started, Marcus was supposed to be the leader, no questions asked. Dr. Reynolds is smart, though. He saw that the citizens wouldn't be happy with anything like a military dictatorship; no one wants to live under a police state."

"So Kay is in charge and Marcus reports back to Dr. Reynolds everything that isn't quite right with the program," I filled in.

"Yeah, that's what we think. We're extra careful around Marcus and the Elite Eight, not that we do anything wrong to begin with," Gareth said, shooting me a sideways glance. "Except for training you. Kay must have a grand plan to put herself at risk like that."

"Maybe Dr. Reynolds won't care," I offered.

Gareth shook his head. "He sets the rules; he'll definitely care about them being broken. But he may weigh the benefits."

"What do you mean?"

"Training you isn't that bad in the grand scheme of things. If he puts a stop to it, he'll expose his spy and lose an almost-trained Guardian."

We reached school and I turned to Gareth to say goodbye, glad to know he was someone I could trust. "Thanks for helping me out back there."

"Sure, just . . . take care of yourself, honey," he said with a wink, back to his normal, teasing self.

"I will." I grinned, but my amusement faded as he walked away.

After scanning the grounds, I spotted Baby and ran to her side, engulfing her in a giant hug. I kissed the top of her head and walked her to class, though I really wanted to take her in my arms and run away. But away to where?

CHAPTER TWENTY-TWO

I wake up screaming. There are hands on my shoulders, holding me down, and another pair on my forehead, trying to calm me.

"Amy . . . drink this," Dr. Thorpe commands. She is at my side with a cup of water.

"They're here. The Floraes—" I yell as tears stream down my face.

Dr. Thorpe flashes a light in my eyes, examining me. "You've just had a bad dream," she assures me. "You're safe here."

"We're not safe!" I yell. "Where's Baby? I have to save Baby from the Floraes."

"You're having an adverse reaction to your treatments."

"Do you want to die?" I cry. "They'll kill us." She doesn't understand the danger we're in.

"Amy, calm down."

"Let me go!" I yell at the top of my lungs, pushing Dr. Thorpe out of the way. I fall out of bed and crawl toward the door.

An orderly stops me before I make it more than a few feet. He picks me up and drags me back to my bed. I scream and try to fight, but my blows are wild and powerless.

He holds me down while Dr. Thorpe straps me to the bed, securing my wrists and ankles. She steps away, watching me as I struggle.

"You paged me?" Dr. Reynolds enters the room, eyeing me.

"Ms. Harris isn't reacting well to her treatments," she says loudly, upset. "The electroshock therapy has obviously worsened her condition."

"Please," I beg. "Let me go."

"The trial treatments were a mistake," she tells him, frowning.

"How were we supposed to know that?" Dr. Reynolds asks calmly. "She seemed like a promising candidate."

"Perhaps we should continue with her original medication," Dr. Thorpe suggests.

"It was ineffective against her psychosis." Dr. Reynolds glances at me. "Maybe if we up the dosage?" Dr. Reynolds scribbles on my chart before he hands it to Dr. Thorpe.

She reads it and stops. "But that's nearly twice the dosage!"

Dr. Reynolds looks at her. "Do you disagree with my prescription?" he asks coldly.

Dr. Thorpe flinches slightly. "No . . . I agree completely."

Dr. Reynolds leaves, but Dr. Thorpe stays and stares at me for a moment. She takes a deep breath before stepping outside my room, returning a few moments later to give me a shot. The sedative takes effect almost immediately. I begin to lose myself.

She stands over me as I try to keep my eyes open.

"Please . . . ," I whisper. "If you tie me up, I can't escape from Them. Please . . ."

Dr. Thorpe's figure blurs as the medicine takes hold. "There is nothing to worry about," she tells me as I lose consciousness. "Everything is just fine."

•••

The past few weeks were hell. Kay was riding my ass even harder than usual. On top of that, my mother was almost never around. If it wasn't for Vivian, I would have been lost. I'd drafted her to help me babysit and sometimes she slept over. We talked about everything we missed from Before. Baby loved our sleepovers and tried to stay up with us but always conked out long before we did.

That evening, though, I was alone on the couch in my pajamas, reading. My muscles ached and I was tired from training. All I wanted to do was relax.

Amy. Suddenly Baby was standing over me, back from the bedroom. *The noise has stopped.* Baby looked half relieved, half frightened.

What do you mean? I asked.

The noise is gone. Baby explained. *The humming.*

What hum–? I sucked in a breath as I realized what she was trying to say. The sonic emitters. If it was quiet, it meant . . .

My thoughts were interrupted by a scream that sliced

through the silence. I jumped off the couch, flipping off lights as I went. *Baby, stay there,* I told her as I ran to our bedroom. I looked out the window into the courtyard below.

A chill settled over me and I began to tremble. A pack of Them was in the Quad, feasting. I crouched down, my head in my hands, rocking back and forth. I couldn't let myself completely break down. Baby watched me from the doorway.

Baby, it's Them. They're here now.

Baby shook her head, not wanting to believe me.

I froze and tried to think. We couldn't run, I knew that much. We couldn't wait either. Wooden doors didn't offer much protection. They would be busy for a few minutes with the people outside, but They'd managed to spread across the world in a matter of days. It wouldn't take Them long to wipe out the population of New Hope.

My mother would be prepared for something like this. I took a deep breath to calm down. Then I remembered Adam, in his room. *Baby, check on Adam. If he's awake, make sure he's quiet.* She nodded, her instinctive survival skills resurfacing.

I ran down the hall and surveyed my mother's room. She would have a gun somewhere, but she'd want to keep it away from Adam. My eye caught a metal box on the highest shelf in the closet. I pulled over her desk chair to retrieve it.

Please don't be locked. Shaking, I fiddled with the catch.

The box swung open and I half laughed, half cried out. There was a gun and a full clip of bullets. It was a Guardian gun, completely silent. The kind I'd been practicing with for months. I quickly loaded the clip and ran to check on Baby.

She was standing over Adam's crib, silently watching him. She turned when I entered the room, though I hadn't made a sound.

The noise is back now, she told me. The emitters were on again, but that wouldn't help with the Floraes already inside New Hope. It would only agitate Them.

I have to go. I have to find Them. The ones that got inside. The people of New Hope were loud and ignorant. They didn't know how to deal with the Floraes in anything but theory.

Should I come? Baby asked. *I can help you hear Them.*

No, stay with Adam. He needs you now. Make sure he's quiet. If one of Them gets in, hide.

What if he cries? Her face was desperate. She loved him too.

Make him understand. If you have to, leave him. As soon as I signed the words, I regretted them, but I didn't have time to rethink my decision. I couldn't allow Baby to die. It was better one of them survived than neither. I shook the dark thought from my head as I hurried downstairs.

I silently slipped through the door and quickly scanned the area. They were everywhere in the Quad: at least ten had already found victims, several more crouched, ready to run down anything They heard. One loped toward me and I reacted automatically, aiming for its head, just like in target practice. I squeezed the trigger.

It fell, twitching, and two more pounced on it, tearing into its yellow-green flesh. There were quite a few feeding, but I left them for now. They wouldn't be done for a while and I was more concerned with the creatures still looking for food. After, I could go back and pick off the feeding Floraes one by one.

I heard one behind me and spun around to fire.

"Cool it, it's just me."

Kay's voice came from the hood of a synth-suit. She blended in with the night and I had to squint to make out her form.

Her voice carried across the Quad, and several Floraes looked up at us, torn between their fresh kills and the promise of more meat. I sprinted quickly to her side and placed my head next to her ear.

"What is happening?!" I whispered desperately.

Kay shook her head. “I wish I knew.”

“Do you have an extra synth-suit?”

“At the Rumble Room . . . I can’t spare a Guardian to go with you, but I could give you my keycard . . .”

“That would take too long. Forget it. I’ll be fine without one. I’m used to this.”

“Good luck,” Kay whispered, and disappeared into the night. Hopefully the Guardians were prepared. This wasn’t search and rescue, this was war. The Guardians were accustomed to meeting the Floraes with other Guardians as backup. We had to protect the people of New Hope now. They were absolutely defenseless.

I felt dangerously exposed with the moonlight reflecting off my pale skin and white pajamas. But at least I had a gun. I snapped into focus.

There was a Florae to my left. I knew it had spotted me because of its frenzied snarl and its sudden galloping strides. I turned and shot it in the shoulder, which barely slowed it down. I re-aimed and managed to get its neck. Its momentum threw it forward and it fell at my feet, its head flopping to the side. Black-green blood spurted and I jumped back. I didn’t want the scent of blood on me.

I needed to make every shot a head shot, or I would just

piss them off. That's what the Guardians taught me: to kill a Florae you have to shoot it in its head or slit its throat, detaching the head from the body. I remembered every training session. *Don't fear Them. I am the one with the gun.*

More screams tore into the night from across the Quad. The world was ending again. I fought my urge to run and hide, like I did so many times in the After.

A blur of yellow sped by me, then one of red. I killed the two Floraes following the children, whose jumpsuits reflected the moonlight so they were lit up like beacons. They were running home, to their dorm, but the movement only attracted more Floraes. *How are there so many? How long were our defenses down?*

I crept along the shadows to the school, where dorms took up the two top floors. Those kids were all sitting ducks, but I didn't know what I would do when I ran out of bullets. I had no knife; besides, I doubted I could actually kill a Florae with just a blade, even though I'd been training for it.

I reached the school's main entrance, and from the splintered wood it was clear the Floraes were already inside. My heart stopped. The children in their beds would have nowhere to hide. They would be slaughtered.

I rushed inside and down the hall, keeping as silent as

possible. Most of the yellow and orange doors were closed. Upstairs past the red doors, I crossed back to the stairs that led to the dorms. I was in too much of a hurry. I didn't hear the heavy breathing until it was almost too late. One of Them was nearly upon me when I spun around to fire. Luckily my shot found its forehead. Its yellow eyes, fierce and burning, extinguished as it fell to the floor.

I took the stairs sideways, trying to keep one ear above and one ear below. When I heard whimpers, I burst through a door and skidded into the room, almost falling. When I regained my balance, I realized why the floor was wet; it was slick with blood.

Crazed, I scanned the room, shooting the feeding Floraes one by one. There were no survivors. I wasn't thinking straight; I should have started at the first room and worked my way down. I stepped back into the hall, leaving a trail of bloody footprints behind me. I heard a noise from behind a closed door.

I leaned in, listening. I heard a whimper, then a soft "Shhhhhhh."

I opened the door and stepped into the room quickly, closing the door behind me with an almost inaudible click. The Floraes would be there soon. If I heard, They did too.

The room looked like a kindergarten classroom: lots of little tables surrounded by small chairs. There was a door at the far end. I listened for noise, breathing, anything to tell me where people were hiding.

Near the far wall I heard a gasp, and when I ducked low, I saw them under a covered table. A Minder and two toddlers in pink stared at me fearfully. I looked under the other tables, where more little children crouched, frightened.

I motioned for the Minder to come out and she crawled forward on her hands and knees, painfully loud. I put my mouth to her ear.

"What's through that connecting door?" I whispered.

"Class Two dorm room," she said, her whisper loud with desperation. "There are kids in there now, under the beds. We came from the room next door when we heard the screams outside."

"Get the kids in there," I said. She looked at me blankly. "Now. Quickly and quietly," I ordered in a hushed tone.

The Minder waved the children out from under the tables and herded them into the adjoining room. I helped, but stayed focused on the door. We were making a lot of noise and it was only a matter of time. I searched the small kitchen they used for snack time and found a couple of knives. I shoved one in my waistband and handed the other to the Minder before she left the room.

"Keep silent," I cautioned. "If one breaks through the door, go for its neck." She took the knife with trembling hands. "And turn off the lights."

She nodded once and quietly closed the door. It was silent as a graveyard, but the Floraes knew we were there. Within seconds there was a scratching at the door, then a frenzied panting. With the sonic emitters back up and running, They were agitated. There was nowhere to hide from the noise.

In a few short moments, the creatures were almost through the door. I didn't know how many there were, but I was guessing more than I had bullets for. I took a deep breath. I'd hold them off for as long as I could. If I wounded a few, They would start feeding on each other. I could buy some time.

The door creaked and pressed inward. I aimed, ready to shoot as soon as it broke open, as soon as I saw the green gleam of a Florae's head. My heart thudded, but my hands didn't shake. I knew I could kill Them. They'd bottleneck through the door, and a bullet was still faster than a Florae.

Then, abruptly, it stopped. No more noise, no more

scraping, no more snarls. I stepped back cautiously, keeping my gun raised. Then the door began to open.

"Amy!" Gareth yanked off his hood, shocked. "What the hell are you doing in here?"

"There's a bunch of Class Twos in the other room." I motioned over my shoulder.

"Stay here with them while we clean up. We think we got them all, but the Elite Eight are still on the prowl outside."

I nodded, weak with relief, too exhausted to speak. He looked at me. "Those dead Floraes in the other room . . . ?"

"I took care of them, but I couldn't save the chil–" I didn't want to cry. Not there. Not yet.

"You did a good job," Gareth told me. He pulled his hood back up and stepped lightly out of the room.

I backed against the door, slid down, and collapsed in a heap. I began to shake as the adrenaline left my body. I wondered how many people were dead. I hugged my knees and waited for Gareth to come back and tell us it was all over.

• • •

"Is it over?" I ask Dr. Thorpe.

She leans over my bed. "Is what over?"

"The attack." I look up at her.

"That was months ago," she tells me. "You're in the Ward now."

I close my eyes. "My mind is full of holes," I say.

"I'm sorry for that. It's partially an adverse reaction to your shock treatments and partially the medication that you're on." I can feel her hovering over me. "Amy, I'm going to untie your arms now. Do you understand?"

"Yes." I open my eyes. There are several other people in my room. A nurse and a couple of orderlies.

Dr. Thorpe follows my gaze. "They're only here as a precaution," she explains as she frees my wrists from the restraints.

I flex my hands. "Thank you, Dr. Thorpe."

"You're welcome, Amy." She turns to the orderlies. "Would you mind standing outside? I think Ms. Harris will be more comfortable if it's less crowded." As they leave she calls after them, "Stay close, though."

The nurse stands near Dr. Thorpe as they look over my chart. "I just don't understand," Dr. Thorpe mutters. "The medication that Dr. Reynolds prescribed doesn't seem to be helping her. She continues to be confused and unresponsive."

"Do you think Dr. Reynolds's diagnosis was wrong?" the nurse asks doubtfully.

"No, of course not," Dr. Thorpe says hurriedly. "I just fear that Dr. Reynolds may be a little too liberal with the medication. Keep her on the restricted dosage for now. We'll see how she does."

"And her other restrictions?"

"Let's leave her to her room for today. If there are no problems she can begin to mingle with the other patients tomorrow. Make sure she's escorted by an orderly at all times. We don't want Ms. Harris to become overwhelmed."

Before she leaves, I ask Dr. Thorpe again about the attack. "Why does it feel like it was only yesterday?"

"It's part of your condition, Amy. Unfortunately for you, the electroshock treatments only made things worse."

"Will my memories come back?" I ask, my voice betraying my anxiety.

"I don't know for certain," she admits. "But maybe if you focus on what you do remember, it will help to fill in the blanks."

I take her advice and think back to the night of the attack, trying to remember.

•••

It was an hour before the Guardians were sure New Hope was secure. When I got home, my mother was waiting for me, cradling Adam in her arms. "Amy," she cried, making a strangled noise.

"Mom! Are you okay?" I ran to her and hugged her and Adam at the same time. I reached for Baby as well, squishing her to us.

"Amy, what possessed you to run off like that? You could have been killed!" My mother pulled away and peered into my face, gripping my arms tightly. "Are you hurt? Did one bite you?"

"No, I'm fine." I didn't know how to explain. "Mom . . . I had to help." The more Floraes I killed, the fewer people they could slaughter. "They don't know how to deal with them. No one here . . . Rice–is he okay?"

"Yes. Rice was working late in the lab." She paused. "Oh, Amy honey, I know that you survived out there with the Floraes, but you're not a Guardian. You don't have the proper training, the right equipment." She sighed heavily. "I'm assuming you're the one who took the gun from my room?"

"I had to," I say, unable to meet her gaze. "The Guardians took it from me, but I'll get it back."

"I'll take care of it." My mother rubbed her forehead with

her palm and I could see the strain and guilt etched on her face. "Now that you're here, I'm sorry, but I have to go. We're in a state of emergency . . . I can't believe this happened."

"I understand, Mom. It's all right." I reached for Adam. "You can go. I'll stay put."

"Okay." She placed Adam in my arms and kissed his head. He was awake but subdued. She leaned in to kiss the top of my head as well. "Amy, I'm proud of you for trying to help," she told me. "But I'm more grateful that you're safe."

I grimaced. I didn't even think of my mother when I went to fight the Floraes. I didn't wonder if she was okay or how she would feel if I died; it was like I was back in the After, with no one but Baby.

My mother gathered her computer bag and looked at me with a sad smile. She kissed Adam again, then me, before heading to the door.

"I love you." I needed her to know it.

"I love you too, Amy." She stopped at the door. "I'm sorry I wasn't there," she told me without turning around.

I didn't know if she meant tonight or three years ago. It didn't matter. The nightmares of Them had returned and I wondered if they had ever really left.

• • •

"Frank, you know you have to take your meds." Dr. Thorpe is talking to someone in the hall. I peek out my door to get a good look at him. He's about my age, maybe a few years older. He has dark skin with curly brown hair.

Later, in the common room, I sit across from him, staring. Trying to remember. Dr. Thorpe was right. If I focus long enough on a memory, the rest comes to me. Sometimes slowly, sometimes in a flash. It took me all afternoon to piece together what happened after the attack, but I remembered my time in the Ward in a rush, the parts I was conscious for anyway.

Suddenly it hits me, who the young man is.

"You're Frank?" I ask.

He looks at me, his dark eyes dull.

"I heard about a Frank who was in my Advanced Theory class."

A spark of understanding glints in his eyes and he speaks without turning toward me. "I'm not crazy. I'm in here because of what I learned about the Floraes."

"What did you learn?" I whisper, my chest tight.

He turns to me. "You don't want to know."

"I do . . . I do want to know. Tell me," I plead.

"You don't." He raises his voice. "You don't want to know." He was yelling now, and the orderly who escorted me from my room rushes over and tries to calm him. I sit in my chair, concentrating, wanting desperately to understand.

"Amy, you're sweating. Did Frank upset you?" a nurse asks.

I nod vaguely and she leads me to my room, where I'm left to wonder what Frank discovered about the Floraes, what he's afraid to say out loud.

•••

School was canceled the next morning while New Hope recovered. We weren't supposed to leave our apartments. I tried to call Vivian, but a voice kept prompting me for an emergency access code. All the lines were being held for official use.

I watched the news for a while, but I couldn't stand hearing the names of the dead read over and over, each time with new additions. They announced them alphabetically, so Vivian would be near the front. After they skipped over Alvarez for the third time, I flipped to cartoons for Baby.

There was a knock at the door and I yelled, "Come in." Rice appeared in the living room. "Rice!" I was so happy to see him I jumped off the couch. I ran at him, nearly knocking him off his feet with a leap of a hug.

"I'm so glad you're here. My mom told me that you were okay. I thought we weren't supposed to leave our homes," I said, giving him an extra squeeze.

"The director's assistant gets special privileges." He was holding me tight and kissed my head. "I had to stop by, especially after I heard about what you did last night."

"My mother told you?" I asked, breaking away.

"Haven't you been watching the news?"

"I needed a break from the death toll and I didn't think it was good for Baby."

"Here." Rice took the remote and switched the channel. Baby was watching us, grinning.

I'm happy you're here, Rice.

To my surprise, he replied, *Hello, Baby. I show Amy television.*

"Rice, I didn't know you were learning our sign language." I was impressed. I realized I'd have to watch what I said to Baby around him.

". . . she saved us," the TV blared and I recognized the Minder from last night. "If it wasn't for her all those children would have been killed. I would have died." The Minder was crying and someone handed her a tissue. "She's a hero."

"That's not what happened," I started to say, but then the newswoman continued.

"There are rumors that Amy Harris plans to take the Guardian test after she classes out. The director has no comment at this time."

I turned to Rice. "Did you mention to anyone that I wanted to be a Guardian? Like maybe Dr. Reynolds?" Dr. Reynolds saw me leave the Rumble Room, but what good would announcing it do? I was sure he would have control over what was said on the news. Wouldn't he rather no one knew I was breaking the rules?

Rice shook his head. "No . . . I knew you were up to something with Kay, and after all of your Guardian questions at the party, I'd have to be pretty dense not to figure it out. I haven't told anyone, though."

"You don't think Vivian said something, do you? She's the only other person I told." I couldn't imagine Vivian gossiping after she promised she wouldn't.

"I don't think she said anything, but Amy, I have to tell you something. It's why I came over." His face turned dark as he took my hand, squeezing it softly.

"What?" I asked, even though I got the feeling that I didn't want to know. "What is it?"

"Amy, I'm so sorry. It's Vivian," he said, looking into my eyes. "She's on the list of the dead."

CHAPTER TWENTY-THREE

"Amy." Rice takes a seat next to me in the common room. He looks at me with a kind smile. "It's me, Rice."

"I know." I smile back and my heart pounds loudly. "How are you?" I try not to sound too excited.

"Good. I just came from visiting Baby. . . ."

"Baby! How is she?" I ask desperately, any pretense of composure discarded. I haven't seen her for a while, not since her visit with Dr. Reynolds. And how long ago was that?

"She's fine. I promised I would help her."

"You promised to protect her," I say quietly. I focus on the

memory, but it eludes me. Why does Baby need protection? I try hard to concentrate. "You told me something. . . ."

"Shhhh." Rice motions with his eyes to the corner of the room and I follow his gaze to the camera mounted in the corner. Standing underneath it, an orderly watches us. I nod, understanding that I need to be careful.

I lick my lips and choose my words cautiously. "There was a medicine that I was given; it was very effective. It improved my condition."

Rice turns his blue eyes on me again. "I'll speak with Dr. Reynolds about your treatment options." He puts his hand in mine and signs, Be patient and play nice.

I take a deep breath, trying not to react. I will, *I promise him. He must have learned our secret signing from Baby. How much does he know?*

"I just get confused sometimes. I have trouble remembering everything. There are huge gaps in my memories. I don't even know how long I've been in here."

"Nearly two months."

I stare at the floor warily. How long will they keep me here? More drugs? *I ask, but he doesn't understand, so I try again.* Send Kay with good things?

Hard to get lots. *He squeezes my hand.* Help soon. Be strong.

I nod with a frown. I'm weak and tired. I don't know if I can last much longer. "I remembered," I tell him sadly. "About Vivian. And everything else."

"I'm sorry, Amy." He continues to hold my hand as I cry softly. "Just trust Dr. Reynolds. He only wants to help you." He leans in and hugs me. I breathe in deeply, remembering his warm, soapy smell—comforting. "Take your medicine and let Dr. Thorpe know if your depression worsens. They can prescribe you something for it."

I know he's only saying it for the cameras and whoever else may be watching. With his hand he tells me, We love you. I lo— *He pauses for a split second.* Just hang on.

Okay. *I wipe my face, but the tears keep coming. While Rice holds me, I mourn for Vivian once again.*

•••

On the outside, Memorial Hall looked like any other building in New Hope, but inside it was just one big, bland, white room. Chairs were set up facing the platform and podium and the overflow of mourners stood in the back and along the sides. I wanted to hide in the back but my mother made Baby and me sit up front with her and Adam.

What are all those TVs for? Baby asked. I studied the walls; flat screens lined the length of the hall. Each had a desk and keyboard underneath.

I'm not sure. My mother stood to give her speech. I tried to listen but it was impossible when all I could think about was Vivian and how agonizing it must have been for her at the end. While my mother talked about the strength of New Hope, I felt the opposite–drained and weak. As she spoke, the names of the victims appeared one by one on a screen behind her.

I finally gave up trying to stop the tears. I wiped my face with my sleeve and thought how inappropriate it was that I was wearing red to a memorial service. Baby's yellow jumper was just as ridiculous; it was like we were all in a cult.

After my mother's speech, Dr. Reynolds stepped forward. "Thank you, Director Harris. Will everyone please feel free to access individual names at any of the consoles located around the hall. Don't hesitate to add an epitaph for friends and loved ones. In order to heal, we must first remember." Dr. Reynolds nodded crisply at my mother and they left the platform. My mother came over to retrieve Adam before she was swept aside to speak to someone I didn't know.

I spotted Kay and headed over to her while my mother

was distracted, Baby trailing behind me.

"Hi, Kay," I said, wondering who she lost during the Incident. None of the Guardians, but a friend maybe. Did Kay have friends?

"We probably shouldn't be seen talking together," she muttered to me between clenched teeth.

"Why not? It's out that I want to be a Guardian. . . . My mother hasn't even said anything about it." I watched her, across the room, looking stressed but composed. "Do you think . . . maybe we should just tell my mother that you're training me? She seems okay with me trying out. She might feel better if she knows I'm prepared."

"Absolutely not." Kay lowered her voice. "I'm sure that as your mother she'd want you to be safe, but as the director she would have to make an example of you for not following the rules."

"You break the rules all the time," I told her, incredulous.

"I never break the rules," she stated firmly.

"Right . . . never."

My mother appeared at my side and took me by the shoulder, away from Kay. "Honey, why don't you go write something for Vivian? I'll watch Baby." She gave me a tender look. "It will make you feel better."

I doubted it, but I nodded and went over to wait in line. After a while, the crowd thinned and I found an unused console. I typed in *Alvarez* and Vivian's name immediately popped up. I highlighted it and watched a video of her, showing her Advanced Theory presentation for the synth-suits. She looked calm and poised, but I knew she was nervous by the way she fiddled with her necklace.

After the short video, I highlighted the pencil in the corner of the screen and saw that Tracey had already left an epitaph. GOOD-BYE, VIV. YOU WERE ONE OF A KIND AND YOU WILL BE DEARLY MISSED. It reminded me of the messages written inside the high school yearbook I found ages ago, while scavenging in the After.

I clicked NEW MESSAGE and thought about what to write, but ended up just staring at the blank screen for a very long time. Finally I typed: FOR IN THAT SLEEP OF DEATH, WHAT DREAMS MAY COME, WHEN WE HAVE SHUFFLED OFF THIS MORTAL COIL. SWEET DREAMS, VIVIAN. LOVE, AMY.

"Hamlet is a fitting tribute," a voice behind me remarked. I quickly saved my message and turned to find Rice looking over my shoulder.

"It doesn't sound cheesy?" I asked, embarrassed.

"No, it's not cheesy. Who wouldn't want to be remembered

with beautiful words from Shakespeare?"

He studied me, then went to the console and typed, O'BRIAN, KATHERINE. A young woman appeared, just a photo, no video. She had strawberry-blond hair and dark freckles scattered across her nose and cheeks. She had several messages under her name, one of which Rice highlighted.

TO DIE, TO SLEEP NO MORE; AND BY A SLEEP TO SAY WE END THE HEARTACHE. KATIE, I WILL LOVE YOU ALWAYS–R.

"You and I are very similar," he told me with a sad smile, reaching for my hand. His touch warmed me, but I didn't find much comfort in it. My thoughts were still on Vivian. I closed my eyes tight.

"Amy, are you all right?"

I started to cry. "I feel like I've lost everything all over again," I told him. "Only this time it was worse. I thought we were all safe here, but any one of us could have died." I paused. "Don't you ever feel guilty that you're alive?" I asked him.

"Every day," he admitted. "Is that why you want to be a Guardian?"

I shook my head but I didn't explain that my intentions were not so noble. I wanted to be a Guardian for selfish reasons, for the freedom that being a Guardian would provide.

"I'm always crying on you. You must be tired of it," I said.

"I don't mind," he told me. "It's nice to be useful, even if that use is as a tissue."

"And what does my mother use you for?" I blurted, surprised by my harsh tone.

"What do you mean?"

"Well, you're obviously used for something. So, what do you assist the director with?" I raised my voice. I couldn't stop myself. "You know, Rice, you never give me a straight answer. What do you do to the Floraes? Where did they come from?" I was almost shouting. "You must know!" I dared not say what I was really thinking, that somehow the creatures they used to study managed to escape. That this was all their fault.

I expected him to push me away, but instead he pulled me into a tight embrace. His fingers dug into my skin. People were starting to look at us and I saw Dr. Reynolds turn away from his conversation to stare. I knew I was out of control but I couldn't stop.

"Amy, calm down." He stroked my arm. "It's okay. Everything will be fine."

"No, it isn't okay." I pulled away from him. "Nothing is okay, Rice."

Feeling claustrophobic, I pushed past Rice and rushed

outside into the warm air. I started to run, kicking off my shoes when the buildings thinned and the trees began. I'd find them on the way back. I just wanted to be free.

• • •

After Rice leaves, I sit in the common room, watching the other patients. When Frank comes in, I find an excuse to sit next to him. He mumbles to himself and I try to listen to what he says, but it's indistinguishable. Except for one word over and over again: Florae.

"Have you seen one?" I ask him without looking at him. "A Florae? Up close?"

"You don't have to see them to know them," he replies.

I try again. "What do you know about them?"

His hand clenches into a fist and he begins to hit himself on the thigh. I reach over and touch his leg, attempting to comfort him.

"DO NOT TOUCH ME!" he yells, jumping up. He continues to pound his fist into his hip.

"I'm sorry. I didn't mean to upset you," I tell him quietly.

"This whole damn place upsets me," he shouts. An orderly takes hold of him and wrestles him to the ground so a nurse can give him a shot.

Dr. Thorpe appears, her hand to her ear. "Mr. Jones needs

his treatment now. Ready the machine."

I know I should stay quiet, but against my instincts I stand and stumble into Dr. Thorpe's way. "Amy, please. Not now," she says.

"Sorry. Where's Frank going?" I ask.

"It's okay. He's going to have treatment."

"Not electroshock?" I ask, horrified.

"No. EMDR . . . I don't have time for this now." She pulls away from me.

"EMDR?" I mutter.

"Eye movement desensitization and reprocessing," someone says at my shoulder. I turn to find the nurse at my side. "Was that too much? Do you need to go back to your room?" he asks.

"No. I'm fine. What is EMDR exactly . . . ? Maybe it could help me," I add hastily. I know I am walking a fine line.

"Frank is obsessed with the Floraes. During his treatments we show him a picture of a Florae and negatively enforce the association . . . ," he trails off. "This may be a little complicated for you, but don't worry. Frank's treatment is working. He's getting better."

I nod and sit back down. Rice assured me help was on the way and urged me to play nice, but it's hard not to try to help Frank. I could only imagine their version of negative reinforcement. Whatever Frank is going through, I know it is making him worse, not better.

• • •

School resumed a few days after the Incident. That's what everyone around here was calling it. The final death count was 418 dead, no wounded. The Floraes didn't leave wounded. They killed and devoured and moved on to kill again. And after the memorial service, more information was released about the cause.

The Incident occurred because two contiguous sonic emitters failed and were out for four days, giving the Floraes enough time to wander into New Hope. It must have seemed like heaven to them, all the loud people, all the light.

But I wasn't buying it. Rice monitored those emitters constantly, and I knew he'd be full of regret if he were to blame. He was extremely upset, but not guilt-ridden. And Baby said that the emitters were out for about twenty minutes before she decided to tell me, not four days. How could so many Floraes make it through in twenty minutes? And why would they lie about what happened?

I sat in class, still stupidly hoping that Vivian would walk through the door, even though I knew it was impossible.

"Amy," someone called across the room. I looked up to find Tracey staring at me, dark circles under her eyes. I wandered over to her desk. "I know what you did," she told me. "Upstairs. You saved those children."

"I didn't do anything," I explained. "I sat in a room and waited to die. Luckily the Guardians took care of the Floraes first."

"Vivian tried to help too. She heard the little kids screaming. She ran out of our dorm room. She wanted to save them."

"What?" This hit me like a blow to the stomach. Vivian hadn't stood a chance.

"I hid," Tracey told me, ashamed.

I shook my head. "You did the right thing."

"The Floraes never made it into the Class Five dorms. The Guardians got to them first, but they were in the hall. I heard them. . . . I was so scared." She began to cry.

"Vivian was brave, but she did a very stupid thing," I told her. "You hid. You survived. There's nothing wrong with that."

"You helped," she said, sniffling. "You faced the Floraes and lived."

"Tracey, I had a gun," I explained. "I know how the

Floraes are, how they act."

"I'm so miserable, Amy. I can't sleep. I can't concentrate on my projects." Tracey wiped the tears from her face.

"It's okay. You need time." I hugged her and hoped it helped a little.

"My psyche-eval is up. I don't want to be sent to the Ward."

"You won't. It would be strange if you weren't sad and distracted right now." I thought about Dr. Reynolds and my body tensed. "If you're worried, though, try to focus on the good of New Hope, like all the great things Vivian accomplished before she . . ." I couldn't bring myself to say it. "Vivian was pretty kick-ass," I told her.

Tracey smiled weakly. "Yeah, she was. I just miss her so much."

"I miss her too." My voice caught in my throat and I swallowed hard. "We'll be okay," I said. "We've already survived the end of the world. . . . We can get through this too. There's nothing to worry about. We have a strong community here." Tracey looked at me like she believed what I was saying. For her sake, I hoped she did.

CHAPTER TWENTY-FOUR

The next day, a girl with black hair and pale skin is wheeled into the common room. I stare at her until her face blurs. I know her, but I don't know how. I try to concentrate, but it doesn't come to me. Frustrated, tears well up in my eyes.

"Amy, why are you crying?" Dr. Thorpe bends down in front of me. "Are you in pain?" She holds my wrist in her fingers, checking my heart rate.

"No . . . I . . ." I look to where the girl sits in her wheelchair. "Who is she?" I ask, motioning toward the newcomer.

"Just another citizen who needs to get better. We've

moved her from another floor."

"Do I know her?" I ask, frowning.

"If she's upsetting you, we'll have her removed." Dr. Thorpe finishes examining me and walks to the girl, swiftly wheeling her from the room.

I stare after her, but I can't trigger a memory. I hope I can remember to ask Rice when he comes. Maybe he knows who she is. Maybe he can help me remember. I try to think back again, and this time Kay comes to mind. I let myself focus on her instead.

• • •

"They're bringing in a group of post-aps if you want to tag along," Kay told me a few weeks later. "I can show you our protocol for arriving survivors." Something shifted that night when the sonic emitters broke. Her nasty edge was gone, and while she was still on my ass in training, she was more serious than sadistic. She even promised to take me out in the hover-copter so I could learn the controls. It was like she already considered me part of her crew.

We headed over to the hover-copter landing pad and waited for the post-aps to arrive. "Don't touch them," she warned me. "A lot of them aren't used to human contact. And obviously, keep the noise to a minimum."

"Obviously," I confirmed. I remembered too well what it was like to emerge from the hover-copter, freaked out and helpless. It was only a few months ago.

"It doesn't seem like you took this much care when you brought me in," I commented.

"I already knew you were a special case . . . and I wanted to punish you for shooting me. Twice."

"You're never going to let that go are you?"

"Not anytime soon, sunshine," she told me with a smirk.

"Kay, how did *you* make it here?" I asked. I'd never thought about it before.

"I was here when it happened, visiting my brother." Her expression changed and I wondered what she was remembering.

"Your brother worked for Hutsen-Prime?" I asked.

"And now he works for New Hope. He's such an overachiever. My parents always loved that about him." I detected a hint of jealousy in her voice.

"They didn't care that you were a superstar?" I had a Kay Oh and the Okays poster when I was twelve. I loved her blue hair.

"I was a joke." She didn't sound regretful exactly, more annoyed. "I'd rather be here, doing this." It almost sounded like she preferred the After. "I mean, it was awesome at first, don't get me wrong. They remade me, turned me into a sex symbol. I had stylists and assistants and assistants to my stylists."

"Sounds awful," I said sarcastically.

"It was, after a while."

"I don't understand," I admitted.

"No one ever does. You know, I wanted to be a cop," she told me. "When they started the Guardians, about a month after they announced the world was over, I was first in line to try out. It was great. Everyone thought I would fail horribly. People don't expect a small Japanese girl to be able to break a man's arm."

"They didn't assume you were a ninja?"

I was rewarded with one of Kay's rare laughs. "No. Of all their assumptions, ninja was not high on the list." She pointed toward the rising sun. "Here comes the copter. When they open the door, be prepared to detain the post-aps if they bolt, but only use violence as a last result."

"I never thought I'd hear you say that," I told her.

The hover-copter landed almost silently, only making noise when its bulk hit the soft ground. The door slid open and a child stepped out. He was about ten, sickly and malnourished. It was clear he was frightened. I smiled at him and to my surprise he smiled back, relief evident on his face.

The next person off was a woman–young and pale, with black hair. She looked around, bewildered, then found me. Her eyes went wide and I froze. Betrayal and hatred instantly flooded my system. "You!" I barked out.

I covered the distance between us in a few strides and within seconds my hands were around her neck. My fingers squeezed, her face turned red. She couldn't breathe but I didn't release her. I saw nothing but the girl's darkening face. My anger tuned out every sound but her last gasps for breath.

Like lightning, Kay's arm shot around my neck and the other Guardians grabbed my wrists. Something hard hit the base of my neck and I fell into blackness. The last thing I saw before my vision blurred was her, gasping for air.

Amber.

"Let me see her," I insisted from my hospital bed in the clinic. Kay brought me, told my mother I fainted on my morning run, that the heat was too much.

"You almost killed her. What the hell?" Kay asked.

I recounted all that had happened, a deep bitterness in my voice. I still despised Amber for her betrayal. I hated her for taking from me the one thing, the only thing, that was normal–my home.

When I finished, Kay whistled and shook her head. "Now I get why you wanted to choke her. There's no way I'm letting you near that girl."

I tried to sound calm. "I won't hurt her, Kay."

Kay raised her eyebrows at me.

"I *want* to hurt her, but I won't. I promise. I just need to talk to her and ask why she did it. Baby loved her. I trusted her." I couldn't continue. I wanted to cry and it was hard to swallow after the choke hold Kay had put on me.

Kay considered me. "You can see her, but only if I come along," she said at last.

"Agreed," I said quickly. "Where is she?"

"Two doors down the hall. She needed medical treatment too."

I stood, woozy. I held on to the bed for support until my head cleared. Eventually I was able to stand without fear of falling over. "Let's go."

"Be calm," Kay warned, motioning to the door, and I walked inside a room identical to mine. Amber was in bed, her eyes closed tight.

My eyes narrowed. "I know you're not sleeping," I told her. She still pretended, but I heard her breath quicken. "You sound like a bullhorn when you sleep."

She opened one of her eyes, then the other. "Are you here to kill me?" she asked, annoyingly innocent.

"I'm here to ask you why." I stared into her eyes until she looked away. "How could you do that to me and Baby?" I demanded.

"I didn't expect your voice to be so sweet," she told me. "You were so stubborn about not speaking with me . . . I always thought you'd have an irritating voice, high pitched, you know."

"I'm not here to discuss my voice," I said between clenched teeth.

She sniffed. "Oh, Amy, I didn't want to do it. But how could I say no to Paul? They saw you and Baby one day. They wanted to know where you were staying. You'd survived so long on your own and you didn't have a gang or bows or anything. They wanted to know how you did it. I thought about telling you the truth, staying with you and Baby, but I couldn't leave my brother. After what happened, when that Florae almost got you the night I left . . . I didn't think you'd want me around anyway. I had to go back to my brother, even though I hated the basement."

"What basement? I thought it was a bomb shelter. Did that not exist?" I growled.

"It did. Paul and I lasted six months in there. He protected me until we made our way to the city, and then he found the group to hook up with. He found us a safe place to stay. He saved me. We lived in the basement of some bank building. The Floraes couldn't get through the bars. . . ."

"How do you know to call them Floraes?" I asked. Until I came here, they were nameless creatures. They were just Them.

"That's just what everyone calls them in the other city."

I glanced at Kay, who levelly met my gaze. "What other city?" I asked. "What is she talking about?"

"Fort Black," Amber told me. "It's in Texas. That's where Paul and I were before we headed east and found our gang. They have walls surrounding the whole area."

"How many people live there?" I asked. *An entire other city.*

"I don't know. A lot. It's like the Wild West in there. That's why Paul and I left, to take our chances somewhere else."

"And where's your gang now?" I asked. "Why didn't you stay at my house?"

"They died there, all of them. We knew those copter things were picking up people so when I saw one, I ran at it."

I shook my head at her. She was lying. I couldn't listen any longer. I had to leave or I would hurt her again. I turned to the door.

"Wait. What about Baby?" she called. "Can I see her?"

"I will never let you near Baby again," I sneered.

She grimaced. "I've seen that mark she has . . . the one on her neck."

"What?" I froze.

"I've seen it on other children, in Fort Black."

"You are a liar." I clenched my fists, and Kay grabbed my shoulder, pushing me toward the door. In the hall, I paced back and forth.

"Let's go to the Rumble Room," Kay told me. "We can talk about things there."

"She needs to be watched," I told Kay as we walked. "I don't want her to be alone for an instant."

"Why?" Kay studied me.

"Because she'll make it her priority to fit in and find out how New Hope works. One day she's going to disappear and when she comes back, it will be to destroy everything we have."

"Look, Amy, even though you hold a grudge against that girl, you have to realize that New Hope is not some unprotected house in the middle of a Florae-infested city."

"No, at least I had a fence." New Hope was completely unprepared for the recent Florae attack and lied to cover it up. If the emitters weren't faulty, they must have been sabotaged.

I looked at Kay and wondered how much she knew, what she was keeping from me. My mother told me nothing, Rice only slightly more. Rice, who paid so much attention to Baby and noticed her scar right away. Did Amber tell the truth about other children with the same mark?

"We've increased security measures since the Incident," Kay said as we reached the Rumble Room. She scanned her key card with a glance over her shoulder and opened the door for me. "A teenage girl is not going to bring down New Hope."

I walked through the door, wanting to believe her. She was so confident. But I knew better. Amber was trouble.

"She wasn't lying about the city in Texas," Gareth told me later as we huddled together on a bench in the locker room.

He pulled me aside at practice after seeing how upset I was and I told him everything that had happened. "The Guardians know about it, but we were told to keep it a secret. I went there with my crew to see it with my own eyes."

"Everyone in New Hope thinks we're the only ones left," I said. I stood and began to pace, nervous energy coursing through my veins.

"Listen, Amy, it's better that way. Fort Black is a cesspool. There's no law or order. The strong prey on the weak." I watched him massage his left knee. It was giving him trouble lately but he didn't want anyone to know.

"And what is it here? People are lied to. People are given a reality that isn't real."

"Ignorance is bliss," Gareth said. "I'd rather not know myself. Believe me, it's much better here."

"Amber mentioned something"–I knelt to meet Gareth's eyes, choosing my words carefully–"about children in Fort Black being marked. . . ."

"What, like branded?"

"Maybe. Something about the back of their necks."

He looked at me blankly. "I didn't see anything like that." He shook his head. "Amber probably lied. She doesn't want you to go check it out so she's made up a story about children being mistreated so you'll stay here with Baby. If her brother died, she might see you as family in some crazy-cakes, delusional way."

"I know Amber was lying about her brother being dead." I continued to pace. "I see the way she talks about him, you know? If she's capable of love, she loves him. When she said he was dead, she said it like she was telling me the time."

"So you think we need to watch her?" Even Gareth sounded doubtful. "Did you tell Kay?"

"Kay said we had twenty Guardians and too much to do."

"You think that her gang can hurt us?" He raised his eyebrows.

"Look what two malfunctioning emitters did to us," I said. "Sometimes ignorance isn't bliss. Sometimes it's just dangerous."

"That doesn't change the fact that we don't have the manpower. I have to agree with Kay."

I sighed, giving up. I would keep an eye on her by myself if I had to.

"I have to tell you something," my mother said. "I know you've decided to become a Guardian." She didn't sound angry, more resigned. She stared down at the coffee table, deep in thought. She looked tired, with more wrinkles than I remembered.

"I think it's what's best for me," I told her.

"I agree," she said, to my surprise.

"You do?"

She looked at me wistfully. "I'm concerned, of course, but I think you'll be an excellent Guardian. You've always been a quick thinker and you've gained certain skills living with the Floraes. . . . I think this is the best way for you to help New Hope." She reached over to hug me.

"And there's something else we need to discuss." She hugged me closer. "When you class out, Adam is going to need his room back."

"Of course," I said. "Baby will move in with me."

"Baby can't live with you, not if you are going to be a Guardian," she told me quietly.

"What?" I pulled away from her. "Why not?"

"Guardians can't petition for parental rights. Their jobs are too dangerous. They don't keep a regular schedule."

"Neither do you," I said. "How much time do you spend with Adam? How much time did you spend with me when I was little?" I meant for it to hurt her and I could tell by her pinched face that it did.

"I'm just telling you the rules," my mother said.

"You help make the rules." I took a deep breath. "Can't you just move into a bigger apartment, so Baby can stay with you?" I asked. "Adam already thinks of her as a sister."

"I think it would be best for Baby to move to the dorm," my mother said.

"The dorm? You just don't want to be responsible for her," I accused.

"I love Baby," she told me. "But I have to help run New Hope and work on my research. I cannot be responsible for a six-year-old mute."

I looked at my mother, too angry to respond. I pushed back my chair and stalked off into the bedroom. Baby was asleep, oblivious that her fate had just been decided in the other room. I didn't know how she'd cope without me by her side. What's worse is that I didn't know how I could survive without her.

CHAPTER TWENTY-FIVE

I wake to my door opening. Someone slips silently into my room. I freeze, my breath catching.

"Honey. It's me," a smallish man with silver hair whispers and steps forward. Gareth. I exhale with relief.

"Is it time to go?" I ask hopefully.

"Not just yet, but I brought you these." He hands me a small orange envelope the size of my hand. "Keep it

somewhere safe," he whispers.

I take the package. Inside are a few dozen pills.

"Take one a day," Gareth instructs. "They counteract the meds they're giving you here."

"The cameras." My joy turns to fear.

"I've disabled them for a few minutes. Put the envelope under your mattress. Take the pills when you're in bed, under the covers."

I nod and he winks at me. "It won't be long."

"I'm scared," I admit.

"We're doing what we can for now." He stands and pauses by the door. "Stay sharp, Amy."

I take a pill and tuck the rest under my mattress.

• • •

In the following weeks, I ran. I ran and I trained and I took care of Baby and Adam. I didn't bother to go to class anymore. No one cared. I avoided my mother and Rice. It was easier than being with them and wondering what they knew.

I ran to the boundaries of New Hope and sometimes beyond. The sonic emitters were checked daily after the Incident. But still, no one knew why they failed that night, or at least that's what they said.

I was at an emitter, beyond the farm. I'd never run that

far south before and I was eager to explore. The ground was grassy there, though there were plenty of trees, and I wondered if the forest was a transplant, a way to hide the compound. It was probably all done Before, when New Hope was a university funded by Hutsen-Prime. If it was a top secret research facility, they would have wanted to keep it shielded from curious eyes.

I stopped at the sonic emitter to stretch, and I heard faint voices. My first impulse was to leave, not wanting to be around people. But then I recognized one of them and crept closer, careful to remain quiet and unseen behind a tree.

"But I like it here. You don't understand what they–"

"We stick to the plan, Amber," a male voice interrupts her. "We've already made the decision."

"But this place is different from what we're used to. It's organized; the people are good. They don't have to hurt each other to get ahead. They're all working together."

"Because they have what everyone else wants. Safety and supplies. They take all that's left out there. Is there anything they don't have a surplus of?"

I peeked out to watch them. The man was tall and pale with shadowy black hair. He looked like Amber and I knew that this must be her brother, Paul.

"We could leave the gang. You can live here too. We can tell them everything, break away, get on their good side."

"Oh, come on, you can't be serious. I wouldn't want to live here with these brainwashed idiots. It's worse than a cult, Amber. Besides, what would we say? 'Sorry we trashed your precious anti-Florae devices. Sorry all those people died. . . . We'd like to join your comfy little society now.' I'm sure they'd welcome us with open arms," he spat.

"We could leave out that part," Amber pleaded.

"Enough." Paul shook his head. "You'll get in line or I'll tell the rest of the gang you turned on us."

"You wouldn't," Amber said, horrified.

"I may not have a choice," his voice softened. "Not if you decide to ruin everything."

I backed a few steps away, blending into the woods. As much as I wanted to run away, I didn't. Amber couldn't be allowed to disappear again, it was too dangerous for all of us. I moved back through the trees, their leaves catching at my clothing as I forced myself to make noise.

"Hello?" I called, stepping into the clearing. "Is someone there?" I made a hell of a racket before emerging. Even so, Paul barely hid in time and I pretended not to see him.

"Amber! I thought I was the only one who ran this far

out here," I said loudly.

"Oh," Amber's face was frozen in shock. She looked down at her sandals and sundress, unsure. "Yeah, I was out for a run."

"Well, I'm glad we ran into each other, pardon the pun." I forced a laugh. "Listen, Amber, I've been meaning to have breakfast with you, to welcome you to New Hope." I made my voice sweet and hoped Paul would be convinced and think that all citizens of New Hope were trusting and gullible.

Amber stared at me, then glanced to where Paul was barely concealed. She was debating whether or not to bolt. I moved forward and grabbed her hand.

"Come on," I said, pulling her back toward New Hope, away from Paul. "I think there are pancakes this morning."

I led her by the hand until we were nearly to the farm. I listened carefully, making sure that Paul hadn't followed us, but I waited until we got back to the buildings to really talk.

"Amy, it's not what you think," she pleaded.

"Was that Paul?" I asked. She looked away. "You said he died." I didn't bother to hide my disgust.

"I lied," she said, looking up with tears in her eyes. Crocodile tears.

"I heard your conversation," I told her. "I know you're responsible for the Florae breach. I also know you and your brother have something else planned."

"It's all Bear's idea," she blubbered. "He's in charge. I didn't want to be their spy, but they made me. I told them we should just live here like normal people, but no one ever listens to me. Not even Paul."

"Look, Amber, I think you've let bad people influence you in order to survive. But you're here now and you can do more than just get by. You can live."

She swallowed, wiped her nose on her arm. "I do like it here." She looked up at me, hopeful. "If I tell you everything, can I stay?" she asked.

"I don't see why not," I assured her.

"And Paul?" she asked. "I don't care about the rest of them, but I want Paul to live here too."

"I'll talk to the director about it, but Amber"–I made sure she understood–"you have to tell the truth. You have one chance to get this right. If I find out you've lied, I'll take you out beyond the barrier and tie you to a tree. Then I'll set off a car alarm just out of your reach."

She considered, trying to decide if I was bluffing or not. The thought of making anyone Florae bait was abhorrent, but I could make an exception for Amber.

"Okay," she finally said.

"The first attack was meant to cause panic, make the people here doubt the system." I explained what Amber had told me as precisely as I could. She'd already been apprehended and taken by the Guardians to a secure location.

"Terrorists," Marcus muttered. The meeting room was occupied by several Guardians as well as Rice, my mother, and Dr. Reynolds. There were also a bunch of people I didn't know. The ones in lab coats were probably researchers who worked with my mother and helped make decisions. The remaining handful were more imposing, and even silent they maintained a commanding presence. Ex-military personnel, I guessed.

"Amber said that they estimated only a few people would die, not hundreds. When they found out how much damage they did, they realized how unprepared we are for an attack of any kind. They're planning another sonic emitter outage tonight. They want to push the Floraes toward us, then show up and save the day. Thanks to Amber, they know who the key players are here. They plan to take you all out, leaving New Hope without any leadership or direction. Since they will have saved New Hope and have a lot of firepower, they assume that they can fill the power void."

"They want to destroy everything we've worked for," Dr. Reynolds said, his doughy face grim.

"How many are there?" Gareth asked.

"Amber said forty-two men, eighteen women, and two Class Four children." The categorization slipped automatically from my mouth. "And they have a lot of firepower. Guns when they want to make noise and bows when they don't."

"Which emitters are they going to hit?" Kay asked.

"All of them." I paused. "Just like last time," I stressed, letting them come to the realization that I knew the true details of the earlier attack. I knew that the story about only two emitters failing was a lie.

"They will enter to our south and split up, working their way around us to disable the emitters. A main force will stay put, just south of the farm. That's where I found Amber today. They plan to push the Floraes in from there. Unfortunately I don't know if they'll change their attack strategy now that Amber didn't leave New Hope to meet up with them. I heard her express her unease with their plan to her brother. If he tells the rest of his gang, they may assume she's turned on them."

"Thank you, Amy," Dr. Reynolds said, his voice crisp. "If you remember anything else, let us know immediately. You can leave now."

I swallowed hard. "No."

Dr. Reynolds's eyes narrowed, and next to him my mother's mouth dropped open. Kay smiled. My mother recovered first. "Excuse me?" she asked as though she hadn't heard me properly. "What did you just say to Dr. Reynolds?"

"I'm staying to hear the plan."

"Amy, your presence is no longer required."

"This is what you have," I told them. "Twenty Guardians against sixty-two armed thugs. You have synth-suits and technology, but they're desperate killers who are herding the Floraes back toward us. They let hundreds die without blinking an eye. How are you going to patrol the entire perimeter of New Hope with twenty people?" I asked.

"Cameras," Rice said. "Can we set up cameras in time?"

"We can try," Gareth offered. "It will take too long to make a run to an electronics store; first we'd have to find one that hasn't been ransacked. Maybe we can take the cameras from the research buildings and move them to the outer perimeter."

"That will alert them to what we know," I warned.

Kay stood up. "We need to deal with this now. If we spook them and they run away, we don't know when they'll attack again, or who they'll tell about us. Next time, there could be a hundred armed thugs. We should take most of our people and wait at the place Amber indicated. We'll catch them before they start to disable the emitters. We can have volunteers, trusted people, at certain strategic locations around the perimeter. They can radio us if anything looks out of place."

"I volunteer," I said immediately.

"Kay, what's your opinion on us accepting my underage daughter's assistance?" my mother asked.

Kay looked at me and sighed. "She's a child. She can't help us." I glanced at her and she gave me a hard look. Kay still didn't want my mother to know she was secretly training me.

"I agree," Marcus said and, one by one, they went around the room and said that I was too young. Rice was the only holdout.

"We need her," he told the group.

"There is not enough evidence to suggest you will have a major effect on the outcome, Amy." Dr. Reynolds commanded everyone's attention. "We cannot sacrifice our children to fear. We have made our decision. Please leave the room."

I forced myself to stay silent as I got up and walked to the door. Why did they get to decide what I could do? I was the one who spotted Amber and her brother. I was the one who got Amber to tell me all she knew.

The door shut. I was once again in the dark.

CHAPTER TWENTY-SIX

I take one of the pills Gareth gave me every morning. Along with being clearer, the memories are coming back more quickly now. I'm careful when I speak to the nurses and Dr. Thorpe, not to seem better or worse. I play nice, just as Rice advised. I've managed to fool them so far, even under the watchful lens of the cameras.

I haven't seen Frank around, but I notice Amber in the

corner. I know it's Amber now; she's triggered a lot of memories for me. I go to sit next to her. No matter how I feel about her, she's something familiar in this awful place.

"How are you?" I ask a little resentfully.

"I'm fine. Just fine." She looks at me. "Are you a nurse here?"

"No, Amber, it's me, Amy." I drop the attitude. "Don't you remember me?"

She stares at me. "You're Amy. . . . You had a sister, right?"

"That's right. Baby," I prompt.

"Did they kill her too?"

The blood rushes to my head as I panic. "What do you mean?" Rice said Baby was doing fine. Amber ignores me so I shake her shoulder. "Amber, what do you mean about them killing Baby?" I ask desperately.

She looks at me sadly. "They killed my brother, you know. Then they put me in here. I thought maybe the same thing happened to you."

"Oh." I try to relax, but my heart still races. "No, I don't think I'm here for the same reasons you are."

"Then why are you here?" she asks.

I glance around the room. In addition to the cameras and the watchful gaze of the orderlies, Dr. Reynolds has arrived and is observing us. I sit back, making my face passive.

"I don't know," I whisper.

Dr. Reynolds comes over. I do my best not to look as agitated as I feel.

"Hello, girls." He smiles at us. "I hate to interrupt, but it's time for Amber's treatment." He holds out his hand for her and she takes it, almost eagerly. Dr. Reynolds leads her away without a backward glance at me.

Where are they taking her? *I stand to follow them, but the orderly is watching and I sit back down, on edge. I don't want to think about all the things they could be doing to her. I distract myself by trying to remember again. There was another time I was being watched, not in the Ward, but in my mother's apartment. I focus, willing my mind to clear and for the thought to become a memory.*

•••

I knew they would send someone to keep an eye on me, but I didn't think it would be her. I knew they couldn't spare a Guardian. I was hoping for a Minder, or someone who didn't know me. My mother, on the other hand, was more than capable of seeing through my bullshit. Not that she was just sitting there watching me; she was working on her computer and talking on the phone. She tried to whisper so I wouldn't hear, which drove me crazy. Even while engrossed in her work, she knew my every move.

"Where are you going?" she asked, not bothering to look up from her computer.

"My bedroom. Chill out." While out of her sight, I grabbed the tiny headset I took from my synth-suit earlier and shoved it in my pocket.

Baby, can you help me with something? I asked.

Sure, what?

Let's go up to the roof and I'll explain.

I held Baby's hand and approached my mother at her desk. "I can't stand it in here," I said. "I need some fresh air. I want to go up to the roof with Baby."

"Absolutely not," she said absently.

"Do you seriously think I would do anything to harm her?" I argued. "I just want to be outside, not cooped up."

"Fine, I'll come with you." She stood.

"Mom, I kind of want to be away from you right now." It sounded hateful, but I needed her to stay. She shook her head.

"You can watch us go up," I told her. "I wouldn't leave Baby alone on a roof. Also, I don't have any weapons and I don't even know if you all changed the plan after I left the room. I'm many things, Mom, but I'm not stupid."

"Fine, Amy, go. If I find out you're up to something . . ."

I rushed out the door before she could change her mind, dragging Baby behind me.

We found a spot next to the solar panels and sat down. *Why are we up here?* Baby asked. *It's hot.*

I know, but I want you to listen very hard for me and tell me if you hear anything strange.

There are two people arguing downstairs about a broken cup. . . .

No, I signed, *I mean if you hear the emitters turn off again, or a truck . . . something weird like that.*

We sat on the roof and waited. I knew Baby was bored. *Have you made a lot of friends at school?* I asked her, although I already knew she had.

She nodded and named them all, spelling out their names. I was impressed with how fast she'd learned her letters.

Do a lot of your friends live in the dorm?

Yes. Most.

I worked up my courage and finally asked, *Would you like to live in the dorm?*

She looked at me, surprised. *I want to live with you and Adam.*

What if you can't? I was a little ashamed because it was my decision that would land her in the dorm.

Then I guess it would be okay. I'd get to be with my friends at least. She paused, staring at me. *Where are you going?* she asked, worried.

Nowhere. Next month is my birthday and I won't be a red anymore; I'll be an adult. I may not be able to take you.

Why not? She stopped suddenly, tilted her head.

What is it? I asked.

A noise, like when we found Amber, only louder. She meant a truck.

Where?

She pointed and I grabbed the earpiece from my pocket and pressed the little button on the side. "Kay," I shouted.

"Owww, what? Who is this and why are you yelling?"

"Sorry." I lowered my voice. "It's Amy."

"How did you . . . ?"

"Never mind. Look, Amber was wrong or they changed the plan. They're not coming from the south. They're northwest right now, near the lake. They're in trucks."

"We're on it," she responded. The earpiece went dead.

It only took me a second to make my decision. I hurried to the corner of the roof where I'd stashed a bag earlier. I took out the black clothes from the bag and hastily put them on.

The creatures are back. I'm going to go help, I signed quickly. *You stay put. You'll be safe here.*

Baby nodded. I grabbed the last thing I stashed–my mother's newly recovered Guardian gun. *You just listen for Them and hide when They are near.*

She nodded again and signed, *I know, Amy, like how we used to live.*

I made my way down the fire escape and hit the ground running, heading quickly toward the lake. On my morning jogs, it took about twelve minutes to get out there. I made it in ten.

It took me a moment to understand what I was seeing. The Guardians weren't fighting Floraes; they were fighting ordinary people. Where were the creatures? The Guardians were being careful not to use their weapons, trying to subdue the gang without killing them. I tucked my gun into my waistband and rushed toward the nearest Guardian in trouble. Even though he was in his full synth-suit and I couldn't see his face, I knew it was Gareth, fighting three large men.

I tackled the nearest assailant and put him in a headlock the way Kay had taught me. By the time he was knocked out, Gareth had already incapacitated the other two men.

He tossed me a handful of plastic handcuffs and I cinched one around the unconscious man's wrists.

Flooded with adrenaline, I hit the ground and crawled forward on my hands and knees. Someone, a woman, tripped over me and I jumped on top of her, struggling to keep her down. Pressing sideways with all my weight, I managed to rock her onto her stomach. She groaned loudly as I shoved my knee between her shoulder blades and handcuffed her as quickly as I could.

Crouching low, I made my way forward, more carefully this time. The trucks were now in sight, and a Guardian was trying to wrestle a man from the driver's seat. The man got free for an instant and slammed the Guardian's arm in the door. I recognized the resulting yell as Rob's and I hoped his arm wasn't broken. I was about to go help them when I spotted a group of Floraes in a cage in the back of the truck.

I reached for the gun at my waist, ready to shoot, but the creatures were bizarrely placid. They stood almost still, rocking slightly as if in a gentle breeze. Creeping up to the cage, I peered closely at Them. The creatures were wearing headphones over their almost nonexistent ears, held in place with duct tape wrapped securely around their heads. This was how they did it? Noise-reduction headphones?

Suddenly two gunshots rang out and I turned in time to see Gareth crumple to the ground. Behind me the Florae were going berserk. The gunshots were loud enough for Them to hear through the headphones. I glanced at the cage, which was holding, before I ran to Gareth.

"Are you all right?" I helped him sit up, scanning for the shooter. Kay already had someone on the ground and was kicking him repeatedly in the ribs.

"I'm . . . fine. . . ." Gareth told me between gasps. I pulled up his hood to examine his face. "The suit . . . stopped the bullets . . . but it hurts. . . ." He coughed loudly. "Hurts like hell." He gingerly rubbed his chest and then tried unsuccessfully to stand. I helped him get to his feet and let him lean on me, supporting most of his weight.

"He okay?" Kay asked, pulling off her hood as she jogged over.

"I'm just peachy." Gareth's attempt to smile turned into a pained grimace.

Kay looked at me. "You shouldn't be here."

"I know. I wanted to help. . . . Are the Floraes secure?" They'd quieted down since the gunshots.

"Yes, as long as they're wearing that headgear. How did you know which direction the trucks were coming from?"

There was no reason not to trust them, but I noticed Marcus hovering nearby. I motioned with my eyes toward him.

Kay understood my hesitation. "Marcus," she yelled, "you and the Elite Eight should do a quick run of the perimeter. Make sure it's secure." Marcus glared at her, but grunted an affirmative. After he'd gone, Kay turned back to me expectantly.

"It was Baby," I said at last. "She has extra-sensitive hearing."

"She heard the trucks?" Gareth asked, unbelieving. He winced slightly. "From halfway across New Hope?" I nodded. "Honey, that's not extra sensitive, that's supersonic."

I watched their faces nervously, hoping I hadn't made a mistake.

"Don't worry," Kay said, "we won't tell your mother."

"Why would my mother care?" I asked uneasily.

Kay and Gareth gave each other a look. "Believe me, this is something you do not want her to know. She would incorporate Baby into her Florae research."

My blood ran cold. "What? Why?"

Kay frowned. "Listen, Amy, your mother *only* sees what's good for New Hope."

I swallowed hard, pushing down my sudden anxiety. I

was still shaking my head slightly.

Kay reached past me, guiding Gareth to lean on her, relieving me of his weight. "You'd better hustle so you can get back before the director notices you're gone," Kay told me. "I'll wait a few minutes to report in."

I gave Kay and Gareth a curt nod before I took off at full speed. When I reached my building, I hurriedly climbed up the fire escape and frantically changed into my jumpsuit on the roof. I quickly shoved my dark clothes and gun back into the bag. I barely had time to stash it before my mother appeared on the roof.

"I guess everything went well," I said, trying not to look nervous or guilty.

My mother studied me. "Everything is fine, Amy. You shouldn't worry about it. Trust me."

I smiled weakly, unsure. Kay warned me *not* to trust her. My own mother. Unconvinced, Baby and I followed her downstairs.

The next morning, I caught my mother before she left for work. "What's going to happen to Amber?" I asked. "Where's her gang?"

"Amber was released. The others were taken care of,"

she said, closing her computer before I could see the screen.

"Were they sent to the Ward?"

"The Ward is where citizens can go to get the help they need," she said irritably. "It's not for criminals."

"Then were they expelled?" I asked, confused. What punishment would releasing them be when they already survived so well in the After?

"No," my mother muttered, annoyed. She didn't want to tell me.

"What about Paul, Amber's brother? Is there any chance he'll be released?"

"No," she said with finality. My mother wanted the conversation over.

"Can't you rehabilitate them?" I pressed. "There's got to be some work they can do for the community, some way they can contribute even if they aren't freed."

"No, Amy, there is no chance that any of them will live in New Hope."

"Why not?" I demanded, refusing to back down.

She turned to me and sighed. "Because they're dead. All of them," she told me quietly.

I looked at her, shocked.

"Dr. Reynolds and I . . ." She rubbed her temples.

"Sometimes the people in charge have to make difficult decisions."

"Spare me the rhetoric," I sneered.

"Would you rather they were let loose on New Hope? Can you imagine the damage?" She tried to defend herself.

I shook my head, sickened. "But you let Amber go."

"Dr. Reynolds will keep her under close observation. He said that she might eventually fit in here."

"Did he?" I asked angrily. "And is he the one who decided the others should die or was that you?"

"Amy, I . . ." She moved toward me and tried to hug me, but I shook her off.

"Dad protested against things he thought were wrong, like capital punishment." I glared at her. "How do you think he would have felt about this? About New Hope's policies? About forced psychiatric evaluations?"

"It's different when you're responsible for the last members of the human race. We don't have the luxury of your father's kind of thinking now."

"It doesn't help our numbers to sacrifice them."

"We collected their genetic material first. . . . We need a cohesive community here. It's essential."

I looked at my mother in disgust and rushed out of the

apartment, repulsed by her clinical detachment about what anyone else would call murder.

• • •

Rice hasn't come to visit for a while—I think it's been days—and there hasn't been any word from Kay or Gareth. I try not to show my fear, but I'm becoming more and more nervous. I have trouble sleeping and Dr. Thorpe has commented on the dark circles under my eyes.

I try to keep my mind busy. I watch the doctors, the nurses, the orderlies. I wonder which of them really think they're helping us, and which know our treatment is an act.

I also study the other patients. There are thirty on my floor. I sit in the common room and wonder what they each did to be put in here. I change seats to sit next to Amber. She doesn't acknowledge my presence.

"Amber?" When she still doesn't move, I go on. "I saw you the other day."

She continues to stare forward. I put my hand on her shoulder, take her head with my other hand, and turn her toward me. Her eyes are blank, unseeing. The side of her head is shaved, revealing a long row of stitches. I drop my hands, horrified.

"Oh, Amber." I feel like I'm going to be sick. Breathing

heavily, I place my cold hands on my flushed face. I can't get enough air and feel faint. I begin to hyperventilate, but make myself slow my breathing, desperately trying to remain calm.

When I've composed myself, I look again at Amber. A glob of drool gathers at the corner of her mouth, and I use my sleeve to wipe it away. "I'm so sorry that this happened to you," I tell her.

I hated Amber for so long, but now I only pity her. She was just trying to survive. No one should suffer this. No one deserves to be forced into oblivion.

•••

"Did you know?" I asked Kay. I'd waited for her all day to come back from her secret mission, which was most likely making sure there were no more gangs in the surrounding area, ready to pounce on New Hope. I finally caught her in the locker room.

"Hello to you, too." Her voice lacked its normal bite and when she looked at my face, she dropped the sarcastic tone altogether. "I didn't know what they were going to do with them, no."

"It's barbaric," I spit.

"It's necessary." Kay looked around the Rumble Room, lowering her voice. "I thought we should detain them, put them in the Ward to recondition them, commission a couple of guards, but I'm not the big boss. The director and Reynolds make the final decisions."

I hated how everyone rationalized the massacre. Even Kay. I needed to be alone. Away from the propaganda and the blind loyalty. I ran out to the edges of New Hope, wandering restlessly. I stayed out well after sunset, reveling in the darkness, comforted by the quiet. When I got home, I went straight to my room and shut the door. Baby was already in bed so I curled up next to her.

"Amy?" I heard my mother calling from the other room, but I ignored her. "Amy," she said again from the doorway. "I . . . we have to talk."

I turned on my side to glare, but when I saw her worried expression, I sat up. She motioned me to come into the living room, where she sat on the couch. I settled in as far away from her as possible. I stared at the floor.

"Amy, look at me. Dr. Reynolds expressed some concerns to me. . . ."

"What? What concerns?" I asked snippily.

"That you don't respect authority," she told me unhappily. "That you like to pry into things that don't concern you. That you may not have New Hope's best interests in mind."

My head snapped up. "Dr. Reynolds wants to send me to the Ward?" I asked, horrified.

My mother pressed her lips together and nodded. "But he won't just yet, as a favor to me. Because my research is so important, he doesn't want me distressed in any way."

"So the only reason I'm not in the Ward is because of *you*?" I let that sink in. "What about Baby?"

"Baby is fine," she assured me. "She's fitting in with all the other children, learning to read and write, to communicate. We're confident her vocal skills will come eventually. I thought it would be best for both of you if we began to sever your connection to her."

"What? No! That's crazy." I wanted to jump up but I had nowhere to run to. Instead I folded my arms across my chest and tried to stay calm. I knew that I couldn't afford to freak out again. "Is that why you want her in the dorm?" I asked, my voice trembling. "Do you think that's really necessary?"

"I don't know, Amy. I just want you to be safe." She reached for my hand. "Becoming a Guardian will be a good start. You can prove yourself. Until then, you have to try harder."

"I will, I promise," I told her, all my fight gone. I held on to her, still in shock about how close I was to losing Baby.

"Mom . . . I have to know."

"I can't tell you about my research." She squeezed my hand.

"No, it's not that. I want to know if you're really on board with all of this."

She let go of my hand and gave me a hard look. "I did what had to be done. Before you got here, Amy, New Hope was my whole life. Even Adam was a result of a regulation *I* helped establish. We have to protect New Hope. It's the only possible future of humanity. Otherwise, we should just let the Floraes in. It's not only about us. It's about the generations that will follow. It's about our future."

I looked into her shining eyes with a sad understanding. I knew now that Kay was absolutely right. My mother could never learn about Baby's incredible hearing. Finding me in a restricted area wasn't harmful to New Hope, so she hid it. My becoming a Guardian will not only show that I can fit in, but will help protect New Hope. Everything she did, she weighed with the benefit of New Hope in mind. If she thought they could use Baby, study her, dissect her to find out how she ticked, she would do it willingly.

"I love you so much, honey. It's hard, I know, but we will

make it . . . and so will this community." She hugged me tightly and kissed me on the top of my head.

I closed my eyes and wondered which my mother would choose if it came down to it: me or New Hope?

CHAPTER TWENTY-SEVEN

I see Dr. Samuels in the hall, but I try not to make eye contact. I want him to think I don't know who he is, that I'm sufficiently drugged. He comes to me, though, looks me up and down.

"Amy, I want to apologize." He clears his throat. "I was wrong to recommend your electroshock treatment. There's a reason it's only used to treat extremely severe cases of

depression. I should have considered your circumstances more carefully. I shouldn't have let Dr. Reynolds influence my professional opinion."

The pain, the torment I endured, comes flooding back and it takes everything I have not to lash out at him.

"I've begun to think . . . ," he continues in a whisper, "that Dr. Reynolds may not have your best interest in mind." I can't help but flinch when he puts his hand on my shoulder.

"Don't touch me," I say between clenched teeth. Dr. Samuels stares at me. He sees the hate in my eyes and begins to back away.

"I was only trying to help," he tells me guiltily.

"If you want to help me, get Rice." I glance at the cameras in the hallway. "I miss him. I wish he could visit more often," I say loudly.

"Yes, of course." Dr. Samuels studies me, and I can tell he sees beyond my drugged act. Still, his remorse seems to outweigh his loyalty to Dr. Reynolds and he says, "I'll let Rice know you've been asking for him. Or perhaps, one of the Guardians?"

My head snaps up. "Kay or Gareth," I whisper. "Not Marcus," I breathe, hoping the camera microphones won't pick up what I just said.

He leaves me, with a curt nod. I continue down the hall, careful to shuffle my feet and keep my head low.

•••

The Guardian test was on my birthday. I'd thought of nothing else since my mother and I had our talk three weeks ago.

I looked in the mirror. I was seventeen, an adult according to New Hope, but I still felt like a child. Baby had already moved into the dorm and I'd soon have a one-bedroom, picked out in a building near the Rumble Room, where the Guardians lived.

I stretched and put on my running clothes. My mother had left me a note on the kitchen counter: *Happy Birthday, Amy, and good luck. You can do it! See you tonight at your party. Love you.* I slipped on my shoes and headed out the door, stopping by the dorm. I stood under Baby's window and whispered her name as low as I could. In just a few seconds, she stuck her head out the window, waving at me excitedly.

Happy Birthday, Amy! she signed. *Test today?*

Yes. I'll see you afterward for my party.

Good luck! She turned back to her roommates, her new friends. She had no idea how important the test really was, but it was probably better that way.

I noticed a lot of people on the way to the Rumble Room, way more than could be coincidence. Gareth was there, clutching a clipboard and making ticks across the paper.

"What's up?" I called to him.

He grinned. "Biggest testing day ever," he told me.

"How many applicants?" I asked, trying to get a glimpse of the list.

"Two hundred and nineteen. I get to check everyone in and record times for the distance run. Joy," he said sarcastically.

"How many do you think will make it?" I asked.

"Hell, I'll settle for ten trainees and one spanking-new Guardian." He winked at me and I hoped his trust wasn't misplaced. "Go on. Line up with the fresh meat."

It wasn't long before Kay got on a loudspeaker. "Okay, everyone, we're going to put you into groups now. If you fail a trial, you're cut. If you stray from the group, you're cut. If you whine or complain, you're cut. Group one," she hollered. "All adults between the ages of seventeen and twenty-one, you're with Jenny." Jenny was waving her arms, indicating who she was.

"Okay, guys," Jenny told us when everyone was gathered around. "We're going to do a five-mile run now. I'll set the pace, but you can go ahead if you want, the path is marked. Anyone who can't at least match my pace will be cut."

I smiled and kicked off my shoes. I started off with the group, but soon pulled ahead. We followed the markers, bits of orange plastic tied along the trees and in bushes. I began to outpace everyone but a tall guy with annoyingly long legs. Little by little I inched ahead, pushing myself harder than I had ever before. My legs started to hurt and my chest ached with each breath.

When I saw the finish line, Gareth standing with clipboard in hand, I forgot all the pain in my muscles and chest and ran like I was being chased by a Florae. I finished first, barely, the tall man right on my heels. Gareth recorded our times on his clipboard. I wanted to collapse on the floor, but instead I kept walking so my legs wouldn't cramp.

"Save something for the other tests, guys," Gareth chastised, but I knew he was proud I'd won.

When I'd recovered, I searched for Kay. She was busy speaking with some of the other Guardians, but when she saw me she raised her eyebrows. I held up my index finger to indicate I was first, and she smirked, pleased. I was no longer Amy. I was a reflection on the director and the Guardians. And I knew that would be my ticket to freedom.

• • •

The next day I spot Frank's dark curly hair from across the hall. I haven't seen him for a while, not since his last outburst. I follow him to his door.

"Hi." I glance up at the camera. "I'm Amy; we've met," I tell him, wondering how I can ask him about the Floraes without giving myself away.

"Oh, hi. Would you like to see what I've been working on?" he asks me with a grin.

I'm surprised by his mild manner. It's almost as if we're in Advanced Theory and I'm looking at his idea. I step into his room and stare at his wall. He's managed to draw all over it. At first it looks like scribbles but there is a method to the madness. Diagrams and numbers. Chemical structures.

"They let you do this?" I ask.

"It gets painted over sometimes, but Dr. Thorpe thinks it's therapeutic."

I step closer. "What does it mean?"

"This"—he points at an equation—"is the basic structure of a Florae cell."

I study the numbers. "I'm sorry. I don't understand," I tell him. "What does it mean?"

"It means . . ." He grins. "That the human race is doomed."

He starts to laugh hysterically. "Don't you see it? It's us. We're the problem. Not them!"

His sudden change in behavior scares me, and I back out of the room before the orderlies arrive.

Frank's outburst has triggered a memory, though. It is almost clear. . . . I think back to the day of my Guardian test, trying desperately to remember.

•••

After the first trial, only twenty-five people in our group remained. Our next two tests were marksmanship and hand-to-hand combat. I did fine in both, but quite a few more people were cut, including a girl who almost shot herself in the face while peering into the barrel of her gun.

Next, Jenny led us outside to a rope ladder that snaked up a tree trunk and was strung between two trees like a bridge, with bells tied in various locations. Jenny explained the stealth trial, telling us we had to cross the bridge. If you rang a bell, you were out.

Applicant after applicant failed. Finally Jenny yelled my name.

"Harris." She looked at me, with a nod, and said, "Show them how it's done."

I walked to the ladder, shaking out my hands and feet,

still barefoot from the run earlier. I took a deep breath and reached for the rope, clearing my head of all doubts.

I made my way carefully up the ladder, mindful of keeping my weight evenly distributed. My heart was beating so hard, I didn't notice anything beyond the task. I scurried across the bridge, cautious not to disturb the rope and ring a bell. At the end, I lowered myself using just my hands. My feet touched the dirt and I spun around to face the people who were left.

Jenny smiled. "See. It can be done," she told the group.

I breathed a sigh of relief. In the end, only four other people passed.

"Last trial, guys." Jenny yelled. We followed her back into the Rumble Room and up the stairs to the second floor, where I'd never been before. She sat us in a room, then came to collect us one by one. I saw the others leave and wondered what was going to happen next.

"Amy, you're up," Jenny said, smiling. I followed her down the hall to a black door.

"Go inside," she ordered. Taking a deep breath, I put my fingers on the handle and pushed. I entered a small room with a large machine. Old-fashioned headphones hung off it, dangling toward an empty chair.

"Have a seat, Amy," Nick said. "We're just going to test your hearing."

I barked out a laugh. "A hearing test? Shouldn't you do this first?"

"Just put on the headphones," Nick grumbled. "You're going to hear several beeps, sometimes in your left ear, sometimes your right, and sometimes both. If you hear a beep in your left ear, raise your left hand. If you hear a beep in your right ear . . ."

"I think I've got it," I snapped, feeling silly I'd gotten all worked up over a stupid hearing test.

After passing, I went back downstairs, where all the surviving applicants had gathered. Of the two hundred–plus people who began, only about twenty remained.

Kay appeared. "Congratulations! You have today to move your things into the barracks. You'll begin your training first thing tomorrow morning . . . unless any of you think you're ready to take the final trial. We highly recommend that you train first."

"I'll take it," I said. There were a few sharp intakes of breath but none of the Guardians were surprised.

"All right, kiddo." Kay smiled. "Let's get you suited up and ready to go. The locker room is this way," she told me as if I didn't already know.

I followed her and headed to the locker where my synth-suit was already waiting.

"You did remarkably well today," Kay said. I ignored the rare compliment and pulled open my locker. After I retrieved the contents, I shakily slammed the door. "Are you okay?" Kay asked.

I turned to her. "I'm just . . ." I searched for the right word. My entire future depended on how I performed next. If I didn't get control of my nerves, I'd be in trouble. I couldn't afford to fail, not if I wanted to stay in New Hope.

"I can't tell you what the test is, Amy. You need to succeed by yourself, or we can't make you a Guardian. This isn't fun and games. You could get seriously hurt."

"Has anyone died during this test?" I hadn't allowed myself to wonder about the physical danger I might be in.

"Just put on the synth-suit and meet me outside."

I pulled on the soft, strong material of the synth-suit. It hugged my body snuggly and I was comforted by the softness against my skin. I stretched, shook out my arms and legs, trying to stay calm.

I rechecked my weapons: a Guardian gun and two knives. Both knives were intact and real, no practice knives this time. I tucked one into each leg sheath and walked slowly back to the Rumble Room, where Kay and the Guardians were waiting. Everyone was gathered around Marcus.

"What's going on?" I asked Nick.

"Not sure, but your test has been postponed."

"It's more important now than ever," Marcus was almost shouting, "that the Guardians are one cohesive unit. The final test needs a higher level of rigor for the security of us all and the greater good of New Hope."

I heard a snort behind me and turned to catch Gareth roll his eyes.

"Dr. Reynolds has devised some new tests, trials that each potential Guardian will have to pass. These tests are still in the works, so until then, there will be no new Guardians."

"What about Amy?" Kay asked. "She has to have her test. . . ."

Marcus looked at me, already in my synth-suit. "I think Amy has proven herself time and again."

"Well, that's for damn sure," Gareth said from behind me.

"Unless you object, Kay, I think we should approve

Amy's Guardian status." Marcus looked at her levelly. "It's your decision."

Kay met his gaze, her face stony. "We'll have to get the committee's approval. . . ."

"We can bring it to them tonight." Marcus's smile was mocking. "I'm sure they'll give their consent."

Kay considered. "Amy's in," she said at last.

I released the breath I was holding. "So that's it?" I asked. "I'm a Guardian now?"

"Looks like." Kay patted me on the shoulder and the other Guardians clapped. She leaned in and whispered, "I don't know what Marcus and his military cronies are up to, but you do deserve this."

I wanted to hug her but I knew she wasn't the hugging type. I let my exhaustion sink in. I just wanted to go tell Baby and my mother that I passed.

Marcus approached me with a weird, satisfied look on his face. "Okay, Amy, your first job as a Guardian is to retrieve the trail markers we used for the run. You can put them in the Rumble Room office."

"All right." I was tired and disappointed to have to do such a tedious chore, but at least I was a Guardian.

Five minutes into my task, I heard Marcus's voice again. "Amy!"

My hand went to my communicator in my hood at my ear. "Yes. I'm here."

"We're going to do some stealth training. When you're done, meet us out by the dairy farm, in the western field. Do you know it?"

"Yeah, sure," I told him. I quickly gathered up the rest of the flags and dropped them off in the Rumble Room. After that, I hustled toward the pasture. When I reached the field, I immediately knew that something was wrong. There were no other Guardians. They should have already been there.

"Hello?" I called uncertainly. I reached again to the communicator at my ear. Pressing it anxiously, I realized it was disabled.

I heard a sound across the field. Drawing my gun, I turned quickly and scanned the field, trying to find the source of the noise. "It's not smart to taunt someone with a loaded gun," I yelled. Too late I realized my mistake.

I took an involuntary step back as a flash of green shot across the field, headed straight for me. I aimed and fired, but my gun jammed. I pulled the trigger several times before I tossed it aside, wasting precious seconds. I fumbled for my knives, finally grabbing them from my leg sheaths. I gripped them tightly, taking a wide stance as I was taught. This was real. That bastard Marcus set me up. *I had to fight a Florae.*

Too fast, it ran into me at full force and I was knocked to the grass. Claws raked across my abdomen, trying to eviscerate me. My synth-suit protected me from being torn to shreds, but pain came every time the creature dug into my body. As it pummeled me, I took my knife and thrust upward, cutting into soft tissue. The Florae didn't care. It continued to tear at me, trying to sink its teeth into my flesh. Hot putrid breath hit me. Panicked, I stabbed at its head and managed to slash the knife across the creature's face. I thrust again and the blade hit its eye socket, meeting little resistance. It was like cutting through soft butter. If I could just get to the brain I knew I could kill it, but the creature pulled away.

Screaming, I pushed with all my strength and the creature fell back awkwardly. I jumped to my feet. I only had a few seconds–but something about the Florae was strange.

There was a glint at its neck, familiar but out of place. I didn't have enough time to ponder, because the creature was on top of me again. It went for my face and the stink from its mouth made me retch. Its remaining eye looked right at me, yellow and milky.

It tried to bite my chin and the force alone left me gasping from the pain. I sliced upward, aiming for its neck, knowing that was the only way I could escape, the only way I would make it out alive.

I jabbed again and again, and I could feel the warmth from the creature's blood through the synth-suit. It refused to give up. I delivered blow after blow, but each of my stabs was less effective.

Finally I pierced the Florae's neck and I dug in the knife. The creature fell backward. I dropped to my knees, sucking warm air into my lungs, fighting to stay conscious. I could breathe again.

The creature's arms and legs were wriggling, twitching disturbingly, and I was filled with a hatred so intense my chest burned. The Florae reached for me as I approached, but its head was twisted, half of its neck cut away. Its claws weakly scraped my leg, but there was no longer power behind its swipes.

I brought my knife down again severing its neck while blood squirted onto the ground. A putrid scent hit my nostrils, like rotten eggs.

Only when its head was completely removed did it finally lay still, its hunger extinguished. I collapsed on the ground.

Eventually I heard someone calling my name. I looked up. Kay was running toward me from across the field. "Amy, I swear I didn't know!" She was out of breath and looked more unsettled than I'd ever seen her.

"Was that my test?" I asked dumbly.

"Yes." She crouched down beside me. "Normally we would do it in the Rumble Room with snipers trained on the Florae. I don't know what Dr. Reynolds is playing at, but he forced this on us at the last minute. Said it would be more . . . true to life. I had complete faith in you and we made sure you were equipped properly, that you had a synth-suit and a gun." She looked at the carnage of the decapitated creature. "The knives were supposed to be for backup."

I felt deadened from what she was telling me. *Dr. Reynolds.* "My gun . . . jammed." I pointed to where I'd tossed it earlier and Kay retrieved it, examining it closely.

"You're missing the firing pin."

"Is that part of the test too?" I asked shakily. I was still working to process the information. That was my test. I could have died.

"No . . . Marcus," she growled. "That bastard must have sabotaged the gun. Why?"

It all came together. Marcus did it because Dr. Reynolds

wanted me out of the picture. Sure, my death would distress my mother, but she'd be proud if I died trying to defend New Hope. Better than having Dr. Reynolds commit me to the Ward, where I'd always be at the back of my mother's mind. Better to get rid of me for good.

"I think we should tell everyone that the gun malfunctioned." I looked at Kay. "Tell them that I will make a fine Guardian. That I'm dedicated to defending New Hope." I knew I'd have to make them trust me. I couldn't live my life always looking over my shoulder, wondering which of the Guardians were trying to kill me.

Kay studied me for a moment, nodding her agreement. "All right. That's what we'll tell the other Guardians, but I promise, Marcus isn't going to get away with this."

Kay helped me to my feet as the sun glinted off something on the gory ground, the same sparkle I saw before, caught in the terror of the fight. I knelt next to the dead creature, studying its slashed neck.

My blood ran cold at what I saw in front of me. I reached down and picked up a small gold cross on a gold chain.

Vivian's necklace.

CHAPTER TWENTY-EIGHT

I've been taking the pills that Gareth gave me for two weeks. All the gaps have been filled in, all the fog has cleared. I remember everything now. It came to me in bits and pieces, returning slowly, painfully real. Sickening. Why did it take so long?

Because I didn't want to remember.

A part of me was happy to sleep all day, to become nothing.

I look at the pills in the cup the nurse hands me. It would be so simple. I could just take them and stop taking the antidote. I could forget again. But I won't.

If I did, I would be no better than them.

I had wanted the truth so badly. I thought it would be easier to face the world as it was, Florae infested, if I just knew where They came from. What They were.

I lie on my bed and stare at the ceiling. Gareth once told me that ignorance was bliss and I'd responded that ignorance was dangerous. We were both right. But which was better?

If I'd chosen to remain ignorant, would I be happier? If I'd chosen to leave it alone, not to pry, would I still have my family, still have Baby? I knew that was not an option. I would never have left it alone. I would never have given up.

I made my choice and there is no going back.

•••

"Where is my mother?" I asked Rice. I caught him just as he was leaving a restricted area.

"Amy, I thought you had your training test today. What happened? How did it go?" He regarded me, bewildered. I'd showered and changed out of my synth-suit, but I know I still had a wild look in my eyes.

"I passed," I told him. "I'm a Guardian now."

"That's great! I knew you would." He grinned and hugged me, and I almost lost my resolve and melted into his arms. But I pulled back quickly.

"Where is my mother?" I asked again.

"Working." His smile faded. "Why? What's wrong?"

"Take me to her."

"I–I can't. She's in a restricted area."

I willed myself to appear calm. "I just want to tell her that I'm a Guardian now."

"She'll be really proud." Rice nodded. "But you know I can't let you inside."

With a flash of insight I decided to change tactics. I grabbed him in a bear hug. "I'm just so happy, Rice. I've wanted this for so long. . . ."

"Oh . . . I know, Amy. I think things are really going to work out for you now." When I let go, he looked flushed but relieved.

"You're coming to my birthday party later, aren't you?" I asked. "Baby will be happy to see you."

"Of course. We have even more to celebrate now."

I nodded and walked away, pretending I was heading for home, but then I ducked around the building and waited for Rice to leave. I felt bad deceiving him, but I had no choice.

After he was gone, I headed back to the black door, armed with the key card I'd stolen from his pocket.

I didn't remember exactly how to get to my mother's office, but I opened the door nearest the elevator and ducked inside to gather my thoughts. It was a small, empty office, and I spotted a lab coat thrown over a chair. I grabbed the coat and put it on, figuring it would make me less conspicuous. I heard voices in the hall and I peeked out the door. Lab assistants. I followed them at a safe distance.

Eventually they led me to the hall where one side was lined with doors, the other with glass. The hall with the cells, each holding a Florae. The creatures shuffled slowly, circling their confined spaces. I kept going down the hall. At the last black door I turned the knob and entered my mother's office.

She was at her desk and looked up, startled. "What . . . *Amy*?" Her hands froze above her keyboard. "How did you get down here?"

I pulled out the necklace. It was still covered in the black-green blood of a Florae.

She looked at the object and back at me, the shock and puzzlement clear on her face. "What is this? Where did you get it?"

"I found it around the neck of a Florae." I told her. "After I decapitated it to pass my final Guardian test."

"Amy! I knew you would. . . . Wait, you took the final test today? I thought–"

"That's Vivian's necklace," I said, cutting her off. "Why would a Florae be wearing Vivian's necklace?"

My mother let out a long sigh and rubbed her face with her palms. She got up and walked over to the office door, glancing outside before closing and locking it. Then she returned to her desk and settled wearily into her chair. "Vivian didn't die during that awful incident. Not technically anyway."

"The Floraes aren't aliens, are they?"

She paused. "No." My mother looked into my eyes. "Vivian was bitten by a creature and became a creature herself."

Minutes passed in silence or perhaps it was only seconds. I reached back toward the wall, grasping for support, trying to process it all.

My mother looked at me and sighed again. "We were developing a strain of bacteria," she finally explained. "Something the military commissioned, Dr. Reynolds in fact. They wanted a bug that would impair enemy soldiers without killing them."

"Biological warfare," I said.

"I wanted to save lives, Amy. The project was supposed to be an end to violence. The soldier would be sick for a few days, then recover completely. Even a short amount of time can give any military a huge advantage." She was staring intently at me, willing me to understand.

"What happened?"

"It wasn't ready. There were side effects. First it turned our test subjects' skin green from the phytosterols. A few died before we realized they needed direct sunlight. I modified the bacteria, but then the subjects became incredibly hungry. They craved protein and could not be satiated. I was so close to developing a solution.

"I sent a sample to our New York office and a young lab assistant broke the slide. He cut his finger. Once it was in his bloodstream, the bacteria took hold and it was the beginning of the end. He turned into a bloodthirsty creature and infected everyone in the lab. It takes only one bite. They infected the city, then the country, then the world."

"Why wasn't there a quarantine?" I asked, my voice weak. "How did it spread so fast?"

"The bacteria mutated and became airborne. Some people began to show signs of the infection right away, but in others it lay dormant. Do you know how many people you can contaminate in an hour? Someone got through airport security. As soon as that happened, it was over. That's how it traveled so quickly, why there are so many of them. The airborne strain soon died out, but the original strain remains. Now it can be transmitted by bodily fluids, most usually by saliva."

"The creatures, they're people," I whispered. I finally allowed myself to say it.

"No, Amy, not anymore. Once you're infected, you change; you're no longer a human. I've studied them. Every ounce of humanity disappears."

"So it's all lies." I regained my voice, raised it forcefully. "How many of those creatures actually got into New Hope and how many were our own citizens? What really happened that night?"

"It's not *all* lies, Amy. Those thugs disabled all the sonic emitters. Using members of their gang as bait, they lured a dozen Floraes into New Hope."

"A dozen Floraes? But there were so many people killed."

"Some were killed. Most turned, then killed others."

I thought back to the first day, sitting alone on the couch, seeing the horror of the Floraes for the first time. "But I saw the ship, the spaceship in Central Park."

"That wasn't a spaceship; that was a new piece of installation art. Some idiot newscaster decided it was a spaceship and that's how the story spread. We decided it was better to portray the Floraes as an outside threat, not a plague manufactured by the government. The misinformation was a fortunate turn of events. Right now only a select few know the truth, those who can help us in our quest to eradicate the infection."

"You did it," I said, still trying to comprehend what she had told me. "You're the reason all this happened. You're the reason Dad died." She watched me, her eyes full of pain. I glared at her, no longer knowing who she really was, what she was capable of.

She closed her eyes, exhaling through her teeth. "It was an accident, Amy. None of this was supposed to happen. We're working on something now that will stop the infection. Don't you see that's why I'm here night and day?"

"A cure?" I asked, daring to hope.

"We can't find a cure. We tried to develop an antidote at the beginning of our research, one that we could use on our own soldiers so they wouldn't become infected. It was never effective, and now the original strain has mutated. If someone is bitten by a Florae, they're irrevocably changed."

"Then what? Something to slay them all?" I couldn't stop thinking of them as mindless killers, but I'd also begun to think of them as people. They were all human, once.

"Unfortunately they are still too similar to humans. Anything I could develop to kill them would kill us as well. What I'm working on is a vaccine," my mother explained.

"How do you test something like that?" I wasn't sure I wanted to know the answer.

My mother crossed her arms, pinched her lips together. I wanted to cry then.

"You used those people the Guardians caught, didn't you? Amber's brother, his gang?"

"I did what was necessary. I will always do what is necessary."

"Even if it means killing innocent people?"

"I would sacrifice the few to save the many, yes."

I paused, afraid to ask the next question. "Does Rice know all this?" I whispered.

My mother looked down, then up at me. "He knows about the infection, what the Floraes really are."

I sucked in a breath. I felt betrayed. Sickened, I could no longer stand to be in the same room with her. I made a break for the door.

"Amy, wait! Let me walk you out of here. If you're caught . . ."

I ran out the door and down the hall. When I finally reached the elevator, I was shaking so badly I could barely hold the key card.

At the first floor, the elevator doors opened and I was staring straight into the face of Dr. Reynolds. His eyes widened when he recognized me, taking in the lab coat, my trembling hands.

"Hello, Amy. What are you doing here without an escort?"

I couldn't even look at him. "My mother walked me to the elevator and sent me up. It's my birthday."

"I know. I also hear you passed your Guardian test. Congratulations."

No thanks to you. I pushed past him, desperate to reach the outside.

I heard him call after me: "Good-bye, Amy. I'll see you later." From his mouth it sounded like a threat.

• • •

When my mother comes to visit me, I pretend to be drugged. I don't look at her when she sits next to me or puts her hand on my shoulder.

"I've asked Dr. Reynolds to give you another psyche-eval. He's going to, as a special favor to me," she tells me.

I look at her sharply and I can see she is surprised. I try to dull my face, act uninterested. "That's nice, Mom." I turn back to the television.

"I just want you to know, Amy, that all the things I did . . . I have to make up for them. I know what I'm responsible for, and I can never forget it." There are tears streaming down her face now.

I stare straight ahead until she gets up to leave, kissing me on the top of my head.

• • •

I wasn't back in my mother's apartment for more than a few minutes before there was a knock at the door. When I didn't answer, Rice came in anyway, looking jubilant. He thought we were going to have the mother of all parties tonight, to celebrate my birthday and my becoming a Guardian.

He stopped dead in his tracks when he saw my tearstained

face. "What happened?"

"I found out my mother is responsible for the apocalypse," I whispered.

"What . . . ?" His jaw dropped.

"I know the secret . . . about the Floraes. I know what they are." I reached into my pocket and fished out his key card, holding it up. He took it back solemnly and sat next to me on the couch.

"I killed Vivian," I told him, unable to meet his gaze.

"No you didn't. Even if you killed a Florae that used to be Vivian . . . it wasn't her. Vivian is gone." He reached out to me but I shrank away. "Have you told anyone?" he asked.

"Not yet, but people deserve to know the truth."

"Amy, come on. Let's talk about this. . . . I think you just need to cool off. There are a lot of things you think you may know, but really you have no idea."

"Like what, Rice? What else could I possibly not know?" I was close to sobbing again.

He put his hand on my back. "I . . . ," he began just as Baby burst through the door.

Happy birthday, Amy! she signed, running over to us. *Did you pass your test today? Are we having a double party tonight?*

She turned to Rice. *Hi, Rice. Do you want to hear about school today? It was fan. We were put into groups and had to solve a puzzle. My group was the fastest. . . .*

"Hannah, not now. I have to talk to Amy–" Rice clapped his hand on his mouth, alarmed.

Baby took a step back, her eyes wide. She stared at Rice with an intensity I'd never seen before. Then she opened her mouth and sounded out the syllables.

"Han-naaa." Her voice was soft and hesitant. I couldn't believe the sound came from her. *That's me,* she signed slowly, *Before.*

I leaped up and hugged her, the tears pouring down. Baby could talk. She had a name. I turned to Rice, who was watching us with a look of dread. "How did you know her name?" I demanded.

Rice was breathing heavily. "I think maybe you should sit back down, Amy."

I went to the couch and pulled Baby onto my lap, unwilling to let her go.

"I . . . I don't know where to start. . . ." He took off his glasses and cleaned them on his lab coat before returning them to his face. "Baby–her name was Hannah then–was in foster care, just like I was. Hutsen-Prime chose us. Some of us, the older kids, they tested us and singled us out. We were given special treatment, an education beyond anything we could ever hope for. Some of the children . . . the little ones . . . they took care of them. They also used them for experimentation."

Baby was an experimental subject? Suddenly it was all clear and the truth hit me like a brick. "Is that why she has that mark on her neck?" I asked.

"Yes. The research team your mother was working with was not only looking for a weapon; they were looking for an antidote. Something ally soldiers could take to keep them immune from the bacteria."

"What does that have to do with . . . ?" I sucked in a breath. "They were testing the bacteria *on children*?"

Rice sighed. "Children who had no family, who were lost in the system. Children who wouldn't be missed if they had an adverse reaction. The mark is the injection site."

I hugged Baby close. I couldn't bear to think of her as Hannah, as some test subject with no parents to protect her. "And you were a part of all that?"

"To a small degree, yes. I was still only a child myself." He looked at Baby. "They lost so many of their original research subjects. . . . When I saw Baby that day, when I saw the mark, I remembered her. She was always so playful, so friendly with the other children. She was one of my favorites. Amy, I knew her. I have been trying to protect her."

"Do you think she is immune?" I thought of the wound on her leg. Was it a Florae bite?

"I . . . don't know. I've been secretly testing her blood but I haven't found anything that would help us."

"You've been testing her? Rice, if my mother found out . . ." *If Dr. Reynolds found out.*

"I don't know what they would do to her," he admitted. "I've tried to keep her under the radar."

"You've been keeping her safe," I said, seeing Rice with new eyes. "Please, you have to keep helping her. I might not always be around." I started to tell him about Baby's hearing.

"I know." He smiled. *Baby told me,* he signed. "I'll protect her."

I was only allowed a moment of shock before the door opened loudly. I turned, expecting my mother had come to check on me, but instead I was greeted by Marcus and two members of the Elite Eight. I scrambled to my feet but immediately Marcus grabbed me and pulled me away from Baby.

"Sorry, kid," he said, "I have to follow orders."

"Rice!" I looked to him, pleading.

"What is this about?" Rice asked, his voice surprisingly forceful. He moved closer to me and took my hand.

"I don't answer to you," Marcus sneered.

"Not yet, but you may one day," Rice reminded him.

Surprisingly that made Marcus pause. "Talk to Dr. Reynolds. He gave me strict orders." Marcus dragged me toward the door.

"Rice!" I screamed as my hand slipped out of his.

Baby tried to follow but I signed, *Stay with Rice. He will keep you safe.* The last thing I saw was Rice's horrified face as he clutched a crying Baby.

In the hall, they shoved me into a large body bag, and Marcus hefted me to his shoulder, carrying me like I was a sack of laundry. I wanted to fight, to lash out, but I knew I couldn't take on Marcus plus two of his muscle-bound cronies. I was shoved onto a hard surface and heard a motor start.

After a short ride, they carried me somewhere inside a building–I could hear doors opening and closing as I was moved around. They dropped me and untied the top of the bag before they left, locking the door. I wriggled out of the bag onto a cold linoleum floor. The small room was dark but I could make out a bed, a sink, a toilet. I lay still and miserable, unable to bring myself to move. Hopeless, I closed my eyes and wrapped my arms around my head, hoping to drown out the world.

CHAPTER TWENTY-NINE

"You seem different, Amy." Dr. Reynolds is sitting across from me again, in my room in the Ward. This is my latest psyche-eval, the one my mother orchestrated. "Perhaps your treatments have been more effective than we anticipated."

"I am different." I smile. They haven't given me medication in days so I'd be clear enough to talk to Dr. Reynolds, not knowing that I'd neutralized the pills weeks ago. "I understand now what you're trying to do here."

"And what's that?" he asks, curious.

"Maintain humanity."

"Not just maintain, Amy. Improve."

I have to concentrate hard not to laugh. "Improve, yes, I see that."

"Your mother seems to think that you've handled certain information quite well."

"Such as?" I don't want to give anything away.

"That there are Floraes in New Hope. That we perform tests on them."

"Yes. I've adjusted my way of thinking. I know it's for the good of the community." I'm keeping my responses short so I don't mess up. I just have to convince him. I just have to get out of the Ward. I can squirrel away supplies, learn how to fly a hover-copter. One night I'll sneak Baby out. We can live like we did before we came here.

"Do you know why you were placed here, Amy?"

Because your first murder attempt failed. "Because I needed help. This is where citizens go to receive the help they need."

He flips through his notebook. "When we first spoke . . . I flagged you as possibly subversive," he says, surprisingly blunt.

"I was just interested in learning about New Hope," I try to explain.

"Yes, I noted that as well." He reads from his book. "A. Harris has an extremely curious disposition, prying into matters that are beyond her clearance level as a new citizen of New Hope."

"What else?" I ask, unsure why he's telling me this.

"A. Harris has an unnatural attachment to a post-ap she calls Baby. This child has a chance to live a happy, fulfilled life as a citizen, unless unduly influenced by A. Harris. She also has severe PTSD, causing many anger issues and an irrational resentment toward the structured society that defines New Hope. She should be monitored closely for violent behavior and rebellious conduct." He snaps his notebook shut.

"And now, because of my treatments, I'm much better," I tell him.

He looks at me pointedly. "No. You're not."

I try to stay calm. "I don't understand."

"Amy, your mother is very important to us. Her research is invaluable. If we are to take back the world from the Floraes, we need people like her: smart, dedicated, and loyal. Since you arrived six months ago, your mother has lost some of her focused commitment to New Hope. Now she worries about you . . . for your well-being."

"But now I can fit in," I plead. "Especially if I'm a Guardian. I can devote myself to New Hope. I can defend it." My voice is strained.

Dr. Reynolds shakes his head. "Amy, you and I both know there is only one thing to which you are devoted." I swallow. He means Baby.

"I'm not getting out of here, am I? This was all for show, to placate my mother."

"It's a shame really, Amy. You're so smart. You have so much to offer us, but you just can't be trusted. I know you think that one day, maybe not too far off, you'll escape from the Ward and leave New Hope behind with Baby at your side."

Shaking, I refuse to look at him.

"I have scheduled a small neurosurgical procedure for you next week."

"Neurosurgical?"

"I have decided we must go in and perform a minor lobotomy."

A lobotomy? This can't be happening. "I am not psychotic," I whisper.

"You are extremely violent. Even on your medication, you killed a nurse in an attempt to escape."

"What?! I never . . . Is that what you'll tell my mother?" It suddenly hits me that Dr. Reynolds is, at heart, a sadist. Nothing more, nothing less. He's only telling me his plans because he wants to revel in my helplessness and my terror. Despite my chill, I feel a warmth rush to my face. I can barely contain my rage.

He nods. "Yes, and we've already told a different story to all of New Hope. That you were wounded while on a mission and are recovering in the Ward from severe injuries. People are inspired by you: the director's daughter willing to sacrifice life and limb for New Hope. You've helped to strengthen our cohesive community, Amy." His smug smile is sickening.

"You've turned me into a phony martyr," I hiss. "Why are you telling me all this?"

"Because I've been gauging your reaction."

My head snaps up.

"This was part of your evaluation, and it's fair to say you have not responded positively."

"That was part of my psyche-eval?" I ask. "And the procedure?"

"That's entirely up to you, Amy." He stands to leave.

"We'll see how well you behave."

I bite my lip, trying to appear resigned. "How long will I have to behave, to prove myself?"

"Indefinitely." He smiles as if I should be pleased by this.

"Will I ever . . . Can I see Baby?" I ask desperately.

"No," he says, enjoying my misery.

He thinks he's won. He thinks he knows me, but he has no idea what I am capable of. If I can survive the After, I can survive the Ward.

I'm not surprised that he comes. Even if Dr. Samuels didn't relay my message, I knew Rice would be back. I sit quietly, pretending to be medicated.

"Amy." He takes my hand. I act as if I'm oblivious, focusing in the general direction of the television.

I know we're being watched. It's a constant thought at the back of my mind, as is Dr. Reynolds's threat of the lobotomy. Amber's blank, uncomprehending face flashes through my thoughts and I shiver.

I give Rice's hand a tentative squeeze. *Rice. I can't stay here. Reynolds wants me gone. It's not safe. Help me.*

I will, he signs into my hand. *I want to do more, but I'm being watched too. We all are. We have someone on the inside now.*

In the Ward? Dr. Samuels? A glance tells me he's talked to Rice; he's on our side.

We can do this, Rice signs. Our eyes meet and I have to look away before I start to cry. *Kay has a plan.*

Yes, I sign. *I'm prepared. I'm awake and ready.*

"I should go," Rice tells me, trying to let go of my hand, but I squeeze it tighter.

Promise me you'll look after Baby, I sign. I know she's found her real name but I'll never stop thinking of her as Baby, the toddler I found in the After.

I will, Rice assures me. He pauses and studies the ground. He looks like he has a decision to make and I wait, tense and desperate.

Rice reaches up to his hair, rubs the back of his neck. He turns slightly and then I see it: a small, diamond scar at the nape of his neck. That's why he wears his hair so shaggy, to cover the mark. I gasp, then catch myself and try to look drugged and uninterested.

Then he's gone and I have to pretend that I have no feelings. All I can do now is wait. Wait and hope.

I don't know what time it is when they come for me. It's after lights-out, and I'm already in bed when two Guardians appear. These are my colleagues. I'd trained with them for four months.

"How did you get in?" I whisper.

"Look, sunshine, we don't have a lot of time." Kay looks around the sparse room. "Grab what you want to take, quickly."

"There's nothing."

I mentally prepare myself for what is to come. If we're successful, I'll never see this place again.

"I've disabled the cameras," Gareth tells me from the door. "We have five minutes to get out."

"I'm ready."

We make our way silently from the building. Kay uses a key card to open doors and run the elevator. I smile when I see Dr. Reynolds's name on the side. When they check the system, it will look like Dr. Reynolds himself broke me out of the Ward. *How did she manage to get it?* Then I grin. *Dr. Samuels.*

When we're out of the building, I head toward the dorms, but Kay stops me. "No, Amy. You can't take her with you."

"I can't just leave her here." I can't abandon Baby.

Kay gives me a hard look. "Would you really endanger her like that? You have no choice. She does. Which do you think she'll choose?"

I know Baby would choose me. She would willingly leave New Hope and go back to the After, just to stay by my side. But with a realization that almost destroys me, I know I can't do that to her. She's no longer Baby. She's Hannah now. I think of her smiling face. She loves it here. She's happy. She fits into New Hope better than I ever could. She has her own past and her own future, and someone who will look after her. Unlike me, she is safe here. She has Rice.

I silently nod as the tears stream down my face. Before I can change my mind, I turn away and run to the grove of trees where Gareth is waiting.

The three of us quickly make our way to the outskirts of New Hope. "The hover-copter is by the lake," Kay whispers. "Marcus has taken to patrolling the perimeter with the Elite Eight, so keep silent until then."

I nod, feeling the heaviness lift and the exhilaration of the night air on my skin. I am no longer in the Ward.

We soon reach the hover-copter, and Kay and Gareth climb inside. I stop at the door, suddenly choked up again. *Baby. Can I really leave her behind?* I need to find another home, another place we can live in safety, then I'll come back.

"Good-bye, Baby," I shout at the top of my lungs as we

take off. I desperately want her to know that I love her, that I'm not leaving without thinking of her. "I'll come back for you!" I yell. I know she will hear me. No matter what lies they make up, even if they tell her I am dead, she'll know the truth.

Soon we are in the silent night sky, surrounded by stars with the dark world below us. We are all quiet on our journey and I am grateful. I know that Kay and Gareth–and Rice–have risked everything for me. It's a debt I can never repay.

The hover-copter trip takes hours and I fall in and out of a fitful sleep. When we land, I am jerked awake. The door opens and I step out into the new day. Kay and I stand together in the warm morning sun. I smile when I think of our last ride, so many months ago.

"Thank you, Kay, for getting me out of there. How did you manage to get the hover-copter?"

"We were ordered to head south and find fresh Floraes for the director." Kay reaches into the back and starts pulling out supplies. "So that's what we're doing. Orders are orders."

"And you always follow orders."

"Always." She throws me a large, black pack.

I place the bag on the ground and rummage through it.

It has everything I need: a synth-suit, a Guardian gun with extra ammunition, a small bow with arrows, and a water filter. There are also dehydrated food packs used for camping and a bunch of rechargeable batteries with a solar-powered charger.

"Rice thought you could trade some of that stuff for supplies later. . . . Neither of us knew what the post-aps were trading these days."

"What post-aps?" I ask. Right now I'm more concerned with Floraes.

"You're about thirty miles north of Fort Black." Gareth points to the south and then runs a hand through his silver hair. "You'd better take this." He tosses me a small black box that looks like an old-school transistor radio. I turn it over in my hands, baffled.

"It's a personal sonic emitter," Gareth explains. "There aren't many Floraes out here, so it should work like a charm to keep them away. If they hear you coming, they'll flee. You'll want to keep it always running, if you turn it on and there's Floraes inside the sonic radius, they'll go berserk."

"What's the range?" I ask, filled with overwhelming gratitude to have such an amazing gift. I just may live after all.

"Only about a hundred feet. It's got about forty hours of battery life, but you can charge it while it's on." He shows me how to pull out the solar panel and how to tell when it's done charging.

"Thank Rice for me," I say. I suddenly realize that I may never see him again. After everything that happened, after sharing a kiss that, at least to me, promised more, this could be the end. I shake my head to clear the thought and force myself to swallow the sting of finality.

"He said to tell you that this is one of the first prototypes. He wanted you to know the original idea was one of Vivian's." *Vivian. Vivian is now going to keep me alive.*

I give Gareth a big hug. "I'll miss you," I say as I start to cry softly. I turn to Kay and hug her as well. I can tell she's tense, but then I feel her body relax, hugging me back. When I look into her face, her eyes are wet and shining.

"Be careful out there. Fort Black is not New Hope," she warns.

"That's what I'm counting on," I tell her, wiping my eyes. "Thirty miles is nothing. I can be there by tomorrow morning."

"She's tough and smart," Gareth tells Kay, giving me a wink. "She'll be fine."

"We've got to get back," Kay says. "We would take you closer, but we're working under tight time restraints. They'll check to see how many miles we traveled." Gareth waves good-bye and heads back into the hover-copter. Kay stands on the same spot, watching me.

"Amy, one more thing. The director visited me when you were first sent to the Ward. She told me what floor you were on. Your mother knows the problem I have with authority. She knows I'm fond of you."

"You think she planned on you helping me?" I ask.

Kay nods. "I do."

The tears come again as I remember my mother's face when she first discovered I was alive. Then I shake the thought from my head. I don't have time for contemplation. Right now, I have to focus on staying alive. I switch on the sonic emitter.

I watch the hover-copter take to the air and disappear in the distance. Quickly I change into my synth-suit and strap on my pack. It's a little heavy, but I'm fit and I know I'll need the extra supplies.

I stretch my legs and listen. No Floraes yet. I set out at a walk, hoping that the emitter will shield me until I reach Fort Black. If not, I have my gun and my knives, though I am loath to kill Them, knowing They are people. Were people. But if it's my life or theirs, I won't hesitate.

I start to run, slowly at first and then faster and faster. I quietly disappear into the After.

Keep reading to find out what happens . . .

IN THE END

CHAPTER ONE

I long for the comfort of night.

The sun feels warm on my face. Before, sunshine was a good thing. But this is the After, and outside of New Hope, the light means only one thing if you're not armed: death.

It's early spring, but in the place that used to be Texas, it gets oppressively hot early in the year. I stop walking and open my canteen. The water drips from it and sizzles on the asphalt when I take a drink.

My synth-suit shields my otherwise bare feet from the burning ground, though my calluses also offer protection. I always wear my synth-suit in case I come across someone unfriendly–and out here, everyone's unfriendly. In the After, I learned to live without noisy shoes, and continued to run without them while I was in New Hope. I'm grateful I kept up with my running, or I wouldn't have made it out here these last three months. Even a simple supply mission like this could turn deadly.

I close my canteen and scan the area. On the horizon, I see a strip of houses that lies by a dried-up lake. I haven't hit this neighborhood yet for supplies, and as it's a fair way from the main road, I'm hoping no one else has either. As I get closer, I see that at some point this must have been a cozy little community. The walls of the houses are stucco, the roofs red tile, as if designed to look like a Spanish village. An old swing on a backyard jungle gym sways, its metal links creak in the wind. The houses, obviously cheaply made, aren't suitable for shelter anymore. After just over three years, many are missing doors and windows.

Houses like that don't stand a chance against Them.

At about a hundred feet away, I break into a full run. There seem to be more survivors in this area, more than I ever saw in Chicago. They won't be active during the day, but if someone's staking out this place, I don't want to give them time to catch me. There's no sign of anyone, so I flatten myself against the wall of the first house and peek inside. No hint of life, not even a breeze.

As I make my way inside, I let out a sigh. The place is wrecked. It's not the old bloodstained walls that sadden me. Evidence of past Florae attacks have become so commonplace, I barely even register scenes of death anymore. I'm just disappointed that the house has been ransacked already. The cabinets are thrown ajar and empty, the couches overturned. Even the pillows have been ripped open, the stuffing strewn across the floor.

Some people are worse than Them, I sign, then bite my lip to keep the tears back. I'm talking to Baby in our secret language. But she's not here with me anymore.

A quick check of the other houses reveals nothing but a half-empty bottle of vodka. I toss it into my pack. You never know when you need disinfectant or a Molotov cocktail. My time with the Guardians taught me that.

At the last house, I freeze when I see it in the backyard: an orange tree, full of fruit. I haven't seen fresh fruit in a long time, not since New Hope. Hands shaking with anticipation, I pick every one. When I can't fit any more into my pack, I sit on the ground, peeling orange after orange and jamming the sections into my mouth. The sweet taste helps the emptiness for a while. I eat until my stomach feels like it will burst.

I rest in the shade of the tree, satisfied. My contentment is fleeting, though, and soon the emptiness returns, not just a gnawing in the pit of my stomach but a hollowing out of my entire being. It's impossible to avoid the loneliness that has haunted me since leaving New Hope, so I let it wash over me. I nearly give in to it, and sit under the tree, waiting until something hostile finds me. In the end I fight the despair, pushing it down inside where I don't have to deal with it. I stand, determined not to give up.

Time to go, I sign to the empty air.

CHAPTER TWO

On a shady side road, I make my way back toward the place I've made my home. I pick up my pace, anxious to return before nightfall. I used to be afraid of the day, but the sonic emitter that Kay gave me keeps me safe from the Floraes. Night is what worries me now, when I hear the occasional voice nearby or a gunshot in the distance. There are people out here. Not many, but enough. They are alive in the After, which means they were either smart and figured out the Floraes' behavior, or they are just mean enough to survive. I don't want to find out which.

When I reach my new home, I bypass the large plantation house and head to the backyard. Beyond the overgrown tangle of grass is a field. I scan the area for any sign that the yard was breached while I was gone. I'd set traps, pressure-activated alarms that would send the Floraes running. So far, no one has disturbed the yard and my luck seems to be holding; everything looks as I left it. I sprint to the overgrown tree in the far corner and scramble up the trunk, into the tree house.

The tree house, a remnant of Before, has held up well. It barely creaks as I walk across the wooden floor and make my way to my sleeping bag in the corner, careful not to overturn the stack of books next to my makeshift bed. The tree house is large, larger than my room in the Ward, with two giant glass windows, one facing the house, one facing the field. Seems silly to have glass windows in a tree house, but judging from the mansion up front, that family had money to spare. There was a rope ladder that I cut down. I can scramble up the tree without it. It's not ideal, there's no running water, but the tree house is sturdy and hard to spot in the mess of leaves and branches. Even without the emitter, I wouldn't have to worry about Floraes up here.

In the three months since I've left New Hope I've had too many close calls. The first couple of nights were sheer terror. I thought about going to Fort Black, since Kay had dropped me so close, but I didn't see the point. If it was as bad as everyone said, I wanted to stay away. I had nowhere else to go, so I wandered aimlessly. At least I didn't have to worry about Floraes. The emitter kept them at bay.

One night, while I was scavenging a house, I heard voices, whispered but deep. I hid in the bushes and waited, knowing what kind of men banded together. The kind who Amber brought to my home in Chicago, the kind who attacked New Hope. Still, I wanted to check them out.

When I looked at them through the leaves, I could see there were no women with them. Not a good sign. After they moved on, I ran in the other direction. I've had a few encounters since then, but I always hide. I was lucky to find this place. Anyone looking to scavenge will head straight to the mansion up front.

This place is only twenty miles from where Kay said Fort Black would be. After I decided not to go there, I started to feel the loneliness. It was small at first, just an itch that I knew I couldn't scratch. But now it's an ever-present sadness. Even if I don't feel safe going to Fort Black, I like at least being *near* other people. In New Hope, I grew used to being in a community, to being part of a family again. As much as I was mistreated there, as much as I don't want to admit it to myself, the horrible truth remains. I miss New Hope.

And now, I am all alone.

I try not to feel sorry for myself, instead passing the time by working out to stay fast, or by reading or scavenging for supplies. But the memories come back. I think of my mother, who loved me, but not enough to save me from Dr. Reynolds. I think of Kay, my real friend.

I think of Amber, who betrayed us all and paid a horrible price. She brought a gang to the doors of New Hope, and they tried to create a panic, kill the leaders, and take everything we had. I forced her to tell the truth, and for a brief moment I thought I'd done something good. I'd saved New Hope. But then I found out all the people in the gang were put to death, without so much as a trial. And Amber, she was unmade, given a lobotomy to keep her placid.

Sometimes I even allow myself to think of Rice, how good and safe it felt to be held by him–then I stop. I can't let myself think of that or I'll go crazy. And I think of Baby, who I love more than anyone, who's safe in New Hope. I wanted to take her with me, but Kay talked me out of it. That she was better, safer, where she was.

Suddenly I freeze, holding my breath, not moving a muscle. Outside something is rustling the long grass in the field near the house. I silently crawl along the floor, peeking up out of the window. A lone Florae shuffles slowly. I stand up behind the window, turning on my flashlight. The monster swivels toward me and immediately begins loping. At one hundred feet away, it will run into the sound waves from the emitter.

With shaking hands, I reach to the emitter at my hip and switch it off. My pulse races and every nerve screams against what I am doing. For a moment I feel truly alive, awash in adrenaline. For a moment I forget my loneliness.

The green monster crosses the hundred-yard line, creeping menacingly, its yellow teeth bared. Looking up, it knows exactly where I am. And I look curiously into its horrible eyes.

You used to be a human.

What are you now?

The creature circles the tree house, and I peer out over the doorway. It tries to climb the tree and makes it up a few feet, surprising me. Startled, I come back to my senses. What am I doing? I fumble with the emitter, pressing it on. The creature falls from the tree and staggers back, unsure of which way to run to escape the sound. It darts toward the house at first, and I fear it will set off one of the alarms, but it changes direction and speeds back to the field, not stopping when it breaks away from the sound radius.

I exhale, realizing I had been holding my breath, and shakily sit down. Was I that desperate to see another person that

I would risk my life . . . or was it something else? Something darker that I don't even want to begin to think about? I shake my head. No. I want to live, even if it's this solitary existence. I sneak a look out the window, searching for the Florae, but it's long gone.

Leaving me alone again in the black, hot night.

I spend the next two days roaming through the surrounding neighborhoods, searching through houses I've missed or skipped before. Supplies are getting dangerously low, and I've combed through the area too thoroughly. If I want to keep living this way, I'll have to start traveling farther out to scavenge. I make it home with nothing more than a dented can of spinach and some shampoo. There's a pond I found a while back that I've been using for water, but I'm sure I can spare a couple of bucketfuls to wash my hair. The synth-suit keeps my skin clean, saps sweat away from my body, but my hair is another story, especially if I don't wear my hood often.

As I settle into my sleeping bag, I hear a familiar crackle. It's my earpiece. Kay remotely turned off the communication ability, so Dr. Reynolds couldn't track me. It has a solar-powered microbattery, though, good for years, and I've been using it to amplify faraway sounds, keeping it in my ear at all times. It's been so long since I've heard anything, I forgot that someone might actually try to use it to contact me.

"Sunshine? Are you there?"

I sit up in anticipation. It was nothing more than a whisper, but I know who it is. "Kay?"

Just the thought of talking to someone friendly makes my eyes flood. But she doesn't answer.

"Kay?" I plead. "Kay?" Nothing. I slide back to the floor, my head in my hands.

And then, after a few minutes, she's back.

"Sunshine?" She's whispering, but there's something else, a tone in her voice, something I never thought I'd hear. Kay sounds scared.

"Kay! Are you all right? Did you guys get in trouble? How's Baby? How's Rice? How's my mother?"

"Amy, I don't have a lot of time. Gareth hacked me in to the system so I could contact you . . . but I'm being watched closely."

"By Marcus?"

"No time, sunshine. You making it okay out there?"

"I'm handling it."

"Good girl. Listen, I need to tell you something. . . ." She pauses so long, I think she's cut out again.

"Kay, what is it?!" I ask desperately.

"It's . . . Baby."

My stomach turns over as dread seeps into every pore of my body.

"Dr. Reynolds has Baby."